Author's not

As the adage gc ue events. That is to say, I have kept as close to the facts of battles/people/dates etc where possible. I've also allowed myself artistic freedom as this is not a history lesson. I have used original place names where possible (my hometown of Tonbridge reverting to Tonebricge and Sevenoaks to Seouenaca by way of examples). My aim is simple – drop you, the reader, into unfolding events as they happen. I was there when I wrote it. I lived every moment. Life was not easy back then. It was downright brutal at times, but I like to think humans were the same as they are now. They laughed in the face of adversity, as we do today. They also died unnecessarily. Love, hate and humanity were as strong a quality then as they are now, although some traits were more apparent than others.

Would I have liked to have lived back then? Hell, no – although there is a part of me that would. I should probably speak to a therapist.

J W Phillips

CHAPTER 1

The corpse swung from the makeshift gallows, a grotesque marionette in the fading light. It's my first vivid memory. At four years old, my brother and I watched from below as the woman's legs kicked, her face turning from red to purple as she released her bowels. She was a witch, or so the townsfolk said, but to me, she was Lunete, the kind lady who gave me apples and whispered tales of far-off lands.

The crowd gathered, their shouts drowning out any cries for clemency, convinced she was responsible for the blight on our crops and the strange illness that had claimed old Mathis. They said she danced with devils and cast curses on the innocent – so this was fitting justice.

Our father grinned, a broad smile splitting his face, buoyed by the spectacle. It was the first time he had taken us out for the day, and he revelled in the chaos. "I told you she could fly!" he laughed, pointing at the swaying body.

Beside me, Paul watched with an intensity that sent a chill through me. His expression was oddly indifferent, yet a spark of excitement flickered in his eyes. Father told us to watch and wait; when the cheering crowd dispersed, there would be a chance to steal her rancid clothes. He would return.

Three hours later, he did, the smell of ale and fish mingling with the stench of death. It was dark. He lifted me up, holding me at arm's length as I stripped the body, passing the tattered rags down to my brother on the ground.

As Paul took the fabric, a grin crossed his face, a deep shadow dancing beyond my understanding. I couldn't shake the memory of Lunete's kind smile, her gentle touch.

Life progressed from there.

*

There were two of us at birth. It was the year of our Lord, 1329 although I cannot vouch for that date. I was the product of low-born serfs moments after my brother, Paul, entered this life. Memories, good and bad, flood back as I speak his name. How I miss him.

Since that day I have witnessed the passing of two kings, a plague sent from hell, and the dawn of a new millennium – life evolves with or without my input. I am assured that the gospel of Romans 10:9 tells us in part that "If you declare with your mouth, thou will be saved." Therefore my salvation may be achieved through confession. So be it.

You have been warned.

As I speak this testimony, Brother Michael scribes the words onto parchment in the monastery's library. My rigid fingers limit even basic tasks these days. The scar on my palm reminds me of a violent past, and the candle's smoke does nothing for my failing health. It is a laborious commitment, as Brother Michael often reminds me. Father Nicholas Budwith, the Bishop of St Mary Magdalene Parish, has assigned him this duty and assures us he will read every word before pleading God's forgiveness on my behalf. He is a devious old man but I keep such thoughts to myself. He has an unnatural interest in my story and I have no idea why he believes my soul is worth saving. But I am thankful. A bishop's endorsement to God must count for something.

As days will turn to weeks and summer to winter I am sure he will lose interest, but I will continue. Brother Michael has been ordered to strike nothing from my testimony so I am talking directly to you.

Hello.

Paul and I looked identical at birth, but our mother never had time to acknowledge such detail as she died giving me life. I would like to think she forgave me, but our father never did. Her name was Eleanor and I am told she was ugly. I have no way of knowing if that was true or whether it was just the taunts of children who overheard vindictive chatter and used it against us. Children are cruel – but they also learned that cruelty directed at Paul and me impacted their health.

She chose the name for a boy, Paul, long before giving birth, but my father named me.

Ailred.

I have always hated that name and swear he gave it to me as punishment for killing his wife. On more than one occasion I woke to find him staring at me in whatever rat-infested barn we slept the night before with a mixture of loathing and sadness. People say she was the one person he showed affection towards although he beat her unconscious in between.

Our formative years were survival. Anything our father did had an ulterior motive – if he gained nothing, he did nothing. Without the charity afforded by the nuns at St Mary Magdalene's Priory and the occasional slice of bread by folk with pity in their hearts, we would have perished. That would have saved many future lives but that is the nature of things.

The winter hardships tested our resolve and the undeserved beatings took their toll. How can a father punish his children for his own inadequacies and sleep at night? Over time, Paul and I learned to depend on one another and it forged our lives. It is why I am still here today.

It pains me to recall my father but I must include him as he shaped us. You need to understand.

He had spent the early years of his adulthood as an archer in the service of King Edward the

Second but was wounded in the leg in some long-forgotten melee. It left him with a limp that became worse with age. I did not care.

After being discharged he found employment working for Lord Thomas de Clare, enacting disciplinarian duties around our home town of Tonebricge in Kent.

Father was a colossal man due to his years mastering the English war bow. The power required to launch arrow after arrow in short succession took years of dedication, and that shaped his body into the giant sinuous killing machine it was. It was the only skill he possessed and to watch him practice was a thing of beauty. I stated earlier that he did nothing for us but I will add a proviso. He taught us archery. I say 'taught', but he would make us fetch his arrows from the target and then test his accuracy by attempting to get close to us without drawing blood. Under such conditions, you learn to study trajectory and the finer details of an arrow's flight. I still have a scar on my thigh. I am sure the original reason was part of some long-term scheme that would benefit him but it gave Paul and me grounding in the art. It later saved our lives. King Edward had decreed archery practice compulsory for all males over the age of fifteen but in those days it was our childhood passion. No one needed to force us – we were obsessed. Father had stolen a half-sized war bow, or baby bow as we called it, and we honed our skills whenever we could. It frustrated Paul that he could fire an arrow further than me, but I had the keener eye.

He gloried in conflict, and as children, we witnessed beatings meted out to poor wretches who had fallen into debt or been unlucky to meet him on a bad day. So many times we washed blood from his clothing and bandaged his skinned knuckles. Not once did he show regret or gratitude. I always shied away but Paul was different. He watched with fascination. His eyes transformed into an emotionless expression, seizing him until the violence stopped. I did not think anything of it at the time but came to wonder if it was provoked by childhood trauma.

It was a sign of things to come.

Father had no friends. He did have a brother, Uncle Peter. They had fought together and Peter came to stay with us after he left King Edward's army. It did not take long for him to fall out with my father. They all did.

I awoke one morning with Paul next to me, snoring. Father was pacing up and down, his nostrils flared as he punched the barn door.

'What's wrong?' I asked.

'That dirty fucker.'

'Who?'

'Who do you think – that slimy bastard, Peter.' He lost control and focused on me, his eyes glazed. He looked like he would attack me but stopped as Paul woke and sat up. Father turned his attention to him. He ran at Paul and pulled him up by his neck, choking him and screaming into his face. 'This is all your fuckin' fault. He's stolen all the money and fucked off.'

I jumped to Paul's defence. 'Why is it his fault?' I tried to hide my fear but how convincing can a petrified ten-year-old sound?

He stared at me and nodded, a sickening smirk on his face. It frightened me. He dropped Paul and said, 'Ask him,' and stormed out.

I looked at Paul. He shrugged and went back to sleep.

We never saw Uncle Peter or the money again.

By that time, Paul and I looked very different. It was strange. The other twins living in the parish were identical. Paul was an inch taller than me, his curly dark hair and hardening face contrasted with my blonde, almost white hair and baby-faced complexion. Whereas I was lean, Paul was showing signs of our father's size and strength. To this day I have no idea why we were different, and have never found anyone who has an answer beyond, “It's God's will”.

And it was God's will that ended my father’s life.

As we entered our teens he forced us to collaborate in ambushes on travellers or drunken folk as they left the Chequers Tavern. The tavern was sited in the middle of a row of wooden buildings, pillared between the smithy and butchers. Merchants would stop here whilst travelling between London and ports on the south coast of England that served lucrative markets across the channel. These wealthy people were prime targets for my father's greed.

By this time he had long since been lost to alcohol, his unpredictability ending any chance of employment. These local robberies, and the intimidation of easy-prey individuals, were his sole means of income.

His robbery plan was simple, but we used it many times to good effect.

But simple plans, enacted often, are doomed to failure.

Unbeknown to us, Lord Thomas de Clare had been partitioned by a group of local peasants led by the owner of The Chequers Tavern, Tom Brewer. They wanted rid of my father and the negative image his actions had instilled. Word spread between merchants that Tonebricge was a dangerous place to travel through and they bypassed the town, stopping off in nearby Medestang or Seouenaca, denying much needed earnings. This impacted the lord's tax revenue and he agreed to act. It so happened that Sir Hugh le Despenser, Lord of Glamorgan, along with his page boy, Jacques Stafford, were staying at the castle at Sir Thomas's invitation. Being unknown in the area, he offered to pose as a wealthy silk merchant in an attempt to lure my father into Sir Thomas de Clare's trap.

And on this day, my father took the bait.

*

I was about fifteen. My father and I were towards the back of the tavern playing dice. It was dark. An aroma of stale ale mixed with stale piss clung to everything and everyone. Not every drunken customer made it to the privy. A broken chair remained where it had been smashed over Lee Smithy's head the night before. We spent day after day there, waiting for a suitable victim. Our money had dwindled to nothing, the last coins being spent on alcohol in my father's obsessive pursuit. Wearing the only clothes we owned, we attempted to fit in. We smelled terrible. Nobody would sit near us. I did not blame them – I would not sit near me given the chance.

Alongside the local faces were several others I had never seen before.

One man, sitting with a bored-looking boy of similar age to me, kept falling from his chair. He was tall, taller even than my father, with a narrow, hard face. He wore an elaborate blue and white checked surcoat over a light-coloured tunic, bound around the waist by a heavy leather belt. I could see no weapon, but that was not unexpected as patrons were required to hand them over until they left. In between bouts of drunken revelry, his clear cold eyes scanned the room. He was anything but drunk. I had a good view as my seat was positioned in his direction, but my father faced the opposite way. I kept him updated. He had spoken with the merchant and the boy earlier and sensed an easy target.

I could see what was going on. Tom Brewer, the tavern's owner, was in league with this man, giving him weakened ale and charging nothing for it. Tom's son, Richard, who was a couple of years older than me, was at his beck and call, keeping his tankard filled. The merchant was the worst-acting drunk I had ever seen. Add to that the number of extra men present and I could only draw one conclusion – entrapment.

It was at this point that I made the most crucial decision of my life. It was time to break free from our father. He had all but destroyed our lives until now and we might never get a better opportunity.

So I said nothing.

'Are you sure they're the right ones?' my father asked, throwing the dice and gazing across at me.

I looked at the stranger. He was speaking to the boy, his drunken antics stopped as he scolded him. The boy shrugged. He did not care. The man lost his temper, bringing his arm up to strike him but glanced over and reined in his anger. Composing himself, he stood and started singing an out-of-tune ballad, back in character. I looked at Tom Brewer. Our eyes met and I nodded and smiled. His face showed confusion for a second, then recognition. He understood. I was with him.

'Yes, Father, they're perfect.'

Downing his drink, we picked our way

through the crowded tavern. As we exited, I had one final glance towards Tom who was cleaning tankards with his apron and I gave him a wink, then followed my father out the door.

Paul was sitting on an empty half-barrel across the street opposite the tavern. He was listening to the sound of pigs having their throats cut in the butcher's next door and throwing stones at a family of ducklings. As we approached he looked up.

'I managed to kill one of the little ones,' he said with a snigger.

Our father gave him the pair's descriptions and we dashed to our pre-arranged positions.

Paul's job was to signal when the victims left the tavern. I in turn would forewarn our father who was waiting further down the street armed with his knife and cudgel.

We left the rest to him. Simple.

*

Paul's whistle sounded clear in the early evening stillness. It had not taken them long to follow us out of the tavern. It was an overcast day in early October. I heard the man singing as they followed the muddy street heading towards us, the boy trailing behind looking dejected. Peeping from my hideaway I watched as they came into view. The man was wearing a brown cape that covered him, but I could make out the form of a sword beneath. His right hand gripped its handle and he walked with a swagger. Draped across his shoulder he carried a leather pouch, the type that was slung over a horse and tied under its belly.

I broke cover and ran ahead. In previous attacks, I would be sure to keep to the bushes, but this time I strayed into the street. I wanted the man to be forewarned of the danger.

'They're coming, and he's unarmed.'

My father rummaged on the floor and had difficulty finding his weapons. The hours in the tavern had affected his judgement.

'Good, now fuck off and let me work.'

I turned and left, intending to make my way back along the river in a large semi-circle to meet with Paul.

I stopped. Turning back, I found a place to hide about fifty paces from my father. There was still light left in the day. I watched and waited. I had made the decision and would see it through.

It happened in seconds. As the victims drew level with my father the man paused and I saw his hand edge the sword inches from its scabbard.

In the past, my father would leap from his hiding place with such speed that the victim was unconscious before they knew what had happened.

Today was different.

His blood-curdling attack scream fell on deaf ears. He stumbled from his hiding place – his old battle wound and drunkenness making this surprise ambush anything but. The boy following ran back towards the tavern.

In an instant, the man's sword was drawn. He stepped to one side as my father blundered past, and he took a defensive stance. He swayed side to side on his toes, loosely tossing the sword from one hand to the other, twirling the polished blade effortlessly in either hand. This man was no stranger to violence. His smiling face should have served as a warning to my father, but he was committed. He would not back down.

He had the cudgel in one hand, dagger in the other. He always bludgeoned his victims – the blade only there as a threat. Today would be different. His opponent was ready. He was more than ready – he beckoned my father on and was enjoying the moment.

As my father lunged forward and swung the heavy stave at the man's head, he stepped backwards and it whistled past his face, exposing the side of my father's body. The man brought the sword up, twisted its blade and used the heavy pommel at the end to smash my father in the face. I heard his blackened teeth shatter as he tried to regain his position, spitting shards and trying not to choke on fragments.

By then it was too late. The man stabbed a short seax blade into my father's groin and thrust the narrow blade up to its hilt. I had not even seen a second weapon. Father's eyes widened in terror as he realised his mistake. He wobbled for a second before the man darted forward and head-butted him on the bridge of his nose, knocking him down like a rag doll.

I felt terrible shame. It happened as I planned, but reality sickened me. This was all my doing.

The man stepped forward, pulling the seax from its wound, and stamped on my father's right hand – the one holding the dagger. He dropped down with all his weight onto his chest and began stabbing into his eyes as my father screamed for mercy.

I could not move. This was nothing like Paul and I play-acted when we were young.

As I was about to run away I heard another cry. It was the high-pitched battle roar I had heard as a child. This time it was real. Looking towards the carnage that was my father, I saw Paul come running. The man was still in a state of frenzy with blood covering his face when Paul charged into him. He caught him off balance. They fell forward across what remained of my father, Paul grasping the man around the neck with his forearm. For a few seconds, Paul pinned him to the floor and choked him.

I dashed the remaining distance and arrived at the same time as Tom Brewer and the rest of the tavern's menfolk.

We stood bewildered as the man shook himself free from Paul's grasp. He threw Paul onto his back and turned the blooded blade to him. Paul was winded and immobile, staring up at his assailant with a blank expression.

It was the same look I had seen on Paul before at times of violence.

The man forced the tip of the blade into Paul's mouth and moved into a position in which to deliver the death blow.

'STOP!'

It was a shout of authority that had a Norman accent.

Sir Thomas de Clare tapped the flanks of his horse and pushed through the group of men watching. The jet-black beast became unsettled and he pulled on the reins.

'Woo, woo...' he commanded, never taking his eyes from the man on top of Paul. 'You seem to be rather enjoying yourself, Sir Hugh.' he said, suppressing a smile beneath his short-cropped beard. He used the French-Norman language spoken by the ruling classes, but I understood enough. 'I'm aware who the gentleman on the floor over there is,' he nodded toward the bloody mess that was our father, 'but might I enquire as to who this boy you're about to open up is?' He stroked his horse's head. 'I hate to spoil your fun, but sometimes it's nice to know someone's name before you stick a knife down their throat.'

Sir Hugh took his stare from Paul and acknowledged Sir Thomas. 'I'm sorry my Lord, I didn't ask,' he said, trying to show respect. 'I don't always remember to ask someone's name when the bastard attacks me from behind.'

Sir Thomas removed his bycocket hat and

smoothed back his long greying hair with his spare hand. He was about forty years old with a long straight nose and steely eyes, his broad shoulders and dress sense showing a lifetime of physical training and privilege. He was not angry, just intrigued to know who Paul was.

I stepped forward.

'His name is Paul, my Lord.'

He glanced across, raising his eyebrows, and nodded.

'Ahh, Paul,' he mused, switching seamlessly into English. 'That's a good Christian name.' He looked towards my brother as he struggled to release himself.

'This bastard is no Christian, my lord, he's a son of a bitch...' Sir Hugh started to reply, digging his forearm into Paul's windpipe, but was cut short.

'You there!' Sir Thomas shot a stern look towards me.

I went to remove my hat only to find it wasn't on my head, so tugged my forelock instead.

'Yes, Sire?'

'Can I assume you are some relative of this good Christian fellow, Paul?'

'Yes, Sire, he's my twin brother.'

'Then it follows you're related to Sir Hugh's friend over there lying with his eyeballs removed – yes? Only a relative would be stupid enough to attack a nobleman carving up a total stranger. You're his son, perhaps?'

'Yes, Sire.'

'Now,' he said, addressing his words to Tom Brewer at the front of the crowd. 'You told me the sons of Mr Eyeballs over there were complicit in his crimes. Is that so, Tom?'

He looked at me with a solemn face. 'Yes, Lord, but I think these kids might...'

'No buts, Tom. You wanted rid of this gang and that's what we're doing. You there...what's your name?'

'Ailred, Sire.'

'Ahh, Ailred...a tremendous old Norman name. Well, Ailred the Norman, I'm afraid we're going to have to hang you and your brother, Paul the Christian. We can't have the likes of you growing up to be like your father.'

My mind went blank. How could this be? I had thrown my own father into their trap and now Paul and I were to pay the price. My body started to sweat and shake.

He pointed to me and a couple of bystanders rushed over and grabbed me before I could run.

Sir Hugh pulled Paul up out of the mud by his ripped tunic and dragged him over to me.

Lord Thomas looked down from his horse. 'String them up in front of the Chequers, it will act as a deterrent.'

I kicked and bit at my captors trying to break free, but it was no use.

'But, but, Lord...we...'

Lord Thomas had no time for my pleading.

'I'll leave the details in your capable hands, Sir Hugh – I have an appointment with the Earl of Northampton at the castle and I'm running late.' He hesitated as if distracted. 'Speaking of Northampton, where's that bastard son of his?'

'I've no idea, Lord, he disappeared at the first sign of trouble. He's worse than useless,' Sir Hugh replied, shaking his head and raising his eyes to the sky.

Sir Thomas tutted to himself and started to trot away. 'That will never do – anyway, my work here is done.'

There was movement from within the crowd, and the boy, Sir Hugh's page, appeared with a broad smile carrying a rope.

'Here you are, we can use this to hang the thieves.'

By then, a small number of his soldiers and guards had arrived and were ushering the town's folk away.

'SIRE, before you go…may I beg clemency on behalf of the young lad, Ailred?' It was Tom Brewer from behind the short line of soldiers.

Sir Thomas stopped and turned his head. 'Clemency? Damn your eyes, Brewer, you drag me to this shit-hole to rid you of this gang then you want clemency?'

It was the first sign of temper he had shown, but Tom's interjection gave me hope.

'Beggin' your pardon, Sire, but can I just point out that young Ailred was in on the plan to trap his father. He gave me a signal in the tavern in support.'

Paul gave me a confused glare and went to speak, but I grabbed his arm. 'Shh!' I hissed.

Tom continued. '...yes my Lord, he deserves some credit for...'

Sir Thomas gathered his composure and waved a dismissive hand. 'And what would you suggest we do for this young Ailred Norman fellow, uh? Knight him, maybe?'

Tom wrung his crumpled hat in his hands but continued. 'I could use someone to work at the tavern, Lord. I'm happy to vouch for him if you release him into my care.'

Sir Thomas sat for a second looking in the direction of Tonebricge castle, then looked at me. 'Do you pledge yourself on pain of death to this man?'

I did not have a choice, so jumped at the opportunity. 'Yes, Lord Thomas, of course I will...' but he did not let me finish.

Sir Thomas turned his attention back to Tom. 'If he was a party to capturing this wretched man I'll grant you this, but only because I like his name. Do what you will with him but the other bastard hangs for them both. Be assured, if Ailred the Norman here breaks any of my laws in future I'll hold you responsible. You understand that, Tom Brewer?'

I could see Tom's son, Richard, remonstrating with him, red-faced and waving his arms about, but he was not to be deterred.

'Yes Sire, thank you, Sire.'

Sir Thomas nodded at the two soldiers holding me and they relaxed their grip. Shaking them off, I moved away and turned to Paul.

'My brother was also part of the plan...' I pleaded and looked for support from Tom. He was moving towards me and grabbed me by the arm.

'No, he wasn't. Now come with me boy, before I change my mind.'

'But...but...he's my brother, I can't just let him hang...' I cried, tears welling up.

Sir Thomas pulled hard on his reins, turning the horse's head and trotted off to his meeting with Sir William de Bohun, Earl of Northampton, at Tonebricge castle.

There was to be a hanging.

*

Paul stood without emotion as Sir Hugh's page tied the noose around his neck. He had been dragged to the Chequers by soldiers under supervision from Sir Hugh. There was bruising around his face, with one of his ears was partially torn off. The page boy spat and slapped him but he refused to react, choosing to stare through bloodshot eyes.

The front of the tavern was busy as town folk came to watch the execution, bringing their children to the spectacle.

I felt powerless. Through my stupidity, I was

about to watch my brother die. I had already killed my mother and father. I cursed my existence. My hands shook as I grasped Tom's arm and pleaded.

'Please do something, I beg you.'

His son, Richard, stood on the other side of him, questioning his father's decision to save me.

Tom snapped.

'What the fuck do you expect me to do?' he screamed at me and then turned on Richard. 'And you can shut the fuck up, too. You heard Lord Thomas, we can do what we like with him – we have free labour and all you can do is fuckin' complain!'

'You've put us in danger though, Pa.' he bellowed, putting his hands on top of his head. 'If this idiot puts one foot out of place, we'll be hanging next to him from that scaffold.' He pointed to the wooden cross-beam attached to a post outside the tavern. It had been used many times before. The page boy had slung the rope over, through an iron ring, and was tying the end to Sir Hugh's saddle as he sat waiting.

The boy's hands trembled with excitement as he secured the rope. He looked across at Paul. This was more than watching someone die. This was power. Seeing my distress added to his pleasure. He grinned and looked up at Sir Hugh sitting on the horse.

'May I have the honour of leading your mount off?' He spoke with assurance, in English, so we could all understand.

I wanted to run. I could not bear to watch my brother choke to death, but deserting him would be a betrayal. I was helpless.

Sir Hugh looked towards Paul, who was still silent and defiant, his hands tied behind his back.

'You there, Paul Christian, do you have anything you want to say before I carry out the sentence?'

'...before *I* carry out the sentence,' the page boy interrupted.

Sir Hugh looked down at him. He had not said a word to the boy since the attack, but now he did. 'You could learn a lot from Paul, Jacques Stafford.'

The boy looked up in surprise. 'I could learn a lot from a common serf? I am Jacques Stafford, the son of Sir William de Bohun...'

'Bastard son of Sir William,' Sir Hugh cut in.

'Granted – but son, never-the-less. Soon I will be your squire. In time I will be your equal and you are belittling me in front of these... *people*?' he spat the word.

Sir Hugh looked across at Paul again. 'A squire is brave and honest. Today I saw your true character.' He stared hard at Paul, who never once lowered his eyes.

'I...didn't run away, just went to fetch Sir Thomas.' The page was adamant.

'Oh, you ran away, I will swear to God on that.'

The page, Jacques Stafford, trying to break the

tension, said, 'When you raise me to your squire, Hugh, you'll see my true worth.' He lowered his gaze and patted the horse, then looked towards Paul. 'Shall I lead off now and hang this filth?'

'I am *Sir* Hugh to you, boy, and I care nothing for who your father is. In battle, I need men I can trust, men who will die for me. What would you do if faced with a thousand screaming Welsh or a horde of Frenchmen? I know exactly what you'd do.'

Stafford looked close to tears, his frustration at boiling point. He was being humiliated in front of people he despised.

'That is ridiculous, I'm fearless, as I will prove soon enough. Now, *Sir* Hugh, can we hang this peasant and be gone? My father is expecting me after he finishes his meeting with Lord Thomas.'

Sir Hugh sat pondering something, then dismounted and walked over and faced Paul.

'One question. Why did you attack me to defend that no-good piece of shit back there?'

Paul refused to answer, lifting his chin and staring Sir Hugh in the eyes.

'You will answer me, boy, or I will break both your legs and put you through so much pain you'll be begging to be hung.'

Paul did not reply or lower his gaze.

Sir Hugh swallowed hard and slapped Paul hard across the face with the back of his studded glove drawing blood from a shallow cut across his cheek.

'Last chance,' he hissed, moving his face within inches of Paul's.

Paul thrust his head forward and went to bite him but Sir Hugh jerked back just in time, Paul's teeth snapping at thin air.

Sir Hugh laughed. He grabbed Paul by the tunic, dragged him over to the nearby blacksmith's forge and threw him down next to the large anvil. Lee Smithy went to speak but the look on Sir Hugh's face silenced him. Lee put down the large hammer he was working metal with and stepped aside.

'Hold him still,' Sir Hugh commanded, pointing to two of his guardsmen.

They knelt on his shoulders while Sir Hugh pulled Paul's legs up and over the anvil so his kneecaps were central.

Still, Paul did not struggle or speak.

Sir Hugh took up the hammer and held it in front of Paul's face.

'Why did you attack me? You wanted to save a man who destroyed your life?' His voice was calm.

Silence.

He raised the hammer above his head with both hands and I looked away. I heard a loud clang as the tool struck.

Silence.

I looked back. Sir Hugh had the head of the hammer resting on the end of the anvil next to Paul's knees. He was Smiling.

'Release him,' he said, nodding his head.

Paul stood and resumed eye contact.

'I know the answer,' he said, handing the tool back to the smithy and nodding thanks. 'He's your blood. You hate him but you have loyalty to the point of death. I just wanted to see if you would say it.'

He looked towards Stafford who was standing looking bewildered.

'This Paul Christian fellow has the qualities to make a better squire than you, regardless of his upbringing. You have been my page for the last four years and have learned nothing – all because of who your father is.' Stafford looked horrified and went to interrupt, but Sir Hugh concluded. 'You say you are brave – fearless was the word you used. Am I correct?'

'Yes.'

'In that case, you will be willing to fight Paul here, will you not? He is of similar age.'

Sir Hugh's change of direction gave me real hope.

Stafford's laugh was hollow and unconvincing. 'You are joking, Hugh?' My father will never agree to that.'

'*Sir* Hugh to you, boy, and your father is not here. I am willing to face any consequences arising from this. It's about time you learned to stand on your own.'

He walked to Paul and stood close. He smiled and moved his face a little further away from

Paul's teeth, and said, 'You have shown bravery and loyalty – they are invaluable qualities in a man.' He released Paul's binds.

Paul massaged his wrists and walked to the middle of the street, never once taking his eyes off Stafford. His face was still emotionless.

Stafford raised his arms, the palms of his hands out in appeasement. 'This is ridiculous...'

Sir Hugh ignored his continued protestations.

'Winner becomes my squire. It's that simple.'

Both were unarmed.

Stafford stayed close to the horse. He looked ready to run, his eyes flashing in all directions looking for an escape route.

By now, the assembled crowd were enthralled. It was rare to witness disagreements between the ruling classes but to see a young Norman humiliated in this manner was unheard of. They had come here expecting to see Paul hang but now he was their champion, fighting on their behalf.

Seeing he was cornered and with no alternative, Stafford moved to within ten paces of Paul.

'If you touch me I'll have you hanged.'

I laughed out loud. I could not help myself. Even Sir Hugh suppressed a smile.

Paul's face remained unmoved.

Stafford stamped his foot on the ground pretending to rush Paul, hoping he would run away, but Paul stood staring.

Then it happened. It was like winter's worst storm, when lightning and thunder flash and boom together and you think the world will end.

Paul exploded.

He ran the short distance between them with such speed that Stafford did not have time to react. He punched him in the face with incredible power, knocking him unconscious. He was snoring before he hit the ground. I looked towards Sir Hugh and saw him smile before making his way to attend the stricken boy.

But he had underestimated Paul. Within seconds, Paul was standing above Stafford stamping on his head, his eyes glazed, grinding his heel into his face. Sir Hugh ran the last few feet and dragged him off, only for Paul to slip his grasp and jump with both feet onto his head until he was subdued by four of Sir Hugh's guards.

'You're an animal, boy,' he said once Paul had regained his composure. He laughed to himself for a second. 'You remind me of someone. You and I are going to make a dangerous team.'

CHAPTER 2

I have been silent for the past few days as Brother Michael has been unwell. At my age such delays could prove calamitous, therefore we continue in haste. He says he is fine, although his persistent cough is a distraction. I am easily distracted. I wish he would replace these guttering candles but Father Budwith assures us that they are too expensive. How costly can they be? This priory has never recovered from a robbery years ago, and subsequent Bishops have come and gone, each professing poverty. I suspect the problems are down to bad management, although the loss of such wealth must play a part.

Brother Michael is glaring at me, so we resume.

*

I did not see Paul for a year.

He had been mounted onto Jacques Stafford's horse and then he, Sir Hugh, and his entourage trotted out of town towards the castle. It was getting dark.

Jacques Stafford was not dead, but close. He had been given basic medical attention but was in no condition to travel, so Tom Brewer offered to give him a bed in his tavern until his father, Sir

William de Bohun, could organise a long-term recovery plan. Sir Hugh would have some serious explaining to do on his return to the castle. I did not envy him.

As for me, it became apparent what my future was. From the minute we were alone, it started. Tom had my life mapped out.

'Boy, take Stafford to the tavern. Put him in the first room on the right as you go upstairs, and tell whoever is staying there to vacate by orders of Sir Hugh. We need to keep this kid alive until they collect him. God help us if he dies.'

I stared at him. Why was he telling me what to do? He stood with his hands on his hips as his son, Richard, joined us. I was standing next to the unconscious body of Stafford, his face unrecognisable.

'You don't get it, do you?' Tom looked at Richard and they laughed.

I was still confused. He had risked his reputation to save me from the gallows, for which I was grateful.

'You're mine now, boy – I own you. Lord Thomas handed your existence to me.' He looked at Richard and nodded. 'Show him.'

Richard pulled out a short length of birch from his breeches and struck me across the thigh.

That hurt. Not so much the pain from the smack, but the realisation of my plight. And I had no brother to support me. It was the first time in our lives we had been apart and without him, I felt lost. I owed this man my life but feared for my future, my only comfort being the knowledge that Paul was safe.

God knows how I managed to carry the unconscious Stafford upstairs. I received no help. His breath was deep, which was a comfort – if he died Sir Hugh would have little defence. Paul's case to become his squire would die, as might Paul. And where would that leave me?

The present occupier of the room, an elderly man of poor health, was furious. He would have punched me twenty years ago, as he kept telling me. He had paid for the night and refused to leave. I explained the situation, but he was adamant.

'I'd have punched you twenty years ago,' he said again.

'I know, Sir, you've told me three times already.'

'What did you say, sonny?'

'I said you said you'd punch me,'

He baulked and stared at me. 'I never touched you!'

I pointed down to Jacques Stafford on the floor. It made no difference. Whatever I said, and however I said it, he refused to move. It was hopeless. I was about to give up and fetch Tom when a young woman appeared.

‘What’s going on here then?’

The old man looked pleased to see her. 'He says I punched him and this man twenty years ago.'

She was of a similar age to me, about fifteen,

and wore a full-length white gown typical of a serving maid. She spoke in a calm, assertive manner, directing the question towards the older man, rather than me. I answered anyway.

'He won't leave,' I said, having no idea who she was or on what authority she asked the question.

She frowned at me, flicking her long blonde fringe out of her blue eyes with a sweep of her head, and put two full chamber pots down next to Stafford.

'I was speaking to this gentleman,' she replied, sounding polite whilst still managing to reprimand me. 'Now, Sir, I know it's an inconvenience, but a young fella such as yourself shouldn't be staying in this room!' She spoke and laughed at the same time, fluttering her eyelashes and moving towards his belongings that were in a satchel at the end of the straw-filled bed. 'Let me help you with these things – we'll pop you in our master bedroom tonight, free of charge – how does that sound?'

'Do I have to punch anyone?' he asked.

She gathered his belongings and ushered him out of the door, speaking all the time and leaving him no opportunity to argue. It was masterfully done.

In that second I was smitten. I needed to make a good impression.

Moments later she returned. Without a word, she began making the bed. Once finished, she placed the chamber pots to one side, moved to

Stafford's legs and picked them up. She looked at me and raised her eyebrows.

'You want me to pick this end up?' I asked, regretting it the moment the words left my mouth.

She rolled her eyes and let her head slump.

'What do you think?'

Picking him up under the armpits, we manoeuvred him onto the bed. The blood was drying on his face, and his nose was bent at a strange angle. He would never look the same again. I almost felt sorry for him before remembering his joy when he was about to hang my brother.

'I'm Ailred,' I said, straightening up and feeling my sore back.

'I know who you are and what you are,' she replied, looking at me with contempt. She turned her flushed face away and picked up the pots. 'Get him undressed, boy, or do you expect me to do that too?'

I blushed. 'Yes, Mam.' It was another statement I regretted. As she turned and left the room I made one more attempt. 'What's your name?'

'I'm Mam to you, boy.' She closed the door behind her.

*

After undressing, cleaning, and making Stafford as comfortable as a man with a bludgeoned face could be, Tom Brewer and his dragon of a wife, Emma, had me running around doing every job his family did not want to do. It was hell. I had never had to work for someone else before, always living hand-to-mouth with Paul and our father. I hated servitude and being belittled. Richard was the worst. From that first night, he resented my presence. To him, I was invading his territory and being two years older was determined to show dominance. So he did. At every opportunity. The tables were not cleaned well enough, the human excrement behind the tavern needed removing, and anything and everything required attention. And he always had that birch – which he used without a second's thought.

Emma was no better. She was an enormous lady with a gigantic bust that she flaunted at any drunkard in the tavern. She was known for it. By her smell, she never washed but I learned that if a woman had a big enough chest drunken men had no scruples.

As the evening grew into night, hunger took over. When I asked Tom or Emma for something to eat they laughed. They did a lot of laughing where I was concerned. One of my tasks was delivering food to the customers' tables, so I stole mouthfuls from each plate. The poorer customers tended to order the house pottage, a slow-cooked stew that comprised anything edible added to the pot and thickened with flour. I had been brought up on the stuff.

I did not see Mam for the rest of that

night. I was hoping I would. She had been the one member of staff who had shown me the slightest measure of respect. She was the only other member of staff. By the time the tavern had emptied and I had finished cleaning Lee Smithy's vomit from the front door, she had not reappeared.

'Ok, boy, we're going up to bed. When you've finished down here you can have the rest of the night off.' Tom laughed as he and Emma walked upstairs.

'Which room is mine?'

There was more laughter before Emma put me straight. 'You're in the stables, boy, with the other animals.'

*

With their incessant laughing still ringing in my ears and carrying a lantern, I unbolted and pushed open the barn doors. It was situated behind the tavern, built from rough-sawn timber and accessible via a passageway between the tavern and the neighbouring smithy. To the rear of that were the stables where patrons who stayed at the tavern would board their horses overnight. The barn was full of animals, all fenced in according to their species. It stank, but I did not mind – because I had no intention of staying.

I went through the barn, and, using the back door, entered the stables. My plan was simple – steal a horse and get as far away from this soul-destroying hell-hole as possible. Beyond that, I had not thought.

There were three horses that night, all with their heads peeking out from above the low doors of their enclosures. Each seemed docile enough and looked like they expected feeding.

I looked around for a saddle, although I had no idea how to harness a horse – or ride one for that matter.

'So you're a horse thief too, are you?'

The voice came from behind me, and I spun around in surprise.

It was Mam. 'They'll hang you, you know?'

She was holding a bowl of warm pottage in one hand and a mug of ale in the other.

'I…I was looking for some food to feed them.'

'Of course, you were,' she said, scowling and putting the food and drink on the floor. 'I had a feeling you would…' she gestured towards the horses, '...you would *feed a horse* tonight, so thought I'd come and dissuade you.'

I realised there was no point continuing the lie.

'I can't live like this, Mam. Those three will kill me. I'd rather take my chances and run. I don't know how you can work for those bastards. I know he saved me from hanging, but this is no life.'

She cocked her head to one side and stared at me. 'I don't think you've grasped the situation you're in. When Lord Thomas pardoned you he entrusted you to my father...' I went to interject but she held up her hand. 'Yes, I'm Tom and Emma's daughter, and in saving your life he now owns you. If you run away you're not only insulting my father but also Lord Thomas. Both will come looking for you and both will hang you.' Again, I went to cut in but she continued. 'You have two choices. One, make the best of working here, or two...' she tipped her head sideways and mimicked someone hanging.

I leaned against the stable wall and let myself slide down. She picked up the food and drink and handed them to me, leaving a delicate fragrance of lavender behind. It was gorgeous – no woman ever smelled so good.

‘They're not so bad,’ she said, sitting on an anvil close by. ‘Once they get used to you and you show them respect you'll be fine – well, at least my Ma and Pa will be. Just do as you're told and if you have any questions ask me. *Do not* ask Richard. He’s...well, just don't ask him anything. There's things about him...’ She did not finish the sentence.

She smiled. It was the only pure image I had seen that day and was the only reason I abandoned my plans to leave.

She stood and gathered the now empty plate and mug and went to leave.

'What's your real name?' I asked, more in hope than anything else.

'Mam,' she replied, then added, 'but you can

call me Philippa.'

She left.

*

I found a spare stall in the barn that was used to store straw. It became my new home. There were horse coverings piled in one corner, used to keep them warm in the depths of winter, so my bed was comfortable enough. My life until then had never been settled so this was no hardship.

After such a traumatic day, I slept well.

I was woken the next morning by Richard. He was pissing on me. It took a few seconds to realise what was happening and then I lost my temper. Jumping to my feet, I screamed abuse and ran at him, my fists clenched and arms whirling. He sidestepped me and grabbed me around the neck as I passed, wrestling me to the ground and forcing a submission. It was humiliating.

While I was subdued, he hissed into my ear. 'Stafford is awake, boy, and has shat himself overnight. Guess what your first job of the day is?' He laughed. 'And we're expecting Sir William to pick him up at some point, so you'd better do a good job.' He squeezed my neck tighter, almost choking me. 'Not so tough without your brother, are you?' He released me and stood. 'And if I see you speaking to my sister, I'll fuckin' kill you.' He spat at me and left.

I tried not to show fear, but deep down I was terrified. He was older and stronger and I realised he could kill me and face no consequences. I was expendable.

Getting up and brushing myself down, I made my way out of the barn. I had a young man covered in shit to clean up.

*

He stank. Hearing me enter the room, he turned his disfigured face in my direction and tried to speak. It sounded gibberish. It was a slow quiet voice, but I could just about understand what he said. 'Where am I? Who are you?'

'You're in the Chequers Tavern. You've been injured.' I found myself speaking as if talking to an old deaf person. He did not recognise me, which was a relief. 'I'm going to clean you up now before your father comes to collect you and take you home. You'd like that wouldn't you?'

'I'm not a fuckin' child, you bastard,' he slurred, moving his head back onto the blood-stained pillow and looking towards the ceiling. 'Come closer, I can't see well.' Moving next to his head, I knelt, putting my ear closer to his mouth. 'If you mention this to anyone outside this room, I'll have you skinned alive.' He gulped, licking the dried blood from his cracked lips. 'Do you know who I am?'

I edged away.

'No, Sir'.

'Good.' He closed his swollen eyes. 'Now get on with it.'

*

At midday, Sir William de Bohun arrived. He was accompanied by members of his household guard and his physician. By that time I had finished with Jacques Stafford and was mucking out the stables, Philippa having been given the task of keeping Stafford comfortable now he was clean. I stopped when they appeared and moved closer to the tavern's front door where Tom was waiting looking anxious.

'Greetings Lord,' Tom gushed, bowing low as Sir William dismounted.

He was a short, stern-looking man, his long curly blonde hair just visible under his bright red chaperon headwear, and his mannerisms supported my assumption.

'Where is my son?' he demanded.

Tom averted his gaze and nodded towards the door.

'He's upstairs, Sire, and he's fine. I'll get the girl to show you up.'

'Get out of the way, you idiot.' He looked towards his physician who had dismounted and was opening his horse's saddle bag. 'Hurry up Joel, get whatever you need and follow me.'

He pushed past Tom and stormed up the stairs.

'Philippa, Philippa…!' Tom shouted, looking around. He saw me watching and beckoned me over. 'You, boy, get up there and see if His Lordship needs anything.'

I bounded up the creaking wooden stairs and

stood outside the open door. Sir William was standing bedside as Joel, the physician, was tending to Jacques Stafford's wounds. There was silence as he worked – a silence which I broke.

'Sir William, do you know what happened to the boy that left with Sir Hugh?'

Even now, fifty-six years later, I cringe recalling that moment.

'WHAT?' he screamed, turning towards me red-faced and eyes blazing. 'YOU WANT TO KNOW HOW THE FUCKIN' BOY WHO TRIED TO KILL MY SON, IS?'

He flew at me as I backed away, tripping and falling backwards, down the stairs.

Everything went black.

*

When I awoke I was still dressed and lying on the straw that was last night's bed. I had a lump at the back of my head, but closer inspection revealed no blood. It was a relief. I tried to stand but my legs had other ideas. Looking across the barn, I could see two of everything. I blinked. Still two. I closed one eye and the two of everything became one. It was something that Paul had suffered years ago. He had cracked his head whilst falling from a tree, experiencing double vision and a headache as a consequence. It had not taken long before he returned to his boisterous self so I was not concerned. I tried to get up again as I was sure Tom or Richard would come looking for me, but it was not possible. As time went by, no one came.

I slept again.

The next time I awoke it was twilight and I was undressed. Philippa was standing close by with her arms full of clothes. I blinked and was relieved to see just one Philippa, although I had an awful headache.

'Nice to see you alive,' she said, throwing the clothing down next to me. 'Put these on, you smell terrible.'

'Did you undress me?' I asked, looking down at my nakedness and blushing.

She laughed. 'Don't worry, Ailred Norman, you've nothing special!'

The threats from Richard came rushing back. 'Where's your brother? He said he'll kill me if I talk to you.'

She put a finger to her lips to hush me. 'I know, he's told everyone, and I wouldn't put it past him – the sadistic bastard.' She looked away and said quietly, 'I doubt he'd stop at just you.'

'He's threatened to kill you too?'

'I wasn't talking to you,' she snapped, 'you talk too much. Put the damn clothes on.'

'Yes Mam.' I knelt and rummaged through them. Finding a beige tunic, I pulled it over my head and tied it at the waist with a length of cord. It was rough and uncomfortable and a little large for me. 'One of Richards's old hand-me-downs?'

'Yes, it's too small for him now – he won't miss it.'

There was an awkward silence. She had gone through all this trouble to look after me. She must like me, so I said, 'It looks like we'll be seeing a lot of each other, maybe we could...'

She stopped me there and shook her head. 'You *really* are a bit slow, aren't you?' I looked blankly at her. 'You're so dumb. You don't know when to speak or keep quiet...'

I was confused. 'So you want to keep me safe from your brother?'

'There you go again, you open your mouth and stupid words fall out.'

I looked at her and went to speak, but decided against it. I did not want to prove her point.

'You need to grow up. Don't mistake my good nature for weakness. I just need you to stay alive and remain here – is that so hard to grasp? Every job you do is something I don't. Hell, I even managed to attend the Sunday afternoon service at St Mary's church today – that's not happened for months. If you die or run away I'll be the one shovelling shit and working until midnight.' She saw the hurt in my eyes. 'By the look on your face, you're beginning to understand. Just work hard and keep yourself to yourself.' She turned and went to leave. 'In time I might think of you as human.'

It was a harsh truth to learn and explained my leisurely afternoon. The rest of the family were out enjoying their Sabbath.

Life away from the protection of my father

and brother was going to be difficult.

*

I went about learning the family business. At first, the long days and hard labour destroyed me and I considered running away, but as time passed Tom and Emma began to treat me with compassion. Sort of.

It started when they gave me time to attend the funeral of my father. He had been left to rot where he fell but monks came and cleared up the mess when people complained about the smell. It was a cheap affair conducted by Father Jeremiah, the sub-prior of St Mary Magdalene's priory. He and I were the only attendants. He was buried in an unmarked grave at the back of the cemetery, and there were no flowers on that wet morning. It was a brief service and any hope-filled words the eulogy offered gave little optimism for his long-term soul.

As weeks went by I started to get most Sundays off.

After the Sabbath's church service, along with many of the men of Tonebricge, I would practice archery. It was law. Knowing I was keen and could make life difficult for him, Tom allowed me the time. He even loaned me a bow. It was, strictly speaking, Richard's, but he would always skip practice. He was not alone. Many local men did not adhere to the law, but Sir Thomas de Clare was lenient if there was good cause. Impacting work on his estate was deemed good cause.

And every Sunday I improved. It became rare that anyone on the archery range got close to my accuracy.

A few local Tonebricge residents still shunned me, unable to forgive my past, but over time I earned the respect of most.

Philippa lived a parallel life, ignoring me most of the time, and my need to ask her advice dwindled. Richard continued to be a thorn in my side, never showing me a second's grace.

And still, I had no contact with Paul. Every time a member of Lord Thomas's or Sir Hugh's cortège came through the town I would enquire. I had no idea if he had become Sir Hugh's squire or was buried in an unmarked grave somewhere near my father.

One morning things changed.

Simon called me over. He was the son of the Butcher who owned the establishment on one side of the tavern and was a friend of mine. We practiced archery together and he knew I was desperate for news about Paul. On this day, he was chatting with a man and a young lad wearing the livery colours of Lord Thomas's household. They were buying cuts of meat and loading them onto a low cart that was piled high with vegetables and firewood.

I put the broom over my shoulder and walked over. 'What's up, Simon?'

'This gentleman has information regarding

your brother.'

By then they had finished stacking the meat and were about to lead the horse away. It was a scorching July day, and the meat was already smelling.

My spirit lifted.

'Excuse me, Sir, is it true – do you know something about my brother, Paul?'

The man grabbed the horse's bridle as the apprentice sat on the cart, making sure nothing fell out the back, and said, 'I can't hang about talking to the likes of you. If we don't get this meat back soon, it'll go off.' He sniffed the air. 'If it hasn't already.'

I ran after them as he led the cart away.

'Does Sir Hugh have a new squire?'

'Look, I told your friend all this earlier, I'll be damned if I'm going to go through it again, ask him,' he grunted and carried on leading the horse toward the castle whilst the apprentice pulled faces at me.

'But, Sir, just answer me that one question... please.'

He stopped and turned around, resignation on his face. 'Yes, Sir Hugh has a new squire. From what I gather his name is Paul Christian, now leave me alone or I'll take my whip to you.'

He left.

'Thank you, Sir, you're a good man.' I shouted after him and gave the boy a genuine smile, regardless of his gesturing insults at me.

So I knew.

I rejoined Simon and over a free mug of ale, questioned him on whether the man had been any more forthright with him. He had. Sir Hugh had refused Lord Thomas and Sir William's plea to reinstate Jacques Stafford as his page. He had made Paul Christian his squire, thus creating friction between himself and Sir William. Lord Thomas was not really bothered who Sir Hugh employed. He was, however, keen on keeping the peace as there was talk of imminent war between England and France and he needed to assemble an army to contribute to King Edward's claim to the French throne. He was hoping to unite Sir Hugh and Sir William under one banner but this conflict was threatening the plan. Both were obstinate and had returned to their fiefdoms with the issue unresolved. In short, they hated each other.

'So Paul must be in Glamorgan,' Simon said.

'Where the hell is that?'

'Damned if I know. I just know Sir Hugh is Lord of Glamorgan, so assume that's where he'll be.'

That made sense.

I had little knowledge of the ongoing conflict between England and France due to my upbringing, but Simon was well-versed on the subject. His plan was to join the army when he could, so took a keen interest. He brought me up to date on the two country's relationship. Or lack of it. Politics was not my strong point, but as Simon put it, 'It gives us an excuse to kill Frenchmen – what's not to like?'

'That's why I'm so dedicated to our war bow practice,' he concluded, finishing the ale and handing the mug back. 'With the aim you have, you should think about it too.' He put his arm around my shoulder. 'We could go together.'

'And get killed in a poxy field in France? I'll stick to the tavern, thank you very much!'

Simon grinned and strolled back to the butchery whilst I picked up the broom and returned to sweeping the tavern's floor in preparation for that evening's service.

I was beginning to feel at home.

I had a smile on my face for the rest of that day, which annoyed Richard when he turned up for work. For the first time in a long time, I was happy.

CHAPTER 3

It was October and the day of Tonebricge Castle's market, a monthly affair that traders from all over the borough attended, each paying Lord Thomas a fee to set up their stalls on the castle's lawn. Until now, Tom had not allowed me to attend. He restricted my work to menial jobs around the tavern, but as the months went by he began to trust me. He even paid me a small wage, keeping it hidden from Richard as he feared his reaction. I did too.

Tom and Emma's stall sold ale to market-goers. At this time of year, the sun had lost its heat with business slowing as people drank less. This month, Tom left the rest of his family to run the tavern and took me. I was honoured. That morning, we chatted as near-equals whilst setting up. I still had wary glances from passers-by, those who would never forgive my upbringing, but on the whole, people accepted me. Life was good – and was about to get better.

Our stall was located between a fleece merchant and a bootmaker, with both doing brisk business with the oncoming of winter. It was late in the afternoon and stallholders were beginning to pack away their unsold wares when I heard a cry of joy.

'Ailred!'

I knew straight away.

Spinning around I saw a group of soldiers in the colours of Sir Hugh le Despenser's livery trotting their horses through the thinning crowd. At the head were Sir Hugh and Sir Thomas riding side by side, and behind was Paul. He leapt from his horse and ran to me, sweeping me up in his arms. We embraced before becoming self-conscious. We stood back and looked at each other. I had not seen him for a year and in that time he had grown. Not just his height but in stature. He had a swagger and confidence about him that I had never seen, and the new clothing added to his transposition. His red and yellow checked tabard was tied around his waist by a thick leather belt that held a scabbard and sword to his side. On his chest, he wore the crest of Sir Hugh, who was sitting in his saddle watching.

Before I could comment on his good fortune, Paul spoke. 'You look well, Al.' His voice was deeper than I remembered, with a calm assurance to his words. 'And how you've grown.' That statement came as a shock. I had not considered my appearance, and, on reflection, I had grown into Richard's hand-me-down clothes and they were now too small. He moved over, grasped me by the shoulders and shook me.

'You've been practising haven't you – your chest size gives you away!' He mimicked the actions of firing an arrow and laughed.

We reminisced, asking questions in rapid succession, neither of us listening to the other's answer until we were interrupted.

'A little help over here when you're ready, Ailred.' Tom was keen to get me back to work.

'It would seem you're busy,' Paul said, glaring at the man who had refused to save him from the gallows and was unable to meet his gaze.

'I'm not paying you to talk to any old stranger when there's work to do.'

Paul bristled but held his temper. It was a marked difference from the Paul that had been whisked away all those months ago. That Paul would have, in all honesty, attacked him.

'Master Brewer, it's so lovely to see you again.' Sir Thomas kicked his horse a few paces forward and removed his garish cap. He looked at me and smiled. 'I see you still have your pet monkey on a short lead. It's good to see he's honoured his pledge not to run away.' He brushed the top of the large velvet hat and teased the feathers. Nodding towards the two of us, he continued. 'I'm sure you wouldn't miss the apeman for a short time while these two young lovers fuck each other senseless.'

Sir Thomas burst into laughter at his own quip, along with Sir Hugh and the two soldiers, leaving Paul and me red-faced.

Tom stopped packing the unsold ale barrels away and considered Sir Thomas's request. 'Of course, Sire, I'm sure I can spare them five minutes together.'

'I pity Mrs Brewer, Sir, if you manage to fuck her senseless in just five minutes! They may need a little more time than that.'

This sent them all into more childish hysterics.

There was a feigned cough from behind the group which brought silence.

'Ahh, greetings Father Rhys, I didn't see you standing there,' Sir Hugh stammered, as Sir Thomas was uncharacteristically lost for words.

'So it would seem,' he said. He spoke in a broad Welsh accent and frowned at Sir Thomas.

'Just a little humour between comrades in arms, Father, nothing more,' Sir Thomas said, hoping to placate the Archdeacon of Brecon.

'I see nothing humorous in the act of fornication between men.' He crossed himself and kissed the cross he wore around his neck. 'It is the work of the devil, and must be stricken from the face of God's earth.'

I noticed him look at Paul as he spoke.

'If you allow me a few moments to straighten this gentleman out, Father, you will have my undivided attention thereafter. A deal, your Holiness?'

Archdeacon Gruffudd ap Rhys raised his chin, then nodded.

Sir Thomas dismounted and approached Tom.

Tom looked nervous. 'I...I...of course he can have...'

'I'll tell you what, Mr Brewer, if you allow young Ailred here the rest of the night off I'll buy your remaining ale. How does that sound?'

Tom looked at me, and then at the barrel and a half of ale that we had been unable to sell, and smiled. 'Of course, Lord, he can have the rest of the night off.' He looked at Paul. 'And they're free to do whatever they want to each other.' He laughed and looked towards the others in his attempt to join their smutty humour, but was greeted with silence, and a disapproving scowl from the Archdeacon.

Sir Thomas ordered one of his entourage to pay Tom what he owed and to instruct him where to deliver the barrels.

'Be back at your quarters by midnight Paul, and don't get yourself into trouble. You have a bad reputation here, so be on your best behaviour. You represent Sir Hugh, and if you let him down...' He let the threat hang.

Grasping Paul's horse's bridle, he led them, Father Rhys, and the rest of the group towards the gatehouse, chatting as they left.

I looked at Paul and grinned. 'Let's get drunk.'

*

'So start from when Sir Hugh took you away the night you nearly killed Stafford.'

Paul had his boots off and was wiggling his toes in front of the fire. We sat overlooking the river Medway as it snaked its way around the castle and drank ale from a small barrel I had bought from Mark Peterson who owned the rival tavern in town, The Royal Oak. We used to sit in the same spot in times of trouble when we were younger. It felt comforting.

I had finished updating my life away from him, which he had listened to with interest, only interrupting to clarify small details.

He downed his ale and began his story.

Sir Hugh was furious that night. After killing our father, which he admitted enjoying, the situation with his page, Jacques Stafford, had come to a head. He had never wanted Sir William's bastard son as a page from the start but had agreed only to please Lord Thomas. Then, after comparing Paul and Stafford's merits that night, had made that bold decision leading to Stafford's mutilation. Sir William had to be physically restrained from attacking Sir Hugh the next day, demanding an armed duel to the death which Sir Hugh accepted, only to be overruled by Sir Thomas as the actions were within his estates. There had been an uneasy truce ever since.

I had asked what happened to Jacques Stafford when he left the tavern and was told he had been laid up for weeks. He was lucky to be alive. By the time he was fit enough to leave his room, Sir Hugh and his retinue, which included his new squire, were back in Glamorgan.

Paul's days were filled with swordsmanship training and etiquette lessons, and he was being taught French by a Basque scholar. ‘They speak French to each other, so I have no choice,’ he said. I was stunned – he had never shown interest in learning anything in his life.

He continued.

Sir Hugh was a hard but fair master, with a brutal temper. He did not have the wit of Sir Thomas, but Paul said there was no one in the world he would rather have by his side in battle. He was looking forward to his chance to serve.

And, from what Paul understood, that time was not far away. King Edward was in the latter stages of assembling a massive army, formed from every part of England, to take the fight to the shores of France. There was even talk of employing Welsh archers. Sir Hugh was to be an integral part of these plans, although he was not sure if the coalition between Sir Hugh, Sir William and Sir Thomas was still ongoing considering the present hostilities.

‘You've come a long way, Paul. I can't believe how lucky you've been.’ I tipped the barrel at an angle to extract the final dregs, whilst Paul prodded the dying embers.

'For the thieving son of a no-good bastard, yeah, I've done all right.' he agreed. 'And I've only just started.'

He spoke with such passion. I do not think I had ever seen him this happy in his life and was pleased for him. Then that voice in the back of my head wished it was me. Only for a second, but for that moment, I was jealous. I do not mind admitting it.

'And what's the story with this archdeacon, Father Rhys? What's he doing so far from his priory in Wales, wherever that is?'

Paul stiffened and spat in the fire.

'He's nothing. He's been preaching the evils of Frenchmanship to his flock in Wales, recruiting their archers for our upcoming jollies with France. They might be uncouth sheepshaggers, but they can fire an arrow as well as any Englishman. He's here to update Sir Thomas on his progress. I couldn't imagine going to war with them but if there's money to be made those bastards will be there, you mark my words.'

'And why did he look at you while preaching the sins of man?'

'I wouldn't give that...that...' he was lost for words, 'that spawn of Satan, the satisfaction of your interest, Al. Forget him. Stay clear.'

He had no intention of continuing the conversation, so I changed it.

'I think I'm in love.'

This impulsive statement caused him to snort the remains of his ale out of his nose in a fit of laughter. I had not intended to mention it to him, but it came out. If I'm honest, I had not admitted it to myself, but the ale was working its magic and I was feeling good.

'It's not me, is it? Sir Thomas was only joking, you know.'

I punched his arm. 'You're just my bit on the side.' There was a moment's silence as Paul wiped snot and ale from his short wispy beard before I continued. 'Her name is Philippa.'

'Is that the wench you mentioned earlier, the one who works in the tavern?'

'Yes, although she's not a *wench* – she's Tom's daughter.' I had not told him about Richard's hatred towards me, and his threats if I ever approached Philippa. I feared what Paul might do.

'Does she love you?'

I sighed. 'She doesn't know I exist. Actually, she does know – she just wishes I didn't.'

He leaned over and squeezed my arm. 'Give it time, little bro – things change. Hell, look at me! One moment I'm a thieving bastard, hated by everyone, and now I'm a squire, soon-to-be soldier. Who knows, if I prove myself to King Edward, I might be knighted one day.'

'I hate to say this Paul, but around here you'll always be a thieving bastard.'

That comment hurt him and I wished I had never said it.

'In that case – fuck 'em. The less time I spend here the better. I'm going to be a powerful man one day Al, you wait and see.'

The rest of the evening was spent in typical boisterous banter as the alcohol hit the mark.

That night was probably the best night of my life and wished it could have gone on forever, but Paul looked up as the moon slipped behind an unseen cloud and started his goodbye.

'I'd better get going Al, they'll come looking for me if I don't get back to the barracks soon.' He stood and brushed his livery down as my elder brother transformed into Paul Christian, the squire.

'Can't you stay a bit longer?' I sighed. It was earlier than I expected.

'We're going back to Sir Hugh's estate in Glamorgan at sunrise, so I need to show respect,' he replied. 'I guess I'll not see you for a while.'

I scrambled to my feet as he stood in front of me. He was in control. All of our lives I had been the one dictating events and reassuring Paul, but he had turned the tables. At that moment I felt alone and frightened. This could be the last time I ever saw him. I felt a tear well in my eye and looked away. I had wanted to say so much that day when he had been led away but none of those words came back to me. I wanted to hug him but knew he would hate that, so I looked at him.

He smiled. 'I know, brother, and I'd love to say the same things to you if I could.'

I smiled as a tear ran down my cheek.

'Never forget, Al, you're the smart one, you'll find a way to get what you want.' He looked me in the eyes. 'You'll find fortune one day – but you'll have to be patient. It might be when you least expect it.' He pointed to the ground where we stood. We'll always have this spot here. This is ours.'

I lowered my head. 'Just take this chance you have and don't fuck it up,' I said. He turned and walked away. 'Oh, and bring me back a Frenchman's head.' I saw him chuckle.

Then he was gone.

*

I was asleep the second my head hit the straw. I was still sleeping in the barn, but there was talk of moving me into the tavern's cellar, as Tom and Emma had come to trust me over the past year. I only hoped that afternoon had not ruined my hard work.

That night I dreamed of my father. He was hunting me with a bow and arrow and I bounded through the forest like a deer. It was bizarre.

I had met Simon Butcher on my way back to the barn the previous night and he was going hunting, using his archery skills to supplement their meat supply. He carried a large bag, so anticipated a good night. We chatted, and I told him about my evening with Paul. He had been sympathetic, although in a hurry to make his first kill. Speaking to him made me realise how good a friend he was, and that must have influenced my dream.

I opened my eyes. It was getting light. I always woke early as the barn's animals would disturb me, but this morning was different. Today I was roused by a kick to the stomach and dragged from the hay by my hair.

'You thieving bastard.'

I could not make out who was screaming at me, but it did not matter. There must have been five or six soldiers standing over me, and behind them stood Archdeacon Rhys. And it was he who spoke next.

'Bring him.'

'Bring me where?' I cried, fighting to grab the soldier's arm who was dragging me by my hair. 'What have I done?'

No one answered.

After having my hands bound behind my back, I was led from the barn, only to be halted by Tom. He was semi-dressed with one boot on, and standing in our path.

'What the hell is going on – where are you taking him?'

The lead soldier, dressed in the colours of Lord Thomas's household, stepped forward.

'Step aside Sir, this man is in the custody of the church, under the protection and authority of Lord Thomas and the King.'

Tom looked at me with confusion. 'This man is an employee of mine – I need him. There must be some sort of a mistake. What's he supposed to have done?' He looked to me for the answer.

'I don't know, these bastards won't tell me anything.'

'Strike the heathen, man, I demand that you

strike him. Insulting me is akin to heresy. I *will not* tolerate it I tell you.' Archdeacon Rhys was red-faced and pointing towards me as if I were the Devil himself.

The lead soldier acted out the instructions with brutal efficiency.

There was a soft voice from behind me. 'We must deserve some sort of explanation, your holiness?' It was spoken with great respect. It was Philippa.

'You stay out of it, I'll deal with this,' Tom said.

But the archdeacon was in no mood to listen to him. 'You would be wise to adopt the humility of this young lady, Sir, or you will be joining this thief.'

'Thief, what do you mean, thief? I haven't stolen anything,' I screamed and looked to Philippa for support. 'You *have* to believe me.'

The look on her face suggested she did not.

*

I was dragged through the main street, past the market square, and down towards the priory. If Archdeacon Rhys had hoped for an angry mob to stone me he had mistimed his actions, as most people were still asleep. I looked around, hoping one of the Brewer family was following to show support but was disappointed. I should have known no one would help.

And still, no one told me what I was supposed to have stolen.

But I soon found out.

As we approached the monastery of St Mary Magdalene on the outskirts of Tonebricge we were met by dozens of monks and nuns. The community turned out to witness my arrival, and I feared for my safety. The Archdeacon had the soldiers lead me through the gatehouse and into the courtyard. The priory had been damaged by fire a couple of years earlier and I had vague memories of watching the flames eat away at the church, but it had since been repaired, and it was through these hallowed doors I was taken. I stood in the vestibule, the tranquillity calming my captors' treatment towards me. I too ceased to struggle.

'Ahh, master Ailred Norman, isn't it? Nice to see you. I'm not sure if you remember me – we met, oh, about twelve hours ago. I managed to have you released from work duties to f... frolic with your brother.' Sir Thomas de Clare was standing in front of the altar, his husky voice echoing to all corners of the vast church. Next to him stood a clergyman, his grand dress suggesting high office. 'Cut his bind if you would be so kind,' he continued, 'we are in God's house now.' He beckoned us towards where they stood. 'And bring him down to meet Bishop Wyville, please.' The leading soldier unshackled my hands and led me down the nave, standing me in front of the imposing pair. 'Father Wyville here would like a word with you if that's all right with you, Ailred?' He raised his eyebrows and waited.

I was in no position to refuse. 'Of course, Lord, but I think there has been a terrible misunderstanding…'

Sir Thomas raised his hand. 'Bishop Wyville, he's all yours.'

There was a moment's silence, the church's aura amplifying it tenfold, and then the bishop spoke. He had a slow but thunderous voice and I thought God Himself was talking to me.

'We are all sinners, my child.' He paused as if giving a sermon to an audience, then continued. 'Some sins go unnoticed and are easily repented, but others are blasphemous.' He looked at me. 'Are *you* a heretic?'

He was wearing the full robes and regalia his position afforded and was pointing his pastoral staff at me.

'No, your grace, I am anything but…' I was terrified. I had long learned the dangers of accusations of heresy. Many innocents had been burned alive or tortured into false testimony. 'Please, Father, can you tell me what my supposed crime is?'

There was a raised voice from the rear of the church. 'You robbed the priory, you thieving…'

'Silence, Father Rhys, I will ask for your input when it is required,' Bishop Wyville commanded.

I turned my head and saw Archdeacon Rhys still standing in the vestibule, desperate to involve himself.

'As Brother Rhys states, a considerable sum of

money was stolen last night. Do you have any knowledge of this?'

So that was it. No wonder the priory was in turmoil.

'Of course, I don't,' I snapped, 'no one in their right mind is going to rob the church – that would be crazy!'

'Crazy or not, someone did last night. You must be truthful my child, God listens to your every word, and come judgment day, you will be held to account.'

I looked to Sir Thomas and then the bishop, before pleading for my life. 'I will swear on the holy bible that I have no idea who stole your money.' I moved forward to take the holy book from the hands of the bishop, but he struck me with his staff, making me wince and step back.

'That will not be necessary,' he said, recovering his composure.

Sir Thomas removed his gloves. 'Where were you last night?'

'I was with my brother, Sir Thomas, as you said earlier. Why am I here? Was I seen stealing anything...because if I was they're lying. Tell me who it was...I bet it was that Richard, the slimy bastard...'

Sir Thomas lost his composure. 'SHUT UP. We're not here to answer your questions, boy, just speak when spoken to. Your brother left with Sir Hugh hours ago and is miles from here, so it's you we are talking to.' He stepped forward and struck me across the face with his heavy gloves. He was a frightening beast when afire.

'There will be no violence in this house of God,' the bishop boomed, ushering Sir Thomas away.

I knelt before the two. 'Thank you, your grace, and apologies my Lord, I meant no disrespect. I was just trying to defend my innocence.'

Lord Thomas put his gloves into his tunic pocket. 'You can defend it from the castle. I have no time for this here. Father, with your permission, I will have this boy interned and we will pursue this matter in a more suitable environment.'

'So be it Lord, but we *have* to resolve this thing in haste. This priory will struggle to function after such a substantial loss. Without its return, this priory will suffer for a generation.

The bishop was showing humility but I was close enough to see the sweat on his brow and hear the panic in his voice. There must have been a vast amount stolen.

Seeing he was not going to be invited, Father Rhys walked down the nave towards us.

'Allow me to handle this matter, Lord Thomas, and save you the inconvenience. I have a history of success in issues of persuasion.'

'I am well aware of your powers of *persuasion*, Archdeacon, but I have a reputation for fairness in this parish and I intend to keep it. I will, however, allow you to be present at the questioning.'

The archdeacon looked disappointed, but said, 'As you wish, Sir Thomas, I was only thinking of your Lordship's pressing schedules.'

I was led in the direction of Tonebricge Castle.

*

It started formally. Sir Thomas put me into a small cell in the castle's undercroft. It was not a dungeon but was fear-inducing all the same. It was cold and damp, the only light afforded was via a small barred window cut into the heavy door. I had no water, no food and had to squat in the corner to relieve my churning stomach. A scattering of straw covered the flagged floor, and I could not begin to imagine sleeping there. I did not have to. After a few hours, the doors opened.

‘I hope your stay has been pleasant so far, Ailred Norman?’

It was Sir Thomas, and with him was a young man a little older than me. Both were casually dressed and seemed in no hurry.

Archdeacon Rhys, still wearing the grand vesture of his church, edged his way past the two and pulled me violently up from where I sat.

'You did it, you and that evil brother of yours… admit it before God,’ he screamed into my face, spittle making me look away. His frustration was hysterical, but Lord Thomas ushered him out, to the archdeacon's annoyance. ‘I cannot impress upon you enough the seriousness of the situation, Lord, the longer this interrogation goes on the less chance we have of recovering the money. We need it to pay my countrymen to join the King's army. Without that, they'll never come to England.'

Sir Thomas sighed. 'Yes we know all this, Father,' he rolled his eyes at the young man next to him, 'but we have methods of doing things here, and I want my son Nathaniel to learn from this experience.'

'Of course, Lord, Nathaniel and I are well acquainted. He is a God-fearing member of my congregation when I am in this priory, and has sought my advice on many occasions in his battle against Satan.'

He turned to Nathaniel and offered him his hand, which he kissed and bowed his head.

Turning to me, he said, ' We need results, Lord. The greater time spent here listening to this lying...'

'So you think the thief might be escaping as we speak?' Sir Thomas said.

The archdeacon became animated. 'Yes, Lord, if we can...'

Sir Thomas seemed confused. 'So you think this might *not* be the robber then? You sounded convinced a few seconds ago.'

I stood listening as he dismantled Father Rhys's certainty.

Any hope soon died.

Before Father Rhys could retort his put-down, Sir Thomas barked, 'Take him to the dungeon, jailer.'

His tone was flat and decisive. He was enjoying watching the adulation on his son's face.

I was taken further into the depths of the castle, past the oubliette, which was a small barred hole in the floor where condemned people were thrown never to see the light of day again. I prayed to God I would not end up there.

We entered a dark oppressive room with coal burning in a small kiln in one corner, a poker inserted. It made my blood run cold. There was a table at the centre with a single wooden stool on one side and a pair of high-backed chairs on the other. Various chains and ropes were scattered about the floor and a set of shackles was fixed to each wall.

'Take a seat, Ailred, if you please. We'll try not to detain you long,' Sir Thomas said as he and his son sat down.

I sat on the stool.

'I promise, Lord I never robbed...' I stuttered but was stopped.

'Not so fast, Ailred, let me speak – if that's all right with you?'

I looked down at the table.

'Good. Now, you're a proven thief, yes?'

'Lord, that was a long time ago, Sire, and I was only doing the bidding of my father. He made us rob people.'

'Yes, I remember that night well, which brings me to my second point, your brother.'

'My brother? He's not even here, Sire, he's with

Sir Hugh.'

'True, and he is of high standing now, so I just wanted to know if he was with you the entire evening?'

'Yes, Lord, we stayed together all night, first we...'

He wagged his finger at me. 'If you keep your answers short and to the point, we'll be out of here all the sooner.'

I nodded.

'Now, Ailred, did you see anyone else last night that can uphold your story?'

Father Rhys lost his patience. 'It's his brother, Lord Thomas, I tell you, he and this man are demons from hell – *they* robbed the church.' He turned and looked at Nathaniel. 'Think of your son, Lord, the more time he spends with this man the closer he is to hell!'

Nathaniel shuffled uneasily in his chair.

'SHUT UP...' Sir Thomas snarled, before taking a deep breath. 'Apologies, Father, but I would like to do this my way.'

Archdeacon Rhys was prowling up and down, thumping his staff on the floor. 'As you will, Lord, but I 'm telling you...' he murmured, more to himself than anyone else.

'As I was saying, did anyone see you?'

'I bought ale from Mark Peterson at The Royal Oak.'

He nodded.

'Oh, and I saw Simon Butcher on my way back

to the barn.'

'And both of these men can attest to that?'

I nodded.

He looked at me and scrunched his face. 'What do you think, Nathaniel? Anything on your mind?'

His son stood and straightened his clothing. He was taller than I with long straightened hair and a more than passing resemblance to Lord Thomas. Even his mannerisms were similar.

'Well, he seems a personable fellow, although he smells terrible.' He chuckled to himself. 'The question is why would someone rob a church, beyond the Devil's accomplice,' he looked at me, 'and then stay around waiting to be caught? If I was him, and by his smell I'm glad I'm not, I'd be miles away by now.' Sir Thomas gave a knowing smile. 'And nothing has been found to tie him to this. *But*, being a seasoned thief, who planned robberies in the past...'

'May I speak in my defence, Sire?'

But the Archdeacon was having none of it. 'SPEAK...of course you cannot, I'll have your tongue ripped from your head and drive that hot poker...' he slammed his staff onto the table.

I jumped.

Just then there was a knock on the cell's door.

'What is it?' Sir Thomas shouted.

'Sorry to interrupt, Lord, but there is some urgent business that requires your attention.'

He sighed, 'I'll be as quick as I can.' He looked at

Nathaniel. 'Carry on here, Nate, if you would be so kind.'

He had one glance at Father Rhys and left the room.

Nathaniel continued the interrogation, all questions looking for weaknesses in my story, but could find none.

'There must be dozens of thieves in Tonebricge!' I said, as Nathaniel sat down and stared across the table at me.

'That there is, Ailred, but they are all petty criminals that could never achieve this level of audacity.' He stopped and looked at the archdeacon who had been quiet for a while, then continued. 'To break into the church's vestry, gain access to the treasury's vaults and get away with fifty pounds of gold doubloons takes a lot of planning.'

I choked. No wonder the church was in pandemonium. That level of loss was unthinkable. Whoever stole it would be rich for the rest of their lives. I wished I *had* stolen it.

Archdeacon Rhys waited for this moment to speak. 'Well, I think we have all the proof we need.' Nathaniel and I looked at him in surprise. 'Do you not see what this devil is doing? He is enchanting us. Surely you can feel his eyes bewitching you?' He stared at Nathaniel. 'Oh, my God, this demon has you under Satan's spell already – you just do not realise.' He crossed himself and moved to Nathaniel's side. 'You must cast this devil's thoughts from your mind.' He licked his finger and made the sign of the cross on Nathaniel's forehead. 'He is using his eyes to infect your soul.' He covered Nathaniel's eyes with his hands. 'Look upon this creature no more. We must remove this beast's eyes, lest he sends you straight to hell.'

Nathaniel turned and looked away. 'I...I didn't realise Father. What can I do?'

'We must chain it to the wall so it cannot gaze upon us.' He placed the staff on the table, and pulled me over to the wall, smashing my face. 'Bring me the shackles in haste, and do not look into its eyes.'

Before I could do anything, I was manacled to the wall, my face pressed against the rotting stonework. I turned my head sideways.

'Don't listen to him, Nathaniel,' I begged. 'He's crazy. I'm no more a devil than you are...'

Father Rhys laughed. 'See, Nathaniel, see what this fiend will do to poison your mind. He's using Satan's voice now. Can you hear it? Can you hear the unmistakable voice of the devil?'

'Yes...Father, yes, I can hear it – please save me, Father, I beg of you.'

I was unable to see either of them but could feel the hysteria as he manipulated Nathaniel's mind.

'Cover your ears, my son, cover them, and leave this cell of the damned. I will summon God's strength to fight this...this, thing, alone. Be gone good Christian, and do not re-enter this house of Satan until I have sent Beelzebub's spawn back to hell.'

'Thank you, Father, I thank you…'

I heard the door open and close, and then silence.

'I am no devil, Father, and you know it…' I heard footsteps, and then the sound of the hot coals being disturbed. Still, there was silence. 'Father Rhys, for God's sake, you must believe me, I had nothing to do with the robbery.' I was petrified – this madman could do anything now we were alone.

'It was you, I know it was you and your brother. Your brother took my key.' The voice was in my ear and I could smell his stale breath.

'I…we, had nothing to do with it Father, nothing I tell you.'

'If you did not know, which I doubt, then your brother did it alone. Either way, you must atone. God will judge me if I allow this sin to go unpunished. I will have your eyes, but first I will bring you pleasure. God will want you to feel his love before I darken your world.' I felt his hand lift my tunic and rub the inside of my thigh. 'Does that feel good? Does Satan like that?'

His voice was in the other ear and I could sense his excitement.

'What, what are you doing?'

'Your brother liked it when I did this to him,' he said as he stroked my cock. 'Will you not get hard for me? Your brother did.'

Before I could say anything else he moved away and I heard him pick something up from the table. I felt him lift my tunic and a finger penetrate my arse. Then two.

'Father, please...' I begged, but all I could hear was rasping breath, then the sound of him spitting onto something.

'By God's decree, I fill you with his love.' He released the words as if he was climaxing, and I felt the end of his pastoral staff inserted into me with great force.

I screamed in agony.

'Let it out my child, let God into your soul.'

He was holding my shoulder with one hand so he could thrust the staff harder and I felt his hand shuddering.

'Take God's love, take it all...'

He was licking my neck, his hand now reaching around and stroking my cock.

Through my screams, I heard the door open.

I just about heard Lord Thomas's voice. 'What the...?'

'Help me, please help me,' I begged.

I felt his hands detach and the staff made a nauseating sound as it was removed, the intense pain easing.

'Get out, Father – this man is innocent,' Sir Thomas bellowed.

'Innocent? He is *not* innocent! I am God's spokesman on earth, who are you to contradict my testimony? I act on Christ's behalf.' His speech was high-pitched and rambling.

'It was the butcher's son, Simon. I just had word from his family that he went missing last night and he stole their business savings too.'

Stillness descended. I rested my cheek against the cold chalky stonework.

Father Rhys made one final attempt. 'It was him and his brother...'

'Take that poker from him and get him out of here – and unshackle this man, Nathaniel. You should *never* have left him alone with this...' he stopped to choose his next word carefully, '...this maniac.'

CHAPTER 4

Well, that was difficult. Reliving those moments was something I thought I would never have to do, but the burden has lifted. I have carried the weight of that day most of my life. Brother Michael turned a shade of pale I have never seen before, which I take as a personal triumph.

Bishop Budwith, who instigated this project, took the manuscript away for three days and has just returned it. He scrutinised it and asked many questions which I will not transcribe here. To summarise, he wants to know if everything I say is true. I will repeat to you what I asked of him – why would I lie? I am old, and if you have not deduced that already you should be reading something else. So, yes, everything I say is true.

After that confirmation, his interest in this confession is waning. It leaves me wondering if my narrative is to blame or whether there was an ulterior motive in his initial investment. He has no interest in any of this story outside the robbery.

*

I was taken from that place of iniquity and returned to sanity.

It was Philippa who secured my release, allowing Simon Butcher's mother to cry on her shoulder long enough to retrieve the information and relay it to Sir Thomas in time to avert the removal of my eyes. For that, I will be forever indebted.

And so it was that on that evening I stood opposite Philippa in the Chequers Tavern, sitting being too painful, and started the next chapter of my life.

'How did you know I was innocent?' It was an obvious question.

'I didn't. I thought you were guilty as hell.'

I chuckled to myself. It's surprising how you can laugh after the fact. 'So why did you help…?'

'Because…'

'Great answer.'

'You didn't let me finish. Because…'

I shrugged. 'Well, at least I know.'

'Because I needed to know who or what you were.'

Again I shrugged. 'Well, Philippa…' I picked up my mug and raised it in front of my face. 'I thank you from the bottom of my heart.'

She looked at me and twisted her head sideways, then dissolved into a fit of laughter.

'Oh, I thank you from the bottom of my heart,' she mimicked me and held up a pretend mug.

I scowled at her for a second before realising my ridiculous offence and joined her mockery.

'Where is Richard this evening?' I asked when

we had stopped ripping into one another.

'Who cares?' she said, getting up and walking over to the counter and leaning over to pour herself an ale. 'He's no doubt drowning his sorrows that you're not eyeball-less.'

There was no one in the tavern as it was late and Tom and Emma had long since gone to bed, leaving Philippa to lock up. They had been happy at my release, but were upset that Simon Butcher had robbed his parents and the Priory. They, like everyone else, found it hard to accept. They had known him from birth and could not believe he had committed such a crime.

'Good luck to him,' she said as she gulped down half the mug, wiping her mouth on her sleeve. 'He'll be set for life.'

I rolled my eyes at her. 'If *I* had done it, you'd have called me every name under the sun and danced on my grave after they'd hung me!'

'Yes,' she laughed, 'but he's better looking than you.'

I shook my head and groaned.

'Don't worry, you have your strengths.'

I smiled. Someone had looked beyond my past for the first time in my life. It was a step forward.

'So you think I have strengths?' It was a dumb question by a dumb person.

She looked at me and stared deep into my eyes. 'Your strength is in your...smell.' She held her nose and waved her other hand in front of her face. 'Go to bed, Ailred Norman, you have a busy day tomorrow. See if you can stay out of trouble.'

With that, she stood and finished her drink.

'Good night, Mam,' I said, my injury causing me to walk gingerly from the tavern in search of my hay-filled bed as she finished wiping the surfaces down.

*

The following morning I awoke to the sounds of Richard's abuse and went to sleep that night with his rantings in my ears. He never let up. You would think someone would tire of squashing bugs, but he was intent on grinding them into the ground. I dismiss it now, but at the time it was hell on earth.

And so it went on, week after week. And with each passing day, I learned more about the business. I would attend church each Sunday at St Mary's with the Brewer family before archery practice. I missed Simon. We had competed on the range and pushed one another to improve, and I still found it hard to believe he had robbed his own family and the church, but deep down wished him well. The thought of him sunning himself on the coast of a foreign country made me smile.

And Philippa made me smile. She would tease me daily, flaunting her body and making me laugh. She had a quip for everything, and we spent hours ribbing each other. Whatever I did she would do better, although she never provided a scrap of evidence to back it up. I never asked. If ever I woke with a hangover she had a worse one, and to this day I swear she threw up on demand.

Yet still her brother bore into me. Day after day, he stamped on the insect that I represented.

And then one day everything changed.

'I'm pregnant.'

'What do you mean, I'm pregnant?'

'What do you think I mean?' She looked at me as if I was stupid. Which, looking back, I was.

'But...but...that means...'

She shook her head. 'You're so dumb, Ailred.'

I did not know what to think. This was Philippa, my Philippa, the person I adored. She was pregnant. Which meant...I could not bring myself to think beyond that.

'Yes, I'm going to have a baby, Al.' She looked coldly at me. 'And no, it's not yours.'

I was crestfallen, I don't mind admitting. Strike that – I was devastated. I knew it could not be mine, because, well, I think you can work that out.

I took a large number of deep breaths, before asking, 'Who is the father?'

'Don't worry, you don't know him,' she said but seemed distracted.

'I might.'

'Well, it could be a couple of guys if I'm honest...'

My world crumbled. I got to know this woman so well in the last few months. She had saved my life and we had become close friends, but...

'I'm sorry,' she said.

I looked at her and smiled. It was fake, but I did it anyway.

'You never did hide your emotions well, Al.'

'You shouldn't apologise, Pip, it's your life – but you'll need help and support through this. Whoever the father is will need to know.'

She gave me the most genuine smile. 'Thanks, Al, I want this baby. I don't care who he is.'

I held her hands. 'I love you.'

'I know, and I love you too, but in a different way.'

I looked at the floor and could not stop a tear rolling down my cheek.

'You'll always be *my* Ailred,' she laughed. 'Now I need to tell my parents.'

'I'm always someone's backup,' I said, more to myself than her.

We had been mucking out the stables at the time, and she was gathering her things together.

'What was that, Ailred? You mumble so much, you drive me crazy sometimes!'

I looked at her as she scurried about, tidying.

'It doesn't matter,' I said, 'it's just me.'

The rest of that day was spent in the barn. I did not want to be around when she told her parents as they needed privacy. I wondered how they would take it. It would come as a shock, as it had to me, but I suspected they would come round to the idea in time.

Then it struck me – what about Richard! He was bound to think it was me…

I was right.

'WHERE THE FUCK IS HE?' I could hear him running towards the barn.

I was sitting on a bale of hay and jumped up as he careered into sight. He was red-faced and blowing. I think he had been drinking.

'You fuckin'…' He grabbed a pitchfork off the floor and ran at me. 'You raped my sister, I'm gonna fuckin' kill you.'

He lunged at me but I managed to dodge his first effort, ducking around the back of him so I was not penned into the stall. I needed to escape and started running towards the barn door. Just as I made it there Philippa came running in the opposite direction and we collided, our heads smacking hard. I saw stars. She fell unconscious to the floor. I was dazed but alert enough to understand her plight – and my own.

'Wait, wait, she's hurt.' I shouted, holding my head and waving a defensive hand as he approached.

But he did not stop.

'I'll fuckin' kill her after you, the whore.'

'It's not my baby, it's not mine…' but by then he was upon me and was thrusting the fork towards my face. I was seeing double and having trouble fending off the blows. Then it happened – one of the narrow prongs went through the palm of my hand and stuck fast.

I screamed in pain, which made him madder as he tried to release the iron spike. I was hanging on to the other prongs. Even in my bewildered state, I realised if he pulled it clear he would continue the assault on my face. He kept screaming, 'I'll kill you both, I'll kill you both.'

Blood was spraying over the floor and covering me.

I tried to calm him, appealing to his sense of reason, but he had none.

And I feared for Philippa. She did not move as we fought over the pitchfork.

'STOP RICHARD, STOP THAT RIGHT NOW.'

Tom came charging in with Emma close behind. He attempted to grab the pitchfork, while she scrambled on the floor attending to Philippa.

'IT ISN'T HIS CHILD YOU FOOL...LEAVE HIM BE.'

Richard stopped and stared at his father, and then at his mother as she was feeling Philippa's forehead.

'SHE'S A FUCKING WHORE,' he screamed, dropping his end of the pitchfork and running out.

'Did he do this to her?' Tom asked looking to chase after his son, but I stopped him.

'No, no, we clashed heads when I tried to run away. He's a lunatic.'

That calmed him and he joined his wife kneeling over their daughter.

I pulled the spike out of my hand and looked about for something to stem the blood, finding a short length of material which I tied tightly.

'Is she all right?' I asked, crouching beside them.

She stirred and opened her eyes. We let out a collective sigh of relief, and I stood back.

'It looks like she'll be fine – but I need to get this tended to. It's bad,' I said and looked around the corner to check if Richard had gone. He had.

I left and jogged towards the priory. The clergy were the only people I could think of who had any knowledge of healing and I was desperate. I had seen many people suffer infection after the most innocuous of injuries, so I feared the worst.

By the time I reached the priory gates my jog had turned to a walk and I was lightheaded. The blood had soaked through the bandage and was dripping a trail behind me. It was not far but the pain had grown and my hand throbbed.

I was met at the gate by a novice monk. His stare told me he recognised me as the man who had been accused of robbing the priory a few months before.

'You are not welcome here, Sir.' he said, before noticing my bloodied hand.

'I...I need help,' I begged, as I felt waves of pain.

I could make out his voice calling names and felt myself fall. I blacked out.

When I awoke I was lying on a straw-filled bed. As my senses returned I gazed around. I was lying close to an old monk, his shaved head perspiring as he looked to be fighting some kind of infection. He was mumbling prayers to himself. There was the smell of vomit and faeces and urine.

I lifted my hand and looked. There was a poultice bound front and back and the blood had been washed away. It still hurt but the throbbing had stopped, which relieved me.

'Ahh, Master Ailred, I see you're with us again.'

I looked towards the sound of the soothing voice. It belonged to a young monk who was standing next to Philippa. She had a lump on her forehead that had been treated with some sort of herbal paste.

'We were beginning to wonder if you would ever return,' Philippa said, smiling. 'How are you feeling?'

'I've felt better,' I replied, trying to flex my fingers to see how much control I had, 'but seeing you helps. How long have I been asleep?'

'You came in yesterday,' the monk said, walking over and studying my hand. 'Stick your tongue out.' I did and he nodded. 'Good, good – I'm Father Jobe.'

I looked at Philippa. She looked tired but the lump on her head was her only visible injury.

'How long have you been here, Pip?' I asked, trying to sit up.

Father Jobe eased me back, 'She came looking for you yesterday and has been here ever since.

She's been fretting. Now, you must rest – you lost a lot of blood.' He looked at the hand again. 'I stitched it up the best I could before applying those poultices.'

'You put stitches in my hand?' I was stunned. I had heard of it being performed but had never seen it.

He glowed with pride. 'Yes, you're my first attempt and I'm rather pleased with how it went. I used catgut.'

'Well, can you thank the cat for me when you see it?' I replied.

He suppressed a grin. 'If all goes well you can come back and I'll remove the stitches in a week or so.' He looked at Philippa. 'Just keep your husband out of trouble will you?'

We both laughed and I lay down and closed my eyes.

'Go home, wife, and I'll come back when Father Jobe says I'm fit enough to leave.'

There were a few seconds of silence.

'Richard has gone,' she said.

'He'll be back. It can't carry on like this. Either he leaves or I will. We can't live together, we all know that.' I waved her away. 'Now go and get some rest, you look like shi…' I looked at Father Jobe who raised his eyebrows. '...you look like you need the rest.' He nodded in appreciation.

She turned and left as I closed my eyes, the dying monk's chanting lulling me into a deep sleep.

*

I thanked Father Jobe and donated the only money I had to the priory as I left the infirmary the next day. I was unsteady on my feet and my hand still hurt, but was otherwise fine.

After a slow walk back, I met Tom as he was opening the tavern. We chatted. He'd had no contact with Richard since the incident and was struggling to cover his workload. My absence had not helped. Emma looked out from the door with a concerned expression.

'I know he's hot-tempered but he's still our son,' Tom said.

'He tried to kill me.' I waved my bandaged hand in front of his face. 'More to the point, he would have killed Philippa if you hadn't stopped him.'

He pulled the window shutters open, letting the warm spring sunshine into the murky tavern. 'Oh, he was just trying to scare you. If he wanted to kill you he would have.' He stood and put his hands on his hips. 'And he loves his sister, I know he wouldn't have hurt her.'

I shook my head. 'You're kidding yourself, Tom. He's dangerous.'

He shrugged.

Emma came out but would not make eye contact.

'Am I still welcome here?'

They exchanged glances. 'Well, we certainly need the help, and while he's gone you're safe, but when he returns...' He hesitated. 'We can't turn away our son.'

I thanked him and went into the barn. The blood had been cleaned away as it would attract more rats. There were enough already. I tried to put the previous couple of days behind me.

That afternoon I went back to work, serving people in the tavern and delivering food to the tables, anything I could do one-handed. Richard had damaged my left hand and I favoured the right, so it could have been worse.

As days went by my wound healed. And there was still no sign of Richard.

Things returned to normal.

Every morning I would wake and start my chores. Whatever I was capable of at first, but that increased as my injury improved.

Tom and Emma worried about Richard, but that was understandable. Philippa would not mention his name.

After two weeks, Father Jobe removed the stitches and I could see the wound. He was more than happy with his stitching experiment. So was I. The skin had knitted together well. There was no sign of infection and I was heartened to hear the worst risks had passed.

I was assured I would be able to use the war bow, but not for a while.

And every day Philippa grew larger.

'You can't avoid the obvious forever,' I said one afternoon when I saw her struggling to replace hay in one of the tavern's beds.

She stopped and looked across at me. 'And that obvious thing being…?'

'The father will have to get involved with the baby when it comes. Or at least contribute.' I hesitated. 'Whoever he is.' It was a petty thing to say, I know, but it still hurt.

'Well, Mr Norman, my constant reminder of guilt, I told the two…' she pulled a quizzical face, '*…people* involved, and they both disappeared within a few days. My guess is they joined the army and are en route to France or Scotland or some other god-forsaken place.' She laughed. 'It has to be better than helping to bring up my bastard child.'

'Have you told Tom and Emma they left?'

'No, and I'm not going to until the time is right.' She frowned at me. 'And you mustn't either.'

'They won't be happy,' I said.

She straightened and put her hands on her hips. 'Nope. It'll be just another mouth to feed.'

*

Before long, Philippa and I were running the tavern. Tom and Emma were happy to let us. With the perks of running a tavern came the perks of running a tavern. Ale and wine. Whenever I wanted it. And I wanted it. At first, I used to finish the patrons' leftovers. It was simple. No one noticed. Then I would pour myself wine. Again, no one cared.

If I could smile on parchment I would do so now because that was how I felt most of the time. Through alcohol, the world opened itself to me and I socialised. I had always been a loner. Paul had been my only companion but now I found myself at ease. It was an awakening.

I would go to sleep every night without a care, and wake the following morning feeling guilty – but by midday the cycle would repeat.

I moved into the tavern. The rats in the barn would miss me. I was hoping for Richard's room but was disappointed. His room was rented out to paying customers with the proviso that he could move back whenever he returned. His parents would forgive him. Philippa was different. Weeks passed and he did not appear, so all was well.

*

'That's three each, Al. I thought I'd never see this day.'

It was a scorching hot August Sunday and I was straining to see the target a hundred paces away. I had attended church with the family and was endeavouring to relieve Bart, the Butcher's new employee, of his hard-earned pay on the archery range. The damaged hand had healed to the point I was able to return to my love of the bow, and after a few practices, my aim was back to its best. Well, I thought it was. Bartholomew was good, but it had never occurred to me that he might beat me. No one beat me. Ever.

'Double or nothing on the final round?' I snapped.

He looked at me with disappointment. We had been to the range often since Simon had run away and were beginning to forge a bond. He was new to the area, having been brought up by his mother in nearby Seouenaca. I liked him.

'No need to get tetchy Al, you're just having an off day,' he said, lowering his bow and taking the arrow from the string.

I picked the half-empty jug of ale from the floor and downed it.

'If you think you'll lose...' I shrugged. 'I'm always better under pressure.'

He looked at me, and then at the distant target.

'There was a time when I couldn't get close to you, Al.' He pondered for a few seconds, then blurted it out. I knew it was coming. 'Do you think drinking might affect your aim?'

I tossed the empty jug to one side and nodded. 'You too? Everyone thinks they're my mother these days.' I picked up an arrow and placed its nock on the string. 'One shot,' I said, gesturing towards the target. 'If I win, will you shut up?'

He nodded. 'I'm hardly banging on about it, but yeah, if you win I'll shut up.'

'Good,' I replied, and stood straight, my feet planted, as I weighed up the shot. There was a northerly breeze but my mind had accounted for that.

He stepped forward and lowered my bow. 'And

what if you lose?'

I had not even considered the prospect. 'If I lose?'

'Yes, if you lose. It's not a bet without a forfeit.' There was silence for a few seconds before he said, 'You stop drinking for a week.'

I laughed. 'Good one, Bartholomew. I'll tell you what – if I lose I'll…'

'No, Al, if I win, you stop drinking for a week. Unless you think that's too hard?'

'Fuck off, Bart.' He was beginning to get on my nerves.

He sighed. 'You can be such a prick sometimes, Ailred, just shoot the arrow.'

I lifted the bow and looked at the round wicker target in the distance. Placing the broad-headed arrow's nock onto the string again, I drew the bow to its full capacity as I had thousands of times before. It was second nature to me, my body now powerful enough to fire twice as far as the simple shot I was about to make. It was all instinct. Just before I released the string, I noticed a tremor in my hand, only for a second, and then the arrow was airborne. A split second later it embedded itself in the red ring that encircled the bullseye.

'That'll do,' I said, picking up the discarded jug and tipping any remaining drips onto my tongue.

'Good shot,' he admitted. 'So all I need to do is hit the bullseye.'

I smirked. 'Nothing gets past you, Bart.'

He stepped forward and I passed him an arrow. His routine was similar to mine, although he looked longer at the target, visualising his task. He was bigger than me, his chest and shoulders sculpted from the effort of lifting and hacking slabs of meat in the butchery.

'Get on with it.'

He let the arrow go, my intent to break his concentration wasted.

He looked at the target, then at me, but said nothing.

'Fuck off,' I said and walked away.

*

When I arrived back at the tavern, Philippa was sitting at one of the tables chatting with a middle-aged man with a greying beard. I had not seen him before. He looked as though he knew Philippa well, as they laughed and played tafl, a popular board game. Apart from him and a couple of regulars, it was a quiet Sunday afternoon.

She looked up and smiled. It melted my heart.

'Ahh, you're back.' She stood and held her enormous stomach. 'I just can't get comfortable today, baby Robbie here is kicking the living daylight out of me.'

'You've named him Robbie?'

'Yep, I like the name.'

'And if he's a girl?'

'He's a boy.'

'You don't know that.'

I leaned over the counter and helped myself to a mug of the strong ale.

'We'll see,' she said. 'Anyway, this is Benedict.' She took me by the hand and stood me next to the man she had been talking to. 'He's here to ask if...'

The man, Benedict, stopped her with a playful tug of her arm. 'I can speak, you know!'

She laughed. 'Sorry!'

He stood and shook my hand. 'As the lady says,' he winked at Philippa, 'my name is Benedict and I am Lord Thomas's lead huntsman.' He sat back down. 'I'm in the process of organising the Lord's upcoming hunt.'

'Happy to meet you, Sir.'

'Call me Benedict,' he said, 'we're all friends here.'

I nodded and smiled.

'I used to drink in this tavern for years before I was given my current position and then moved into the castle. I watched Pip grow up.' He looked around. 'And where's that brother of yours – still fighting one another?'

Philippa picked up his mug and went to refill it. 'He's gone, Sir, I mean Benedict.'

'He's gone? Where?'

She finished filling it and handed it back. 'Tell Ailred why you're here.'

He shrugged. 'Well, Ailred, I'm looking for beaters and bowmen for the hunt.' He took a large swig. 'And from what I hear from Pip here there are few better marksmen than you on the range.'

'You're too kind, Benedict.' I leaned over and poured another ale. 'Does it pay?'

He sighed. 'Yes, lad, you have the honour of serving your Lord.'

I realised I was being rude. 'Then yes, Sir, I am at your disposal.'

He smiled. 'And there *will* be perks, don't worry.'

Whilst he and Philippa continued their board game, he gave me a rundown of the event. The hunt was in three weeks and was being held on the estate of Lord Robert De Knole. He and Sir Thomas were friends and he was allowing Sir Thomas to use his vast estate, situated north of Tonebricge close to Seouenaca, on the promise he respected the area and his tenants and gave half his hunting spoils to Lord Knole's kitchen.

'I don't know that area very well,' I said.

He grimaced. 'I'll be honest with you Ailred, neither do I, which will make my job all the more difficult. Organising a hunt is hard enough as it is, and Sir Thomas is *so* particular about them – I can't allow any mistakes. That's part of the reason I came to you. A skilled bowman can be the difference between a successful hunt and me losing my job.'

'You honour me Sir, but I know another fine archer too.' I poured myself another drink, allowing just the right time to elapse before concluding. 'And he has an in-depth knowledge of Seouenaca and Lord Knole's estate. May I suggest I might...'

But he was ahead of me. 'That's ideal, Ailred. Yes, by all means, bring him along.' He was more than happy.

He finished outlining the details of times and places and what would be expected of Bartholomew and me, and he left.

'Time to celebrate,' I said, raising my tankard.

*

The day of the hunt arrived. I was excited. I had found a local trustworthy man to stand in for me at the tavern and Tom had been fine with me taking the day off. It reflected well on him and the Brewer family. Philippa had by now stopped any stressful tasks and settled for serving behind the counter.

'Good morning Al, it's a fine day for a hunt.'

I greeted Bartholomew as he met me outside the tavern. He was carrying his unstrung bow and a quiver of arrows and had a bag hitched over his shoulder. Alongside a butcher's knife, he had a leather water pouch attached to his belt. I carried similar equipment, and we were pleased that Benedict had arranged to have us picked up by a cart and team of horses as Seouenaca was a fair journey.

'Thanks for thinking of me for this outing Al, I'll be in Sir Thomas's good books after today.'

'It's a good chance to impress,' I agreed.

The cart turned up and we scrambled aboard, making room for a couple of women who had also agreed to help.

The journey to Seouenaca took about an hour, and the four of us speculated on the day. The women had attended a hunt before, both being on the catering team and said it was always a good day. They said that Sir Thomas had planned an open-air feast straight after in which all the huntsmen and their wives would finish the day. That was their job, to help make sure it was a success.

It was an overcast day with more than a hint of rain. I hoped it stayed fine, as wet bow strings were liable to break or stretch and arrows often warped or flew irrationally due to moisture adding weight.

We met with Benedict and a number of his underlings and were assigned jobs. He looked stressed. It was Bart's and my responsibility to go ahead of the hunt with the beaters and protect them from any wild boar or wolves they might encounter. We were there as protection. Simple.

There were about twenty beaters with us, all local men. We were sent out an hour before the main hunting group. The terrain was wooded with thigh-high bracken making it difficult to walk, let alone run, sloping hills giving way to deep valleys.

At first, the banter was constant. We poked

fun at one another and speculated on who might scare up the biggest deer or boar, but as time went by the landscape forced our silence. It was thirsty work.

After an hour we had beaten out a few deer and pheasants, attempting to funnel them towards the following hunters and we stopped for a drink. I had filled all my containers with wine and had been sipping at them throughout. It had not affected me as I drank every day by then and was used to it. Beating and battling our way through the countryside had caused my hands to tremble and drinking helped steady them.

We could hear the hunt as it thundered closer, the horns and shouts of excitement confirming we were achieving our task. At this time, Bart and I had our bows strung. Up until now, there had been no sign of danger so I had finished my first pouch of wine.

'ARCHER!' The cry came from one of the beaters.

I picked up my bow, dropping my drink in my hurry to nock an arrow.

The beater was standing behind a tree as a wild boar was attempting to attack him, while nearby a brace of piglets scurried around in fright.

I decided there was time to pick up my drink and replace the stopper, which I did. When I looked back the boar had managed to circle the tree and had knocked the man to the ground and was goring him with its sharp tusks.

I laid the arrow on the string and fired. The arrow flew straight and true, but missed, embedding itself into the tree. There must have been a gust of wind otherwise it would have killed the animal.

I grabbed another arrow and was in the process of firing when there was a terrible scream from the boar. I looked up and saw it rear in pain as a second arrow struck its neck, followed by a third which brought the beast to its knees.

'What the...' I shouted at Bart as he ran to the aid of the injured man. 'That was my kill.'

Bart was furious. 'What the hell were you doing? If this man dies it's on your head, Al.'

By the time I got to him the boar was in the final death throes, kicking its legs as it tried to stand and protect its young. Bart was kneeling next to the man who was groaning in pain, his right leg shattered below the knee, the jagged bones protruding from the skin at right angles.

Bart drew his knife and cut the boar's throat, a great gush of blood spurting out and ceased its movement.

He moved back to the man.

'Right, hold him still Al, and I'll try and set this leg.' I stood above them looking down. 'Well come on, get down and help. This is your fuckin' fault.'

I knelt beside Bart and put my hands on the

man's shoulders in an attempt to steady him as Bart moved towards the wound.

Bart made a sniffing sound. 'Can I smell wine? Has this man been drinking?'

I nodded. 'Yeah, I think so.' By this time the lead beater had joined us and was helping. 'Go find the chirurgeon,' I shouted into his face.

He frowned. 'It's you – you stink of wine.'

'Rubbish!' I stood up and looked around. 'I'll go and look if you won't.' I picked up my things and ran off in the direction of the hunt as Bart and the beater continued to comfort the man.

It did not take me long to find them. It was led by Sir Thomas and Lord Knole, both riding white stallions and leading a small group of men and women.

I stood on the track they were following and waved my arms above my head to catch their attention. Both men reigned their mounts in and slowed to a halt.

'Out of the way man,' Lord Knole shouted, 'or I'll have you whipped.'

'Begging your pardon, my Lords, but we are in great need of a chirurgeon,' I said. 'Do you have one in your party?'

'Who the hell is this man?' Lord Knole shouted, looking around at the following group.

'His name is Ailred Norman, Lord, and he is always in places you least expect.' Sir Thomas looked at me and scowled.

'Well, Ailred Norman, get out of our way.'

'I'm sorry my Lords, but we have a seriously hurt man in the field. One of your beaters has...'

'Well go and help him, man, and stop your infernal babbling.'

I looked towards Sir Thomas.

'You heard his Lordship – off you go.'

I stood aside and let them pass. They did not even consider helping.

After the last of the party had passed I opened my second pouch of wine and took a few large gulps. I had earned it. I did not think there was much point in going back to help as I had nothing to offer. Besides, Bart had everything under control. So I decided to walk in the opposite direction. It seemed the right thing to do at the time. I started to fall often and the wine was running low. I had heard that the after-hunt feast was being held at our initial meeting point, so decided to go help set up. I could be of benefit there – they would be pleased. I followed the tracks that the hunt had created, so it was simple to find my way back.

After about an hour my wine pouch was empty. The sky was dark, with drizzle beginning to drift across the forested landscape, and soon I fell across the feast site. Literally.

I was met by a woman in an apron, holding a dead chicken. 'What are you doing here, Ailred?'

I stood and stared at her. 'How do you know my name?' I asked. 'Are you a witch or something? Are you going to cast a witchy spell on me?' I waved my arms around in what I considered a spell-casting manner.

'Oh my god, you're drunk! You and your friend Bartholomew travelled with Margaret and me in the cart from Tonebricge. How could you have forgotten that already? Where is he now? He needs to get you away from here. If Benedict or the gentry see you in this state you'll be in serious trouble.'

I laughed. 'So you're not a witchy? Bart is somewhere over there.' I pointed in the opposite direction.

'Just go…' she commanded.

She turned and left. There were several large fires scattered about the clearing with spits fixed around them, as various meats sizzled above. Women were scurrying like ants, transforming the site in preparation.

'ANTS,' I shouted, and walked towards a large striped tent. I peeked inside. It was empty except for some casks lying on their sides on a makeshift table, each with a tap fitted. The rest of the table-space was taken with mugs and tankards of various sizes. I was thirsty.

*

I awoke with a vicious kick to my stomach. I vomited. Sir Thomas was standing above me with Bartholomew behind being held by a couple of household staff. There were casks of wine and ale lying on the floor close by where I must have knocked them off the table before collapsing.

'Take these two and get them out of here!' Sir Thomas shouted, dragging me towards the tent's exit. 'I will have you both flogged for this...you have humiliated me in front of Lord Knole.'

He threw me onto the muddy floor. It was still light and it had been raining. The fires were smouldering as the catering staff tried to cover them in any way possible, but the wet conditions were proving disastrous. The looks I received were a mixture of contempt and apprehension that the feast was ruined.

Benedict arrived. Even in my drunken state, I knew what was coming.

He ran to me, picked me up by my tunic's neckline, and punched me in the face. I felt my nose explode and could feel blood pouring from it. To this day it is crooked – a visible reminder of that day's shame.

Bart was professing his innocence but was under no illusion he was guilty by association. His bow, arrows, and knife had been confiscated and the pair of us were physically kicked out of the camp.

It was a sobering experience.

'You fuckin' drunkard bastard...!' Bart took me by the throat as we trudged in the direction of Tonebricge. I did not fight back. 'He'll come looking for us once this day is through, you know that don't you? Sir Thomas will have us whipped and hung.' He threw me to the floor. 'You've killed us.'

I said nothing. Everything he said was true. The only reason we were not dead already was because he did not want the sight of mutilated men at the site of a feast. Wives might object to having a skinned man hanging from a nearby tree as they ate.

I stood and walked off. He followed twenty paces behind berating me, but then turned silent.

And still it rained. The day would be a washout. Sir Thomas would blame us. Me. As my drunken state turned to the first stages of regret I realised what I had done. I had not even asked how the man with the broken leg was. Things would change. Tom and his family would come to hear of my drunken antics and feel I had let them down – which I had. My mind turned to Philippa. I hung my head.

After a couple of hours of silence, Bart caught up to me.

'Will he lose the leg?' I asked without looking at him.

'What do you care?'

I did care. Now the mind fog had lifted, I looked at myself with the eyes of others.

'I'm sorry.' It seemed so hollow.

I heard him sigh. 'I'm not sure what we should do now.'

'I'll plead on your behalf.' It was the least I could do. 'He's been lenient to me in the past, so he might be reasonable.'

We walked on through the downpour. It was twilight and we were approaching Tonebricge. We had followed the same track home as we had taken there, but Bart knew a shortcut to bypass the final half mile. It was through the marshland. The last time I ventured deep into the wetlands surrounding the town was as a child when Paul and I had played there. It was dangerous, but Bart said he knew the firmer ground.

'Let's just keep to the path,' I said. 'At least we know we'll get home that way.'

But he was adamant, so I agreed.

He pushed deep into the marsh and in my semi-drunken state was beginning to wish I had insisted we stayed on solid ground before Bart stopped dead. I walked into the back of him.

'What's this?' he asked.

I moved past him. It looked like a bundle of rags. I prodded it with my foot but it did not move. There was a bow and a quiver of arrows nearby, and a large shoulder bag.

My heart fell.

'What is it?' Bart asked, sensing my mood.

I bent down and pulled the bundle over.

Bart stepped back. 'Fuck...poor bastard. Any idea who it is?' He looked at me. 'Or should I say, was?'

I knew who. 'It's Simon Butcher.'

His throat had been hacked open, only a few tendons holding his head to what was left of his decomposing body. Animals had been feeding on him over the months but there was no hiding the fact he had been subjected to a frenzied attack.

‘Who the fuck would do a thing like this?’ Bart looked appalled.

‘I...I have no idea.’ I said.

Then it dawned on Bart. ‘So if Simon Butcher is lying here dead, he didn’t rob his family or the priory.’ He shook his head. 'And his sudden disappearance and the theft of his family savings is the perfect alibi for someone.'

'I have no Idea.'

He looked at me. 'You didn't want to walk through this part of the marsh, did you?'

I stared at him. 'What's that supposed to mean?'

He looked back at the corpse. 'Well, someone killed him and robbed the priory – and they're still out there.' He stepped away from me. 'And you were the first person blamed...'

'I swear to God, Bart, I had nothing to do with this.'

But he was gone, leaving me alone with the mutilated body of my old friend.

CHAPTER 5

Again, Father Budwith has taken an interest. Whenever the subject of the robbery is broached he takes the parchments away for days at a time before returning them. I am not sure what he hopes to gain, as I have said from the beginning – I have no idea who stole that money. If he thinks I will have an epiphany after all these years he is deluded. God knows he can be annoying.

Brother Michael wants to strike that last sentence but I am adamant we keep it in.

*

It took an age to find my way back to town. I tried to follow Bart's trail but found myself knee-deep in marsh water as mosquitoes attacked every part of my visible body. So much for it being a shortcut.

When I reached the sanctuary of solid ground I was towards the north end of town. It was dark and the street was deserted. I could hear a commotion coming from the direction of the tavern. Since Bart had left, all I could think about was the body we had found. He accused me of having something to do with it, and I was certain he would report the find. Simon Butcher's family would be devastated and conduct a search, and I would once more be the prime suspect. That, added to my drunken antics during the day, meant my time in Tonebricge was numbered. I cursed my stupidity.

As I walked towards the tavern the words spoken by Archdeacon Rhys as he assaulted me with the pastoral staff came back. He *knew* Paul and I had robbed the monastery – and something about a key. I forced the memory of that cell away but it kept returning.

Then I considered Paul. Could he have done it? I knew I had not; but was I sure about him? No, he had left me at midnight and gone straight back – there wasn't time, although if he had a key...

Before I could answer that question I turned the corner and saw the tavern a few hundred paces away. People were milling outside holding lanterns. Amongst the shouting, I could hear the wails of a woman screaming.

As I drew nearer, the figure of Bart came into view. A couple of townsmen were holding him in front of Benedict and some of his hunt organisers on horseback.

I slipped into the shadows of one of the houses and eased myself into a position to hear what was being said.

'I keep telling you – I saw the body,' Bart was shouting, and again I heard the screams of a woman. It was Simon Butcher's mother.

'I don't care about the fuckin' Butcher's son, where is Ailred Norman?' Benedict was leaning from his horse and waving his riding crop at Bart, while one of his followers jumped from his mount with a coiled rope in his hand.

'I...I don't know Sir, I last saw him in the marshland as we...'

'You two destroyed my life today. I've been dismissed because of you bastards.' He was physically shaking with rage. 'Now, where is he hiding?'

'I'd tell you if I knew Sir, I promise,' Bart pleaded, but Benedict had not come to hear that.

'You know...string the bastard up until he tells me.'

Bart tried to break free from his captors but they were too strong. The rope was thrown over the tavern's wooden cross-beam, and a noose was tied to one end.

'Last chance, boy, tell me where he's hiding,' Benedict shouted.

Bart was crying. 'Please Sir, I...I don't know. Please, for the love of God.'

'You know where he is, you just need persuading.' He nodded to one of his companions.

'Have mercy on him please Benedict, for my sake.' I knew the voice well. It was Philippa. She was being held back by her mother but managed to free herself.

He glared at her and I could see real hatred on

his face. 'Do not call me Benedict, you stupid slut. You call me Sir. This shit is down to you – you vouched for them. If I don't find the bastard, be sure I'll come for you.' He was angry but had a fixed smile on his face. 'I will hang you too – with or without your baby.'

'But...but...' She was lost for words.

He laughed. 'Do you think I'm your friend or something, you miserable bitch?' He laughed again and turned his back on her.

A man looped the noose over Bart's head and pulled it hard, almost knocking him off his feet. Benedict jumped down and pulled the rope's slack and started to pull. He lifted Bart a few inches from the floor as he fought to get his fingers under the rope to loosen it. All the time Benedict laughed.

After a few seconds, he loosened his grip and let Bart fall to the ground.

I breathed a sigh of relief – he was just trying to scare him.

'Where is he you piece of shit? Next time I won't release you.' He started to tie the rope's end to his horse's saddle. 'Think before you answer.'

Bart coughed and spluttered, taking in great gulps of air but was unable to speak.

Again, Benedict laughed. It was at that moment I realised he would hang him regardless.

Philippa had gone inside the tavern with her parents and most people present were leaving, sickened at the spectacle. Bart did not know the answer, it was clear to everyone.

Benedict remounted. He backed his horse up as Bart was hoisted a few feet from the ground. His hands were free and he tried in vain to lift his body weight off the rope around his neck. He would manage to release the pressure for a few seconds before his hands would lose grip and he fell back.

And all the time Benedict laughed.

Bart kicked and spluttered for so long, his free hands prolonging the agony.

Benedict sat watching. I could not see his face anymore as most people with lanterns had left, but I knew he was smiling.

In time, Bart's kicking slowed and one of the more merciful huntsmen walked over and hung onto his legs, adding his weight to Bart's, and ended his suffering.

*

I stayed hidden as Benedict and his followers remained, hoping I showed myself. They were disappointed.

There was no mistaking what would happen to me if I was caught. My choice was simple. Leave. Get as far away from Tonebricge as possible. At that moment my decision was made. I would go to Glamorgan and meet with Paul, he being part of the gentry there. The thought of seeing him lifted my spirits. I would miss Philippa, but I could always get word to her when

I had settled...

Benedict's words came back.

"I will hang you too – with or without your baby."

If I left, her fate was assured. On account of me.

I needed to speak to her, but could not risk being seen at the tavern. Over time, Benedict and his companions had drifted away and I made sure each had left town and not doubled back.

Bart remained hanging from the post in front of the Chequers as no one dared cut him down.

When I was sure it was safe I edged my way towards the barn. She had anticipated my movements that first night when she knew I would run and I was counting on her doing the same now. She could also use that same logic to have me captured, but I had no alternative.

'Hello?' I whispered into the barn's gloom.

I was met by silence.

'Hello, it's Robbie boy, although I'm not kicking you from inside.' It was the only covert message I could think of.

'Ailred – I'm back here.' It was Philippa.

I took a deep breath and moved towards her voice in the stall I used to sleep in.

'I...I thought it might have been one of Benedict's men,' she said close to tears and hugged me.

I squeezed her and we kissed. It was a kiss between two desperate people.

Then she stood back and punched me in the face. Even in the darkness, she managed to strike me on my already broken nose.

'You bastard. Why would you do that? You've ruined everything.'

I searched for the right words. 'Sorry.'

I heard the wind as another punch grazed the side of my face.

'I have to go...,' I whispered.

'And leave me to hang?'

'...and you must come with me.'

'GO? GO WHERE?'

'Shh,' I whispered groping for her mouth.

She shook me off but remained silent.

'We'll go to my brother. Sir Hugh has land in Glamorgan and Paul is his squire. I can get work there, maybe join their archers and serve.' The words came to me as I spoke them.

'I don't even know where Glamorgan is,' she said, 'and I'm nine months pregnant. I can't travel to wherever this place is in my condition.'

'We can't stay here. We *have* to go.'

There was silence.

'I could start shouting and you would be captured.'

'I know.'

More silence.

'I'll get the horse from the stables – there's only one paying customer staying tonight. We might as well be hung for horse theft as anything else.'

I kissed her again and cried.

*

We left within the hour. Philippa added her finances to mine. It was something, however small. She had refused to steal anything from her parents who were snoring in bed as we left. The trauma of the night had sent them to the bottle and were in the process of sleeping it off. She shut the rear door and patted it.

'I'll miss you both. I'm sorry.'

I would miss them too. What had started as a punishment had ended in mutual respect and a sense of belonging. Until I wrecked it.

The sun was making itself known as I led the horse and Philippa in the opposite direction from its rising. I remembered Paul telling me that Glamorgan was west, in Wales, and Sir Hugh's seat of power was based in Cardiff Castle. He said it was a long journey. That was the sum of my knowledge as we set out that morning.

Philippa had gathered anything that she felt the baby would need when it came and I did the rest. Alongside blankets and rations of food, I collected clothing for both of us. Tom's bow and a quiver of arrows, my short knife, and the axe, all fitted onto the horse. Beyond that, we were at God's mercy.

'Do you think they will come looking for us?' I asked after we had left the town, keeping to the hidden trail that temporarily ran parallel to the main road. Philippa looked comfortable enough, but I suspected that would change.

'I've been thinking about that,' she replied. 'Neither Lord Thomas nor any of his men were involved last night, so Benedict's actions were his own.' That had not occurred to me. 'And if Bart had found Simon's body,' she looked at me and I gave an acknowledgement, 'then Lord Thomas would be furious with Benedict for killing Bart as no one can lead them to his body.' She looked at me again. 'Hell, the priory money might still be near the body.'

It was something else I had not thought of.

'I didn't look if I'm honest.'

'And you're nothing if not honest, Al,' she laughed.

I did not feel like laughing. In the short time we had been moving she had highlighted my lack of awareness, and I was worried she would regret her decision.

We travelled on in silence. The sun rose behind us and the concealed path we followed curved in and joined the main road. Once on that, we were visible to all.

We passed a few people and were given wary looks but otherwise no one showed interest.

After a few hours, Philippa said, 'We should stop here.'

'Why?' I wanted to get as far away as possible.

'Because this horse needs a drink and some rest.' She looked at me. 'And I'm pregnant – I don't know if you've noticed. There's a river over there, it's the perfect spot.'

I looked in the direction she was pointing.

I had done it again – shown my lack of judgement. My self-worth shattered. 'Are you sure you want to go on with me?'

She brought her arm down.

'What are you talking about?'

I wanted to tell her my feeling of inadequacy but that would make me look weak.

'Don't you go getting second thoughts now, Ailred Norman. We have a long way to travel and the last thing I need is to carry a quitter. We have a baby to support and I can't do this alone.' She pointed at me. 'This is your baby now, so stop doubting and get this horse fed and watered and pass me some food.'

She slid from the horse and stormed off into the undergrowth.

'Yes, Mam.'

I had been told.

It was a warm day and Philippa's mood softened. She never stayed angry long.

'We could stay here the night?' I said. It was a suggestion but I was not sure if it was a good one.

'It's been a long day and I can't see them travelling this far out to look for us, so yeah, good idea.'

I patted myself on the back and started to drag the blankets off the horse.

We moved closer to the river, away from the road and any prying eyes, and lay them on the floor. It was a warm summer evening and we had covered a good distance. The horse grazed nearby and was tethered to a long rope, while we ate food. It was idyllic.

'Do you still think it's a boy?'

'I've told you already, I know it is.'

I lay back on my blanket and looked up. The sun had set and a few early stars were visible.

'Your family will be disappointed to miss the birth.'

'Stop mentioning family. My *parents* will be disappointed.'

'What is it with you and your brother...you seem to hate him. Is it because of what he did to me?'

I could hear her teeth grind. 'I don't want to talk about it.'

I did not press further, suspecting there was something dark hidden.

We chatted for a while. We spoke of our plans and hopes for a new life together, then there was silence. As the remaining stars appeared and a half moon rose we settled down to sleep.

"A new life together". It was the first time we had said those words.

We slept.

*

'I didn't sleep a wink last night.' Philippa was up and about gathering our things together. 'Robbie boy made sure of that.'

I felt guilty – I had slept like the dead. When in doubt, show empathy. 'Yeah, me too.'

'He kept you up all night too?' She rolled up her blanket and dragged mine from under me. 'He's a busy lad, is Robbie. Come on – get moving.'

I went into the undergrowth and answered the call of nature and drank from the river. We shared the last of the bread and chewed on some cold mutton, then set off.

After about three hours we stopped. It had been my idea because I had seen a small pond off the road and thought it was time.

Philippa opened a pouch of water and took a swig, handing it to me.

'There's water there,' I said, replacing the stopper, 'might as well save this stuff.'

'Right idea Al, but if you drink from that pond you'll be shitting for days. It needs to be flowing water. Even then it's not always safe to drink...' She stopped. 'Don't worry, you'll learn.'

I sulked. I was good at that.

We continued on the deserted road until we came across a group of travelling monks. They were going in the opposite direction but stopped and passed the time of day. They were from the House of Austin Canons Priory at Reigate, a town not far from there, and suggested we would be safer in their guesthouse overnight. It was a matter of principle that travellers were made welcome at the priory, and there was ample food.

We gave thanks and bade them farewell.

Over the coming hours, Philippa became uncomfortable as Robbie battered her, and I grew tired. I had never walked so far and my shoes rubbed blisters.

As I thought I could go on no longer, the dusty road split two ways. One continued, the other towards what looked like the priory. We took the second option.

The horse was panting as we entered the open gates. It was late afternoon and the early sunshine had been doused by a blanket of clouds.

We were met by a young monk who welcomed us.

'Good day, Brother.' Philippa said, 'Is there any chance we could shelter for the night, and maybe eat?'

He smiled. 'I am Brother Timothy and you are most welcome to stay the night – especially in your condition.' He pointed to a cluster of low buildings to the right of the church. 'The guest accommodation is over there next to our dormitory. I am still a novitiate, so if you require anything do not hesitate to call upon me. As far as I'm aware, there is still a private room available, so you and your husband can stay there.'

He took the horse's reins from me and led us in that direction.

As we arrived at the guest housing, a tall monk with broad shoulders strode towards us. He had the walk of authority but managed to remain humble throughout.

The novice monk, Brother Timothy, bowed his

head. 'Prior John, greetings. I have told these travellers it will be possible to stay in the single-room housing tonight, I hope I have not spoken out of turn?'

Prior John looked at Philippa. 'On the contrary, Brother Timothy, I insist upon it.' He walked over and helped her from the horse and brushed her down. 'Please take this lady's horse to the stables.'

I removed our belongings before Brother Timothy led the horse towards the rear of the priory, as Father John showed us to our room. It was small, with a single window opening to the side of the lay monk's dormitory. There was a large communal bed in the corner, which had a wool-filled palliasse.

'There is drinking water in the kitchen and the reredorter is near the stables. Please use it and not the side of the wall,' he looked at me, 'it encourages rats and the smell is insufferable at this time of year. You've missed supper I am afraid, and I have to conduct the Compline in church soon, but if you go to the kitchen and tell them Prior John sent you, they will provide pottage. It's rather good here.' As he smiled I noticed a deep scar running the length of his cheek.

We thanked him and he left.

I transported our belongings to our room, after which we strolled to the kitchen, taking time to explore the priory as we went.

Similar to Tonebricge, this was a double priory,

which meant monks and nuns lived in separate communities but shared facilities, and as the monks were attending the compline service, nuns were more visible. We spoke to many and they were more than helpful, offering advice and showing excitement at Philippa's pregnancy.

'Have you ever considered becoming a nun?' I asked as we neared the kitchen. It was more a compliment than a question.

Philippa stopped and looked at me. 'I was one.'

I waited for her to finish the sentence, but she remained silent and walked off.

I ran to catch up and put my hand on her shoulder. She stopped.

'You can't just tell me you were a nun once and then walk away.'

'There is a lot you don't know about me, Al – come on, let's get some food, I'll explain after we've eaten, I promise.'

I walked behind her in a daze.

As we entered the kitchen, a middle-aged nun walked towards us.

'Greetings, my children. Are you staying with us tonight?'

'We are, Sister, we're staying in the guest room near the monk's dormitory,' Philippa answered.

'I notice you are with child, and I was wondering if you would rather move into more suitable accommodation?'

'Are your quarters superior to that of the monks then, Sister?' Philippa asked.

She smiled. 'Indeed not – nothing we have is superior to their surroundings,' she spoke with a hint of sarcasm, 'but I was more concerned about your condition. You look close to due?'

Philippa held her pregnant belly and caressed it. 'Yes, Sister, I think little Robbie will be with us soon enough, but not tonight.'

She nodded. 'I am sure your knowledge is superior to my own, but if you need anything...,' she looked at me and put her hand in mock secrecy to her mouth, '...anything feminine, be sure to seek one of the nuns out.'

I whistled in jest and looked skyward, whilst Philippa and the nun laughed.

'Thank you, Sister...?'

'Mother, Kimberly,' she said adjusting her headwear. 'I am the Abbess here.'

'Excuse me, Reverend Mother.' Philippa lowered her head and curtsied.

I attempted the same but the look on Philippa's face told me I was making an arse of myself.

We parted ways and collected our food and water, which we took to a table in the empty refectory.

I sat opposite Philippa and waited.

She sighed. 'This is not going to be easy for either of us.' Then she began.

*

She was twelve when she asked to enter the Convent at St Mary's Priory in Tonebricge. It was her choice. Her parents were devastated as they had hoped she would continue to help run the tavern and forbade it.

So she ran away. She wanted to serve God.

The convent had an obligation to seek permission for someone that young, but her father refused. The prioress therefore had no option but to return her to her parents.

At home, despite being thrashed and berated by Tom, she refused to work in the tavern.

Her mother, Emma, was the one to relent.

One morning before Tom rose, Emma took the defiant Philippa back and gave her blessing. Philippa had tears of gratitude in her eyes while recalling the story.

She became a novice. Being the youngest, the older nuns fussed over her and treated her as their own.

She was happy.

After six months her mother visited and told her Richard, her brother, had left home to join Lord Thomas's household troops. Her mother had wept at losing him.

Within three days Philippa was back living in the tavern.

She told the Abbess at the priory that she did not have the self-discipline to continue her novitiate period.

Although disappointed, the Mother Superior had wished her luck but reminded her that once she left there was no returning.

'By then you must have known it was the right

choice to leave.' I had commented.

She continued.

On her return to the daily routine in the tavern, she was happy. The happiest she had ever been, despite the hard work and long hours. I had gone to speak but she held a finger up to stop me.

Then he came home. Richard. He had failed his probationary period, Sir Thomas rejecting him on the advice of senior councillors, the reason never being given.

'You must have been pleased to have him home,' I noted.

She looked at me but said nothing.

'What?'

'Think about it, Al. I left for a reason and returned for a reason.

'You left when Richard was still at home and returned when he left.' I was still confused.

She stared into my eyes and they glazed over.

'What could he have done that was so bad as to send you to a convent?'

She never took her eyes off me.

'WHAT DID HE DO?'

She refused to look away.

Finally, I understood, and it was me who lowered my gaze.

*

It had gone on for years. I had noticed the tension, but never the deep hatred. My lack of awareness humiliated me. I threatened to kill him if ever I saw him again, but she said it wasn't in my nature. I was, 'too nice'.

'How did it end?' I asked before my eyes opened wide. 'OH MY GOD...!' I stared at her pregnant body.

'No, no...' she said, 'please, no, this wasn't him, I swear.'

I breathed deeply. I believed her.

'When did it end?'

'It ended the first morning he woke after his return. I was kneeling astride him on his bed. He opened his eyes and the first thing he saw was me with the axe. I held it high above his head. I said nothing.' She smiled. 'He never touched me again.'

We finished our food in silence.

As I collected our dirty bowls together to return to the kitchen, I said, 'Thanks for telling me the truth.'

She stood and kissed me on the cheek. 'He was right, you know?'

I frowned. 'Who was?'

'Father John. He said the pottage was good here.'

I smiled. She had a way of disarming me and the world.

*

We took a stroll back to the room. There were the first signs of rain in the air and it had turned colder. I put my arm around her as we walked and she drew herself close. It was a real sign of affection, the first we had shared until then.

On our return, I picked up the pile of blankets and started to make the bed. She stood and watched. There was a large bowl of water in one corner.

'You can wash first,' I said gesturing towards it.

She did not move, so I looked at her.

'You're a good man, Ailred Norman.'

It took me aback.

'I do my best.'

'Your best is good enough for me.' She started to undress.

I looked away.

'Watch me.'

I turned.

'Help me.'

I walked over. My hands were shaking.

She stood unmoving. I waited but she remained impassive.

'Take this off me,' she commanded.

She was wearing a large smock, and I undid the buttons below her neckline. Pulling it up and over her head, she turned towards me. I looked at her naked body. It was the most beautiful thing I had ever seen. She moved over to the bowl and started to wash herself in silence, washing every inch of her body.

My heart was thundering as she concentrated on her lower half, pleasuring herself.

She looked at me – her eyes glazed and intense. 'Undress.'

I did as I was told in seconds, ripping any

clothing that did not come off easily.

She moved over to the bed and lay on her back, her fingers still working on herself.

I went to wash but she was too far ahead to wait.

She was breathing heavily. 'Come here now.'

She looked so vulnerable, yet her commanding voice and penetrating eyes aroused me to a level I had never experienced.

I knelt in front of her and she held my hands before dragging me forward and biting my neck.

'Do me now,' she said.

I did her.

*

It had not taken long. I was embarrassed but Philippa said nothing critical as we lay side by side on the palliasse holding hands.

My father had taken Paul and me to one of the whores in Tonebricge when we were young. He would only pay for the one as he said it would be a wasted expense. It had been humiliating for me but Paul enjoyed himself before it was my turn. I did not mention any of this to Philippa, although she must have guessed my lack of experience.

'Thank you,' I said.

She chuckled.

'Next time I'll be...'

'Shut up Ailred Norman.'

She had a way with words.

*

I woke. It was dark and had no idea where I was.

Philippa's panting reminded me.

'It's coming,' she gasped.

'What's coming?'

'THE FUCKIN' BABY'S COMING.'

I jumped out of bed and searched for the tinderbox and fire-steel and lit a tilley lamp.

She was kneeling on the damp bed.

'Are you sure it's coming?' I asked.

'My waters have broken and I'm having contractions, so yes, I'm sure.' None of that statement meant anything to me, but she sounded certain. 'Go fetch a nun.'

'Which nun?'

'GO GET SOMEONE WITH A FUCKIN' BRAIN.'

I left the lamp with her and rushed out. There were lanterns scattered around the priory as the clergy attended services at all times, day and night, so I ran to the monks' dormitory as it was the closest to us.

There were beds down each side of the long quarters and I entered. I heard snoring and it smelt of wind and body odour.

'I need help,' I said, but no one stirred. 'I NEED HELP.'

That did the trick.

Within seconds I was surrounded by semi-dressed monks.

'Philippa is having the baby.'

A tall gangly monk whom I had not seen before said, 'Who are you and who is Philippa?'

Before I could answer, the novice monk,

Timothy, joined us.

'Quick, Brother Stephen, go fetch Prior John.' He looked at me. 'Follow me, we'll inform the nuns – they'll know what to do.'

He took me to the church.

'They will be at matins now.'

Matins was the night service that monks and nuns attended at separate times in the church, and it was here we found the majority of the nuns.

Entering through the night entrance we stood at the back of the naive. Reverent Mother Kimberly was standing by the high altar preaching. She looked at my concerned face and understood immediately.

'We will cease this service at once,' she broadcast, and all heads turned. 'Quickly now sisters, we have a baby to bring into this world.'

*

I sat outside the convent's dormitory alone. The sun had come up and I had not seen Philippa for hours. I wanted to go inside and help but was told in no uncertain terms that it was not my place. On occasion, one of the nuns appeared and gave me a rundown of how everything was going but I felt useless. Philippa was being attended by two experienced nuns who had been abestetrix's before turning to God, so was in good hands.

'And how are you holding up?'

I looked up from biting my nails and saw Father John, the prior, casting his shadow over me.

'Not so bad Father,' I answered, 'although it's not about me, is it.'

He offered me a jug of ale which I took and drowned in one. I had not realised I was so thirsty.

'I'll get one of the novices to bring you food. It could be a long wait.'

I returned the jug and thanked him as he left.

After an hour Father John returned with a plate of bread, cheese and cold meats and was carrying a jug with two mugs, trying not to spill the contents.

'I thought I would serve you myself, being that this is the most important day of your life,' he said as I got up and helped put the haul onto the ground.

I had not considered that. Although the child was not mine, I felt an incredible bond through Philippa's emotions.

'You honour me, Father.'

'Sit, sit, my child.' he patted the ground next to him and I sat, our backs to the wall. 'Tuck in, Ailred, you'll need all God's strength very soon. The first days are the hardest.' He reached forward and poured two mugs of wine. 'It's a little early,' he said, 'but under the circumstances...'

He raised his mug and I clinked it.

'Cheers.' We spoke as one.

There was a moment's silence as we ate

and sipped our wine before I said, 'You seem knowledgeable in these things, Father?'

'I had a child once.'

I coughed wine through my nose.

He laughed. 'I wasn't always a monk you know!'

'Can you be a monk and have a family?' I was ignorant in the ways of the church then.

He smiled. 'The church is my family, Ailred. It is *our* family.' He gestured around. 'We give vows but not all of us were born into this. It can be a calling, a voice from the almighty, demanding obedience.' He looked at me. 'And when we hear that command we must obey without question. That is what happened to me.'

I finished eating and took a sip of wine. I had promised myself never to touch wine again after the last time but found it difficult to turn down hospitality from the Prior himself. I liked him. He had a calm mannerism that I felt at ease with, regardless of the circumstances.

'Where is your child now?'

He sighed. 'He is with God. It was a long time ago, and my wife died with him. I felt more pain that day than I have ever felt in my lifetime of war before then.' I looked at him in surprise. 'Yes, I was a soldier before my calling. You look shocked. How do you think I received this?' He turned his head sideways to highlight his scarred cheek.

'I had wondered, Father.'

'As I say, it was a lifetime ago and my vows hold me to God's calling now.'

We drank more wine together and nuns stopped coming out to reassure me.

I started to worry.

'Your life will change.' He sensed my trepidation and tried to engage me.

I sat quietly as I often do when anxious.

'You are a good man by all accounts, Ailred.'

That came as a surprise. 'By whose account – no one here knows me?'

'The Reverend Mother summoned me earlier and asked that I might join her in praying for Philippa.'

His tone showed concern, and I started to panic. 'When?'

'As I was preparing this food. I went and we prayed together at her bedside.' He saw my face. 'But do not worry, she is fine. Trust in God.'

God had not done a great deal for me or Philippa in the past, but I kept those thoughts to myself. I leaned back and closed my eyes.

'I spoke to her for quite some time, my child. She loves you very much, Ailred, but she is afraid. She thinks you can be too, how can I put this, nice.'

That word again! 'She thinks I'm weak?'

'No, no, you misunderstand.'

I sulked.

'I'm going to tell you some things now Ailred, and they are not coming from Father John, the

Prior of Reigate, they are from John de Pyrie, the soldier and survivor of countless battles. I need you to listen and never tell anyone what I am about to say.'

I sat up. 'You have my word, Father.'

'You are going to have to learn to kill.'

The opening statement stunned me to my core.

He saw the look on my face. 'I thought that would get your attention. When all this is through you are going to be this woman and this child's protector. Once you leave here you will be at the mercy of the world's evil – and be sure, the devil is everywhere. If you are not strong and decisive he will send his black-hearted followers for you and your family. You will need all of God's strength to survive.' He took a deep slug of wine. 'If there was one thing I learned from those dark days of war it was you *have* to be ruthless. You can never take a backward step. Never. Your enemies will sense any doubt and it will spur them on. From what Philippa told me, you have been the subject of bullying and intimidation until now and have always done what you consider the right thing. She loves you for it. But when you have a child you will have to change. You *must* change or I fear for your future.' He sipped more wine. 'Do you know how I got this?' he pointed to his scar, then laughed. 'I would be very surprised if you did! I got it in my first battle against the Welsh.' I saw a look of reflection cross his face as he recalled the time. 'I was a member of Hugh the Younger's army at the time, and we were stationed at Caerphilly Castle. We had the entire area locked down tight, none of the locals could move without The Younger’s permission. Anyway, to cut a long story short, the Welsh revolted and attacked the castle and we spent days defending it. A man called Llywelyn Bren had led the uprising, and we nearly lost the castle. There were a lot of brave men killed on both sides, I can tell you. We eventually routed them, hunting down the rogues who dared challenge King Edward’s rule. Towards the end, I came across an injured Welshman who was lying on the ground. He was calling for help. I felt pity for him, so went to his aid. He looked grateful, and as I knelt to attend his wound he brought a dagger out from beneath him and slashed me across the face and tried to bury it in my neck. I was dumbstruck at the time. If it hadn't been for one of our archers nearby he would have succeeded.' He felt the scar. 'I now realise, the devil was working through that man. You must learn never to be fooled by him. You must do to him what he will do to you, but do it first.' He took another sip of wine. 'The archer chopped his hands off and castrated him, leaving him to die a long and painful death. It was a warning to the others who escaped.' His voice was slowing as he continued. I think he was reliving his youth. 'If you walk away from the Devil he will pursue you.

You must learn to kill him and if more come you must kill more. If you do not you will lose your family and everything you love. Kill, Ailred, kill and kill again – you must never take a backward step. The Devil is everywhere, in the French, in the Scots, the Welsh – everywhere.' He stopped and his eyes cleared. 'Forgive me Ailred, it has been a long time since I have allowed myself to remember back. I think you understand what I am saying. Protect the innocent but destroy evil.'

I did understand.

I went to speak but heard a scream from inside the dormitory. It was Philippa. I jumped up. I listened for the cries of a baby but there were none.

Father John stood and put his hand on my shoulder. 'Trust in God, my child.'

Then there was silence. I feared the worst.

I ran to the door and burst into the dormitory. It was dark but my sight soon adjusted. There was a group of nuns, including the Reverend Mother, gathered around a bed at the far end. It was quiet. As I hurried down the rows of beds they turned.

'WAIT!' Mother Kimberly shouted and resumed what she was doing. The authority in her voice stopped me.

Two minutes later I heard a baby cry.

Running the rest of the distance, I arrived in time to see Mother Kimberly, her arms covered in blood, pass the screaming baby to Philippa.

I knelt by her bed and kissed her forehead. 'Are you all right?' Then I looked at the baby. 'And she's beautiful.'

She smiled weakly, but I was barged out of the way as the nuns continued their work. I can never express the love and admiration I have for those nuns and Mother Kimberly that day. They are forever in my heart – even though they did throw me out of the dormitory until they had finished.

*

We stayed for a week. Philippa was exhausted, mentally and physically. The baby had the cord wrapped around her neck and the delivery had been traumatic. They had thought the baby was dead at first but it was the relentless work of the Abbess, Mother Kimberly, that saved her. She had refused to give up. The baby had taken to the breast straight away.

We were happy. Happier than either of us had ever been, but it was short-lived.

'Need we check the treasury?' Father John approached me as I was carrying food from the kitchen. I looked at him in surprise. 'That order of friars that stayed with us last night mentioned a man and a pregnant woman who were being sought in connection with the robbery at St Mary's Priory in Tonebricge.'

'It wasn't us Father, I swear on all that is holy.'

He smiled and nodded. 'I know, but it will be common knowledge that you are here now and I fear whoever you are running from will come for you.'

'How long have you known we were running away, Father?'

'From the first moment you entered the priory. I am not blind, my child. You may stay as long as you wish, you know that, but you should continue your journey soon – for your own sake.' He hesitated. 'You may leave the baby if you feel she will be restrictive. She would have a wonderful life here and be brought up by God's chosen people. A child could have no better beginning in life.'

I was horrified. 'I respectfully suggest you don't say that in front of Philippa, Father!'

He nodded. 'The answer I was hoping for. I'll let you get back to your family. You have much to talk about.' He turned to walk away and then stopped. 'Have you named her yet?'

'Kimberly.'

He smiled. 'After, our own Reverend Mother. That is a wonderful name and she will be honoured.'

*

We baptised Kimberly the next day in an emotional service which was attended by monks and nuns alike, something unheard of in Reigate Priory.

The nuns tried hard to smile as we left the gates. Philippa was mounted on the horse, with baby Kimberly nestled close to her bosom. They had come to regard her as their own, the child they would never have, and I saw true sadness.

'Let's get on with the rest of our lives,' I said.

I did not look back.

CHAPTER 6

Predictable. Bishop Budwith managed half the manuscript this morning before asking if I had omitted anything. He gets more tiresome by the day and has asked me not to add these preambles. It annoys him. Tough. I expect him to lose interest over the coming weeks if not days. I will be happy when he does but fear this story will cease before its natural end. He will no doubt find alternative duties for Brother Michael and you will never learn of truths I am yet to tell. We will see.

*

We had been given plenty of food when we left, the monks running the kitchen filling every available space in our saddlebags.

'From what Father John said, we have to keep heading west,' I said when, after hours of travelling, Philippa asked if I knew where we were going. 'He's been to Cardiff Castle before and says the natives can be dangerous to anyone from outside, especially the English.' I went on to tell her about the Welsh uprisings over the years and the relationship between the English barons and local people.

She was stunned. 'How do you know all this?'

I explained to her that at times when she was sleeping or recovering, I would seek Father John out and, over wine, he would regress back to John de Pyrie the soldier. She had no idea he had previously served. He would give me as much information as he could remember.

'If he was ever called back to defend Christendom he would drop everything and fight,' I said. 'And in all honesty, I think he would enjoy it!'

'Well, I never would have guessed that,' she said. 'And you used that time to learn? You surprise me, Ailred Norman.'

'Meet the new Ailred Norman.' I reached up and squeezed her foot.

She laughed. 'That tickles, and if you think you're having sex with me ever again, you can forget it – look what happened last time!' She pulled the sleeping Kimberly from her nipple and showed her to me.

I laughed.

*

It was morning twilight and I was in a state of near-sleep but aware of my surroundings. It was damp, the dew had settled overnight, penetrating my blanket and clothing. Philippa and Kimberly slept close by, but they had been up half the night as the baby refused to sleep and cried, eventually feeding and falling into a deep sleep giving Philippa a chance to rest.

We had found a small clearing away from the beaten track near water after walking most of the day and tethered the horse to a tree close to the stream, and it was from that direction I heard speaking.

Awake now, I rose from my blanket and edged closer. I saw a young man of about fourteen. He was untying the horse. He was alone.

'What are you doing?' I asked. It was a stupid question. I ask a lot of those.

'I was feeding him.' His dress was shabby, his hair and face filthy, but it held a smug grin. He had no fear.

'Go,' I said, pointing towards the road.

'I think I will,' he said, which came as a relief.

He continued to untie the horse.

'Without the horse.'

He laughed. 'Go back to your whore and the bastard.'

I felt my heart pounding. I looked towards Philippa. She was awake and watching, her eyes fearful.

I walked towards her and back to my blanket.

'What else have you got?'

The voice came from an older shaggy-bearded man as he strode towards the boy from behind a tree where he had been urinating, rubbing his hand down his threadbare tunic to dry them. He had a cleaver tucked into his belt and pulled it out as he neared.

I looked at Kimberly as she slept, then reached

down and picked up the axe. I always kept it close to hand and was hoping the sight would scare them away. It did the opposite. They burst into laughter.

'What the fuck have you got that for – off to chop some wood?' the older man said. 'Just give us what we want and we'll be on our way, ain't that right son?'

I heard John de Pyrie's words in my head. These next few moments would define my life.

I walked towards them and they continued to laugh.

'You haven't got it in you, sonny,' the older of the two said, 'I can see it in your eyes.'

I stopped a few feet away and lowered the axe. He was right, I was not my brother Paul, nor John de Pyrie. I was that nice guy.

The son continued untying the horse while his father walked past me towards Philippa and Kimberly.

'Coward,' he hissed into my ear as he walked past holding the cleaver high as a threat.

I snapped.

As he took one more step and took his eyes off me I brought the axe round in a wide arc and caught him on the side of his head. It was a sharp axe and embedded itself with a sound of splintering bone. I saw parts of his brain spill out as I yanked it free. He had screamed at first but as he fell he let out a deep moaning. I turned him over and stared down. His eyes were glazed but he was still conscious.

'Fuckin' laugh now, you bastard.' I screamed into his face and knelt on him. I heard shouting from behind where the younger man was. I looked around. He had let go of the horse and was begging me to stop. I could have the horse back. They did not want it anymore. We could keep all our possessions. How generous of him.

I brought the axe down with all my might into the man's face, splitting his head halfway through, before prising the rest open.

'If you are in my sight when I stand up, I swear to God you will get worse than this. I spat into the face in front of me and stood.

The boy was gone.

Kimberly slept through it all. Philippa said little, although she pecked me on the cheek. I thought I would be angry or frightened but I was neither. My hands were steady as I gathered our things together and within a short time, we were moving again. I did not bury the body. The foxes or wolves or whatever could have that.

I had visions of the younger man rounding up his kinfolk and coming for us and there was a part of me that wanted it.

I had killed for the first time – killed someone who deserved it. It felt good.

*

We looked out over the fast-flowing water. Far in the distance was land. We were speaking to an old man who had stopped us, begging for food.

He pointed, and said, 'This is the river Severn and that's Beachley over there.' I thanked him and handed him a piece of hard cheese and a hunk of stale bread. He looked pleased. 'But I'd stay clear if I were you, it's close to *that place*.' He was repeating something we had heard many times on our journey west. *That place* was Wales.

'So I hear, and you say there's a boat service that will take us across tomorrow?'

'Eye, that it will. The monks from Tintern Abbey will be crossing back to that god-awful place, but if I were you I'd stay well clear...'

'Yes, I get the picture. Thanks again.'

We had taken days to reach this point, having travelled up and down the river looking for a place to cross. We had been directed here by people we met en route, all with strange accents we had trouble understanding. The town was called Aust and we had discovered it was the only crossing for miles, the alternative being a long landward detour.

We tallied up our money and searched for someone connected to the river crossing. It was not difficult to find where it started as a well-worn track led to the water's edge and a vast chain disappeared into the swollen river. It was high tide now, according to the old man, and all crossings took place at low tide. I was not sure what any of that meant, but I did not like the thought of getting into anything floating in that rushing water. I said as much to Philippa.

'You should tell them tomorrow, Al. I'm sure you know more than them about it. You could design a new boat.'

She was annoying at times.

Close by we found an inn called The Ferry Tavern. I nearly asked Philippa if she thought it was a good place to enquire, but stopped myself. She looked at me and grinned.

'We're looking for a room for the night and access to the crossing thing tomorrow – are we in the right place, Sir?' I asked as we stood at the tavern's bar.

The toothless man looked at me and frowned. 'It's called a ferry, and yes, we have a room tonight, so long as that little 'en don't play up.'

We paid him for the room and a night's meal, and additional coins for the crossing the next day. 'I wouldn't go taking any family of mine over to that place.' He gestured across the water. 'But if you're stupid enough to go, I'll take your money.'

I was beginning to see a pattern emerge.

'Does the Lord of Glamorgan travel this way on occasion?' I asked.

'Eye, Sir Hugh does indeed. He always travels with an armed escort, mind you. He came through here a few months ago if my memory serves. Was down Kent way by all accounts, discussing Welsh archers.' He poured Philippa and me a mug of cider. 'What's this world coming to if England needs archers from over there?' He shook his head. 'They'll no doubt turn their arrows on our boys given half a chance.'

He tutted and left.

After taking the horse to the stables out back and checking it was fed and watered, we sat down in a corner of the tavern and sipped our drinks. Kimberly remained asleep in the sling around Philippa's chest.

'Are we sure we want to go *over there*,' Philippa asked in an accent mimicking the local dialect and pointing towards Wales.

I laughed. 'I don't know why I'm laughing, we must be mad.'

Philippa shrugged. 'It can't be as dangerous as they say, besides, what choice do we have?' Kimberly woke and started to fidget. 'Let me get her upstairs before she starts to scream the place down.' She finished her drink and stood to go upstairs. 'And don't forget to bring the food up when it's ready,' she called back.

'Yes, Mam.'

*

Kimberly slept through the night for the first time. I woke to find Philippa with her ear close to her face.

'What are you doing?'

She put her finger to her lips. 'I'm checking she's still alive.'

'Oh my God...' I went to rush to her side but she waved me away.

'It's all right, she's breathing.' She stood up straight and looked down at our sleeping daughter. 'That's the first time she's slept the whole night. I just assumed there must be something wrong with her. I wonder if all first-time parents are like this?'

I smiled. 'I doubt it, no one would be that stupid.'

She threw a shoe at me that missed and hit the wall, waking Kimberly. She started crying.

'Now look what you've done, Norman. And get my shoe – you better not have damaged it.'

We gathered our belongings together and left. After collecting the horse we made our way to where the ferry started. The inn owner had given us proof of payment and instructions on where to go and at what time, and when we arrived there were a number of monks milling around waiting.

The river had dropped since we had last been there and we could see the long chain stretching from one bank to the other. Four men pulled a flat-bottomed boat into position, readying itself for passengers.

'Quick, get down there and tell them how it's done, Al.'

I knew it was coming and ignored her. 'How are we going to get the horse onto that?'

She nodded her head. 'I'm sure there's a way, let's get moving.'

I tried to speak to some of the monks as we awaited our turn to board, but most spoke a different language except one. He approached us after I managed to chivvy our horse up the gangplank and onto the vessel. 'You must be brave or desperate to make the journey over there,' he said, pointing over the water.

'You too, Brother? I thought you might be a little more positive about the place.'

He smiled. 'I doubt you'll receive a warm welcome, although you may be lucky.' He gestured towards my unstrung bow. 'There's talk of our archers joining your ranks.'

He was a short man of about fifty wearing the traditional brown habit and had the ruddy face of someone who drank. He spoke good English but with a strong Welsh accent.

'You are well informed I see, Brother, but I'm not a soldier.'

'My information is acquired through the study of human behaviour and I have seen much, my child.' He shook his head. 'And believe me, where archers and men of violence are concerned none of it is good.' He turned to Philippa and Kimberly. 'May I?' He held his arms out to receive the baby.

'No disrespect, Brother, but she doesn't take well to strangers, I've only just settled her...'

He made a sad face and drooped his lower lip.

She laughed. 'But in your case, I'm sure she'll behave.'

She passed her over. Within seconds Kimberly was balling. No words of comfort could calm her and after a short time, he admitted defeat and handed her back.

'I have a way with children,' he said with a grin.

We spent the crossing chatting with Brother Rhosier.

Most of his life had been spent at Tintern Abbey. He had been born to a young unmarried local girl who could not afford to bring up a child. She had left him outside the chapter house and the monks had taken him in. In later years, he had counselled her when she came searching for him and he had granted her an indulgence as she was racked with guilt. She died the next day with a clear conscience.

He told us Tintern Abbey was a special abbey. I said I thought all abbeys were special, but he explained that it was the only abbey in Wales and as far as he was aware England, that took in troubled and mentally impaired people and cared for them.

'You mean crazies?' I asked, to which he had looked disapprovingly at me and said they were just people who needed help like anyone else. I had felt ashamed of that. I still do.

As the bare-topped men pulling us across the river neared the bank, I asked, 'Did you ever come across a nobleman called John de Pyrie?'

He looked shocked to hear the name. 'The Devil himself. Yes, most folks around here know of John de Pyrie.' He shook his head. 'You would be wise not to speak his name this side of the water.' He noticed the surprise on my face. 'Yes, he is a prior now in Reigate if I am not mistaken, but his brutal reputation lives on. By all accounts, he is a good man of God and I have no doubt in that, but the people of these parts will never forgive his cruelty.' He crossed himself and looked skyward.

The ferry was pulled into the bank and the four sweaty men slumped across the thick chain as we disembarked. A red-headed man pushed a plank up onto the side and the other monks walked down, Brother Rhosier waiting to help me with the horse.

We stood on the sandy bank as the new passengers took our places on the ferry. 'Thank you for that, Father, it has been a pleasure meeting you,' I said shaking his hand.

Philippa nodded in agreement.

'If you are turned away by Sir Hugh and need accommodations, find your way to Tintern Abbey and you will find sanctuary.'

'Thank you, Father,' Philippa and I said together.

He joined the other monks and slipped back into his native tongue.

*

Brother Rhosier had given us directions to Cardiff Castle, or Castell Caerdydd as he called it, which was in the opposite direction to his abbey. We had hoped to travel with the monks for safety, native-speaking monks would have been ideal companions in hostile surroundings.

The road was well-used and in good repair as

we set off, but soon deteriorated. We passed a few people who nodded, but we made a point of not speaking.

After a couple of hours, everything was fine. And then it was not.

We were on the outskirts of a village, both Philippa and I walking to give the horse a rest. Brother Rhosier had advised we bypass any towns where possible, which until then we had, but we had yet to find an alternative route for this one. As we walked in, we were approached by two young men. We smiled and nodded. They did likewise. Then it happened – it was always going to happen sometime. They asked a question in Welsh.

I smiled and nodded. It did not work, they expected a reply.

I looked at Philippa who made a quizzical face and turned her attention to the baby.

The taller of the two, he was about fifteen with matted hair and a narrow face, pointed at the bow and spoke again.

I gave a knowing nod and laughed. He and the other man laughed too. It was funny. I looked at Philippa. She in turn burst into hysterics. She pointed to the horse and then to Kimberly, and mimicked firing an arrow, before doubling over as if it was the funniest thing in the world.

I seized the moment and grabbed her and we walked off, wiping away tears. It worked. The two waved and continued, slapping each other on the back as they went.

'I'm not sure what that was all about, but these people seem harmless,' I said when we were out of earshot.

Philippa climbed back onto the horse. 'We've been lucky so far, let's keep our mouths shut and carry on.'

Which we did.

*

We slept in a disused shack that night and got wet. We had enough money to stay at an inn but thought it unwise after all the cautionary advice we had been given. It had been dry when we bedded down but the heavens opened during the night and the porous roof gave no shelter. It was not disused for nothing. We had spent most of the night keeping Kimberly warm and dry while the other slept, but Kimberly hated being separated from her mother and cried until she was between her breasts.

And it continued raining the next day.

'At least this weather should keep people off the roads,' Philippa said as we trudged on the next morning, my shoes squelching in the mud. 'We shouldn't have far to go now. Brother Rhosier said it should take a couple of days.'

She was right on both counts, although as we neared our destination we found more people braving the torrid weather.

Cardiff was massive. The castle dominated the town and was positioned between three rivers. It looked impregnable. We could not avoid people by the time we got close, but no one gave us a second glance as they hurried about their daily lives.

We started to hear English spoken by soldiers as they rode past, always in numbers, and I recognised the colours and livery. They were those of Baron Sir Hugh le Despenser.

*

'Can you just get a message to him, it's important. Please?' I asked.

We were standing in the arched entrance to the castle below the portcullis, flanking towers on either side. We had joined a queue of people and animals as they looked to enter, all speaking Welsh and most carrying tools or bringing supplies.

The sentry stepped from the doorway and called his commanding officer over. 'English fella here wants to get a message to Paul Christian.'

He joined us. 'You do, do you?' He was a middle-aged man dressed in full mail with a surcoat displaying the Despenser coat of arms. The other sentries wore similar uniforms and were checking anyone entering for weapons. They looked on full alert.

'Yes, Sir. He's Lord Hugh's squire.'

'Yes, I know who he is, but why do you want him? Most of these Welsh people here want him and would kill him if they got their way.' He stared at the line of people behind us and they looked away. 'Fuckin' Welsh animals...'

'He's my twin brother, Sir. I need him to know I'm here with my wife and child.'

He looked us up and down and nodded. 'You are, are you – you look nothing like him.'

I was about to answer when Philippa spoke. 'With respect, Sir, we've travelled a long way and it's dangerous out here being English. If we are not who we say we are, why would we bother making up a story that could get us into serious trouble – it's easy to prove us wrong.'

He tapped the end of his morning star repeatedly on the ground while he considered the question.

One of the other sentries spoke. 'If he is his brother, we'll be in the shit if we turn them away, Sir. They won't last the night out there being English, Sir. I wouldn't like to be the one who...'

'Yes, very well, go get him, Mark. I think he's with that scholar, Albar, in one of the tower rooms.' He looked back at me. 'What's your name?'

'Ailred, Sir. Ailred Norman.'

He hesitated. 'So you're Paul Christian's twin brother but don't look like him and you have a different second name? Are you taking the piss, son?'

'It's a long story Sir, and I'll happily tell you it when Paul confirms who I am.'

The other sentry, Mark, was walking away but heard the last part of the conversation and stopped.

'My brother can get very angry when he...' I added.

'Go on Mark, but if this man is not who he says he is...' He shook his head and tapped the morning star on the ground again.

I turned back and stood next to Philippa and Kimberly. We waited while others filed past.

A short time later I heard an angry voice.

'If this is some kind of fuckin' joke...my brother isn't married or has a fuckin' kid. I'm going to flog the bastard's skin from his back.' Paul came bounding down the spiral staircase from one of the towers and jumped out of the door next to the commanding officer, his eyes ablaze. He was holding a coiled cattle whip.

'Holy fuck – it *is* you!'

'Jesus, Paul, you scare the life out of me and I'm your brother – God knows what the locals think.'

He dropped the whip and hugged me. 'What the hell are you doing here, and what's this about a wife and baby?' He looked towards Philippa and Kimberly who were standing next to the horse. She smiled and Kimberly burst into tears. 'You have a lot of explaining to do, little bro.' He turned to the sentries. 'Let them pass and be sure to get the horse seen to.'

*

We sat in the tower room with Paul and his language teacher, Albar. He was a thin, timid-looking man in his early thirties, his eyes forever studying whoever was speaking at any one moment. He only looked comfortable when speaking to Paul, and often dropped into French as the two spoke. To my amazement, Paul understood and replied in French, but would apologise.

'Albar only speaks French to me,' he said, 'it's how I've learned so fast.'

Albar smiled. 'He is a good student, although he is prone to temper tantrums.' He had a strong accent and soft mannerisms.

Paul refilled our mugs with ale and leaned back in the high-backed chair.

'That's quite some story Al, and I've heard of the devil's monk in Reigate Priory. I doubt he'd have made it here on foot like you two. The locals would string him up the second he set foot in Wales. You were lucky to get here alive, I can tell you that from experience.' He sipped his ale. 'So why did you leave and take on the responsibilities for someone else's kid – are you mad or something?' He did not even glance at Philippa.

I had left out large sections of the story as I did not want to air them in front of a stranger. I looked at Albar but said nothing.

He understood. 'Would you like me to leave, Paul, Sir?'

'No, no, anything you have to say can be said in front of Albar, he's my closest friend and I trust him with my life.'

'You honour me, Sire.' He bowed his head and turned his gaze to me.

I told him everything.

By the time I finished, Kimberly had finished feeding and fallen asleep in Philippa's arms.

'That explains a great deal. You did the right thing coming here,' he said, 'however dangerous it was. I'll speak to Sir Hugh and see if I can find you work.' He looked at Philippa. 'And as you have serving experience I'm sure we can find you some sort of employment. We'll oust one of the Welsh wenches if needs be.'

For the first time in weeks, I felt safe.

Paul and Albar left to sort out our accommodation and future employment.

'Your brother's nice,' Philippa said, resting Kimberly on a low table, 'although he hardly spoke a word to me.'

I had not noticed. 'He's just pleased to see me. He'll get to know you in time.'

'And he seems to trust his tutor, Albar. I hope it's well-founded.'

'Paul wouldn't have said it if he wasn't sure. They looked close.'

I walked around the small room, idling the time away. There were manuscripts on the shelves and various quills and blank parchment on lecterns. 'Can you read?'

Philippa chuckled. 'What do you think? She laughed again. 'And I'm not going to even ask you that question.'

The door opened. Sir Hugh entered, followed by Paul.

'You get around, Ailred!'

'Sir Hugh – I'm sorry for this unannounced...'

'It's fine. Paul has filled me in on your circumstances and I have given him full backing in accommodating you both.' He looked at Kimberly. 'All three of you.' He smiled. 'Your brother has made an exceptional squire, regardless of the backlash it has caused, but that was of my making. I'm happy to help. It so happens that one of my Welsh wet-nurses just quit, so you're in luck.' He winked at Philippa. He looked back towards me. 'And Paul tells me you're handy with the bow...?'

'More than handy, Sire.' Paul added.

'That's to be seen, but you archers will be in high demand soon. I'm sure I will be seeing you both around, and please don't make me regret this.' He turned and left.

*

We were put to work. Philippa was given the position of wet nursing and housed in the female quarters with a number of other English women. There were numerous babies within the castle from the gentry's wives and lovers and all required round-the-clock feeding. It was not what Philippa had hoped for but she was pragmatic and grateful. Most of the hired help were local women who lived nearby and were paid a fraction of the English wage.

I was assigned anything and everything. I was at the beck and call of anyone who needed service – even Paul. I was boarded with other English menial workers, including Albar. I found myself bedding in the same room as him and found him fascinating. He was a font of knowledge on most subjects and spoke of Paul with high regard.

'He's a fast learner,' he said one night as I sat on the side of the bed and removed my boots. 'I don't think he's ever been given the chance to express himself.' He studied my reaction, as he did with everything we spoke about. 'There's a great deal about Paul that would surprise you. He's not the same brother you grew up with.'

He was right. He walked about the castle as if he owned it. The gentry all knew him and he had the respect of every fighting man. He studied studiously and threw himself into combat training with the single-mindedness of a man possessed.

I lay down in bed at the end of another long and gruelling day. 'He holds you in high regard too.' I said, closing my eyes.

As I drifted off to sleep his final words crept into my consciousness.

'I love him.'

CHAPTER 7

Cardiff held an uneasy truce. For as long as anyone could remember there had been hostilities between the English and Welsh. The Anglo-Saxons had invaded, and, more recently, the Normans. There was always tension as the Welsh resented English rule with a passion and had attempted to overthrow the barons over many years. The last concerted effort was led by Llywelyn Bren who, after surrendering to spare the lives of his followers, had been executed at Cardiff Castle by order of Sir Hugh le Despenser's father who ruled the estate before him. He had been hung drawn and quartered. It was a story every Welsh boy and girl had been told alongside other rebellious heroes. It fuelled a never-ending state of siege.

*

'Try this.'

I drew Dafydd's bow to the tip of my nose and loosed. I felt the hum as the string settled, the arrow striking the target dead centre.

'That's incredible Daf, I didn't realise how much better your bow was.' I looked it over. It was a beautiful weapon, made from Spanish yew and must have cost a fortune.

I handed it back.

'Great – now you're going to claim the only reason I'm better is because of the bow.'

It had taken months to understand his accent and we were friends. His job was similar to mine and he was the only Welshman living within the castle's walls. He was the intermediary between the English and Welsh workers and was trusted by both, although I had never seen him talking with Paul.

We were on the castle lawn and there was a mixture of Welsh and English archers practising. Never-ending talk of an imminent invasion of France was forever circulating. Sir Hugh was in the process of cobbling together a mixture of Welsh and English men to join such a venture. The bowmen, with the exception of Dafydd, practised in groups of their own nationality and never came together. That made Sir Hugh's task close to impossible. Dafydd was acknowledged as the most skilled by both sets. He was a tall powerful man with a barrel chest and huge arms and was able to place an arrow in the bullseye with remarkable consistency. I was jealous. I was also jealous of his wife. I know I should not admit this, but she was a beauty beyond anyone I had seen. She was also Philippa's friend.

'Have you two finished yet?'

I looked up as Philippa spoke. She and Dafydd's wife, Blodwen, walked towards us.

'Just about through,' I called back, sliding my remaining arrows into the quiver and walking forward to retrieve the others from the distant target.

We stood in the afternoon sunshine chatting, Blodwen and Philippa fussing over Kimberly who by now was smiling and attracting attention. The other archers were beginning to pack their bows away and drift off when Paul came striding over. Dafydd and Blodwen went silent as he approached.

'Hi, brother, how was the practice?' He spoke with assurance and I noticed some of the Welsh archers look down and walk away.

I laughed. 'Funny you should say that Paul, I got schooled by Dafydd here. His bow is so much better than mine. Spanish yew puts mine to shame.

Dafydd shrugged but refused to meet Paul's gaze.

Paul held out his hand. 'Pass it here.'

I was shocked at his abruptness but said nothing.

Dafydd walked over and handed him the unstrung bow.

'String it then. How am I supposed to gauge an unstrung bow, Taffy.'

I stepped in, 'Come on Paul, let him be, he's a friend.' He was embarrassing me and making the women uncomfortable.

'I'm only joking Al, we're all friends here,' he

looked at Dafydd. 'You can take a joke can't you?'

Dafydd nodded and brought out a string, looping it over one end of the horn-tipped nock, bending the bow and repeating it at the other. He passed the bow to Paul.

'An arrow?' He laughed. 'I'm not sure we want any Welsh bowmen in France if they don't know you fire an arrow!'

I went to speak, but Paul looked at me and said, 'I'm joking – what's the matter with everyone today?' He put his arm around Dafydd's neck and yanked him, causing him to stumble. 'He's as much a brother as you are.'

He took the arrow offered and placed it on the string. He drew it halfway and stopped. 'This is a serious bow, my friend. Do you mind if I shoot at that target?'

Dafydd said nothing.

Paul drew the bow and loosed, striking the outer ring. 'Not as good as you, my friend, but I think I can do better. Go and fetch it for me. You remember what an arrow looks like?'

Some of Paul's friends had gathered nearby and were beginning to laugh.

'I think we need to go, Daf,' Blodwen said. She was shaking.

'Yes, we'll catch you two up a little later…' Philippa added in an encouraging manner. She could sense the tension and wanted them to get away.

'Leaving already, Taffy? If you want your bow

back, you'll have to fetch the arrow.' He made the sound of a dog. 'Go fetch Welshy, there's a good boy.'

'Come on Paul, that's enough.' I said, starting to walk towards the target. 'I'll get it.'

'STOP.' Paul was cold-faced and staring at Dafydd. He walked over to where I had left my quiver and took out one of my arrows, placing it on the string. Paul's friends went silent.

He drew the string to its full length and aimed at Dafydd's face from ten paces. 'Get the fuckin' arrow.'

Dafydd stared back but did not move.

'I said, get the fuckin'…'

'No.'

I pleaded but it was pointless. He was deaf to my words.

'I have nothing without my honour – so you'll have to shoot that arrow, English boy.'

Paul's face remained unmoved and he swivelled around, aiming the bow at Blodwen.

'Get the fuckin' arrow.'

I stepped forward and stood in front of Blodwen, who was in tears.

A soft accented voice broke the standoff. 'There you are Paul, I've been searching all over for you.'

I looked behind Blodwen. It was Albar.

'Have you forgotten your French lessons? They are more important than these silly archery games you young boys like to play.' He skipped around as if he were a child, running to one of Paul's friends and 'tagging' him before running away.

Paul's friends laughed, breaking the tension.

Paul's hands were shaking with the effort of holding the arrow on the string and so released it, letting it fly past the tearful Blodwen.

He looked towards Albar and his face softened, then glanced at Dafydd and raised his chin.

'We'll need you boys in France. Keep up the good work.' He dropped the bow and joined his teacher.

*

'He's an animal, Ailred.'

Dafydd and Blodwen had gone back to their respective accommodation and Philippa and I were walking by the river that ran close to Cardiff Castle. It was a pleasant Sunday afternoon. It was dangerous walking outside the castle but Philippa was so angry she needed to get away. 'They're our only friends here, and now they won't even come for a walk with us.'

'I'm sure it will blow over. They know it wasn't us.'

Philippa handed the smiling Kimberly to me and I tickled her under the chin and pulled a silly face.

'You know Paul's tried it on with Blodwen, don't you?'

I looked at her. She was serious. 'When? How do you know?'

'She's my friend, Al. He tries it on every time he sees her alone.'

'Does Dafydd know?'

She laughed. 'Of course not. He's a lovely guy, but he'd kill him.'

She was right. He was mild-mannered but knowing Paul was making sexual advances at his wife would tip him over the edge.

I played with Kimbley in case she was affected by the tension.

'There's more.'

I looked up. She looked worried. 'What?' I asked.

'He's more aggressive each time. She's afraid he might do something...'

I took a deep breath. This was serious. Paul was well established here, our preferential treatment being a result of it, but he was beginning to act untouchable.

Then a terrible thought occurred. 'What's he like with you?'

She bent forward and took Kimberly from me but said nothing. I went cold.

'It's not about me, we're talking about Blodwen. I can look after myself.'

'Has he...?'

'He never speaks to me.'

'That's not what I asked.'

She put Kimberly onto the floor and encouraged her to crawl, laughing and beckoning her forward, smiling all the time.

She was frightening me. I needed to speak to Paul.

*

Philippa told me not to mention our conversation about Blodwen to Paul and I told her I was not that stupid.

I was.

By the time we finished, Paul had accused her of lying and manipulating me and called Dafydd a Welsh agitator. I thought he was going to attack me at one point his denial being of such resolve. I believed him.

'Fine, I'll keep my eye on both of them if you think they're dangerous,' I said, 'although that doesn't excuse your behaviour.'

He laughed. 'Oh, that – I was only joking. I'll give him his due – he took it well. Besides, we can't fall out with the Welsh archers now we don't have the money to pay them.'

This was my chance. I took it.

'Did you rob the Tonebricge Priory?'

We were in the same tower room he and Albar conducted French tutoring in and he sat down at the table.

'What did you say?'

'They found Simon Butcher's body in the marshes around Tonebricge before we left. He had been murdered.'

I had omitted that part when we first arrived as I needed to find the right moment to ask.

'I don't even know who Simon Butcher is,

besides, if I had robbed that place do you think I would be here? Trust me, I'd be long gone by now.'

'It was something Father Rhys said.' This part was going to be difficult. 'He said something about a key.'

Paul turned on me. 'Key, what key? When did he say this?' He was angry.

I could not bring myself to speak about the ordeal in the dungeon, so said, 'I spoke to him not long after the robbery. He said something about you having his key.'

He slammed his fist onto the table. I jumped.

'Don't listen to what that devil in a cassock says. He hates me. One of these days I'll fuckin'...; He stopped himself and looked towards the ceiling. 'Just forget about him.'

He got up and walked out without another word.

That went well. I sat down. A few minutes later the door opened and Albar entered.

He looked surprised to see me. 'Where is Paul?'

'I'm not sure, he left.'

He spoke a few words in French, most of which I did not understand, but I understood enough to realise he was due a lesson.

'I'm worried about Paul,' I said. I had come to trust Albar and found him easy to talk to.

He stopped riffling through the parchments he was carrying and looked at me.

'I always worry about him. It is my job. Now

you are here we can worry together.' He looked me up and down. 'You and Paul are close, yes?'

'We were brought up together.' I shrugged. 'I feel I hardly know him now.'

'I think you are not like him. He has high ambitions now and will do anything to achieve them.' He stared me in the eyes. 'Anything.'

The door opened and Paul entered. Albar scolded him for being late. Paul said something in French that I did not understand and Albar laughed and kissed him on both cheeks.

'I must ask you to leave now, Ailred,' Paul said.

Albar was holding Paul's hand.

I left.

*

Life continued. Paul became a virtual stranger and Dafydd and Blodwen avoided Philippa and me. There was always an excuse not to visit. Philippa felt it most. She became depressed most days, the constant feeding of Kimberly and the other children in her care took its toll.

And then things changed. I was mucking out the stables with a group of other men, Dafydd included, and Paul came bounding in.

'Have you heard?'

I stopped shovelling. 'Heard what?'

'It's happening. King Edward is summoning all available troops to Ipswich by June.'

I was shocked. 'So soon? That's only a few weeks off.'

'I know, good, ain't it!' He looked towards

Dafydd. 'Looks like you and your lot will be sailing out with us.'

He said nothing and continued his work.

'It's your chance to earn some money, Taffy. Stick with the English and we'll make you rich.' He turned back to me. 'How are you feeling about it? There's more to war than firing a few arrows at Mister Frenchie, you know.' He drew his sword. Dafydd looked over and flinched. 'You have to be capable of ripping the bastards apart.' He enacted the actions of swordplay, his face a picture of concentration, hacking and thrusting. He was happy.

'I'll be fine.'

He stopped. 'What about Philippa – will she come?'

'Yeah, we've spoken about it and she wants to follow along with the others.'

He looked disappointed but said nothing.

'What about you Taff, taking the little lady?'

He stopped and waved the pitchfork in Paul's direction. 'Leave her name out of it.'

Paul hardened. 'She's a fuckin' pig, anyway.'

I put my arm around his shoulder and ushered him out. 'You need to lay off him, Paul. You'll be fighting on the same side soon. You might need him to save your life.'

'I'd rather die.'

*

Sir William de Bohun, Earl of Northampton and his escort trotted through the main gates.

We stopped working and watched. It was no secret Sir William and Sir Hugh were still at loggerheads, so the sight was not expected. Hostilities ran deep since the day Sir Hugh had replaced Sir William's son Jacques Stafford with Paul as his Squire, and Paul had all but killed him.

'That's Sir William, isn't it?' Philippa walked over and stood beside me. She had a baby feeding from her breast and was holding Kimberly's hand as she continued to learn to walk.

'Yep, and that's Jacques.' I pointed towards the back of the retinue.

'Oh dear, why on earth would he bring him along? He knows Paul's here.'

'He isn't going to leave his squire behind. It's a matter of honour.'

'I just hope Paul keeps out of the way. I can't imagine what they're here to talk about.'

I nodded in agreement.

Jacques looked towards me and stared. His face was disfigured and he had a patch over one eye. He looked as if he was trying to place where he had seen me before.

'OI, JACQUES, GOOD TO SEE YOU.' The shout came from the window of one of the flanking towers.

Jacques Stafford looked around to see who had shouted but his father turned and said something, causing him to stop. He faked a smile and laughed.

'This isn't going to end well,' I said.

They were greeted on the pathway by Sir Hugh who grasped Sir William's arm in friendship as he dismounted. Sir Hugh gestured for me and a number of other workers to join them.

'Take these gentlemen's mounts to the stable and look after them.' We scurried around, gathering the horses as each guest climbed down. I walked to Jacques and held out my hand to take the reigns.

'You're the brother, aren't you?'

'I'm not sure what you mean, Sir.'

'You know exactly what I mean. You tell him I will kill him the first chance I get.' His voice was low, trying to keep the conversation between the two of us.

'Come on, Jacques, don't dawdle.'

'Coming, Sir William, just thanking the boy here for his hospitality.'

He threw the reigns at me and walked towards the great hall with the others.

A few minutes later I was joined by Paul. 'What did he say?'

I was not going to tell him as it might antagonise the situation, but he needed the warning. 'He said he's going to kill you.'

He gave a great belly laugh. 'Of course, he is. You'd better lock Philippa away – those good looks of his will turn her head.'

He continued laughing and walked towards the hall.

I was joined by Philippa. 'He has no sense of

danger has he?' she said.

I led the horses off to the stables with the others. 'He has no sense at all.'

*

It was not long before I was bringing the horses back.

As Sir William and his entourage remounted, Sir Hugh stood at the doors to the great hall and watched. He did not wish them farewell or speak.

With one final look in his direction, Sir William turned his horse's head and rode out. Jacques followed.

I did not see Paul until late that night. There were rumours that Sir William had come as a last-ditch attempt to heal the rift but the problem was insurmountable and he had refused to join with Sir Hugh and the Welsh archers.

That evening Sir Hugh gathered everyone onto the castle lawn and confirmed the rumour. He told us we would be leaving for Ipswich in the morning. It was an inspirational speech.

'The time has come, my friends, to uphold King Edward's rightful claim to the throne of France. God save the King.'

We cheered. In that moment I understood the passion and comradeship of an army. I looked at Philippa as I waved my hat in the air.

She turned and walked away.

That night I got drunk. I still had not spoken to Paul, but I was sure he was doing the same as the rest of us. Even Dafydd toasted our forthcoming campaign with me. Philippa had stayed in the service quarters and was feeling low again.

'How many Welsh archers will come tomorrow?'

Dafydd scowled. 'Not as many as before the money was stolen. They were relying on being paid upfront so they could leave it for their families.' He swigged his ale. 'But there will be a good number regardless. There will be plenty to gain once we're there.'

'Sir Hugh said we'll all come back rich.'

He raised his eyebrows. 'He would say that. The truth is a good number won't come back at all.'

'That's a cheery thought, Daf!'

He laughed. 'We'll be fine.'

We were sitting together near the main gates. It was an unseasonably warm evening, and many had gone to bed in anticipation of a long day ahead. I was about to do likewise when there was a commotion coming from the main gate. I heard Welsh voices shouting.

A dishevelled man walked towards us. There were a number of other people still being held back by the guard detail. He had been the only person allowed through.

'What do you want?' I asked, but he bypassed me and went to Dafydd and spoke to him in his native tongue. He looked distressed.

Dafydd jumped up and shouted, throwing his chair to one side.

'What is it?' I asked but he ignored me and ran

towards the gate.

I followed, moving past the man.

'I would go the other way, Sir, if I was you,' the man said in broken English.

'Why, what's happened?'

He said nothing and walked back.

I pushed past him and joined the group at the entrance. Dafydd was kneeling over a naked woman's body. He was crying. I moved around to see who it was but was unable to distinguish the person.

Then I realised.

'Oh my God, Dafydd.'

Blodwen had been the target of a vicious attack. She had bite marks all over and blood pooled between her legs. Her lifeless body was barely recognisable.

'Who the hell would do a thing like this?' It was insensitive, I realise now, but was the first thing that came to mind.

He turned his head and vomited. He spat. 'I'll fuckin' kill them. I will not rest until I know who did this.'

I was not welcome at this time of grief, the surrounding Welsh folk made that clear. They took the body away.

'Oh, that's a shame.' I turned and found Paul standing behind me. 'She was such a pretty little thing too.'

*

Philippa was in pieces, sobbing uncontrollably.

I tried to console her. 'She was outside the grounds, so it must have been a Welshman,' I said, but it fell on deaf ears.

I picked up Kimberly who was distressed at seeing her mother so upset. Rocking her, I said, 'I spoke to Paul and he said Sir Hugh doesn't have time to investigate as it's too close to our departure to France.'

She sniffed. 'Of course he hasn't, it's only a Welsh woman.'

'I'm sure that has nothing to do with it.'

She lost her temper. 'Think, you fuckin' idiot.'

I looked at her.

'Oh my God Ailred, you're so blind.' She got up and snatched Kimberly from me, causing her to cry. 'It was your crazy brother. He's planned this. He knows Dafydd doesn't know he's been tormenting her for months.' She looked at me through bloodshot eyes. 'But you do. And I do. We could have helped her.' She started crying again. 'He knows you ship out to France tomorrow and knows Sir Hugh won't follow this up.' She moved within inches of my face. 'Your brother is a cold-hearted monster – and you've aided him time and again.'

I did not know how to respond. I went to move but did not know where to go. Then I did.

I found Paul with Albar in Paul's bedroom. Albar jumped as I barged in but Paul smiled. He had managed to get sole use of one of the tower rooms and had a bed in one corner. Other than the gentry, he was the only person with such privilege.

'Did you kill Blodwen?'

'Nice to see you too, Ailred.'

Albar looked nervous. 'Would you like me to leave, Sir?'

'No, stay here, I think I'm going to need you in a minute.'

I paced up and down. 'Well, did you?'

'I will tell you this once Ailred, and then never mention it again. You are my brother and I love you. With these accusations you make me look weak and foolish in the eyes of people I need respect from.' He looked at me with disdain and concealed anger. 'But I will tell you this, although I have no need to justify myself.' His look was one of impatience. 'I, unlike you, was in the chapel all night thanking God and praying for the safe delivery of all our comrades who will travel to France tomorrow.' I went to speak but he stopped me. 'Before you insult me and ask for proof, I was with Albar here.' He looked at his tutor. 'We were on our knees – praying for you.'

Albar nodded.

I left.

*

The next morning I awoke with a feeling of trepidation and excitement. The night before had been a nightmare. I could not find Philippa after I returned from talking to Paul and had no idea where she slept. There was little talk about

Blodwen's rape and murder, all conversation focusing on the forthcoming expedition.

A large number of Welsh had assembled on the castle grounds, most carrying war bows and quivers of arrows. Adding them to the number of English archers and men-at-arms we made a formidable body of fighting men.

I looked for Philippa. If she was not quick she would miss me leaving.

I never saw her before we left.

CHAPTER 8

I was the last to leave. I waited but she never showed. We had agreed she would travel with the camp followers at a later date but I was still disappointed. What if I did not make it beyond the first days – I would never see her or Kimberly again.

Paul was at the front with Sir Hugh and I watched a tearful Albar walk away, back to the sanctuary of his books and teachings. They would be reunited soon as he was destined to travel as a follower. He could keep Philippa company.

I had no horse like the majority of men and filed in.

'Oi, English, you're the squire's brother, aren't you?' The question had a Welsh accent and came from behind. It seems I was not the last to leave.

'I am.' I was in no mood to converse.

'Is it true we're picking up the Earl of Huntingdon and his men en route?'

I had heard talk of an alliance between the two old friends, and Lord Clinton was the Lord High Admiral so it made sense. I was not looking forward to a sea journey across to France. I had never even seen a ship before, let alone travelled across an ocean.

‘I heard that's the plan, yes. Sir Hugh and Lord Clinton go back years.’

There was a moment’s silence. I thought I was safe. I was not.

‘Oi, English?’

I said nothing.

‘Oi, English?’

‘Just speak, Welsh.’

‘You want me to speak Welsh? Will you understand if I do...?

I groaned.

By the time we arrived at Huntingdon, Welsh had grown on me. He was funny. I needed someone to drag me from my state of melancholy. He was the perfect tonic. I had expected to hear Dafydd's voice at some point but did not. In all that time of running banter I never once turned around. Welsh was a faceless voice.

We were met outside a vast mansion by a large group of men.

'Do you think that's the Earl of Huntington?' I asked.

'The one with the massive horse, the armed bodyguards and the Earl of Huntington's crest on his surcoat?' Welsh mused. 'No, I think that's the stablehand.'

I ignored him. 'I hope I'm boarding his ship. If the High Admiral can't captain a boat, no one can.'

'They'll be putting us expendable Welsh boys on a ship and scuttle it as soon as we leave Ipswich.'

I laughed.

'I'm not sure why you're laughing – you're one of us, English-Welshboy.'

There was widespread laughter and others joined in at my expense.

'At least I'm getting paid.' That shut them up. An apple core hit me on the back of the head.

*

We milled around Ipswich harbour. There were thousands of us, mainly English, but many from Wales, and I found myself adopted into the Glamorgan ranks. I think they thought me amusing. I met Welsh face to face. He was a small wiry man of similar age. He had never seen battle other than drunken shots at English guards on the castle walls, like all his companions.

'If I can't get us on Admiral Clinton's ship, I'll see if I can get us posted with my brother on Sir Hugh's.'

I went in search of transport. I found Paul with Sir Hugh at the harbour's edge looking out at the hundred or more ships. It was an extraordinary sight.

'Wow!' It was an automatic response.

Paul turned to me. 'Ah, Ailred Norman. I hope you're well?' It was as if I was one of his squires, or worse, his page.

'I'm fine, Paul.' He stared at me but said nothing. 'Sir.'

'Good, I see you're assigned to the Glamorgan mark?'

'Well, I travelled with them, but I'm not sure that makes me part of their company.'

'I think we'll keep you there if that's acceptable to Sir Hugh?' He looked for confirmation. Sir Hugh nodded. 'Good, I want you Welsh archers in Lord Clinton's ship. It will reinforce our commitment to unity and calm some of the internal politics.'

I did not know what to say. This was Paul giving orders and assigning personnel.

Admiral Clinton approached.

'Ah, Sir Hugh, we have a fair wind to our advantage, I intend to set out as soon as possible.' He spoke in English and was stroking his long grey beard and studying the ships. 'King Edward has surpassed himself – they are a fine fleet of cogs.'

'I bow to your superior knowledge, Lord Admiral,' Sir Hugh replied, shaking him by the hand. 'I wouldn't know a cog from a hulk.'

'Well, you better learn fast if you want your archer chaps spraying arrows into Frenchy later.' He laughed and pulled Sir Hugh aside and started to explain the difference.

I took the opportunity to question Paul. 'What was all that about?'

He smiled. 'I told you before, I have

appearances to keep up. One day I will be leading all this.' He swept his arm, taking in the multitude of armed men and ships anchored off the quay. 'Besides,' he looked around to check he was not overheard, 'I've got you a place on the safest ship in the fleet. You should thank me.'

I had to give it to him, he was turning into quite the politician.

When I got back to Welsh and the Glamorgan archers, there was a stand-off between them and a group of English soldiers led by Jacques Stafford. Sir William de Bohun and his troops were here already. I had no idea what they were arguing about but it was getting heated. I walked into the back of the English men and started to nudge my way through.

'ENGLISH-WELSHBOY,' Welsh shouted.

The front row of Englishmen looked in my direction. Jacques saw me and pushed forward.

That was all it took. It kicked off. The Welshmen piled into the front rank of the English and caught them off guard. At that moment there were more Welsh numbers and their fists and boots were smacking anyone in their way. They were enjoying their day by the seaside. Welsh was behind the front row, who were big valley men with massive hands and vicious tempers.

After the initial surprise strike the English reorganised and fought back, Jacques still trying to get to me. It was mayhem. Men were rolling about the floor grappling whilst others squared up and fought bare-knuckle.

Then it turned nasty. It was always going to. One of the Welshmen pulled a dagger and ran into the heart of the English on his own, slashing and stabbing indiscriminately. Jacques dodged the crazed man and decided it was too dangerous, fighting to escape. That moved the stakes up a level. More English came running over, not wanting to miss out. Once they saw the blade all rules were discarded. Axes and swords were drawn and blood was shed. It went from a common street brawl to an armed conflict in minutes. Jacques Stafford was nowhere to be seen.

I'll be honest, I love a good punch-up but this was turning into an unnecessary battle. People were getting hurt. I saw a couple of Welshmen thrown into the sea as the superior numbers of English showed.

I looked for Welsh. The last time I saw him he was loving life – punching and kicking anyone in front of him, but now he looked troubled. He had a gash across his arm and one of his eyes was closed. And still more English joined. By now the Welshmen were fighting to escape. They were getting attacked from all angles, many of the English screaming murder as they had been attacked first and wanted to exact revenge.

No one touched me as I was wearing the livery of Sir Hugh, and it was he and Lord Clinton who managed to quell the fracas. The sight of the two was enough to stop the English from continuing their assault. Paul was there too, although he had the look of someone disappointed to have missed out.

I dragged Welsh away and pushed him down the street. He was furious, but I could tell he was relieved to escape alive. We looked back and saw a score of men lying on the floor dead or injured.

It was not supposed to be like this.

*

They kept the Glamorgan men separated and herded them onto the admiral's ship.

It had been a sleepless night as thousands of excited soldiers had camped out anywhere they could in Ipswich. The ships and supplies had been fitted out and readied overnight in preparation for boarding this morning. Some of Sir William's men had carried on the quarrel with the Welsh where possible, but in general, both sides avoided further conflict.

I found myself surrounded by Welsh archers on the ship. There were about one hundred of us, the rest of the ship being English sailors and men-at-arms. Lord Clinton barked orders to his understudies and they chivved us into our assigned positions. It was chaos but he knew exactly what was required and gave us confidence. He would be friendly and lighthearted one minute but ball out someone the next if they did not do what they were told.

He was the Admiral.

I was stationed at the forecastle, a walled wooden castle-shaped structure at the front of the ship with Welsh and about fifty other archers, while the rest were distributed at the rear in a similar structure to ours and in the belly of the ship. There were also a few on a high platform on the single mast supporting the sail.

Admiral Clinton wandered about at ease with his English men-at-arms and the Bishop of Huntingdon, Father Fleming, reassuring us and explaining where stores of arrows and the armoury were when the time came. He had to gesture, as most spoke only Welsh. The Bishop was there to give blessings and comfort to any dying man later.

It became real in that instant. I had my bow unstrung and a number of bowstrings ready to be braced when necessary, but I still was not sure I was prepared. There would be no going back now.

As Lord Clinton walked past I asked, 'How long will it take to reach France?'

He looked up at the sail as it eased us out of the estuary and onto the open sea. 'I reckon it will take a couple of days, so you boys can relax for a while.' He went to walk on but stopped. 'You're English aren't you?'

'Yes, Sire.'

'You seem out of place here with all these Welsh boys. What's your name?'

'Ailred, Lord, Ailred Norman.'

'Ah, you must be Sir Hugh's squire's brother.' He looked behind the ship and pointed. 'He's over there in the Margaret.' I looked and could just about make out the figures of Sir Hugh and Paul standing at the front, surrounded by his men. 'And if you look that way,' he pointed ahead, 'our King is there in the Thomas.'

I could not see him, but in truth, I would not have known what he looked like anyway.

Welsh edged past me. 'When do we get paid, my Lord?'

Lord Clinton frowned. 'Sorry, Son, I don't speak Welsh.'

'I was speaking English, Sire.'

He looked at me. 'Can you tell him I don't understand Welsh? Poor chap thinks if he speaks enough I will.'

I turned to translate. I spoke English in my best Welsh accent. 'He can't understand your accent. To be fair, it took me months to figure out what you lot were saying.'

Welsh smiled. 'Tell him he's an English idiot.'

'He says he's proud to serve under you, Lord.'

'Thank him for me will you, Ailred.' He moved away. 'Oh and, Ailred Norman, I will be coming to you when I need to interact with these people. There will be times when I will need fast communication – battles are won and lost on such matters.'

'What the fuck, English! Did he just promote

you to our commander?'

'It looks that way, Welsh – and call me Sir from now on.'

*

'In a few hours, we will engage the enemy.' Lord Clinton addressed the ship's company.

We had spent an uncomfortable night on the deck, sleeping whenever Welsh took a break from snoring. He could snore for Wales. If we sent him in alone, the French would have surrendered within hours. It was a chilly morning, the sky overcast, but Lord Clinton was like a ray of sunshine.

'We are attacking Sluys.' He looked at our faces. 'I realise that not many of you can understand me, but Ailred Norman will translate later. Anyway, Sluys is where we make land and start the campaign. As we all know, Sluys is full of....?' He looked out over our heads and waited, hoping someone might answer. Nothing. 'It is full of French.'

I heard a couple of Welsh voices whisper to one another, 'I knew that.'

Lord Clinton continued. 'So the order of the day will be to...?' More silence. 'It will be to kill as many Frenchmen as possible.'

'Damn, I knew that too. I need to learn to speak up more.'

I turned to Welsh. 'I hope you're taking all this in, I'll be giving you questions later.'

He laughed louder than expected.

Lord Clinton glared. 'It might be funny at the moment, but in a short time you will be up to your necks in blood and entrails and shit, and everything we do now will affect whether you live or die today.' He looked at Welsh and me. 'It's not so funny now, is it?'

We listened as he mapped out the rest of the day, pinpointing the strengths and weaknesses of ourselves and the enemy, ensuring we knew precisely what was expected and every possible scenario. We had laughed at the beginning but after he spoke we realised he was not the Lord High Admiral for nothing. The man was a genius.

*

Word had reached King Edward that the French had chained all their ships together across the estuary feeding Sluys port. It was a crazy tactic according to Lord Clinton, who had laughed when told. It meant nothing to us.

At midday, King Edward's ship, followed by Sir Hugh and ourselves, approached the blockade. All other ships were spread out behind. It looked impregnable. It was three ships deep, each physically chained to the one on either side. There was no way past and I said as much to Welsh as I braced my war bow ready.

His response was simple. 'My guess is we intend to destroy every ship and kill every man in that flotilla.'

It had not occurred to me. I am embarrassed to

admit that now after everything that followed. This was war, not hide and seek. We were here to slaughter humans.

After the Admiral's speech, we were ready. More than ready. He was an easygoing man, but he fired us up like nothing imaginable. I was desperate to be on the leading ship. I got my way.

The wind was behind us as we steered a course towards the static French ships. The mainland was to our right, an island to the left and it looked, at first, as if the admiral was going to simply ram into them. He was approaching the first ship in the link, but as we neared he brought us about and turned broadside. We were about four hundred yards from the enemy and I could see their men-at-arms itching to engage us, a few primed crossbowmen arranged beside them.

Then it started.

'LOOSE.' The admiral screamed the command from his position close to me on the forecastle.

I did not need to translate into Welsh.

A great hum whistled, as two hundred arrows launched. Some fell short but most found their mark. We were close enough to hear screams of pain. It was a pleasing sound. The admiral had no need for other commands. We reloaded and fired again as he took the ship along the front of the enemy line, closing in as he did so.

The next volley of arrows struck the second ship in the link from a shorter range. This time the enemy crossbowmen were able to return, bolts striking the wood nearby but hitting few of our men. Our cogs were higher than their low-lying galleys so we were able to fire downwards into their deck, the platform in our mast the perfect killing angle. And we killed. Time and again my arrows found their mark. I felt no pity. Welsh was next to me and his aim was as good as mine. The Glamorgan archers poured quiver after quiver into the hapless enemy. All down the line our following ships repeated the strategy. It was a storm of arrows.

As we reached the end of their ships, we halted. The King's ship was in the centre of the estuary directing the battle as waves of archer-filled ships sailed close in, raking the galleys. We were now within a few yards and I could see the enemy's faces. They looked crazed, their men-at-arms maddened as they could not get close enough for hand-to-hand combat. It was no coincidence. Their limited crossbowmen were making some kills around me, but we were decimating their ranks.

I looked left and saw Paul on the ship behind us. He was in the front forecastle kitted out in light armour and leaning over the gunwale desperate to get close enough to board. I smiled to myself. To the side of us was another ship, fully loaded with our fighting men, itching for us to finish and allow them to join.

'WE'RE GOING IN GENTLEMEN.' Lord Clinton's voice crackled with emotion.

His sailors ran around the deck distributing axes and pikes and maces in preparation.

But we had more airborne killing to do yet.

My next arrow was a peach. It struck a man who was readying himself for our imminent boarding, in the eye. It buried itself deep and I was close enough to see the eyeball squeezed out the side. He was boarding nothing today.

Closer closer. Their front ranks were demolished. The crossbowmen were edging away, looking to escape to the adjoining ship, their men-at-arms still fronting up as we struck. Grapples were thrown and the sailors pulled us in. Our men-at-arms ran forward and jumped from our gunwale to theirs as we unloaded our final volley before picking up weapons. The ship behind came alongside ours and their men joined us as we attacked. I had been given a mace. It was the first time I had handled one but its usage needed no explanation. I looked at Welsh. He had a graze on his cheek where a bolt had nearly taken him and bruising from the night before, but he was smiling. I nodded. We boarded together.

Our men-at-arms had cleared the main obstacles which allowed us to clamber onto the deck. The majority of the enemy were towards the other side trying to escape, crowding together, so we attacked them from behind. They had no choice – fight or be struck down. At first, it was easy. I reached the bulk of their men and smashed the first man I came across on the back of his head. It shattered his skull and he fell. His initial scream caused others to look around and face us. The next man had a sword and swung it in a wide arc, trying to ward off the encroaching men around me but over-committed and I darted forward and brought the mace round with maximum force into his open face, its jagged points sinking deep into his eye-sockets. Welsh was next to me. He pulled the screaming man out of the way before plunging his pike into the next man's back. He had been climbing over people in an attempt to escape and dragged the next man back with him, making it easy for another Glamorgan man to thrust a sword into his side, opening him up and causing blue and red intestines to spill onto the deck.

By now, Paul and Sir Hugh's ship had boarded the ship our enemies were attempting to escape onto, their archers doing an identical job to us. It was carnage. We were smashing into them from all sides, their numbers diminished at an incredible rate. Some of their ships were trying to escape, but could not as they were chained together. I understood the admiral's laughter now.

Again and again, I destroyed men's heads and faces. Internal organs, blood, brains and shit covered the deck as we slipped and steadied ourselves in an effort to kill. They started to surrender and beg for mercy, but we were in full blood lust, so they jumped overboard. Many had mail or armour and disappeared beneath the red-frothing waves. We did not stop.

Then we stopped. There was no one left to kill.

It had happened as the admiral had planned. We took breath and began congratulating one another.

'YOU THINK THIS IS OVER?' Lord Clinton swung onto our captured ship and stood, hands on hips. 'This is where the battle is won, my beauties, look.' He pointed to ships at the other end of the flotilla. They were far from beaten. 'That's the King's ship, the Thomas, down that end. Between here and His Majesty are a lot of angry Frenchmen. They won't all be as useless as these Genoese.' I had not realised these were mercenaries. 'Now go and crush the rest of these bastards. Make them pay.'

We did not need a second invitation. For as long as I could remember the French had been raiding and murdering across the coast of England. It was our chance to repay the debt.

As our sailors dumped the enemy bodies into the sea we clambered into the next ship. Paul was there, blood up his arms and a detached look on his face. Some of his own men were looking at him in astonishment. He did not acknowledge me at first. I shook him. His eyes cleared.

'Paul, are you all right?'

'Yes, I think so.' He checked himself for injury as Sir Hugh came over.

'Jesus Paul, how are you still alive?' he asked.

'I was carrying out your orders, Sire.'

'I expected you to wait for the rest of us, you mad bastard. Right, follow me.'

He ran across to the opposite side with the intention of climbing into the connected ship. We followed. This ship was manned by Frenchmen, their uniform of a different cut and colour. They were in the early stages of being boarded by another seaward ship and were in disarray. Many of the Genoese men from our ships had fled across already and were crammed together. They saw us coming and prepared to make a stand. Every time one of our men tried to jump across he was either forced back or killed and pushed into the sea. It became a stand-off. At the front of the ship, English archers and men-at-arms began to board, battering their way on. Sir Hugh and Paul moved in front of us and faced the snarling French across the short gap.

'If we don't go now, those bastards are going to take this ship before us, Paul.' Sir Hugh said. 'On three...' Paul smiled and nodded. 'THREE...'

Sir Hugh jumped across seconds before Paul, followed by myself, Welsh, and everyone on our ship. It was time to kill again.

Paul and Sir Hugh, both swinging swords, attacking deep into the body of the enemy like a wedge. We followed. The confidence gained from being led by two brutal fighters was unbelievable. We could not be beaten. The

French did not back away like the Genoese. They fought for every inch of decking but were too crowded to maintain discipline. As Welsh battled with one huge man I managed to lean forward and shatter his shin bone with my mace, turning it at a right angle, the splintered bones breaking through the skin. Incredibly, he fought on, trying to balance on his good leg. At that moment I had total admiration for him, only for Paul to come up behind and chop deep into his neck, biting off his ear as his head tilted sideways.

Sir Hugh grabbed him and pushed him forward. 'Come on Paul, I can see Commander Behuchet on the next ship.'

By now the boarding party had cleared the rest of the ship and joined us looking to move on.

And so it continued. The next ship was equally crowded and determined to repel us, but they could not prevent us from boarding and killing every man aboard. Commander Nicholas Behuchet was one. He was cornered at the stern of the ship and captured. Bound and gagged, he showed restraint, thinking he was being taken captive to be ransomed. His reputation for brutality to past navel prisoners was his undoing. Some of the ship's sailors dragged him to a yardarm and broke his limbs with axes, before tying a noose around his neck and hauling him up to great cheers.

By the time we reached the far end of the flotilla, I was spent. It had taken hours and was getting dark. I had lost sight of Paul and Sir Hugh but was still surrounded by many of the Glamorgan archers. They were following me, and we had killed more men than I could count. The decking of every ship was awash with blood. We happened across Admiral Hugues Quieret in the second to last ship. He had been beheaded and some of the English sailors were tossing his head around like a ball. It was unreal.

I heard a commotion and looked towards the sea. A fleet of small Flemish boats had arrived and were dragging Frenchmen from the sea and killing them before throwing them back. It was their chance for retaliation as they had been persecuted for years by the French and had joined us as allies.

*

It had been a long and exhausting day. Although they had fought us to a standstill at times, we had killed thousands of French and Genoese fighters. Our casualties were limited. The Bishop of Huntingdon, Father Fleming, had wandered the battered ships and administered comfort by anointing the injured and giving the last rites to the dying. He spoke the Commendatio Animae to the dead and administered absolutions. He ignored the enemy. We had taken hundreds of ships as trophies. French naval power had been curtailed and it would take years to rebuild. King Edward had been injured by a crossbow bolt in the leg, but his injury was not life threatening. As

I looked out over the sea it was strewn with the bodies of our enemy. The Flemish had looted all they could, and the sea was pink. I had never seen so many dead people.

King Edward would be happy.

*

'This is Ailred Norman, Sire. He is our link to the Welsh.' I knelt before my King as Lord Clinton introduced me to His Highness. 'He and his Welsh archers fought with passion today and I owe them a debt of gratitude.'

'You honour me, Sire.' I said, keeping my eyes down.

The king's wound had been dressed and he sat back in his chair, his leg raised on a cushion. 'Then, I am also in your debt, Ailred. We have great problems with many of your Welsh friends but at times like this, we are as one.' He laughed. 'Although I'm sure the money helps. They are fierce warriors as I'm sure you are aware, and to be led by an Englishman...'

I looked up. 'I think you may be misinformed, Sire. I am not their leader. They would never accept an Englishman leading them, but I have been accepted by them without being eaten.' I grinned.

He gave a great laugh. 'The Welsh accepted me and didn't eat me! Now that's worth carving onto your gravestone, Ailred Norman.' The rest of the tent joined in his merriment. 'Well, Ailred, go back to your hungry friends and give thanks from their King.'

I rose. 'I will do that, and thank you, Sire.'

Lord Clinton followed me out. 'You made a good impression there, Ailred. Now get back to the Glamorgan boys and count your dead. They would expect you to get drunk and honour them as only a warrior can.' I went to leave but he stopped me. 'Oh, and tell your Welsh friend that if he calls me an English idiot again I'll have him strung up.'

I could not help myself smiling and walked away. He was a great leader of men.

CHAPTER 9

And there you have it. Bishop Budwith has given up. He has yet to reassign Brother Michael to other priory duties but it is only a matter of time. I will miss him. He says he is keen to continue as he has been living a life he would never have known. There are times when I do battle and feel him by my side. He fights for God and I fight for greed, death being the bond linking us. He would make a fine warrior.

You might shake your head, Michael, but killing for a cause is purifying.

*

I returned to the men of Glamorgan. No one greeted me. Not even Welsh.

'Have I missed something?'

'How was the King?' Welsh asked.

'Did you want to see him then?'

He looked at the frowning faces around him. 'No, of course not – he's not our king.'

'I'm confused. You don't want to see him and don't regard him as your king but want to know how he is?' I shrugged. 'He's not great. He was wounded in the leg by a crossbow.' I saw a couple of men smirk. 'But he asked me to thank you boys and said he's indebted to you.'

'Enough to pay us?'

'I'm sure you boys earned plenty today. You were stripping the French clean before they hit the floor.' I had seen them rifling through the dead all day. We all did – it is an integral part of war. 'Stick with it, we'll all get rich.' The other archers drifted away, muttering to each other leaving Welsh with me. 'You're going to have to get this anti-English obsession out of your system, Welshy, it's not healthy.'

'That's easy for you to say, English, you haven't been made a second-class citizen in your own country.'

He went on to lecture me on the evils of the English and some of the stories he told were horrific. I accused him of exaggeration but he said I was blind. I let him burn himself out and he finished saying that he hated all Englishmen, except me. I was the only decent one. So generous of you.

That night we got drunk. Those Welsh boys could drink! We camped next to the battle site as it was late and we still wanted to pick over the bodies of the dead French. I was amazed at some of the places they had hidden their valuables. I found a gold Ecu coin sewn into the undergarment of a dead soldier. It was worth a great deal. I kept the find a secret, fearing for my life if someone discovered I was holding such wealth. We must have missed so much, and so much must have disappeared beneath the waves. The fish would be rich and speak with a French accent.

I found Paul and Sir Hugh's men and flitted between the two groups. The Welsh managed to get into fights with anyone English, then ended up fighting one another. I would have thought they had had enough after all we had been through that day but I was wrong. They compromised by not killing anyone. I put that down as a quiet evening. Even Paul was happy to sit by the campfire and keep out of trouble.

We travelled to the city of Sluys the next day with hangovers.

*

Sir Hugh, Lord Clinton and the rest of his senior advisors spent the next few days in the King's tent that was pitched on a large field in the centre of the city.

Paul sulked.

'You're only a squire, Paul, why would they invite you?'

'Bastards.'

I did my best impersonation of the King. 'We're not sure when to attack Tournai Sir Hugh, let's ask your squire – he's the font of all knowledge.'

'Bastards.'

We had been in Sluys for days as the King and his commanders procrastinated. The Welsh archers were camped outside the town for their own protection as they had antagonised every English baron. Lord Clinton's patience was wearing thin.

Every day Paul would receive snippets of information from Sir Hugh as to what was being discussed. It sounded like they were waiting for someone to arrive before the next step of the operation.

Then he did.

Paul was boarding with Sir Hugh in one of the local taverns and I was staying in the stable. Old habits die hard. We were sitting out front when a group of riders approached. The lead figure was a tall nobleman and behind him rode a dozen or so followers, all dressed in matching livery. I did not recognise the crest.

'That's Robert of Artois,' Paul said as he stood and removed his hat. He looked impressed.

The entourage pulled up beside us and the nobleman addressed us in French. I understood a few words but Paul answered fluently. They laughed together for a few minutes before Paul pointed towards the King's tent. The man thanked Paul and rode off.

'He reminded me of Sir Hugh,' I said. 'Older, but similar mannerisms.'

'They've been friends since he was forced into exile by that French King, Philip,' he replied. He looked excited for the first time since the Sluys battle. 'He's desperate for revenge. Philip has his wife and kids locked up in the Chateau Gaillard in Normandy. If he's here we're moving to a new level.'

'You seem to know a lot about him.'

'Yeah, I do. He's King Philip's brother-in-law, and was robbed of his inheritance.' He laughed. 'He even forged a will in an attempt to get it back, but they found out and tried to kill him. Sir Hugh said he's a ruthless bastard and he models himself on him. Learning history is part of being a squire.' He glowed with pride. He enjoyed being more knowledgeable than me.

'If Sir Hugh thinks he's a ruthless bastard, I'll steer well clear,' I said.

The mention of Robert Artois's wife and child had set me back. With Sluys captured, and in our current state of calm, my mind drifted towards Philippa and Kimberly. I missed them. I had not had time to think about them until now, but a pang of loss gripped my stomach.

I heard Paul talking but could not listen. I got up and left. I walked. I needed to get away from Paul. When we were growing up I never left him alone as he was such a volatile character and without me would always find ways to get into trouble. Things were different now. He was the same old Paul but his character was what made him the perfect soldier. He did not need me anymore.

'Oi, English.'

I looked up from my daydream. 'Where you boys off to?' I asked.

There were five of them. Welsh was in front.

'Just going into town.' I went to speak but he beat me to it. 'And, yes, we'll keep out of trouble…like we always do. You wanna come?'

I thought about it as I had been ignoring the Glamorgan contingent in favour of Paul and his English company, but decided against it. 'Na, I think I'll give it a miss.'

'Suit yourself. Being seen with an Englishman isn't good for our image anyway,' he laughed.

'Oh, and don't go far, we'll be getting news soon.'

Welsh stopped and lifted his chin. 'That brother of yours knows something?'

'Maybe. Robert of Artois just arrived and is with the King now. If he's here it means we'll be moving out soon. There could be trouble.'

'We don't like trouble,' one of the Welshmen said and they all laughed.

They left and headed towards the harbour area where I had left Paul.

*

'Get a chirurgeo, quick.'

Paul was lying on the hay in the stable as Welsh and his companions tried to make him comfortable. It was nearly dark outside, the last of the July sunshine disappearing behind the nearby hills.

As one of the Welshmen dashed off, I called after him, 'And tell him it's Sir Hugh's squire who needs urgent attention.'

Welsh had returned to find me and rushed me

back a couple of hours after I had left him.

I turned Paul's head. He was still breathing, but unconscious.

'What the fuck happened?'

'He was attacked in the alleyway next to the tavern.' There was a red mark around his neck and a knife wound to his back that had been dressed with a crude bandage. It was obvious he had taken a serious beating to his head too. 'We thought it was just the stupid English playing stupid games, but I noticed one guy with a rope around his neck while someone else had a knife. There were three of them. You're lucky we recognised your brother or we'd have stayed out of it. They ran like hares when we steamed in.'

'Who was it?'

'Fucked if I know. English, if that helps.'

One of the other Welshmen walked over. He had blood on his hands after bandaging Paul. 'One of them had a patch on his eye, I know that much.'

'Jacques Stafford. Thanks, I owe you, boys.'

'Can you get that King bloke to pay us?'

I almost laughed.

Paul spluttered and opened his eyes. His face had been battered and there was a lump on his head. He went to speak but could not.

'He's over here.' The Glamorgan man returned with the chirurgeo, who checked Paul over.

'He'll be fine, the stab isn't too deep and someone put on a decent bandage.' The

Welshman gave a knowing smile. The chirurgeo looked into Paul's eyes and got him to follow his finger left and right. 'Yeah, he's good to go. Can I get back to my whore now?'

I thanked him, paid a few small coins, and he left, as did the Welshmen.

Paul sat. He was feeling his neck and rolling his head from side to side. He tried to speak again. This time words came out. 'It was Stafford and some of his men.'

'I know, Welsh and his lot ran them off – you'd be dead without them.'

'Great, I'm indebted to a bunch of sheepshaggers.'

I helped him up and took him back to his room in the tavern where Sir Hugh told us to get lost for an hour as he 'hadn't finished with his filly yet'.

As we milled around waiting, Paul felt his skull and said, 'I felt something break tonight.' He laughed and shook his head. 'I'm sure I can hear something rattling in there.'

*

William de Bohun walked out of the king's tent first, followed by his bastard son, Jacques Stafford. That was to be expected. The sight of Archdeacon Rhys was not. The last time I had seen him he had raped me in a cell with the same pastoral staff he now carried.

'What's he doing here?' I asked nobody in particular.

Welsh turned to me. 'That's Archdeacon Gruffudd ap Rhys. He's one of us.'

I remained silent.

A large group of soldiers had gathered in the field near the King's tent. Word had spread that this was the final meeting before we were told the campaign's intentions. Not before time.

Sir Hugh, Lord Admiral Clinton, Robert of Artois and various other noblemen and clergy whom I had no knowledge of exited, then King Edward. We went down on one knee. I looked towards the Welsh contingent and saw they too had followed protocol.

He left us kneeling.

'My faithful subjects, I know you are eager to continue this quest, and I share your impatience.' He spoke in English and I could hear a few Welsh voices nearby translating. 'I will leave the details to your lords to brief, but in short, I will take the majority on to Tournai where we will take the city. Whilst we're doing that Robert of Artois will lead an army of his men, some of our Flemish troops, and a small contingent of archers into the countryside.'

'That'll be us,' I heard Welsh whisper.

He turned and reentered the tent whilst his lords fanned out to pass on agreed instructions to their respective armies.

'That was short,' Welsh mused as he stood. 'Wasn't worth dropping to one knee for.'

'This is it.'

The loud voice made me jump and I looked around. It was Paul. He had been recovering for the last few days and this was the first time he had left his room.

'You look better, Paul,' Welsh said nodding his head in welcome.

Paul stared at him. 'What's it to you?'

'Come on Paul, these boys saved your life,' I said.

'For fuck sake, I should have let them kill you.' Welsh moved as if he was about to attack him, as did the Glamorgan archers around him. A large contingent of Paul's company edged forward before Sir Hugh and Lord Clinton intervened.

'You boys crack me up...' Sir Hugh was laughing. 'If you fought the French like you fight each other we'd all be home by now!' Both sides settled but stared at each other. 'There you go, all friends again. Right, as you all get on so well I will give you some good news. We'll all be joining Robert of Artois on his holiday around the countryside.' He smiled. 'You children would like that, wouldn't you?'

'With respect Sir Hugh, we aren't archers, we're real soldiers,' Paul said. He was not happy.

'Well, Paul, that is what I said to the King, but these arrow launchers need our protection.'

Lord Clinton stepped forward. 'We're to conduct a chevauchee to bring King Philip out into battle.' He looked around at the confused faces, mine included. 'Chevauchee – we've been given a free hand to cause as much destruction and mayhem as possible and take Saint-Omer in the process.' He smiled. 'And when we run out of things to loot and burn we'll join King Edward in Tournai.'

Paul looked at me. 'Damn, I like the sound of that.'

We dispersed and prepared to break camp.

*

'Your brother's a prick.'

I was walking with the Glamorgan archers and was not feeling the love. I was not sure who said it, but it did not matter. 'He can be, yeah, but you'll be happy to have him on the battlefield.' It was a lame retort and got the answer it deserved.

'Fuck him.'

I did not have a witty response to match that, so continued walking.

We walked for hours. Lord Clinton was as much at home on a horse as he was on a ship, trotting between us Welsh archers and his Englishmen. Paul was with Sir Hugh towards the front, with the Flemish soldiers and Robert of Artois leading.

We had been travelling down a rough track, the ten or so thousand men sending clouds of dust into the hot summer air but found its condition improved. Then we found out why. We were approaching a small rural town and the locals must have maintained the road. There was the smell of burning everywhere. Robert, Sir

Hugh and their men had arrived before us.

'Holy Jesus.' It was the first thing that came to my mind and was appropriate.

Just about every building and every outlying field was ablaze. Dead people, young and old, men and women, lay butchered in the street. Even pets and livestock had been hacked to pieces. I stood rooted.

'This is what war looks like.' Lord Clinton rode past and caught up with Robert and Sir Hugh, who were ahead. I heard a scream and looked towards a burning house. An English archer was dragging a young girl towards an outbuilding that had yet to be torched. He was laughing as she fought to escape his clutches. Then I saw Paul. He was waiting for the pair in the building, holding back another girl. He noticed me as the other man forced the girl inside. He smiled and slammed the door.

*

The army had gone through the town like a swarm of locusts, decimating everything. There was nothing left. We had rounded up a number of pigs that had escaped from a sty and we were deciding what to do with them.

Lord Clinton had the solution. 'Right, you men get these hogs carved up and into the carts. Ailred Norman, take one man and clear out the church cellar. If anyone gives you shit, do it anyway.'

'But they'll be monks or nuns or whatever,

Sire?'

'That's why I'm giving you this job, lad. If you want to be a real soldier you'll need to learn some hard truths.' He steadied his mount. 'Soldiering isn't about glorious battles. It's about working to a plan and removing emotion. It's a business that will make us rich. Now – get on with it, Sergeant.'

I looked at Welsh. 'Well, you heard the man – let's go.'

We left the others as they went about dismembering the pigs and walked to the church. It had already been plundered of anything valuable. Who would rob a church? They were places of sanctuary and respected by everyone. Everyone normal. I was beginning to realise why we had been chosen for this chevauchee. We were considered subnormal.

The priest begged us.

'You speak French, English, what's he saying?'

'He's saying please don't rob us.' I had no idea what he was saying, but it was a fair guess.

We pushed past him and found a door leading to the undercroft. It was locked. I turned to the priest and looked at him. He shrugged. A nun walked by and I stared with menace at her and he relented, producing a key from his cassock and handing it over. We entered. It was ladened with dusty bottles of wine and wrapped cheeses. We went about transporting hundreds of them up and out onto the street ready to be transported. It took the rest of the day and by the time we finished the priest had been joined by a number of other nuns and all were in tears on the steps of the small church.

'It's us or them, Ailred,' Lord Clinton barked as he led us away.

I looked back. It was a painful sight.

'What a lovely sight, eh, Al?' Paul rode past on a stolen horse. It looked like a farm animal that should have been put out to pasture years before. 'This'll bring Philip onto the battlefield.'

He rode on towards the front and joined Sir Hugh and Robert of Artois. They made a happy group.

And so it continued. Every day we brought death and destruction. The further we travelled the less we acquired, each town being forewarned and abandoning their homes, taking their valuables into the countryside. They started to burn their own fields so we could not find fresh food. Our rations were beginning to run low.

Still, King Philip did not come for us.

It was towards the end of July and we received word that King Edward and his allies had reached Tournai and had begun to besiege the city. He had been strengthened by Jacob van Rartevelde, a Flemish statesman and trader. He was keen for Edward to be recognised as King of France as it would benefit his weaving and textile businesses. He had brought a respected army on the promise of payment from our King, Edward.

'We still haven't been paid, Sarg.' Welsh had started to call me Sergeant as banter but after a week it had become his standard address. Lord Clinton was still using me as the go-between and most of the Welsh accepted me as such.

'No one has – I've heard the King's in financial difficulties.' I repeated something I had heard Lord Clinton say to Sir Hugh.

'Is that English for, "we're fighting for nothing"?'

'Pretty much. The Flemish are beginning to question if they'll ever get paid.'

'I know the feeling.'

We were sitting around a campfire at the end of the day drinking one of the liberated bottles from the church. We had burned down a dozen farms and found a small herd of cattle which we had slaughtered and were now roasting. There were about a hundred of us camped away from the bulk of our army as we felt shunned by the English. The Flemish soldiers found the hostility between the home nations a source of entertainment but tended to side with the majority English.

Geraint, a valley farmer who had joined up in the hope of bringing money home to his family, started to sing. For a big man, he had a beautiful voice. We sat listening. He sang in Welsh and it was mesmeric. As he started the second verse the others joined in. It was like a choir had arrived, the sound drifting across the campsite and into the darkening forest surrounding us.

Geraint stood. He was bare-chested in the summer's heat, and, as the lead vocalist, he poured out his heart. He had tears in his eyes. And it was that same heart that a crossbow bolt struck. It embedded up to its fletching, sending pulses of blood across the campsite.

We got up and ran for cover as more bolts flew through the air, the only cover being the surrounding woodland – but that was where the assault came from. There was no escape. Time and again I heard the thud of bolts striking bodies and screams of pain.

I dived to the floor as I realised the men being stuck were those running towards the trees. It worked. I watched the Welshmen fall from my lying position, bolts piercing them from all angles. Owain, the group's only North Wales member was struck through the neck, the barbed head exiting under his chin. He fell, his face level with mine, his eyes pleading before closing. A few men reached their bows and returned fire, but they were chasing shadows. The assailants were like ghosts, picking their target and unloading death.

It stopped as quickly as it started. Paul and Robert of Artois burst into the clearing from one side. They were dragging a boy of about fifteen carrying a crossbow and the rest disappeared into the night.

'Go!' Robert shouted in French and hundreds of

armed Flemish and English men rushed into the woods.

We took breath.

'Count your dead and attend to the injured, Ailred.' Lord Clinton walked over to me. I stood. 'Good.'

'Good, Lord?'

'Yes, it means we're doing our job.' Lord Clinton looked to Sir Hugh and Robert who were standing nearby.

Robert walked over to me and thrust the captured crossbowman to me. He spoke English with a slight accent. 'He's yours. You Welsh took the hit and I'll allow you to extract the answers.'

He need not say anything else.

*

Paul was adamant. 'You need a fluent French speaker.'

Welsh had organised the burial detail. He had included the captured boy and made him dig using his bare hands, and now was time for answers. We had lost seven archers with three seriously injured, and another half dozen walking wounded.

I looked at Welsh as we stood in front of the defiant boy. He was tied to a chair. Welsh reacted to Paul's assertion. 'No fuckin' way you're getting involved with this. I don't give a fuck about your French-speaking abilities.'

The other Welshmen agreed. None of them had forgiven Paul's reaction to them saving his life.

'But Paul's right,' I said, 'we need to know what he says – unless you want me to hand him back to Robert of Artois?'

I knew that was the last thing they wanted. This boy had killed their friends – they needed justice.

Welsh looked at the others. They were unhappy but reluctantly agreed. 'But we ask the questions – he's only here to translate.'

Paul agreed. 'That's all I was offering. What did you think I meant?'

Welsh ignored him and turned to the boy.

'What's your name?' I asked. I thought it better to speak through Paul rather than Welsh.

Paul translated.

'Well, Alain, How many of you are there and who is your commander?

'No, we will not hurt you – just answer the question.'

'Thank you, Alain, now, is King Philip close?'

'Yes, I know about chivalry, but you must answer my question.'

That answer riled Welsh. 'You didn't show chivalry to our men, you fuckin' French bastard...' He darted forward and punched the boy in the face.

I pulled him off and continued.

'Now, let's start again. Answer the questions.'

He did. It took a long time.

He was part of a local group of men who had bandied together through self-preservation. King Philip had nothing to do with them. They wanted revenge for our actions and were angry that he had let it continue for so long. There were about twenty of them and he would not say where they camped. He sat preaching his countrymen's chivalry code and the evils of being English.

It was time for the second part of the interrogation.

I will not go into details. I fear for Brother Michael's soul if he is compelled to write the account. I fear for us all that night.

Paul got involved. Needless to say, he extracted the answers.

As we threw the mutilated body of the boy into the undergrowth, Robert returned.

We gave him the interrogation information. He looked disappointed. 'So Philip is still hiding like le jeune fille that he is.' He shook his head. 'He will come soon. Double the guard from now on, although I doubt this bunch of children will come back once they see what you did.'

He was right.

The next day was like every other but I was beginning to hear descent. It was always about money. Or lack of it. I had started speaking to the Flemish men. They were a friendly bunch, many speaking good English, and had a cruel sense of humour. They would find a weakness in someone and ride them until they were at breaking point and then turn their attention to someone else. They were merciless. But the more we spoke the more I became aware of their apathy. They had not been paid since the beginning of the campaign, and, by all accounts, King Edward was broke. He had allied himself with their leader, Jacob van Artevelde, offering him funds for his newly established government and appealed for an army of a hundred and fifty thousand Flemish soldiers to join him when we landed in Sluys. Word had spread that Edward had overstretched his budget and only a fraction heeded his call to arms.

We were heading for disaster.

CHAPTER 10

By the time we neared the town of Arques, our army had broken into factions. Every small village or homestead we came across was scrapped over. We foraged for food and if we stumbled across a quarry we set upon it without reporting to our commanders. The other divisions did the same. We were low on provisions so anything we found we kept, and being the smallest faction felt ostracised.

It was mid-afternoon and we rested. Sir Hugh and his men lounged nearby, Robert and his Flemish troops languishing somewhere way back. We had been marching all day and found ourselves at a river junction. Robert had told us they were the rivers Lys and Aa and were the boundary between France and the county of Artois – his county. He had told us to wait for him here and together we would attack the town of Arques.

'They're fortifying the perimeter and moving valuables out, Sire.'

Sir Hugh and Lord Clinton listened to Welsh's report. He and another Glamorgan man had been sent ahead to confirm whether there was truth behind rumours that the town was being strengthened.

There was.

'Did you see extra soldiers?'

'Yes, Lord Clinton, they were gathering everyone and taking them in the direction of Saint-Omer.'

Saint-Omer was a larger town about two and a half miles to the southeast. It was where King Edward had ordered us to capture before joining him at Tournai.

Sir Hugh made a fist. 'Then we must hurry.'

He huddled with Lord Clinton and their advisors to discuss tactics while the rest of us prepared.

Paul rode over. 'Looks like we're doing this alone.'

I looked back along the trail and saw no sign of him and his men. 'Not waiting for Artois – he told us to hold back until he…?'

'Nope, It'll give us a chance to front up and gauge their strength.'

It was about time. We had spent the last few weeks preying on the vulnerable and as soldiers were keen to face worthy opposition. There was scant glory in massacring peasants and stealing what little they owned.

Paul was right, we did not wait.

'Archers to the flanks.' Lord Clinton moved ourselves and the English archers to the wings whilst Sir Hugh placed his men-at-arms at the centre. There were about fifteen hundred of us. We left the horses and supplies with a limited guard of injured Welshmen at the river intersection and moved towards Arques.

Our battle dress was designed for speed, light armour and on foot, the forest surroundings dictating events. The plan was to strike with maximum use of archers, the men-at-arms to attack from the centre in an attempt to draw the French out of the town.

We hid in the woods overlooking the main gates, Lord Clinton on the opposite side of the town to us. The town knew we were coming so guardsmen and local citizens manned the surrounding wooden walls.

Half of our men-at-arms in the centre stayed concealed and the other half marched towards the gates, stopping out of crossbow range. The land in front was clear of cover and Sir Hugh led the advanced party with Paul a few paces behind. They had no shields or pavises. If the French rushed out in numbers they would be stranded. I was too far away to hear but could see Sir Hugh taunting the garrison behind the walls, but the gates remained shut.

He moved closer.

Welsh sidled up to me. 'What's he doing?' He had an arrow nocked and ready.

I could see what he was doing but he was opening himself up to a counterattack that would leave him exposed. It was a dangerous tactic.

'He must have faith in us archers, that's all I can say.'

Welsh lowered his bow, taking the strain from his fingers. 'There could be thousands behind that wall, that's just crazy.'

I did not disagree.

Paul moved up to Sir Hugh's shoulder and I could see him pointing his sword and gesturing. He wanted someone to fight him, man to man. I saw Sir Hugh look at him, shrug and stand back.

A crossbow bolt arced out from the gate's tower and struck the ground a couple of feet in front of Paul. He did not flinch but stepped closer. Another bolt struck inches in front. He stood and held his arms wide and head back. He was laughing.

'Your brother's not all there.'

The men on the walls were shouting now, calling Paul on. He put one hand on his hip and made an exaggerated yawning gesture.

The French started to disappear from the walls.

'They're moving,' I said. I was worried. He was so far forward that if they rushed him he would be alone.

The gates cracked open. Paul remained. Sir Hugh started to edge back, as did a number of the men-at-arms.

Cowards. I wanted to shout a warning but was too far away.

Sir Hugh and the rest of his men turned and ran as the gates swung open. Paul looked around, realising how vulnerable he was and gave up his position.

Then they charged. Hundreds of armoured French horsemen, riding down our stranded men.

'NOW...' I screamed.

We loosed. A cloud of arrows filled the sky, our blanket merging with the opposite flank's and hitting the French like a punch to the face. My next flight was in the air before the first struck. I glanced down. Men and horses fell like sythed wheat at harvest time.

I took a second to focus and saw Paul stop and turn as Sir Hugh and his men abandoned their pretence of retreat. They charged forward. We had only seconds to empty as many arrows into the enemy as possible before our troops engaged, at which point we would pick up our weapons and join the attack. I managed four more. I picked up my mace and slung my bow over my shoulder. I had one final look before running down the gentle slope. The French were in disarray. I could not see one horse still standing as so many French knights lay trapped beneath their mounts as they kicked and writhed in agony. The initial charge had been supported by civilians, all eager to take advantage of their military superiority, but when they saw the arrow storm and the hoards of screaming archers descending into them they turned and fled.

'GATES,' I screamed at my fellow Welshmen and we veered towards the right to cut off any retreat, reaching the gates as they began to close. I was first to arrive and wedged myself between the gates, allowing Welsh and half a dozen men to slip inside before they closed. We were instantly attacked by a rabble of local townspeople armed with pitchforks, knives and clubs. They circled us and jeered, hoping we would surrender. That was their first and last mistake. We flew into them. They outnumbered us two to one but as soon as the violence became real they hesitated. Too late. I focused on the leader. He was a big man dressed in an apron and holding a meat cleaver. I attacked him with such force that his companions backed away. It always works – target their champion. Once his aura is destroyed they crumble. He swung at me half-heartedly and I was able to time my response to perfection, striking his elbow with the head of my mace causing his arm to hang limp below the impact. He dropped the cleaver. His other hand reached over to grasp the injury, before holding it up in surrender. He had had enough. I laughed and broke his other arm before swinging my weapon upward into his bent-over face. It raised him from the ground as his face moulded around the mace. All around our men were shattering bodies. As the final man lay dead and Welsh had pulled the axe from his corpse, we went in search of the gate controls. They were easily found. The two men guarding rushed to the door as we approached, knowing it was their only chance to defend. Only one man at a time could enter. I was at the front, almost being impaled on a pike as the Welshmen behind pushed forward. Every time we tried to cross the divide we were warded back, their weapons keeping us at bay. I could see fear in their faces. These were older men left inside as a prelude to retirement. From behind me a couple of arrows hissed past my ear and struck the guards breaking the deadlock. Their early retirement was complete. Stepping over their bodies and entering the gate control room, I looked out at the battle raging outside. The French were fighting tooth and nail, but their bulky armour was a hindrance. Without the mobility of their horses, they were easy prey. From our position high in the tower we were able to resume our arrow onslaught, this time at closer range. We left the gates closed as by now the French realised their battle was lost and were attempting to re-enter. They were crowding around below looking up, only to be rewarded with arrows in the face and neck. Our men-at-arms had the remaining French knights on the run and they too gathered at the gates.

It was carnage. We killed everyone.

I opened the gates.

*

I am not proud of what happened next, but it was inevitable.

Once we opened the gates our men poured in. They had killed every Frenchman outside and it was time to enjoy the spoils of war. And how they enjoyed it.

We left the tower and met the conquering army in the town's square. We were unscathed, bar the odd nick. Robert and our Flemish allies were still nowhere to be seen and I suspected they were camped back at the river intersection. They would not be happy to find out they had missed a victorious battle and the chance to loot.

I thought we might have a post-battle debrief, a chance to assess our tactics in anticipation of the next challenge. I was mistaken. Wherever I went I found men murdering the town's folk, raping women or destroying anything they did not think worth plundering. I'll admit to stealing my share and killing anyone who looked dangerous but much of what happened was wanton. Rape is something I cannot abide but I seemed the only invader with such morals. Even Lord Clinton joined in. I thought he was above such behaviour.

Paul and Sir Hugh did not surprise me.

There was not a great deal to steal as the majority of the town's valuables had been shipped off to Saint-Omer, but the Welshmen found enough to stop them complaining for a while.

Most of the women had also left, which made it worse for those remaining.

As night fell, large sections of the town were ablaze. Bodies littered the streets and naked women and girls lay in distress at the feet of drunken soldiers.

'This is war, Ailred Norman. If we had lost they would have done the same to us,' Lord Clinton shouted to me as he drank from a bottle of wine. 'And good work from you and your men today – we'll make a soldier of you yet.'

I had not seen Welsh or any of the Glamorgan men as they had joined in the looting as soon as it began but knew they would appreciate the compliment. 'Thank you, Lord.'

I searched for somewhere to sleep, finding a small empty stable behind the local tavern. The tavern had not been torched as hundreds of men were crammed inside emptying the wine cellars.

I had a sack filled with whatever looked valuable and I stashed it towards the back of the stable.

And that is where I found her.

'No, no, no...'

My French is not good but I understood that.

'Shh – keep your voice down.' I put my finger to my lips and tried to pacify her.

She stood frozen. It was dark but I could make out the whites of her eye. They were a picture of terror. She was about twenty and was wearing a maid's outfit, presumably from her work in the tavern. 'Stay back there out of sight.' She seemed to understand and moved into the shadows. I checked the door but no one was nearby, so barred it and sat in the hay. 'Do you speak English?' I whispered into the gloom. She remained silent. 'Parlez-vous Anglais?' Still silence. 'Don't worry, I won't hurt you.' My French was not good enough to translate that.

'You are a soldier, you hurt everyone.' She spoke in broken English and sounded as terrified as she looked.

I heard a noise at the gate and a drunken voice shouted something in Welsh. Whoever it was wanted to enter, that much was clear.

'Fuck off, it's me, Ailred Norman. I'm trying to get some sleep. There's nothing worth stealing in here.'

I could hear two men confer.

'Come on English, I heard a filly's voice in there. You must learn to share with your Welsh brothers.' They laughed.

'Just go away.'

'You might have Gareth fooled, but we're not all as stupid as him. Open the fuckin' door.'

I turned my head towards the back of the barn. 'Whatever happens, stay out of sight,' I whispered. I heard her move.

I picked up the bloodied mace and stood beside the duel-fenced door.

They started kicking at the soft old wood. The bolt was not intended to hold out to a concerted effort to break in, and so it proved. After the third or fourth kick, the hinges splintered and a head peered in.

'Come out English, it's a Welshman's turn.' He looked about and then noticed me standing two feet away. 'Where is she – we're going to play a little game with her?'

I gave him one last chance. 'Go away, I've told you there's no one here. We're all on the same side – go and find some gold, I think there's some in the church.' I made that up, but it did not work. His eyes flashed from jovial to venomous.

'We're coming in.'

He pulled the bottom half of the stable door open, crouching to step in.

'Last chance,' I said.

He laughed.

I struck him on the back of the neck and I heard it snap. He went limp and fell forward. The other man gripped the top section of the gate and started to pull. He was growling like a bear, his breath rasping. I held the mace in both hands and smashed his fingers, embedding the shattered bones into the soft wood. He screamed and pulled them free, leaving four fingers behind. He ran, falling every couple of steps due to his drunken state. I followed. I could not allow him to speak to anyone as his testimony would be a death sentence. I caught and killed him, dragging his body back to the stable where I hid him and the other Welshman under the hay.

I shut and secured the gates the best I could.

'They're gone.'

She came back into the open.

'Those two killed my father. He was a good man, but they killed him anyway. I saw them before I ran here.' She started to cry.

'I need you to remain strong. If anyone hears you we're both dead.' She fell silent again. 'What's your name?'

'Why do you want to know, I'm nothing to you people?'

'My name is Ailred.'

'I don't care.'

'All right, but I will do everything I can to protect you – I promise.'

'How – you animals are everywhere.'

'Tomorrow will be different. Tonight everyone is crazy, but in the morning, when everyone is sick from drinking and killing, we will escape.'

She went quiet again, then said, 'I have no choice, Englishman. Merci.'

All night I remained awake as the sounds of chaos and destruction drifted away, only the sounds of barking dogs and blazing buildings persisting. A couple more men tried to enter but I managed to convince them to leave. She remained hidden at the back while I stayed vigilant by the gate.

I woke at first light. I had been determined not to sleep and was disappointed in myself.

'Are you awake?'

'Of course, I am,' she replied. There was a moment's hesitation. 'Why are you helping me?'

'You remind me of a friend. I would want someone to help her if the roles were reversed.'

'These roles could never be reversed,' she said, 'Frenchmen would never act this way.'

That I doubted but said nothing.

I picked up my sack and ushered her towards me. In the light of day, I could now see her. She was covered in hay and still had a frightened expression, but I sensed defiance. She was dark-haired and beautiful.

'This is what we're going to do. I need to tie your hands and lead you out of here.' She looked horrified at the prospect. 'You are my captive and I will take you with me. You must do whatever I say, do you understand?'

'They will attack me...'

'No, they won't. Most will be sick from wine and the blood-lust will have died. You are going to have to trust me.' She nodded and held out her hands. I found a short length of rope in one corner and tied them. 'Ready?'

'No, but I have no choice.'

I pushed open the broken gate and led her out. The sun was already warm and except for the smoke from smouldering buildings, there was not a cloud in the sky. There were a few bleary-eyed men wandering around and the street was strewn with drunken soldiers asleep clutching half-empty wine bottles. No one gave us a second glance.

'Just look frightened and don't let anyone know we came from the stable,' I whispered as I led her towards the town's main gate.

'What have you there, Al?' It was Paul. He was alone and sitting on a horse that looked as if it would collapse with exhaustion. He had a mixture of sick and blood down his front.

'Eyes off Paul, she's mine. I captured her last night and am taking her with me.'

'I don't blame you Al, she's a rare beauty. Were you riding her in that stable last night?' He laughed. 'And don't worry, I'm not interested – I haven't got the energy. Where are you going?'

I looked around. There was no sign of any Flemish troops.

'Robert of Artois is back at the camp so I'll go back there. I think we'll have to return to being soldiers after last night's fun.'

He nodded. 'The last time I saw my Lord Hugh he was banging two young girls at once. I've no idea where he is now.' He smiled to himself. 'Isn't life wonderful at times?'

I had heard enough and started to lead the girl away. 'I'll meet you back there.'

As we left town she stopped and looked back.

'You people are sick,' she said.

CHAPTER 11

I am saved! Bishop Budwith has granted me an indulgence and I am absolved of my sins. He has read and reread my testimonies until now and concluded I am worthy. He does not want to continue. Who would have guessed? He has removed Brother Michael from the task of writing my life and assigned him reredorter duties.

How do I know? Because Brother Michael is still writing. And you are still reading. He slips out at night whenever possible and continues. He feels part of my world now and is desperate to know how it ends. The last thing Bishop Budwith said to Brother Michael and me was that he is resigned to never recovering the money. He is satisfied it had nothing to do with me and lost interest.

There is more to tell, but he will never know.

You will.

*

It did not take long to return to the camp. I was right, Robert and his Flemish troops were already there, as were many Welsh and English men who took part in the battle to take Arques.

Most had been sickened by the aftermath. I was relieved not to be the only one. Welsh was there too. He had a bag of plunder but had refrained from violating women.

I had offered to let the girl go as soon as we left Arques but she had declined, saying she had nowhere to go now we had destroyed her family and livelihood.

We were sitting by the river. It was midday and the sun was scorching. The first part of the day had been assessing casualties from the day before. We had few, the men-at-arms suffering the most, but compared to the thousands the French lost, we got off lightly. They would want revenge.

'Do you have relatives you could stay with?' I dangled my feet in the cool flowing water. 'What about your mother, did she go to Saint-Omer with the others?'

She stood staring into the distance. 'My mother died when I was young. I do not remember her, and all my father's family are gone. We were originally from Gascony, but you people would not know we were sympathetic to your cause as you killed us without asking.' She shamed me for my country's ignorance. 'I will stay with you – it is safer than being alone.'

She was right. There were many women and girls attached to our army – the followers. As we destroyed towns and villages some found solace with the invading force, typically citizens from allied regions of France or Flanders.

She focused back on me. 'You asked my name back in the stables. It's Izelda.'

I nodded. 'In that case, I am pleased to meet you, Izelda.'

She curtsied and smiled for the first time. Its beauty took my breath away.

*

Our men returned in dribs and drabs over the day and it was not until the afternoon that we had a tally.

'Only two Glamorgans unaccounted for,' Welsh said.

I nodded. 'That's not bad, Gareth.'

'Bryn and Glyn are good men.' He looked about at the other archers. 'Did anyone see them after the battle?'

One man stepped forward. 'I saw them in the tavern – they were the first in. They killed the owner. Last time I saw them they were drunk and outside searching for women.'

'Have you found their bodies yet?' I asked and looked at Izelda, who remained stony-faced.

Welsh looked at me. 'What makes you think they're dead?'

'Oh, nothing – they'll no doubt walk into camp soon.'

He shrugged. 'And since when did you learn my name was Gareth?'

'I...I overheard someone speaking about you last night.'

'I suppose I'll have to call you Ailred then.'

'It might confuse me, but if you must....'

He laughed and went about counting his stolen property.

That night the army buried its dead and the next morning we moved on towards Saint-Omer. Robert of Artois told his commanders that it would be an easy capture as there were thousands of his subjects living there who supported him. But that was not the full story. We were hearing contradictory rumours saying King Philip's army was en route to bolster its defences. It did not sound like a welcoming city. We hoped Robert's arrogance was justified.

By the time we reached Saint-Omer two days later the front gates were bolted shut. Robert and a small escort rode close under a banner of truce and gave an ultimatum. Surrender or die.

The answer was a resounding no.

He returned and gathered his commanders and advisors together. On King Edward's orders, he was to take leadership for this attack and was looking forward to it. This was the Flemish army's time to shine.

We waited.

I sat outside our tent with Izelda. She had cleaned my clothes in the river the night before we left Arques and was making a cauldron of pottage for anyone who wanted it. She did not seem concerned at the lecherous looks and blatant stares she was receiving.

'I need to fit in if I am to live through this,' she told me on our first night together. I admired the way she adapted to her new environment. She reminded me of Philippa. And it was for that reason I hesitated to accept the invitation to sleep with her. Do not get me wrong, I did and it was fabulous – but I hesitated. Then I felt guilty. I felt guilty every few hours after that too. What can I say? I'm a weak man and she was a beautiful woman.

Paul had been invited into the tent where the war council was setting out plans. It was a step up – his actions at the battle for Arques elevated him in the eyes of the commanders. I was happy for him, it was everything he had been working towards.

They remained in the tent all morning, only appearing for a short time to eat lunch before resuming. It would seem they could not agree on a strategy.

Gareth approached me as I tended my war bow and checked the arrows. We had used thousands at Arques and recovered any that were still usable. It was our job to make sure they were in good repair, checking the heads, the shafts, and the fletching for any defect. Our lives depended on it. We also carried huge quantities of spares. King Edward was under no illusion how vital we were to his success.

'Do you think we'll siege the city, Ailred?' Gareth often came to me for advice and opinions. My close connection to Paul made me the obvious choice and the reason the other Welshmen sent him over, as they did not want anything to do with the English – especially Paul.

'It depends if the reports of Philip reinforcing Saint-Omer are true or not. Paul says an army of twenty thousand will be joining them soon. If that happens we're in trouble.' I held up an arrow and looked down its line, checking it was true. 'I doubt there's time to siege it out. They'll not want us caught between Philip's army and the garrison in the city.' I passed the arrow to Izelda which she placed with the usable ones before handing me the next.

Gareth looked at Izelda. 'You have a good woman there, Ailred. I'm glad she doesn't speak English or Welsh with some of the things they say about her.' He smiled at her and she smiled back, looking confused. 'If you hear anything from that brother of yours let me know, eh?'

'I will. I'll see you later.' I waited for him to get out of earshot. 'What do they say? I haven't heard anything and you've not mentioned it.'

She shrugged. 'They are all common pigs.'

She passed me the next arrow. That was the last she spoke of it.

*

It was decided. I was right, we were going to act with haste as they could not risk King Philip's arrival.

I left Izelda with the other camp followers and

the division of guarding troops and reassured her this would be a short campaign. We had the support of Robert and his Flemish men, giving us a numerical advantage.

'You sound confident, Ailred,' she said, 'I hope your commander isn't complacent.'

I laughed at that. 'It's his job and I trust him. Now, wait here and keep your head down – I'll be back soon.' I kissed her and she reciprocated.

She held my hand and stopped me for a second. 'Be gentle with the citizens when you break in.'

I left her and joined my Welsh brothers.

In the days leading up to the battle, Robert, aware that the city had a full-strength cavalry division within the walls, had his men dig deep ditches and sink sharpened wooden stakes into the ground to the flanks of his chosen battleground. He was attempting to prevent them from outflanking us and give his men a barrier from any charging cavalry. It was a solid strategy.

He positioned his battle-hardened English men-at-arms towards the centre with us in support. We Welsh, alongside a small division of English archers, were on their right flank, and the remaining archers to their left.

Behind us were three battalions of men from Ypres, Bergues and Veurne, all less experienced but keen to atone for missing the Arques battle. He had decided to hold back a rearguard division of older, experienced, Flemish troops as a reserve to strengthen where necessary.

Sir Hugh was to the centre-left with Paul, and Lord Clinton remained with us. We were set. All we needed was for the Duke of Burgundy and the Count of Armagnac, the French commanders, to attack.

We waited. They did not come. At first, I was exhilarated, desperate for battle and the bloodletting it brought, but as time passed that feeling waned. Were the French generals so skilled as to anticipate our emotions? Morning turned to afternoon and the sun rose, making us sweat beneath what little mail we wore. The men-at-arms suffered the most. They wore heavy armour and carried cumbersome weapons. More proof of a French plan in action.

I watched as Robert brought Sir Hugh and Lord Clinton into the centre front of the stretched army and together they walked towards the city gates. Here we go, I thought. As one, we followed in formation. They were eager to draw our opposition out as they had done at Arques, but the French here were holding firm. I could see them bunched above the gates looking down and jeering, beckoning us to come and die on their walls.

Without warning, and to the dismay of the French generals who I could see shouting counter orders, a division of mounted French knights surged from around the sides of the city walls and galloped towards our left flank. They had fallen for the trap again and lost patience. They always did. The only problem was that we had moved so far forward that within seconds they were on the left body of men. They met the charging knights head-on and hundreds were battered and trampled, causing the remainder to look for retreat behind the defensive ditches and stakes. We wanted to unleash our arrows but the men from Ypres who were defending that side were intermingled with the attackers. We held back. That enforced delay caused the death of many Flemish soldiers. Once their surviving troops returned to the sanctuary of the barricades, we loosed. The French fell. Their horses crumpled. Knights, as they had done in Arques, hit the floor and were crushed beneath their thrashing mounts.

The men of Ypres saw the decimation our arrow storm had caused and craved revenge. The ground was littered with broken Flemish bodies, those who had not retreated in time, so they charged back over the barriers and onto the killing plain once more. We stopped releasing arrows and watched as the left flank broke ranks and engaged the remaining French knights. It was a wondrous sight as Frenchmen were dragged from horses and hacked to pieces.

Raised voices caused me to look towards the city gates. Their commanders were shouting and within seconds the gates opened. Hundreds of mounted French knights galloped out and veered off towards the opposite flank to support their brothers in arms. Again we unloaded our cloud of death but they rode their giant warhorses into the melee, lances piercing bodies and axes removing heads. The Flemish who had broken ranks were stranded. There were enough mounted French to flank them and cut off any retreat. They had nowhere to turn.

We were itching to reinforce them.

'STAY IN RANK,' Lord Clinton screamed. 'The Duke of Burgundy is willing you to break – don't make the bastard's job easy for him.'

He was right. If we had joined the chaos we would be open to a targeted strike and flanking. These French commanders were no fools, even if the initial charge was unplanned. They had adapted well and were gaining the upper hand.

So we watched. That was the limit of our contribution over the next few hours. It was frustrating beyond anything I had endured.

The Flemings fought for their lives, time and again countering the vicious attacks. The battle swayed backwards and forwards, the mounted French knights looking to use their horses as battering rams.

Again I looked towards the city gates. While the Count of Armagnac engaged in the bloody battle on our left flank, the Duke of Burgundy waited. I could see him studying our every move. He had another battalion behind the gates in preparation for us losing our discipline.

I heard a loud French cheer and looked across. The Flemings had broken and were running. The last of their resolve had crumbled and they headed back towards camp. I could see Paul and Sir Hugh in the centre watching as we did, while Robert tried to rally his men.

The retreat began.

The Duke of Burgundy could hold back no more. He left his vantage point. I watched as the city gates swung open. Thank god – he was coming for us. It was our turn. I took one final glance towards Paul who caught my eye and saluted.

They came at us like nothing I had experienced before. These were crazed dogs let off the lead. Soldiers on foot joined the mounted knights, bolstered by city civilians.

We loosed. Volley after volley hit them but still they came. Closer. Our men-at-arms gathered in tight formation and held form.

I picked up my mace and threw my bow to one side. I had killed plenty in the front racks of their charge, now was time to break skulls. All around the Glamorgan men who said they hated the English looked for reassurance.

They hit us. The men at the front linked their shields into a well-disciplined shield wall and the enemy faltered. The horses were unable to penetrate the obstacle and our seasoned campaigners thrust their short stabbing seax blades underneath into the groins and bellies of the French. They screamed in pain and frustration, spitting and reaching over but were met with solid defiance. Spears were thrown, most glancing off shields or armour.

That putrid smell of sweat and piss and shit that accompanied all close-quarter fighting was everywhere.

'STEP.' Lord Clinton ordered above the roar of battle.

Our front row stepped forward five paces as planned, stepping over the prone front rank of their fighters. This was our time. Frenchmen lay fighting from the ground, their thighs, their ankles, their abdomens mutilated as we moved in to kill. I came across a man in full armour. The weight had caused him to fall and he thrust his huge sword at me. In such a confined arena it was useless, its lack of mobility a burden. I smashed his helmet but he remained dangerous until Gareth dropped down next to him and thrust his blade through the visor eye slits. He continued stabbing until the man released his weapon and lay motionless. There was no time to reflect as we fought on instinct. Again, Lord Clinton ordered another five steps forward. We were like a slow-moving entity, killing all who stood in our way. Lesser armoured men came next as the front line of French knights dwindled. The second ranks fell. I battered brains from skulls and ripped men apart. Men lost their bodily functions and screamed for mercy but we moved onward.

'STEP.'

They broke. Our discipline held and now came the spoils.

'KILL THE BASTARDS.'

Lord Clinton need not have said a word. Once our shield wall came down we struck like demons from hell, tearing to pieces all in our path.

I had returned to retrieve my bow and quiver of arrows and with our newfound freedom, we again picked our targets. The French had a limited division of crossbowmen guarding the gates looking to keep us at bay and were inflicting damage, bringing down our front ranks.

'Crossbows at the gates,' I shouted to my Welsh companions. As a group, we stood firm and unleashed a torrent of arrows, dropping many and sending the rest scurrying for cover.

We moved forward, loosing arrow after arrow into the men who stood and fought. The frustration of an archer's attack was palpable. They would stand braced to receive us man-to-man only to be struck in the chest by a barbed or broadheaded arrow and then have their throats cut as we swarmed over them.

I met Paul. He was covered in blood – none of his own.

'Robert and his men have taken a hammering

on the left – we need to rout this lot and reinforce those who are left.' He pointed his sword in the direction of the camp. 'Their failure has given these French bastards a free road. I hope to Christ our rearguard can hold them or our supplies are lost.'

Izelda! I had told her to wait. If the French raided our camp I feared what might happen to her.

'YOU STAY HERE,' Paul shouted. 'DO NOT DESERT YOUR POST.' He could see I was distracted and knew why. The life of Izelda meant nothing to him.

I turned and ran towards camp.

*

When I arrived back, my nightmare had turned into reality. The French had battled through the rearguard defences and reached the camp. They were collecting the horses and mules, the food rations, and burning our belongings.

I was on a hillock overlooking the scene. They had stationed a picket of men around and I could see no way in. There were the bodies of dead guardsmen scattered about but from my limited vantage point could not see Izelda.

They were working at speed to gather everything they wanted, knowing if we won the battle outside the city we would soon return. My only hope was that she had hidden and could wait it out.

'TOI...' The Frenchman came from nowhere.

He was holding a sword and swung it with a relaxed wrist. 'JE VAIS VOUS TUER.'

‘Not if I kill you first…’ I replied, reaching for an arrow but he was upon me.

I managed to duck his initial swing and drew the mace from my belt. We stood face-to-face and I could tell this was a trained knight, his face a picture of confidence. Again he attacked, not allowing me to settle into a defensive position. He was trying to drain my self-belief. It worked. In that instant, I knew he was the better fighter. I could not compete with his years of coaching.

I ran. I am no coward but I have seen enough single combat to know my limitations. Keeping hold of my weapon, I ran towards the line of trees, a narrow gap between two my only exit. I heard him laugh as his footsteps followed. I darted between them and as I did so brushed past a shadowy figure. He could have tripped me or stabbed me but did not, so I continued.

I heard a gasp and turned. The French knight had tripped a couple of feet behind me, his hands outstretched to break the fall. It was the only chance I would get. Then I saw her. Izelda. She had tripped him as he passed her and she ran forward and jumped with both feet onto his sword, not allowing him to bring it around to defend himself. I did not need a second invitation. I was on him, my mace gouging his back open, the small bones of his spine splitting apart and rendering his legs useless.

'LEAVE HIM,' she screamed. I looked at her. She was half naked, what clothes she wore were ripped and she had bite marks and cuts all over. 'He thought I was dead. He's going to wish I was.' I stood back and offered her the mace. She refused. She bent down and picked up the man's sword. 'He told me he loved this sword – it was his mistress. It will be fitting.' She knelt, pulled his face up to meet hers, and said something in French that I did not understand. Then she went to work on him.

*

They stripped everything from the camp and burned whatever they left. We waited out of sight and I helped nurse Izelda's wounds. It would take time – the abuse had been brutal.

We remained hidden. I heard the sounds of horses and men approaching the site as it got dark. The French had left, but we had stayed concealed in case our army had been destroyed. We would have to find our way back to Sluys alone if that was the case. We need not have worried. Robert of Artois, his uniform ripped and helmet missing, led the procession into the devastated camp. He pulled his horse up and I watched as Sir Hugh, Paul, and Lord Clinton joined him. I sighed with relief. Paul was safe.

I led Izelda by the hand and we walked down to join them.

'They took everything, Lord,' I said, approaching the vanguard.

Lord Clinton shook his head. 'So it would seem.' He rode off to survey the damage.

Paul looked down from his white-foamed horse. 'You disobeyed my direct order, Norman. I will have you on a charge.'

'I saved this woman from being murdered, for God's sake.'

He fought to control his rage and his mount. 'What do I care about that woman's life? She is of no benefit to our war effort – I've got a good mind to have her ejected and...'

Sir Hugh sighed. 'Give it a rest, Paul.'

I glared at Paul who did likewise back.

I changed the subject. 'Did we win?' It was a naive question.

Sir Hugh dismounted and led his mount towards the river. 'If you call getting half our Flemish brothers killed and not capturing the city, then yes – it was a resounding victory.'

Paul was seething. 'We met small divisions of the bastards on our return here.' He was alive with nervous energy, the anger of defeat still raw. 'We took back some of the stuff they stole and managed to kill plenty of the filthy dogs, but the others escaped. We have men out looking for them now.' He looked at the meagre consignment of retrieved possessions. 'But I suspect this is all we'll get back.' He jumped down and followed Sir Hugh.

We split up and searched for whatever we could salvage. It had been a baking hot summer's day and the night was still and warm. Sleeping outside would be no hardship. I could tell the leadership's pride was damaged, and no one spoke of the day's events.

I found a few rags that had been discarded and gave them to Izelda and we found a quiet spot away from the despondent army. It was my first experience of defeat and I realised how devastating it was to morale.

Most of the English and Welsh men had survived, the majority of the casualties being on the left flank where the men from Ypres had been deployed. The Flemish defending the camp, once they were over-run, had been chased to a bend on the river Aa and slaughtered in their thousands. Bodies littered what remained of the camp, and the gruesome work of clearing them took hours to complete.

We had dented their army's ability to mount a counter-offensive and our English and Welsh divisions had managed to breach the city's gates for a short period. The French had managed to push them back, but at great cost. They would not be attacking us tonight.

Robert stationed a substantial picket that night regardless. They did not come.

We slept, Izelda choosing to sleep away from me for the first time. Her injuries ran deep.

The next day was the grim job of counting our dead. It was worse than I realised. At least eight thousand Flemish men from Ypres and Bruges had died and there was widespread concern that the approaching French army under King Philip would soon be close enough to finish the job.

Men began to disappear. It was not long before large sections of Robert of Artois's army deserted, most going home to Ypres or Cassel which were in safe areas of Flanders. Even Robert decided to abandon the task set by King Edward.

I was sitting by the river bathing, while Izelda washed her injuries. She had stayed close to me since we had reunited and had said little. Paul approached. He was still angry.

'Artois's going and taking the rest of his cowards to meet up with Edward at Tournai.'

'They still haven't been paid, Paul – nor have we or the Welsh. Can you blame them? They lost thousands yesterday.' I climbed out of the water and dressed. 'I heard some of them talking last night and they intend to cut their losses and go home. They've lost respect for us and King Edward.'

'Fuckin' cowards, the lot of them.'

I sighed. 'Paul, you have to be realistic. King Frenchie is only a day at most away and we're in no fit state to take him on. Can I assume we'll all be going to join Edward – English and Welsh too?'

He turned and walked away. 'You're a fuckin' coward too.'

He was not far wrong. That moment in the clearing facing the French knight had opened my eyes. If it had not been for Izelda I would be dead.

My archery skills were one thing but I was no match for a trained fighter. Paul knew that but refused to acknowledge the fact. He was trained in the art of warfare and thrived on it, but yesterday made me face reality. At some point, my luck would run out.

And I had Izelda to consider. She had saved my life and I was looking for ways to protect her. I was inventing excuses to stay away from conflict – I see that now. At the time I felt responsible and was determined to keep her from danger. I wanted to live.

CHAPTER 12

No Glamorgan men died at the battle of Saint-Omer. It was a miracle. As Lord Clinton lined us up and moved us out, spirits were high. We were happy to be alive. Even the French raid that stripped us of our provisions could not take that feeling away.

'So, the only two we lost were Bryn and Glyn, at Arques,' Gareth said as he shrugged his quiver of arrows over his shoulder and picked up his bow.

'So it seems,' I replied. 'I've no idea what happened to them – maybe they got bored and went home. No doubt on their way back to the valleys as we speak.'

Paul cantered his horse alongside but said nothing.

Gareth looked at me. 'Oh, didn't you hear – their bodies were found in a stable in Arques. They'd been beaten to death with a mace or something and hidden under hay. Bastards.'

I stopped and looked at Izelda.

Paul jerked his head around and pulled his horse to a halt. 'Murdered in a stable in Arques, you say?'

Gareth refused to answer Paul. He was angry.

'Bastard French. Everyone I killed in Saint-Omer was payback for that. They were our friends.'

'Beaten to death with a mace in some stables? Nasty stuff, eh, Welshy?'

He stopped and looked at Paul. 'I have nothing to say to you.' He continued walking.

Paul laughed. 'Then you won't be interested to know I saw two people creep away from a stable the next morning.' He looked at me and then Izelda. 'A man and a woman.' He laughed again. 'If you change your mind, ask Ailred here, he might…' He left a long pause before saying, '...he might come and ask me on your behalf. Beg me for you.'

I looked at Paul who was smiling. He rode away.

'If your brother does know who killed them he better fuckin' tell you…' Gareth was fuming. He looked at me, and then Izelda. 'You were in the town all that night. Did you see a man and a woman near some stables?'

I tried to look nonchalant. 'No, I'd have remembered. He's trying to wind you up, you know what he's like.'

'He's a bastard is what he's like. I'd never go begging to him for anything.'

I was pleased to hear him say that. 'I don't blame you.'

He moved off in an attempt to distance himself from me.

*

We were going to Tournai to join King Edward, about sixty miles southeast. I was happy. Once there I could lose myself and avoid conflict. We carried little as the French had taken or destroyed everything. It would be a long march as we had to find all we needed en route – food, water, shelter. The locals were aware of our tactics by now and left nothing of use. We burned down their homes regardless. It did nothing to ease our hunger. We had to settle for hunting rabbits, birds, and anything that moved, with us archers becoming everyone's new best friend.

After three days of marching and hunting and destroying, we were close to Tournai. Izelda was beginning to open up again. She had been quiet since her ordeal and I could tell she did not want to speak about it. I let her know I was there if she needed to talk.

'Were you married in England?'

It was a subject I knew would come up but still took me by surprise. 'No, but…'

'You were in love?'

I hesitated. 'Yes, but…'

'You are not now?'

Again I hesitated.

'I think you are. I think you will leave me when it is time to go home to England.'

She looked sad, although she did not look shocked. I hugged her and she responded. We kissed.

'That is a good answer,' she said, squeezing me tight before sitting down.

We had stopped by a small brook and the army scattered itself nearby, some hunting, others drinking water and resting.

Paul pulled up bare-chested on his horse. He was with Sir Hugh. I had not spoken to him since leaving Saint-Omer.

'We camp here tonight and we'll reach Tournai tomorrow.' He spoke as if he was in command. 'Our King is besieging the city and we will be joining him.' He looked at Izelda. 'Your wife and child will most likely be there, Ailred Norman. We have reports of a recent arrival of followers from England.' He looked at me. '...and from Wales.'

He smiled, tapped his heels to the horse's flanks and moved on.

She looked at me. 'He is...how you say...a bastard?'

I was beginning to agree. 'Yeah, your English is good. I don't think he knows you speak English or he wouldn't have said that.'

She laughed, 'Oh, he knows all right. You need to open your eyes, Ailred.' She went quiet. 'He will get you killed one day.'

I had no answer to that.

I sat her down and told her about Philippa. There was no point pretending she did not exist now. She listened, never once giving an opinion or asking for clarification. Once I had finished, she got up and picked up our two drinking mugs.

'I'll get some water. It's been a long day.'

When I awoke the following day, she was gone.

*

We reached Tournai at midday. It was the loneliest morning of my life. Thousands of men surrounded me, yet I felt alone and depressed. I spent hours searching for her. She had left a heart etched into the dry soil next to where we slept and made love. That made it worse.

There were no sentries as we entered the English siege camp, nor did there look to be any semblance of order. Soldiers and camp followers mingled. There was an almost carnival atmosphere.

'I expect every man to attend service later and thank the almighty for watching over us.' Sir Hugh pointed to a large white tent with a wooden cross above the centre pole. He was a religious man, which I could never square with the vile actions he would indulge in – usually with Paul.

He dismissed us and we drifted off looking for accommodation and food. As I wandered I noticed many men who were at Sluys. A few acknowledged me and asked about our defeat at Saint-Omer. They said that the siege here was going nowhere and the King and his allies could not agree on anything. It was turning into a farce. As with us, no one had been paid. I asked if they knew of any followers arriving from Wales in the last few days, and they said some had.

I allowed myself a level of excitement.

An hour later that excitement turned to elation.

'AILRED NORMAN!' Philippa ran to me and flung her arms around my neck. Albar, Paul's tutor and scholar, stood behind her holding Kimberly. Any thoughts of Izelda disappeared as we kissed and hugged.

'What a touching reunion – another siege, another woman.' I looked around to see Paul and Sir Hugh ride past and laugh.

Albar gave Kimberly back to Philippa and rushed over to Paul. 'Sire, it is good to see you again. I have missed our...' he hesitated, 'our time together.'

Paul did not stop. He looked down and said, 'I will not be needing your tutoring here, this is a place of war. Unless you've brought half a dozen trebuchets with you, you should have stayed in Cardiff.' He rode on.

Albar's face crumbled. He looked as if he would cry – then did, and ran off.

Philippa shook her head. 'That brother of yours is still a bastard, I see.'

I kissed her again. 'You're not the first person to say that.'

The rest of that day was spent catching up. She had been here a couple of days having travelled with a group from Cardiff. She had heard of our defeat at Saint-Omer and had been sick with worry. That gave me a selfish sense of satisfaction – no one had ever cared enough to care. Maybe Paul when we were younger, but he was turning into a monster. With the knowledge he held over me, for the first time in my life I feared what he might do. How power corrupts the impressionable.

She told me she had seen Jaques Stafford and his Father, William de Bohun. They were somewhere within the encampment. My heart dropped at that news. The antagonism between Sir William and Sir Hugh had never been resolved. Nothing good could come from it.

'Is there *any* good news?' I asked.

'Dafydd came over with us.'

I had hoped Blodwen's husband would stay in Wales after his wife had been assaulted by someone before we left Cardiff. More bad news. It reminded me of that last day before we left and how Philippa had not said goodbye.

'I thought you might not come to France,' I said, throwing Kimberly into the air and catching her. She had grown in the weeks we had been separated.

'I was always going to come, but that final day in Cardiff all but broke me.'

'We still don't know who did those things to Blodwen, do we?' I was adamant.

'You might not, but the rest of us do. Paul raped and murdered her, not, "did those things".' She was angry at the memory. 'And it *was* him. The man has no conscience.' She grimaced. 'Dafydd knows too. I better warn you – he has vowed to kill Paul when he gets a chance. You must try to see...' She stopped herself. 'Sorry, this isn't the time or place.' She kissed me again. 'I just want all this...' She gestured towards the city of Tournai with the siege towers and battlements, '...I want all this to end and we can go home.'

I looked about. There was little sign of victory. King Edward had been besieging the city for weeks and gotten nowhere. He had brought cannons with him. They were worse than useless. It was the first time I had seen them and they were owned and operated by a small number of Tuscan mercenaries who were costing King Edward a fortune. Good luck getting paid, I thought. The city had taken in the evacuees from Saint-Omer. Add to them the local inhabitants and the two garrisons of six thousand fighting men under the command of Raoul of Brienne and Count Gaston, and Tournai's walls were looking like a formidable opponent.

I heard a loud blast from a buisine. It made me jump.

I remembered Sir Hugh's instructions when we arrived. 'That's our call to prayers.' I had lost track of time and needed to attend the service being held in the makeshift chapel. They had been staggered over the day to spread the military personnel, and this was the final congregation of the day. 'If I don't attend Paul will have me arrested for heresy.'

Philippa laughed.

'I wish I was joking.'

'Go, go – I'll be here when you find God and he forgives all your sins.'

I kissed her on the cheek and made my way to the service tent, bumping into Paul as I entered.

'What the fuck was all that about?' I growled, referring to his not-so-subtle inferences earlier.

'Address me as, Sire.'

'Like fuck I will – what's got into you?'

'Show me respect, Ailred Norman or I'll...'

I butted in. 'I'll tell you this, but you don't deserve the warning.'

He smiled at me as if he did not have a care in the world. 'Tell me what, little brother?'

I shook my head. I had no idea what was going on in his brain. 'Dafydd is in the camp and has sworn to kill you.'

He frowned. 'Who's he then?'

'Blodwen's husband.'

'Who?'

'The woman someone raped and murdered back in Cardiff before we came out here, that's who.'

'Oh, I think I remember her.' He grinned. 'Pretty little thing and such a sad incident. And he thinks I did it? I better keep an eye out for this Dafydd fellow then.'

'THE DEVIL IS AMONGST YOU AND I CAN

SMELL HIS PRESENCE IN THIS PLACE OF WORSHIP.'

That was enough to silence Paul. We looked to where the Welsh voice boomed from the altar at the front as hundreds of God-fearing soldiers knelt and prayed before him.

I turned to Paul, and said under my breath, 'What the fuck's he doing here?'

Paul shrugged.

We had not expected to see Archdeacon Grufudd ap Rhys here. He was pointing his pastoral staff towards the two of us, his eyes wide and hateful.

This day was not going well.

The service was short and to the point, Father Rhys preaching the evils of being French and the place in heaven reserved for those who kill them. Whenever he referred to evil he would look at Paul and me. He even managed to mention a robbery in a priory and how the perpetrators of such blasphemy would be cast into eternal damnation. Paul had laughed out loud at that and got up and left, leaving a screaming archdeacon to add an unplanned sermon about how God would punish those who mocked him.

*

I lost contact with the Glamorgan archers. I do not know if they avoided me or if my family's arrival had taken me away from them. It added up to the same thing. I would see them milling around the siege camp, always keeping themselves away from the English. By then Dafydd was part of their contingent. I think he noticed me once but refused to meet my gaze. Another friend lost because of Paul.

Over the next few days, nothing of consequence happened. It was lovely. I had time to reconnect with Philippa and Kimberly. We discovered we had missed one another. I had not realised how much, although my infidelity with Izelda was a nagging source of guilt.

King Edward prowled the settlement with his advisors, assaulting the walls with siege engines and cannons but getting nowhere. Every day men died, either on unbreachable walls or through accident or sickness. It was not long before ill health became the principal cause of death. Our services as archers were only required to give covering fire to suicidal attempts to scale the walls. The crossbowmen in the turrets and on the ramparts added to our death toll. We were running low on provisions too – but it was no secret the inhabitants of Tournai were on the verge of starvation. We cut off their supply of fresh food. Each day King Edward watched from afar and turned the screw, knowing they could not last long.

Then one day they broke.

The doors to the city cracked open. Through the narrow gap, the city discarded its useless mouths.

Philippa stood beside me and watched as

hundreds of men, women, and children filed out. They were non-combatants – everyone not useful to the defence of the city. It was pitiful. When the final child was pushed through the gates the city shut them. I have never seen anything so heartless. They gathered together and walked the short distance to the siege fortifications and begged to be allowed through.

Our boundary remained shut.

Philippa had tears in her eyes as she said, 'The King *will* let them pass, won't he?'

I shook my head. 'He knows that will aid those inside. Many of these people will be the families of soldiers.'

'But he can't leave them in no man's land to starve?'

'You watch. Can you imagine how the men inside will feel if they're forced to watch their loved ones die because they were thrown out? They will hate their own commanders as much as they hate us.'

I was right. He did not allow them safe passage. Day after day they were left to rot. The weather turned for the worst and still, neither King Edward nor the City of Tournai gave way.

Then something happened that would affect this siege and the one King Edward undertook at Calais six years later. It was a mistake that cost him.

I was on the boundary about two weeks later. I was one of the men assigned the duty of ensuring the civilians in no man's land did not break out. They need not have bothered as by then the poor wretches were on the verge of death from starvation.

King Edward was accompanied by Jacob van Artevelde and the Duke of Brabant. Both were allies and supplied a large number of supporting military personnel. I went onto one knee.

'Rise, soldier. How are they bearing up?'

'I'll be honest with you, Sire, they are dying.'

The king shrugged and went to walk away when from nowhere a horse-drawn cart came trotting towards him. Several guards moved forward to protect him but he held up his hand. There was no threat.

The cart was being driven by a Benedictine monk. He pulled up before the King and dismounted, handing the reins to a serviceman.

He fell to his knees. 'Lord, King.' he said in good English, keeping his head down and his hands held in prayer. 'I beseech thee. Have pity on these fellow Christians that have been left in the wilderness.'

The king's bodyguard stepped forward and looked as if he was going to manhandle the monk but the King stopped him.

'What is your name, Father?'

'My name is of no significance, Lord King. I only ask that you show mercy to these poor souls.' He gestured towards the cart. 'I beg of you, supply food so that I may distribute life to the needy.' He crawled forward and prayed at the King's feet.

The King looked down and pondered the request then turned to his two companions.

'What do you think, my Lords – should I show leniency?'

The Duke of Brabant shrugged and gave no response, whereas Jacob van Artevelde was positive to the suggestion, saying, 'It will show you in a good light Lord King, and God will favour your campaign.'

'It would seem you are to be these poor wretches saviour, Father. Go with my blessing.'

Tears ran down the monk's face as he rose and went to thank the King, but was ushered away.

The King turned to me. 'Go with him and give him what he wants.' He hesitated for a few seconds before reconsidering. 'On reflection, give him what we do not need.'

He turned to Jacob van Artevelde, and, speaking in French, said something I did not understand. Jacob laughed and pointed at the Duke of Brabant. Whatever he said, the Duke was incensed. Again, Jacob van Artevelde laughed and waved him away, as if to dismiss the Duke. That was more than he could bear. He drew his sword and looked as if he would attack.

All hell broke loose. The Duke's bodyguard, a stern-looking man missing an ear, pulled his sword. Jacob did likewise, pushing the Duke backwards and squaring up to the bodyguard.

The King stepped away and appealed for sanity but before peace could be restored, Jacob darted forward and drove his sword deep into the bodyguard's neck, severing his artery and killing him on the spot.

I stepped in to protect the King in case the violence escalated. I had no idea what triggered the fracas, but my primary concern was the King's safety.

I need not have worried. The King was enraged, his wrath bringing both parties to a truce. In the background, Jacob van Artevelde and the Duke of Brabant hurled insults at one another.

I could not believe how a simple exchange between two supposed allies could end in such a bloody outcome.

As the scene settled I led the monk towards the kitchen area.

'Thank you, my child,' he said, reclaiming the reins and leading the horse and cart.

I said nothing.

*

Those events changed the course of the siege and King Edward's initial campaign to regain the crown of France.

The monk's humanism towards the stranded civilians shamed Edward into allowing them safe passage. It was an act of kindness that gave strength to the city's defenders, encouraging them to fight harder and longer knowing their kin were safe. It was a rare mistake by the King and one he never repeated.

The coalition fell apart after the killing of the Duke of Brabant's trusted man by Jacob van Artevelde. Jacob was not a knight but a businessman and politician, which made his actions unforgivable in the eyes of the nobility. King Edward had refused to side with the Duke and as a consequence the Duke, and his ally the Count of Hainaut, left, taking their men with them. None had been paid for months. It was inevitable.

So we fought on, only now we were friendless and broke. King Edward was unable to mount any sustained attacks on the walls and word had reached him that King Philip of France and his sizable army were within days of launching a counter-offensive.

Morale plummeted.

With isolation came reprisals. Factions within our army began to implode, each blaming the other for the venture's failure. A sinister civil war erupted, one the King had no control over. We knew it was coming to an end soon and needed to gain as much wealth as possible before any withdrawal or truce. Every man became insular, willing to cut another's throat regardless of nationality.

My position was perilous. I was the forgotten man, neither the Welsh, Sir Hugh, nor any other division felt loyalty towards me.

Every day, the different factions would disappear and look to steal whatever they could find. No one was safe. Most men had accrued some level of wealth while in France, either looting homesteads or robbing wealthy French people. Anyone was fair game. And now was the time for personal grievances to be settled. Under the cover of this dark shadow, men died. The first was Jaques Stafford. He was discovered by his father with his only good eye removed and forced down his throat. He had choked to death. We all knew it was Paul and Sir Hugh, and they made no disguise of the fact.

Men would do anything to earn. Rumours circulated that Archdeacon Rhys was paying men to go out into the countryside and snatch young French boys. He was often seen with the unfortunate children at his sermons and I had heard crying in his tent at night. These boys would disappear to be replaced by others. It was a sickening situation that the nobility turned a blind eye to.

Lord Clinton was attempting to act as a peacemaker but was getting nowhere. He was neutral and still commanded the Glamorgan men who were themselves dragged into the war of attrition. Their survival depended on violent self-preservation.

And so it continued. Death after bloody death. The French must have been laughing.

At this time, the King was in negotiations with

Joan of Valois, who was King Philip's sister, in a bid to agree a truce. Philip was demanding austere terms, knowing he now had the upper hand. He still was not confident enough to risk battle as we still had a capable army.

I feared for my family and could not decide what to do. Luckily, Philippa was there to think for me.

'We need to go home.'

It was an easy decision to make once Philippa made it for me. We had woken after another night of drunken violence. This time the Welsh had been set upon by a group of English men-at-arms. Both sides blamed the other but the result was dead men and another enquiry for Lord Clinton to adjudicate.

I looked at Philippa as Kimberly woke and started to cry. This was no life for them or any normal human being.

I took control. 'Pack your things – we're leaving.'

CHAPTER 13

Bishop Budwith has already granted an indulgence for my sins so I am at liberty to say what I will. That is lucky, as I would never have included this next chapter. And you would never know. Brother Michael, who is an unlikely friend now, tells me he is happy to write whatever I have to say. So I will. He says he has learned much from my confessions thus far and has come to understand violence. This he says without self-flagellation or guilt. He has taken to carrying a dagger when leaving the priory's confines, which is not something you associate with a man of the cloth. He reminds me that Exodus 21:24 tells us: 'Eye for eye, tooth for tooth, hand for hand, foot for foot' and encourages this line of worship. He would have made a fine travel companion back in the day.

*

We waited one more day.

That day the Kings of England and France were deep in negotiations, thrashing out what would become The Truce of Esplechin. It stipulated that Edward would cease hostilities towards France for five years and as remittance

Philip would allow safe passage to England for his troops.

At the time we did not know that. All we knew was that every day the looting and robberies went on and people died. Any day it could be us.

I pleaded with Philippa. I had changed my mind about leaving straight away – I wanted to stay and wait for the truce to be announced then we would all make our way home together. It would be safer.

'Don't talk to me about safety, Ailred,' she said. 'Every time you leave me I get leered at – filthy men looking to molest me at any moment. You will come back one day and find me raped and murdered.'

'But the truce is close now and...'

'How long will it take to organise the clearance of this shit hole? They'll have to secure transportation, then ship thousands of men and god knows what else across the sea. Think Ailred. It will take weeks if not more – by that time anything could happen.' She looked at Kimberly. 'To any of us.'

I could not argue. I was being short-sighted, as usual.

During that day Philippa prepared herself and Kimberly. We would leave early the next morning before the sun rose, but it had to be secret. Even though the army was in anarchy there were still rules, the main being you did not desert your post.

'Going somewhere nice?'

Paul walked over alone. I never could keep a secret from him. Philippa had bundled our meagre belongings into a sack and had it stashed at the back of the tent. I was drying my boots over the fire outside as it had rained overnight.

'Give it a rest Paul, or am I still to address you as Sire?'

He laughed. 'You take life too seriously, Ailred.' He sat down close to the tent. 'Don't mind if I sit with you for a while, do you – I might not get a chance tomorrow?' He looked at me then Philippa.

'The problem with you is you don't take life seriously enough.' I poured a mug of ale and offered it to him, which he took and nodded thanks. 'You will have been out with the others robbing and looting like the rest. How much blood did you shed last night?' I was not going to let him get away without facing up to a few home truths.

He grinned. 'I haven't robbed or looted anyone or anything.'

That surprised me. 'You never used to lie to me Paul, what's happened to you?'

He shrugged. 'I won't pretend I haven't settled a few scores but I'll be going home with as much as I came out with.'

I frowned. 'I find that hard to believe.' I looked at Philippa who picked up Kimberly and walked away. She had had enough. 'You always wanted to be rich ever since you were a kid – you've spent your life robbing people. Don't try and tell me you're a changed man now.'

He downed his ale. 'I don't need it.' He lay back on the damp ground. The months of occupation had turned the once fertile land around the city to mud. There was silence for a few moments then Paul said, 'You remember that last night we had in Tonebricge together, the night before I left with Sir Hugh to Wales?' I nodded. 'Well, that was the best night of my life.'

'That's quite a statement, Paul. All we did was get drunk in our old hideaway and talk a load of soppy nonsense.'

He sat up and looked at me. 'I know, that's what was so good about it. That place is special to me. Go there when you get back and think of me.'

It was a strange request and out of character.

I sighed. 'Things change, Paul. You've changed. You've spent most of this campaign acting like Sir Hugh's puppy and belittling me.'

'I'll be Sir Paul soon, that's what I've been working towards. Don't worry, I'll look after you. Thanks for the drink.'

He went to stand but looked shaky. As he stood, he stumbled forward and his legs gave way. He crumpled to the floor. I waited for him to get up but he did not, so rushed over. His breathing was shallow, his eyes wide and glazed. I slapped him across the face.

'Are you ok?'

He shook his head and his eyes cleared. He blinked. His gaze focused on me.

'Help me up.'

I eased him into a sitting position.

'Has that happened before?' I asked, passing him the dregs of my ale.

He held his head in both hands. 'What's it to you?'

He was staring at me as if I was a total stranger. 'It's me, Ailred, your brother.'

He continued to look at me before recognition appeared on his face. He smiled and clambered to his feet.

'I knew that Al, I was just kidding.'

'Well, has that happened before?' I asked, holding him until he stood unaided.

'Has what happened before? As I said, you take life too seriously.'

He shook my supportive hand from his arm and walked away.

Philippa wandered back holding Kimberly's hand. She had not seen him collapse.

'There's something wrong with him,' I said.

She nodded. 'That's an understatement.'

I watched him walk away and kick a dog that was scavenging through the rubbish.

The rest of the day was spent running through our usual routine. Nothing to arouse suspicion. I did guard duty, fired pointless arrows at our French counterparts, waved goodbye at the end of our turn, and then went back to Philippa. She was ready. If I had changed my mind she would have gone without me and taken Kimberly. I did not blame her.

*

That night I had unfinished business. It involved Archdeacon Rhys. It was something that had to be concluded before I left France or it would haunt me the rest of my life.

I told Philippa I was assigned last-minute guard duty but would be back in time to leave camp before sunrise as planned.

Archdeacon Rhys had a tent near the chapel where he carried out his daily services. He performed any number each day depending on how many people needed guidance and his state of sobriety. If you were brave enough to attend the last service of the day you never knew what to expect. He could rant about any subject under the sun, but would always save a special sermon for the sins of robbery and fornication between men.

By the time I reached his tent, it was dark and quiet. It was an unnatural silence.

I put my ear to the archdeacon's tent and listened. Nothing. I had expected to hear snoring or heavy breathing as the tent was made of thin material. I carried a short dagger and used it to lift the front enough to lay down and roll under. I crawled to his bed. He was not there. I cursed. He tended to surround himself with the abducted French boys and I was surprised there was not one cowering in his bed. He told them God commanded their obedience.

I left. I was about to give up and return to Philippa when I heard a muffled sound coming from the large tented church. Maybe he was tidying or holding an impromptu service? Creeping through the open tent flap, I looked in. There was an oil lamp burning near the front, casting its dim light across the altar. I walked down the central aisle, rows of pews on either side. Something bulky had been left on the altar – an offering to God. As I approached I realised I was correct. Archdeacon Rhys had been tied to the altar. His arms and legs had been anchored to the flood and he lay sprawled out on his stomach like a sacrifice. He was still fully clothed in his religious vestments but the bottom half had been pulled up around his waist. As I drew nearer, the true horror unfolded. His pastoral staff, the one he used to point at Paul and me when he had accused us of various blasphemies, had been inserted up his rectal passage, through his body and exited through his gaping mouth. I walked forward in stunned silence. The brutality was a thing of wonder. Written in his blood on the base of the altar were the words 'HAVE A SAFE JOURNEY'.

I left in haste.

*

Philippa and Kimberly were sleeping when I returned to our tent. It was time to make ourselves scarce. Now the archdeacon had been murdered in such a sadistic and conspicuous manner there would be uproar. Whoever did it had to be caught and would be punished in a public show of solidarity with the church. I knew what that meant. His open animosity towards Paul and me would make us prime suspects. Paul could look after himself.

'Philippa, wake up – we must leave.'

It was too dark in the tent to see, but I heard her jerk awake as if woken from a nightmare. She calmed herself and then spoke. 'Is it that time already? It seems like I only just got her off to sleep.'

'Yes, I think we should leave now.' Rummaging about in the back of the tent I retrieved our travel bag and took everything out of the tent that I thought we might need. We had collected food and that was ready. I slipped a dagger and a small axe into my belt but that was the only protection I could risk taking. I had to leave my bow. It was an extension of me by now and I wanted to take it, but Philippa was insistent. We had to masquerade as a poor family travelling the roads of France and a war bow would attract attention. If that war bow was found to be in the possession of an English archer it would have dire consequences.

Luckily Kimberly did not cry. She was old enough not to grizzle at the slightest inconvenience and looked happy to be awake and 'going on an adventure', as Philippa put it.

The camp was quiet as we slipped past the guards. It was easy. Everyone knew it was a matter of time before the truce was official and we could go home. The French would not be attacking this night. The dangers came from within – and we were about to escape them.

*

We travelled many miles from Tournai before the sun came up. Philippa had wanted to travel to Calais to pick up a ship from there but I thought it unwise. Izelda had told me Calais was under the control of the French so was too dangerous. She said a few French entrepreneurs still traded with the English but they would be expensive to hire for a passage home.

'We'll have to make our way to Sluys and pick up a boat from there,' I said in conclusion. 'They're still friendly, although we're running out of allies by the day.'

'When the money runs out you find out who your real friends are,' she said as she looked over her shoulder for the hundredth time.

'Stop looking,' I said, although I was as wary as her. 'They'll not send a search party looking for us this far out. Hell, they might not even think we were involved.'

I realised what I said the second I said it, and hoped she would not notice. Some chance.

'Involved in what?'

I had not told her about the murder of

Archdeacon Rhys. It would confuse things. I thought I could keep a secret. How dumb am I?

'Oh, nothing...involved in leaving camp, that's all I meant.'

'Ailred Norman – what might we be involved in?'

I gulped. 'Murdering Archdeacon Rhys by impaling him on his pastoral staff – did I not mention it?'

She stopped. 'You did what?'

I took her and Kimberly away from the road and over to a wide river close by. It was turning into a hot September day and this explanation was going to take some time.

By the time I finished speaking, she was red-faced from shouting abuse and was trying to kick me in the balls. She had taken it better than I anticipated.

'So now we are wanted for murdering an archdeacon in France and wanted for, I can't remember what, back home. Holy fuck, Al, is there nothing you can't ruin?'

'I think it was Paul that killed him.'

She fell to the floor with her head in her hands and kicked her feet up and down.

'OF COURSE IT WAS PAUL, YOU DOPEY FUCKIN' IDIOT.'

Kimberly dived down next to her mother and joined in the game, giggling.

I will be honest with you, I did smirk – but she kicked me in the shins.

We sat and cleared the air. It took a while but was worth the effort. The conversation drifted onto Paul. It always did. She told me that on the journey over to France from Cardiff she spent a great deal of time with Albar, Paul's tutor. He was a deep-thinking, sensitive man who analysed everything and everyone. He got drunk one night and confided in her, telling her his inner thoughts. Many involved Paul.

I was beginning to wonder where the conversation was heading.

Albar told her Paul was one of the most intelligent men he had ever met. I laughed, but she hushed me. He told her that once Paul won the position as Sir Hugh's squire he set about doing whatever it took to achieve his goal. Anything. He manipulated everyone. He would find their strengths and weaknesses and exploit them in whatever way would gain him most. In his early days at Cardiff, Archdeacon Rhys was residing there, convincing Welsh archers to join King Edward in his invasion of France. He had taken a shine to young Paul. Paul had reciprocated and would spend hours with the archdeacon.

She looked at me. 'They spent time *alone.*'

Even I understood what she was hinting at.

The archdeacon trusted Paul. When they had first travelled back to Tonebricge, Paul was the archdeacon's companion. I had met them at the market in the castle that day. It was the day the priory was robbed.

I remembered what the archdeacon had said when he chained me to the wall in the dungeon. It made me cringe. It was something about a key and how Paul enjoyed it when he rubbed his… I forced the memory from my mind.

Albar had cried when he admitted he loved Paul. I remembered him muttering it to me once but thought I was dreaming.

'He used Albar for his knowledge and connections and threw him away when he got what he wanted,' she said, getting up and helping Kimberly stand.

'You make it sound like Paul prefers men to women.'

She sighed. 'He uses sex and violence to get what he wants. From what Albar says he can't tell the difference between the two.'

I did not know what to think. If the key Archdeacon Rhys had spoken about was a personal key to the priory's treasury, then Paul would have had access to it. Archdeacon Rhys should never have had a key – only the Prior of Tonebricge monastery was allowed access. If Paul had stolen that from the Archdeacon then that would make him as guilty as Paul. It was something he could never admit to. Paul would have known that. Could Paul be *that* devious?

It was too much for my brain to take in.

She patted my head. 'You're a good man, Ailred. Don't ever change.'

I had a headache.

*

We continued walking. So many buildings had been burned to the ground in the name of King Edward and his claim to the French throne. As I watched broken people attempting to salvage their lives from the ruins, I felt guilt. They clung to the hope that they could undo what we had so meticulously destroyed. I had been responsible for many of the homes we passed.

'You were obeying orders, Ailred.' Philippa had read my mind.

'Yes, but I didn't need to do it with such passion.' I cuddled Kimberly as I watched a young girl about her age crying in her father's arms.

By the end of that day, I consoled myself with the fact that no one had come searching for us. No one was going to travel this far from the relative safety of Tournai to hunt down a stray archer. They had no idea I had anything to do with the death of Archdeacon Rhys and would carry on killing each other regardless.

Thanks to King Edward the Third's rampant army, there was no shortage of places to hole up for the night, so we chose a large house that still had most of its walls and even part of its roof remaining. There was no hint of rain but I always felt safer with a roof over my head.

So we fell asleep with a full stomach and a reassuring roof over our heads.

The initial kick to the face when asleep does not hurt until you wake seconds later, assuming you wake. I did. Lucky me.

The first thing my eyes focused on was Sir William de Bohun, father of the bastard Jacques Stafford, who was killed by Paul. Behind him stood three of his men, two holding lamps and the other gripping Philippa around the throat in the crook of his arm. She was gagged and Kimberly was clinging to her legs with her head buried into her tunic. So much for them not following us this far out.

Sir William picked me up by the scruff of the neck and headbutted me on the nose. He had my attention.

'You and that filthy brother of yours killed God's messenger on earth, Archdeacon Rhys. Where is he?'

I shook my head and blinked my watering eyes. The last time I had contact with this man was when he knocked me unconscious when he kicked me down the stairs that morning his son was brought into Tom Brewer's tavern. He did not like me then and had not changed his opinion. 'Where's who – God?' Man, that was a dumb thing to say under the circumstances.

When I awoke again after Sir William had beaten me unconscious and pissed on me to bring me back, he asked again. This time I was less glib.

'I have no idea, Lord. He's still back at the

encampment as far as I know.' It was still dark, but by the light of the lamps, I could tell he did not believe me.

'He was seen leaving the church tent, as were you. We know you did it.' He slapped me across the face. 'Now tell me where he is.' He turned and pointed to Philippa. 'You're wearing my patience, Norman. If you don't tell me where he is I'll hang this whore in front of you, then burn the child.'

He was not joking. He knew Paul had murdered his son and with proof of what he had done to Archdeacon Rhys, Sir Hugh's support for Paul had evaporated. He had run out of friends.

'I swear to God, I have no idea where he is. He didn't leave with us, you have to believe me.'

He laughed. 'You swear to God, do you? That same god you murdered in such a hideous way? Father Rhys was God's representative on earth.' He kicked me again. 'String the wench up.'

His men rallied and a rope was brought out and flung over the only beam left in the house. Philippa was dragged over and a noose was tied around her neck. Sir William moved over and grasped the other end.

'I…I have no idea where he is, please don't harm her…' I was frantic. The terror in her eyes hurt me more than anything I had ever felt.

'You know.' He turned his head towards his watching men. 'Light a fire back there. We have a child to roast if I don't get the right answer.'

They left one of the lamps with Sir William

and moved back to gather dried wood and debris. I could not take my eyes off Philippa. She was pleading with me.

I attempted to reason with him. 'But you knew Rhys was a sadistic bastard, didn't you? What sort of Holy Man captures young boys and abuses them? How can you...' but he did not let me finish.

'Who do you think organised the round-up of his young flock? We did.' He gestured towards his men. 'I was his shepherd, the only man godly enough to listen to the archdeacon's appeals. He worked on behalf of God. Who am I to question His methods?' He crossed himself. 'How's that pyre going back there – ready for fresh meat?'

'Just about to light it, Sire.' The words had a tone of pleasure to them.

He returned his stare to me. 'Did you and your brother kill Archdeacon Rhys, yes or no?' He gripped the rope in one hand and yanked Kimberly away from Philippa with the other.

'Yes, yes, me and Paul killed Father Rhys, I admit it. Now please let them go. Your fight is with me, not them. They knew nothing about it.' I fell to my knees. 'I beg you, hang me, burn me, do whatever you want, but let these two innocences go.'

'I will be hanging and burning your useless body don't you worry, but if I don't get Paul all three of you will roast. I'll start with the kid.'

He turned around and looked towards the back

where the three men were piling kindling into a mound. There was a spark and within seconds the dry pile exploded into light.

'What the...?' Sir William stammered. Everyone jumped.

The flames from the fire lit the back wall of the darkened house. Silent people stood watching and listening. Dozens of them spread around the perimeter. The only contrast between their dark faces and black clothing was the occasional glimmer reflected from an axe or a sword.

As the flames grew, the three soldiers moved away and joined Sir William. The dark throng remained still and silent.

Sir William, although shocked, wanted to take control of the situation, and said, 'I am William de Bohun of King Edward of England's army. These are my prisoners. They are heretics and murderers and are to be punished.' He repeated the proclamation in French.

From the shadows, a lone man stepped forward. He was tall and powerfully built. He warmed his hands by the fire, rubbing them together, even though it was not cold.

'I am pleased to meet you, William.' he said in English with a strong accent. 'Am I to believe these three are responsible for killing a man of the cloth – a preacher?' I suspected he spoke in English so that I could understand.

Sir William bristled with irritation. 'Yes, Archdeacon Ryhs from Glamorgan, although I don't have to explain my actions to you…person. Go about your business and leave us be, before I…'

The man spat in the fire. 'And how did he die?'

'I will not be interrogated by the likes of you…'

He shook his head. 'I was not talking to you, William my friend, I was talking to him.' He pointed at me.

Sir William was not to be sidelined so easily. 'They made this man of God suffer in a vile and sadistic manner.' He grasped his sword handle. 'But I will be dealing with the repercussions, Sir, not you.'

'You're a feisty little fellow, aren't you?' He spoke with a fake English nobleman's accent. He looked back at me. 'Is this true, you made this man of God suffer?'

'Yes, he bloody well did…' Sir William could not help himself.

The man pulled out a crossbow from under his cloak, loaded it and shot one of Sir William's men in the eye from close range. The man screamed for a few seconds before grabbing the shaft of the bolt and pulling at it, removing the bolt and what remained of his eyeball on the barb.

Sir William and his men drew their weapons, only to be halted by dozens of crossbows aiming at them from the shadowy figures in the recesses of the room.

'I would not do that if I were you.' He walked over to the man who was writhing on the ground and ripped his throat open with a serrated knife. Sir William and his men stopped. 'Where were we? Ah, I remember – how did he die? Did he suffer as my friend William says?'

My only thoughts were to get Philippa and Kimberly out of danger. 'If I admit to this and give you the details will you let the woman and the child go free?'

'Don't start bargaining with this savage,' Sir William said.

Another crossbow bolt sunk into the belly of another of Sir William's men, who keeled over in agony and lay gasping on the floor.

'Will you never learn, William?' He pointed to the man on the floor. A dozen bolts fired by his shadowy companions buried themselves into the twitching body. He looked at me and nodded. 'You have my word.'

I told him the full story of the night Archdeacon Rhys was killed.

'Now please, let them go.'

'And you do not know where this Paul fellow is?'

'No, I swear.'

He looked at Sir William. 'And you say you aided this archdeacon in his flock gathering – I think those were your words?'

'I did as God's representative on earth asked, yes.'

'I thought as much.' He turned to his band of followers and pointed to Philippa, Kimberly and me, then commanded something in French. They moved from the shadows.

I panicked. Rushing forward, I grabbed Philippa and tried to pull Kimberly away. She fell awkwardly. Sir William lost interest in us and made for the nearest hole in the wall with his remaining man. Both had their swords drawn ready to defend themselves. They were too slow. Two big men stood in the gap and shoulder-barged them back. They fell. Within seconds the gang pounced, disarming them and ripping their clothing off. No one touched us. Sir William and his remaining man were raised high into the air on shoulders and carried to the blazing fire. They were shouting and cursing and pleading but nothing distracted them. As they reached the fire they stopped. The tall man stepped forward.

'Archdeacon Ryhs's flock were our children.' His voice showed emotion for the first time. 'You aided that man with the Devil's work and that is something that can never be forgiven.' I thought he might cry as he concluded. 'I will make you suffer as we have suffered.'

They moved the final steps and tossed them head-first into the roaring flames. I watched as Sir William, his hair ablaze, tried to stagger from the inferno only to be kicked back in. He never made a second attempt.

I looked towards the tall man. He had been joined by one of the shadowy figures. It was a woman. He put his arm around her and they kissed. It was Izelda.

CHAPTER 14

The last of the screams died but the smell of burning flesh lingered. I moved to help Philippa remove her gag and make sure Kimberly was all right. She was not. She was lying on the floor crying and holding her arm. Philippa took the noose from her neck and joined us, helping her up and clutching her to her body. Kimberly screamed in more pain. She released her and we looked at the arm she was holding and realised it was broken. It hung at right angles below the elbow.

The tall man walked over with Izelda and studied her arm.

'We must splint that before you try to move her.' He had compassion on his face which was a marked difference from how he had enjoyed watching Sir William and his soldier die in the flames. He shouted something in French and a middle-aged man approached. They spoke for a few seconds before the man came to us. 'He is a barber and will help the girl.' He looked at the concern on Philippa's face. 'You can trust him – English soldiers have given him much practice.'

The barber spoke gently to Kimberly who was

crying.

Philippa was stroking her hair and trying not to cry herself. 'Do what the nice man says.'

He took the weight of the broken arm and led her over to a section of wall that was the right height to sit on and sat her down, speaking in French all the while. Although she was in pain she allowed herself to be guided.

The barber shouted instructions and Izelda ran over with a couple of straight lengths of wood and a thin rope. She looked at me but gave no indication of recognition.

The barber spoke to Izelda. She translated. 'He says he needs you to hold her tight and don't let go until he says.'

I looked at Philippa. She was in pieces, tears running down her face. 'I'll do this,' I said, moving to Kimberly's side.

She nodded.

'He is a good man and knows what he's doing,' Izelda said. 'He will be quick.'

I started to speak to Kimberly, saying anything that might comfort her, but she looked pale with fright and pain. I positioned my body in between her face and her arm so she could not see what was happening.

The barber started his work behind me as I carried on talking to her, trying to get her to answer simple questions. She had not fully mastered speech, but I could tell she understood what was happening. She screamed. I heard a grating of bones and she fought to escape my grasp. She kicked and shouted, and then I heard a click as the fracture was realigned.

Izelda spoke to the man in French and then said, 'The bones are set – we are close.'

I turned my head sideways and managed to witness the rope being wrapped around the splint. By now Kimberly was screaming and calling for her mother. The man spoke again and stood up from his kneeling position and walked away.

Philippa rushed over and took her in her arms, rocking her backwards and forward and singing a lullaby.

*

We were taken to the group's campsite a short distance away. There was household furniture scattered about the site and we sat close to a fire that had a large pot hanging above it. Philippa, with Kimberly on her lap in a high-backed chair, continued to give comfort whilst an old woman fussed over them both, making silly faces at Kimberly and offering us ale.

'My name is Henri and this is my woman, Izelda,' the tall man said, putting his arm around her shoulder. He gave a sweeping gesture with the other. 'And this is where we have been forced to live. All our houses have been burned and you are sitting on the only piece of furniture I managed to salvage.' I looked toward the floor but said nothing. 'Be sure, if you had not killed that pig of a priest you would be roasting in hell too.' I could tell he was angry but he held it under control.

'I am Ailred Norman and this is my wife Philippa, and our child, Kimberly. Thank you so much for the kindness you've shown us.' I looked at Izelda. She stared back expressionless. I understood – we had never met. I was going to apologise for the hurt and destruction we had brought to their country but thought better of it. It would sound empty.

'Well, Ailred Norman, it is good to meet you,' Izelda said, looking at Philippa and Kimberly. 'You have a lovely family. Many of us have lost loved ones to the war and that devil calling himself an archdeacon. You are lucky we found you before some of the other groups camped out in the region. You are welcome to stay with us as long as you want...' She looked towards Henri who nodded his head, '...and it will take a few weeks for the little one's arm to heal enough to move on.'

'Thank you. We will only stay until then, after that, we'll be looking to find a boat home to England.'

Henri sat back and leaned against a tree, swigging his ale. 'I have a cousin who owns a fishing boat. He lives in Calais, but he has suffered like the rest of us. You will need to pay him good money if you want his help.'

I felt the lining of my tunic and checked

the gold Ecu coin I had looted from a dead Frenchman at Sluys was still sewn into it. It was. 'I have money,' I said, hoping no one would ask how I acquired it. They did not.

Henri finished his drink and got up, helping Izelda to her feet. 'We must sleep now, it is late. I wish I could have met your brother, the one who punished the archdeacon. I would have enjoyed hearing how he suffered.'

I laughed. 'You must be the only person in France to have said that. Most people curse the day they met him.' I bade them goodnight.

'You can sleep over there,' Henri said, pointing to a flimsy-looking tent. 'I will ask Maurice to check in on you later. He has more herbs that will take the pain away from the little girl when it comes back.'

Maurice, the barber who had treated Kimberly's broken bones, had managed to persuade her to swallow some powder earlier which had a calming effect, although she was still in pain.

The rest of that night was a blur. We were tired but the sight and sounds of Kimberly's suffering meant we did not sleep. Maurice came and went and it was frustrating that we could not converse with him and ask questions. In the short periods she slept, Philippa and I chatted. We had been lucky until now but we were not safe. Sir William and his men would soon be missed and just about everyone in France wanted us dead.

'If Henri's cousin's boat is in Calais, how are we going to get there safely – someone's bound to realise we're English?' I mused. 'Maybe he could pick us up from Sluys, at least they still tolerate us there?' There were more questions than answers.

We agreed it was not worth thinking too far ahead, the only thing that mattered was getting Kimberly better. I cuddled up to Philippa.

'You introduced me as your wife back there, Al. Are you trying to tell me something, or maybe ask me something?' She laughed at my worried expression. 'It has a nice ring to it, Mrs Norman.'

She looked at me and frowned.

'What?' I asked.

'That Izelda woman – did you notice the way she looks at you?'

I gulped. 'No!' There was more denial in my response than necessary.

'I did. She's a beautiful woman. I hope Henri doesn't see what I saw – he might be the jealous type.'

I scoffed. 'I would have noticed something like that, besides, I've only just met her. You're imagining things.'

She kissed me. 'Luckily I'm not the possessive type – I'd just kill her and then cut your balls off.'

That was reassuring.

We fell asleep for what seemed like five seconds before the sound of Kimberly's pain woke us.

*

Children are resilient – at least this one is. After three days she had stopped complaining and decided to get on with life. She was still taking Maurice's powder mixed into her diluted ale but things were looking hopeful. The arm looked straight. Well, straight enough. I came to the embarrassing conclusion that she made less of a fuss than when my hand had been stabbed by Philippa's brother, Richard.

'She whines less than when Richard skewered your hand with the pitchfork,' Philippa laughed. I could always count on her to read my mind. At least she was worrying less.

In those three days we were given food and accommodation, and Kimberly was treated well. I did not know how to repay them for their kindness. I was to find out.

About a week later when the girls were sleeping on a warm afternoon, I went for a walk. Henri had advised us not to go far from the site but I had no intentions of doing so. As I walked by the nearby stream that served us with fresh water, I looked across to the meadow on the opposite side. There were the remains of a mansion. It must have been spectacular in its heyday. It had been designed to replicate a castle, with turrets and battlements. Lush pasture land surrounded what remained of farm buildings and barns nearby. All had been burned out.

'That was Henri's home once.' I jumped. It was

Izelda. I had not spoken to her since we had arrived. She was wearing a long red gown that hugged her body and had her hair tied back. I had forgotten how beautiful she was. 'You English burned it down and killed his wife.' I looked at her but could think of nothing to say. 'The soldiers took his two sons for the archdeacon. He was a powerful lord once with a wonderful future, but they took it away.' She paused for a few seconds and her serious face dropped. She walked to me and squeezed my hand. 'It is good to see you again, Ailred.'

I smiled and turned to check no one was watching, then embraced her. 'I didn't half miss you,' I whisper into her ear. It was heartfelt and I could not stop myself.

She returned the passion and then stood back. 'That was then, this is now. We must continue to be strangers. Philippa is as nice as you said she was and the girl is a little fighter. You are both lucky to have each other. We must not destroy what we now have. Henri is a fine man but gets jealous, so beware. He is good for me.'

'You always manage to adapt to your surroundings. That was one of the things I loved about you.'

She stopped me with a stern expression. 'You must never talk of love. We were never in love, just lovers – there is a difference.'

'It was a lovely building once.' Henri walked towards us down the gravelled riverbed to where we stood close to the water. He had been too far away to hear our conversation.

‘Izelda was telling me how you once owned all this area and the mansion.’

He shrugged. ‘I did. It was a beautiful place for my family to grow up.' He pointed. 'I owned the land from the hills over there to the forests in the north.'

I tried desperately to think of something sympathetic to say, but as usual, other words came out. ‘Did you find your sons?’ I know, not great. I felt Izelda’s posture slump.

‘I found their bodies dumped on the outskirts of Tournai.’ He was finding it difficult to speak. They had been…’ he could not continue. Izelda put an arm around him and started to lead him away but he stopped. ‘Your free days are over. You will be joining us on our next reconnoitre.’ He looked at Izelda as if the coming sentence was aimed at her too. 'The truce between King Philip and King Edward has been agreed. The English army is breaking camp and marching home towards Sluys. It is time for payback.’ He looked at me hard. ‘That will be your payment to us.’

I returned to the tent. Kimberly was still sleeping whilst Philippa was outside rinsing through some of our clothing. She saw my face and asked, 'What's wrong?' She knew me too well.

'King Edward is leaving France and going home.'

'That's a good thing, isn't it?' She looked confused.

'Henri wants me to help attack our own soldiers.' I looked around the camp. There were about fifty people in total, men and women. 'What can this number do to an army – they'll be destroyed?'

Luckily Philippa was on hand with a brain. 'They won't all go home as one big army. They'd broken into factions when we were with them, so by the time they dismantle the camp and move off they'll travel in smaller groups. He'll ambush the ones he thinks he can beat.'

'I was thinking the same.'

'Of course you were, Al.' She tapped my head and made a knocking sound with her tongue.

An hour later Henri came to me carrying a war bow and a quiver of arrows. I got excited. I had not had a chance to practice for weeks and the calluses on my fingers were turning soft.

'You will need this to kill Englishmen.'

His words dampened my enthusiasm. I took it from him. It was a lovely bow, unstrung and looked to be made of Italian yew.

'Have you not tried it?' I asked as he handed me the hemp string.

He looked embarrassed. 'No, I have no use for one. Crossbows are better.'

I started to string it by attaching the hemp to one end, bending the bow around my body and attaching the other end of the string to the top. It was a powerful bow. He was fascinated. I handed it to him. 'Have a go.' I realised he did not have the knowledge to string it, that's why he looked embarrassed.

He took it and tried pulling the string to his ear. He managed halfway. He was a powerful man but however hard he tried he could not draw it. And that was without an arrow. I could have laughed but knew better. This was not a man to ridicule.

'Ha ha, do you think you're an archer or something, you weakling.'

Paul never did learn when to keep his mouth shut.

*

I sat next to Paul on the grassy hillock. His face was black and blue from where Henri's followers had beaten him into submission whilst subduing him. I had convinced Henri he was my brother but I could tell he had taken an instant dislike to him. Paul was easy to dislike. It must be the first time someone's life has been saved because they murdered a man of God. If it had been anyone other than Archdeacon Rhys, Paul would have been long dead.

Henri had interrogated him about the truce and the army's movements but Paul knew little as he had fled the siege straight after the murder of Father Rhys. Sir Hugh had turned his back on him. He believed Paul had aided me in the murder. Killing soldiers was one thing but supporting the murder of God's representatives saw your soul dragged to hell.

'He thinks I killed the archdeacon with you,' Paul said lying back. 'That's what stopped Henri from killing me. He even thanked me!' He moved his head up and rested on his elbows. 'I wasn't about to tell him I had nothing to do with it.'

I shook my head and frowned. 'But you did kill Father Rhys.'

He laughed. 'If you say so. And I suppose I killed this Blodwen girl in Cardiff too?' He shook his head and lay back down, 'If it stops me from getting killed by these crazy Frenchmen you can tell them I killed Jesus Christ for all care.'

I had no idea if he believed his words. He worried me.

Philippa walked over. I had not had a chance to warn Paul about Izelda, and how I needed to keep our previous relationship a secret.

'Hello, Paul.' She spoke with a regretful tone and did not try to hide it.

'Hi, sweetie.' Paul did not look up or show any interest. 'What's her name again, Al?'

'You can ask me yourself, I'm only ten feet away.'

'Her name is Philippa – you know it is.' It was easier to intermediate.

'That's a nice name, I hope she cooks well.'

'He's only just arrived and you're dancing to his tune, Ailred. You're a fuckin' puppet sometimes.' She stormed off back towards the tent.

'I liked her,' he said.

I gave him a rundown of everything that had happened and the situation with Izelda. He promised not to dispel the illusion but did not seem to know who Izelda was.

'So he wants us to attack our own men?' Paul sat up and took an interest in what I was saying for the first time.

'Yes, it's the cost of saving Kimberly. As I said, she could have died.'

'Kimberly? Who's she then?'

'I've spent the last half hour telling you about her and...' He looked at me with vacant eyes. 'You haven't heard a word I've said, have you?'

He laughed. It had a shrill tone. He looked about and bade me come closer. 'I think he wants us to kill our own men, but don't tell anyone.'

It was the beginning.

CHAPTER 15

Brother Michael has begun turning up to our sessions without robes. That is not to say he is naked, although I have not finished this story so things may change. I am sure there must be a vow governing garment protocol. I have never heard a member of the church swear before, but as I said – he is no ordinary monk. He also has theories concerning parts of my story he shares over strong ale in the darkened tavern across the street. I begin to listen to him as much as he listens to me.

*

It was not long before King Edward's army filed through the area we were camped in. It was a long march to Sluys. Day after day we watched from the surrounding slopes, Henri scanning and looking for weakness. I had asked Philippa if she wanted to join the exodus as it would be safer for her and Kimberly to travel home with the bulk of the army but she had declined. Paul and I had no such option.

'Kimberly is young and her arm is healing well. We'll be safer with you and these French people than travelling with those crazy soldiers.

I shudder to think of the carnage they'll bring en route. I want no part of it.'

She was right. She always was.

Again, the English raiding parties scoured the towns and homesteads looking for food and plunder but found none. It had already been picked over. There were few people left to kill and no reason to kill them but they still did.

I had spoken to Paul over the intervening days about our part in any ambushes. Henri had made clear his expectations. We were to kill Englishmen. It was that or be killed ourselves. I do not think he would have harmed Philippa or Kimberly but I was not willing to take that risk. We agreed.

In our alone time, things were different. I could not bring myself to kill my fellow countrymen, regardless of their intention to hang us for the murder of Father Rhys. I had spent months with these men battling across France and Flanders. Many had died and I felt a close bond. There was no way I would kill.

We would join with any ambush but stay neutral. No one would be watching us in the heat of battle. Once the army had passed through and left his country we expected Henri to return to his land and rebuild his life with Izelda. He had agreed to grant us safe passage to Calais and would ask his cousin to help us return to England at a price. I had it planned. My plan was Philippa's plan.

Paul agreed.

The army stayed consistent with their formation. Henri became frustrated as they never deviated or splintered. He captured and killed several small raiding parties and showed great pleasure and no mercy, but the army was better disciplined. They knew the dangers and stayed close. The commanders still commanded well.

Then one day when Henri had almost given up, he noticed a small group at the back. They lagged far behind the army as if they did not want to be associated with them. I had hoped we would not get the opportunity to enact Henri's plan, but it was not to be.

He gathered us together. He had rallied a few local men to join his venture but had lost many others as their anger lapsed. Hatred is difficult to hold onto for some. People had wanted to start new lives now the English were leaving. There were a few skilled fighters like Paul and me but peasants with nothing to lose made up the bulk. Crossbows were their prime weapon as I had witnessed first-hand but I knew battles were never won with arrows alone.

We stayed in the shadows of the woods lining the wide path the army followed. Dust rose from the thousands of feet that marched past, giving every soldier a persistent cough. They were hacking their way from Tournai to England. I was close enough to see faces in the ranks, people

I knew and had fought with.

And then silence. I looked to my right and saw the small group of wayward troops hundreds of paces behind. They were singing as a choir, their songs becoming louder as they approached. They were Welsh hymns from the valleys.

I looked at Paul. He looked confused. I pulled him aside and whispered into his ear. 'Remember, this is not our fight. Do not get involved.'

'I know, you don't have to keep telling me. I'm not a child.'

We moved back into position. No one noticed, all eyes fixed ahead.

Henri was closer to the path with his more seasoned warriors, his crossbowmen spread out along the fringes on both sides. He had left the war bow and arrows with me over the preceding days and I had practised. I felt like a soldier again. Paul had his sword returned and he held it in a tight fist, his eyes set on the road.

As the Welsh archers drew level I saw my once friends Gareth and Dafyyd singing together at the front.

Paul started to edge forward. I gripped his tunic and tried to pull him back but he would not stop. He drew level with Henri who put his arm across his chest and gestured that he wait for the signal. Still Paul moved forward, Henri grabbing him by the shoulder and pulling him backwards. Paul looked straight ahead. He was looking at

Gareth, the man who had vowed to kill him. I knew what was coming.

He remained silent. He was always dangerous in that state. Shaking himself from Henri's grasp he broke cover and ran into the Welsh, his sword swinging and thrusting, hacking anyone who got in his way. His main target was Gareth but there were plenty to be killed in between. So he killed. They wore no armour and so had little protection from Paul's savagery. Chests were ripped open and heads cleaved from their bodies. He had killed half a dozen before the men from Glamorgan managed to arm themselves and by then the French assault was no surprise. Henri ran forward with his followers as the crossbowmen loosed. It was the only round they had time to fire as by the time they reloaded men were fighting hand-to-hand. I stood back and watched. Paul had not listened to a word I said. He was in the thick of the fighting, his face blank, his brutality frightening. He killed and killed. Men would hold an arm up to fend off a blow or beg for mercy only to have it cut to the bone. He hacked into faces and gouged out eyes and when his sword was buried into a man's rib cage, I saw him bend forward and rip his nose from his face with his teeth.

And then he reached Gareth. I was still in the woods, an arrow nocked and waiting. I stuck to our plan for what it was worth. Gareth had his sword drawn and was fighting one of Henri's better warriors. Both were skilled swordsmen but Gareth was the bigger man and as Paul reached him he cut deep into the man's neck and kicked him backwards, clearing a path to Paul. Even at my distance, I could see recognition on Gareth's face. It mixed surprise with contempt. Paul remained impassive. Gareth held a defensive stance and waited for Paul's attack. It was instant. He rushed forward and swung his sword in a wide arc but Gareth was able to parry, the impact making him wince. Paul's short seax blade was in his left hand and he brought it up towards his groin with lightning speed, but again Gareth was equal to it. Paul had left himself open. Gareth, seeing his opportunity, lunged forward striking Paul on his side. He was wearing light mail so it glanced off and winded him, causing him to step back and take stock. Gareth would not allow him time. Again, he attacked, swinging and thrusting with devastating speed and power. For the first time in my life, I saw Paul backing up. He was in trouble. All around snarling men fought to kill each other, the Welsh managing to stem the premature charge. Axes were pulled from belts in the precious extra seconds Paul had given them. Henri's crossbowmen were in turmoil. The plan was to decimate the Welsh with a massive volley of bolts and arrows and then send the fighters in to slaughter those that remained. Paul had put pay to that. They tried to pick targets but hit their own men as often as not, so ceased.

Paul and Gareth fought on. Then I saw Dafydd. He had decapitated one of Henri's best men and was behind Paul. He had his axe in both hands and was about to attack. He raised it high, ready to embed it into the back of Paul's head when I loosed. It was instinct. The arrow caught my old friend in the side of his neck and the barb exited the other side. It took a few moments before he understood what had happened. He remained standing with the axe high but did not move. He turned towards me as I stepped into the light and nocked another arrow. I have no idea if he had time to comprehend who I was and I had no time to think before sending a second arrow into his chest. Gareth hesitated. He had seen Dafydd behind Paul and waited for his death blow. That pause cost him Paul's life. He would have known the satisfaction of killing him if he had acted immediately. That hesitation was all it took for my third arrow to strike Gareth's eye. He fell backwards. Paul was straight on top of him, tearing at the face of the man who got the better of him. I do not think he could bear looking at him. When he finished most of Gareth's facial skin had been removed.

The attack had failed and Henri knew it. The Welshmen had gained the upper hand and Henri had lost half his men so called the retreat. Paul was the last to leave and he was close to being brought down by the victorious men from

Glamorgan who pushed forward to stop his exit.

We ran.

*

'I knew I should have killed you the moment I set eyes on you...' Henri had Paul pinned by the throat against a tree. We had retreated to our rendezvous and none of the English or Welsh soldiers pursued us. We were in tatters. Most of Henri's men were sitting on the floor nursing wounds. The rest had their heads in their hands. Henri released his grasp and stood back. 'Look at you, you worthless piece of shit.' Paul had a fixed stare and did not respond. 'You destroyed everything, do you understand what you've done?' Paul twisted his head at an angle and looked into Henri's eyes.

Henri gave up and walked away.

Izelda came crashing into the small clearing. 'What the hell happened? That wasn't the plan, why did Paul run into them like that…'

'Ask the crazy man,' Henri said, nodding towards Paul, 'he ruined everything. We're finished.'

She looked at Paul who remained unmoved.

'I know you.' They were the first words he had spoken since before the attack. 'You live in a barn with my brother.' His speech was slow and slurred.

Izelda looked at me with concern. He looked into the sky and walked away.

'What's that idiot talking about?' Henri said,

looking towards Izelda and Me. 'Why are you two looking at each other like that?'

Passions were running high and Izelda needed to calm the situation. 'Can't you see the man's crazy, Henri? Why else would he do what he did? He needs help.'

'He needs putting down like a dog,' he replied but the fight had left Henri. I could see in his eyes that he knew his time avenging his wife and sons was finished. I left and went in search of Paul. He was easy to find. He was sitting on a fallen tree and staring at the ground.

'Are you all right?'

He looked up. 'Why am I cut?' He showed me a gash on his right hand where a sword had glanced off his handle guard.

'You were in a fight, don't you remember?'

He studied me hard. 'Was I? When?'

'We just retreated from it. We were beaten back by the Welsh archers. Do you not remember?'

'Was that today? I remember killing that Welshman Gareth who wanted to kill me. I needed to get him before he came for me.'

That surprised me. 'You remember his name but don't remember you just killed him moments ago?'

He put his head in his hands. 'I don't know what's going on. I remember some things but not others. Voices in my head tell me to do things – and that noise...' He started to beat his head with his hands and I stepped forward and stopped him. He looked at me. 'Can't you hear it?'

His eyes pleaded with me. He looked sad. I had not seen him look like this since we were children.

I heard footsteps and Izelda joined us. She looked concerned.

'Right, you two need to leave now. Henri is asking questions about you and me after what your brother said.' She spoke as though he was not there. 'He is not stupid. I will calm him and we will go back to his lands and begin a new life.' She looked at Paul for the first time. 'He will expose us. You need to take him as far away as possible.'

'Who are you?' Paul asked.

She looked at me. 'You need to get to Calais and find a man called Guillaume. He is Henri's cousin and owns a boat called the Le Roi. If you pay him enough money he might take you back to England.' She turned and went to walk away as Philippa joined us holding Kimberly's good hand.

'What the hell happened...?' She looked at Izelda and saw how serious her face was.

'We have to leave,' I said. 'Henri will kill us if we stay.' I looked at Izelda and thanked her with my eyes. She understood and gave me a weak smile. We both knew we would never see one another again.

She turned and left.

*

We arrived at a junction. We had been walking

north following the army, keeping a good distance behind, and were to the east of a town called Kortrijk. It had been slow progress as Kimberly had wanted to walk, showing us her newfound skill, but after a few steps needed to be carried. The army had turned northeast at this point towards Sluys. We went northwest. It would take a few days to reach Calais. Paul's mental health had improved as the trauma of battle subsided but was far from well.

'We must keep away from everyone and speak to no one – whoever they are,' Philippa said, stating the obvious. 'If they find out we're English...' She did not need to elaborate.

The journey until then had been uneventful. Paul had remained silent and Philippa and I had speculated on our plight. It was not good. She asked me about the look Izelda and I exchanged as we parted. Nothing got past her. I had dismissed it, though she knew there was something more, yet chose not to dwell on it. She knew I was hers. We talked about the difficulties of finding Henri's cousin, Guillaume, knowing there must be thousands of Frenchmen with the same name, but consoled ourselves with the fact none other would own a boat called Le Roi. And we talked about Paul.

It was late September and the first signs of autumn were everywhere. It was warm but the nights were cold. That first night was spent in the open just off the road. It was uncomfortable and if it had rained we would have been in trouble.

The next day it rained. We were in trouble. As we walked along the now muddy road we passed a few people. As had been the case the day before no one wanted to interact with us. After the devastation and hurt the English army had brought I did not blame them. The region was Flemish, not French, but the common people hated us with the same passion, regardless of the ruling gentry's support for King Edward.

We had bypassed a city called Ypers as it was risky and too close to the French border.

We trudged on. Close to a town called Poperinge, we saw a group of travelling nuns walking in the opposite direction. Paul was behind Philippa and me and we stopped speaking as they closed on us. I had Kimberly on my back and could hear her snoring in my ear. The nuns were no threat but we made a point of not speaking near anyone, irrespective of who they were. I nodded a silent greeting, as did Philippa and they returned the gesture, smiling at the sight of Kimberly. We walked on.

'Would you like a drink, Paul?' We had walked far enough ahead to be out of earshot and I took the water pouch from my belt.

There was no answer so I turned, he was not there. I looked further back and to my horror saw him speaking to the nuns. I grabbed Philippa and pointed. She let out a sigh and we hurried back.

When we got close we heard the nuns laughing. Paul was standing in the middle of them conversing in fluent French.

We stood by as they spoke. The nuns were at ease and I realised he was doing what he always did – manipulating the situation. After a short time, the nuns turned and pointed down a narrow track and were nodding their heads when Paul asked them questions. I had no idea what they were talking about. Then they left. They waved goodbye to Paul who did likewise and said something to which they all laughed.

He turned and walked in the direction they had pointed without saying a word.

I looked at Philippa. She shook her head and shrugged. We ran to catch up.

'What the hell was all that about?' I asked, grabbing him by the arm. He stopped. 'We agreed we wouldn't speak to anyone.'

'Did we?' He looked confused.

'What did you say to them? Did they know you were English?'

'They said we could stay the night at Saint Sixtus Abbey. I told them we needed shelter. It's over there.' He pointed down the path.

I did not know what to say. I looked at Philippa who raised her eyebrows, and said, 'It looks like we have a place to sleep tonight out of this rain.' She looked at Paul who looked away. 'Thank you, Paul.' She said. 'And I never thought I'd ever say that.'

He said nothing and continued. We followed.

*

The nuns at Saint Sixtus Abbey were wary. They had seen too many victims of violence to not be. We let Paul do the talking as none of them knew English and by the time he had finished the doors had been opened in welcome. We were allowed to sleep in private shelters. It was the first opportunity to spend time with Philippa and Kimberly in a solid building since she had come over with the followers. Paul was in an adjoining room.

That evening we were offered a strange-tasting food, the Flemish version of pottage I assume. It was lovely compared to ours and the nuns said it was made from mutton and flavoured with garlic. I had not tasted meat for weeks and whatever garlic was, I liked it.

That night, after Kimberly fell asleep, Philippa and I made love. I'm not sure what the rules are about having sex in a Flemish place of worship, but we did not ask. The previous time, in an English monastery, Kimberly had been the result. We hoped for a different outcome this time.

That night I needed to empty my bladder. The nuns had given directions to the reredorter before we retired for the night, so I stumbled out of our small room and went in search. I had already been earlier but in the darkness, it was difficult to find. I pushed a door and found myself in the garderobe where the nuns' linen was stored. I was just about to turn and leave when a thought occurred to me. Travelling through Flanders had been dangerous until now but the rest of the journey through France would be twice as hard. What if we were travelling with a nun – that would be safer.

I looked at the nuns' habits hanging up to dry and had an idea.

CHAPTER 16

We had few belongings in the bag when we left Henri and Izelda. We had decided to leave my bow and apart from a few essentials, we travelled with only the clothes we wore. As we left the abbey I had one more garment tucked away.

We said goodbye to the nuns at first light. They had spent the morning fussing over Kimberly, who was learning to be the centre of attention. Until now, she'd had little chance to shine. I felt sorry for her and hoped it would not be long before we settled and gave her the stability she deserved.

Paul walked ahead as we looked to find the road towards Calais. He was quiet. He had not spoken since last night. I was concerned again.

I stopped and pulled Philippa aside. 'Look what I found.'

I opened the bag and pulled out the nun's habit. I had also found a vail and coif.

'You stole from an abbey?' she said and gave me a stern look. 'You'll roast in hell, Ailred Norman.'

There was no one about so I gave her the clothing and told her to put it on. I say, 'told her' but you do not tell Philippa to do anything.

I suggested. 'You'll make a great nun and would give us a chance to...'

'I get the idea, Ailred, I'm not stupid!'

She went behind a bush at the side of the road and reappeared moments later. I am not sure if this is appropriate, but as soon as I saw her dressed as a nun I wanted to take her back behind the bushes and have sex with her. There must be something wrong with me. Brother Michael has just assured me he gets the same urges these days. I think that says more about him than me. Now I come to think of it, the parchment containing the description of Philippa and me making love in the monastery often goes missing when he is around.

I digress.

'You make a great nun, Philippa.'

Kimberly was staring at her and laughing.

'It feels strange,' she said. 'It takes me back to the days when I was a novice at Tonebricge.'

I had forgotten about that. If anyone could pull off being a nun, it was her.

'Hold on, Paul,' I called. 'We have a new companion.'

He stopped and turned around, waiting for us to catch up.

'Greetings, Sister.'

I smiled at his joke.

He looked at me. 'Is she coming with us?'

My smile dropped.

He continued walking.

*

We crossed the border into France. Sister Philippa's appearance was a godsend. Passing travellers treated us to food and drink and she gave them blessings in return. I had told Paul she was a Scottish nun returning from her Via Francigena pilgrimage to Rome. He believed it without question, never once asking where Philippa was. I asked Paul to explain that story to any French speakers who asked and they would assume we, too, were Scottish. Kimberly's arm was now free from the splint and she had full use of her hand with only a minor bend in her bone.

Things were looking up.

We could have sought sanctuary at another abbey or monastery that night but thought it best not to. Genuine nuns or monks might have seen through our deceit. We decided to spend the night under the stars instead. We calculated it would only be one more day until we reached Calais, so another night in the open would be our last. It had stopped raining overnight and the day had been warm. We found a suitable spot away from the road and settled down.

There was a stream nearby so I took Kimberly for a walk to gather drinking water. When we returned, Paul was kneeling in front of Philippa with his hands clenched in prayer. He was speaking and she was listening.

She looked up as I approached and gestured with her head to stay away. I nodded and

Kimberly and I went back to the stream to race sticks in the fast-flowing current. She beat me, but I let her win. I could have won. Her sticks were better than mine.

When we returned Paul was seated near the fire and Philippa, still in costume, was pacing backwards and forwards. She saw me and when I reached her she pulled me aside.

'What?' I asked. I could tell she was troubled.

'Paul was confessing to me.'

I shook my head. 'He believes you're a nun, doesn't he?'

'He does.' She went silent.

'What?'

'I'm not sure I should tell you some of the things he confessed.'

I laughed. 'You do know you're not a real nun, don't you? The sacramental seal doesn't apply here!'

'I didn't mean it like that. There are things that you don't know about him – things he has been keeping to himself all his life. Some of them explain, well, things.'

I did not know what to think. I thought I knew everything there was to know about him as a child. I found myself jealous. 'What do you know that I don't, then? How do you know I don't know? I bet it's something I know but...'

She cut me short. 'Your uncle Peter raped and beat him most days when he stayed with you as a child.' I stared at her wide-eyed but said nothing.

I could find no words. 'Your father knew about it but let it happen because he paid your father rent.' I sat down on the grass. There was a long period of silence. Paul was sitting humming to himself by the fire and Kimberly ran around in circles flapping her arms, trying to take off. 'I think he has taken too many blows to the head now.' She continued. 'He is damaged. Some of the things he said frightened me. He sees angels.'

I looked across and saw Paul in a different light.

We needed to get him home to England.

*

The next day we reached Calais. It was huge – far larger than I anticipated. The final leg of the journey followed a similar pattern – Paul muttering to himself whilst Philippa the nun gained access to food and unquestioned entry to the walled city. We had a few coins to spend and the gold Ecu was once again stitched into my tunic. That would be our means to travel home. But we needed to find Henri's cousin, Guillaume.

'The only way we're going to find him is to find the boat.' Philippa said as we dodged between the horses and people scurrying around the city. It was market day so the streets were filled with animals being herded from one place to another. French peddlers shouted and customers haggled. It was a scene I had seen in dozens of towns and cities but no two places were ever the same. 'If we find Le Roi we find Guillaume,' she concluded.

Even I understood that. So we searched.

By nightfall, we had checked every boat in the harbour. We did not find it. Some boats did not have names at all, and some were ships. I asked Philippa what the difference was and she told me to ask a sailor, not a nun. Paul allowed himself to be led. At least he was not fighting anyone. We asked him to speak on our behalf if we needed to interact. He did, although his speech was slower and we had to prompt him mid-sentence.

Having given up on our search for the boat, we sat on the long low wall overlooking the narrow inlet that connected the harbour to the open sea. The harbour was designed to allow maximum space for ships to load and unload and curved around the city. It also acted as a wide saltwater moat on the northernmost side of the city. Everywhere smelled of fish. Seagulls in their thousands swooped and scavenged for discarded entrails. As the sun set to our left, I watched as the last of the fishing boats sailed into the quay.

'We'll have to think about finding accommodation for the night,' I said, shooing a gull away from where it tried to peck at crab legs by my feet.

'I was hoping to avoid too much contact here,' Philippa said, 'but I suppose we have no choice.'

'Is there not a convent or something nearby, Sister?' Paul asked.

'No, my child, we will have to...'

'LOOK!' I pointed towards the final boat as it

readied itself to moor. A young man jumped off holding a coiled rope as it drew close and he pulled hard, dragging the boat into the quayside. Securing the front to a large iron peg sunk into the ground, he moved to the back where an older man threw him another rope. He pulled the back in and tied it off. I looked at Philippa as she read the name painted in red writing on the boat's side.

'I think we just found, Guillaume,' she said.

We stayed watching for a while. There were three men on board and they scurried around unloading their day's catch. The gulls around us lost interest in crab legs and hovered over them squawking and diving wherever they had the chance. They had baskets of fish which they hauled onto the quayside and lined up. It had been a good day's work. We were about to go and speak to them when two men in a cart trundled down the harbour to meet them. They jumped off and greeted the older fisherman with a handshake. Together they inspected the catch and stood haggling for a while before shaking hands and heaving the baskets onto the cart. Money was exchanged and the cart turned and left.

We got up and walked towards the boat.

'Just say what I ask you to say please, Paul.' I said as we approached.

'Good afternoon Sir, are you by chance Guillaume, cousin of Henri?' Paul translated.

The older of the three looked up and smiled. That was a good start. He answered.

'Oh, good. Is it possible we could have a few moments of your time, please? Your cousin Henri says you are a kind and understanding man and speaks well of you.' That was not true but I thought it might help.

After Paul's translation, he again smiled and spoke to the two younger men sending them on their way. They looked happy to avoid cleaning the netting and left in a hurry.

I asked Paul to explain our situation, telling him about Sister Philippa's pilgrimage to Rome and our wish to travel across the channel to that dreadful country of England en route to our beloved Scotland. We assured him we could pay a gold Ecu for his services, even though I thought that much overpriced, and Henri had vouched for our honesty.

I have never met a happier man in my life! He agreed straight away. I scowled at Philippa who had told me not to haggle. She stuck her tongue out at me when he was not looking. Very adult. He said we could sleep on his boat that night if we helped him swab it down, whatever that meant. We also had to do all the chores his companions would have done. We agreed.

Two hours later my back ached and my hands were raw. I was not happy. It was dark, but we had an oil lamp to see by. The man, Guillaume, left us after showing us where he kept blankets and some dried food and water. He would return first thing with his companions and take us across the channel, weather permitting.

'What a lovely man,' I said as we looked over the boat. I cannot say too much about it as I have no idea what parts of it were called, but it was big and had a sail – oh, and a steering rudder at the back.

'Yes, he seems different from Henri.' Philippa said, passing the blankets around. 'Seems trustworthy. If anyone can get us home it's him.'

Before we slept, Paul asked Philippa to hear confession again. They went into the small area below the deck. A short while later Philippa emerged shaking her head. 'Paul's going to sleep down there,' she said.

'What did he confess?'

'I'll let you know if I ever need to.'

*

I slept with my tunic on and the coin stitched inside. Guillaume arrived early with his two companions. He introduced them as his sons, and they shook our hands with vice-like grips. They were in their twenties with rugged weather-beaten faces like their father's.

'Would you like to see the money?' Paul translated for me, but he said not to worry as Sister Philippa was a woman for God. All three wore crosses around their necks and would often look at Philippa and kiss them. They were devout men. 'It is our solemn duty to transport His representative on earth to her sacred home.'

I almost felt guilty.

There were four oars on board and after preparing the sails Guillaume asked Paul to sit next to him on one side of the boat. His sons sat the other. Paul looked confused. Guillaume showed him the oars and with calming words, together they rowed out of the still waters and into the choppy sea beyond. Once there they pulled in the oars, raised the sail, and the boat leaned to one side as the wind caught it, causing the mast to creak.

Guillaume laughed at my nervous expression. 'Do not worry, land boy, this is all normal.' Paul's translation assured me. I began to enjoy myself.

*

Paul and I were leaning over the rim at the front of the boat, the hull I think it's called. The wind was gusting, waves showing white horses across their tops, the resultant foam catching the breeze and blowing into our faces. Paul was mesmerised. I am not sure he remembered being on the ship that took him from England to the Battle of Sluys. In his mind, this was his first seaward trip. He was talking to himself in French. Then I heard a different French voice behind us. I turned. Paul remained forward-facing, muttering to himself.

I was faced by the two sons. One held a boathook and the other an axe. Their faces were serious and behind stood Guillaume with

Philippa grasped around the neck with his hand over her mouth. He was smiling and spoke in French, nodding towards me.

'Où est l'argent?'

'Paul!' He remained staring into the distance. 'PAUL – I think these gentlemen want to know where the money is.' He stopped mumbling and turned his head towards me. 'Do you understand?'

He looked at them. His face continued to show no emotion.

Guillaume squeezed Philippa's neck tighter and I heard her begin to choke.

Kimberly, who had been in the small cabin below deck sleeping, appeared and started to climb clumsily up the steps, unaware of the danger.

'Où est l'argent?' Guillaume repeated.

'Where is the money?' Paul translated, although by that time I understood.

I waved my arms and gestured that he eased his hold on Philippa. 'Tell him I'll get the money – it's in my tunic.'

Paul translated in a distant voice and Guillaume relaxed a little.

It did not take me long to rip the gold Ecu coin from the lining. The son with the axe stepped forward and grabbed it from me. He smiled and passed it to his brother who did likewise.

'Donnez-le ici.' Guillaume barked and released Philippa, snatching the coin from his son.

Philippa bent down and scooped Kimberly into her arms and cuddled her.

Guillaume put the coin in his pocket, grabbed Phillippa again, and threw Kimberly to one side. Philippa pleaded with him and tried to reach her daughter only to be flung down the steps into the cabin.

The two sons laughed and looked back at us before closing in together to form a barrier.

One of the brothers made babbling noises and pointed to Paul. He stuck his tongue out and pretended to dribble. Paul smiled back.

Kimberly started to cry and the brothers looked across at her. It was the distraction I was waiting for. It was now or we were all dead.

I dived forward onto both, knocking them backwards, my mind not thinking beyond that initial moment. What I do remember thinking was I hope Paul's instinct was still inside him somewhere.

I got my answer. He erupted.

As I grappled with the man with the axe, Paul was already upon the other brother. They were strong. I was having trouble controlling my opponent as he tried to release his arm to swing the axe. I had him lying on his back with me on top. I had no idea how Paul was coping with the other man. Kimberly was screaming, her high-pitched wail cutting through the violence. I thought I had my man subdued but I underestimated his strength. The next thing I knew he had kicked me backwards with both feet and had reversed our positions. Now he was on top of me and it would only be a matter of time before he freed his arm enough to bring the axe down. I panicked. The initial adrenaline had run its course and reality set in. This man was bigger and stronger and was trying to kill me. I was scared.

He leaned in closer, talking in French to himself. I could smell his breath, his spittle spraying my face. It smelled of the French pottage that I liked. As my final reserves of strength gave out he headbutted me on the bridge of my nose. I saw stars and heard a swirling sound inside my head. My hands lost control of his arm. He knelt on top of me, victorious. Using his left hand to pin my throat to the boat's floor he held the axe above my head.

He grinned at my helplessness. That hesitation was another example of a wasted opportunity. It is a lesson I have learned at other people's expense. Thank God.

A boathook gaffed him. It entered his neck and appeared from his mouth as he was dragged off me, blood pouring all over my face. I moved my body onto my elbows so I could see what was happening. Paul was dragging the man across the deck using the hook through his neck. The man was screaming and kicking, still trying to thrash with his axe. After a few paces, he released his grip on the axe and tried to take the weight of his body from the hook. By the time Paul dumped him next to his unconscious brother at the rear of the boat all the fight had left him and he left a trail of smeared blood across the deck. There would be a full deck swab that evening.

But Paul had not finished. He picked the man up to waist height still using the hook. By now his neck was tearing apart and looked close to losing the head. Paul pushed him onto the rail that ran around the boat and, grabbing his legs, tipped the man over the side.

Guillaume appeared, his head poking through the cabin door to see what the commotion was. He was naked and started to clamber onto the deck. Catching the final act of Paul's unloading of his son into the sea, he shouted something in French and moved the last few steps onto the deck. Paul ran at him and jumped into the air, kicking him with both feet square in the face, whiplashing his head backwards and snapping his neck with a grotesque sound.

I ran to the cabin entrance and pushed Guillaume's twitching body to one side. Philippa was standing at the back clutching the torn nun's habit to her naked body.

Jumping down, I hugged her. 'Kimberly's fine.' I reassured her before she had time to ask.

'Thank you,' she said. I looked her up and down with concern. 'Don't worry Ailred,' she said, 'it's fine, he didn't have time to…' She moved past me and spat in Guillaume's upturned face, his eyes still wide open.

We went up onto the deck. Kimberly was sobbing and Paul was standing next to the unconscious brother towards the back of the boat. He looked frightened of Kimberly's discomfort. As Philippa helped Kimberly up and cuddled her, I joined Paul.

'We've got some rotten meat in the cabin. Do you want to help me feed the fish?'

He did not understand what I meant but helped all the same.

CHAPTER 17

Brother Michael wants more details of the deaths of Guillaume and his son. What I have given is my best recollection. Maybe I missed something, he asks. No, sorry, Brother. He seems disappointed. He also asked if Philippa and I had sex on the boat and if so I should record it for posterity. Maybe I could draw pictures.

You are beginning to worry me, Brother Michael – and stop grinning.

*

We kept the other brother alive. He was to be our sailor, assuming he awoke. Paul had damaged him but he still lived. I wondered if Paul was getting sentimental in his old age.

'We need this man alive,' I said, more to myself than Paul.

He said something in French, then spoke in English. 'Why, who is he?'

I stood back in surprise. Apart from not knowing who the man was, it was a reasoned response – the first he had given in a long while. 'We can't sail this boat, so we need him to get us home.'

'Will our father be there?'

'I'm not sure, Paul. Let's wait and see, shall we?'

I threw a bucket of water over his head and woke him. He spoke some words in French and sat up. I had Paul sitting close by holding the axe but the man did not look capable of causing problems. He glanced about and spoke to Paul.

'He wants to know where his father and brother are.'

'Did you tell him?'

'No, where are they?'

'Tell him they are dead and he will be too unless he sails us to England. I will allow him to live if he does.'

Paul translated. The man looked sad but resigned. He said he would, to which I promised to keep my word.

And I did.

*

The man did not look back as we watched him sail away. He thought we would kill him. The old Paul would have in a heartbeat, but this Paul was an empty shell and was growing worse by the minute.

As we walked up the stony beach I looked around. The sailor had offered to drop us off at Dover as that was where the majority of the English army had sailed into, but we told him to take us further down the coast. The English army was not our friend. He obliged and dropped us here, wherever here was.

'At least you still have the coin,' Philippa said as

she threw stones into the sea with Kimberly.

That was the sum total of my journey through France. It was better than nothing. We had left plenty of men buried or rotting on the battlefields so I could not complain. I pulled it out of my pocket and looked. It was smeared with dirt and blood so I rubbed it on my tunic to clean it, spitting to get the worst off. It shone. It was the only gold coin I had ever come across and had not studied it since finding it on the dead Frenchman.

'What's it worth?' Philippa asked.

'That's a good question. I have no idea.' I replaced it in my pocket. I did not want anyone to see it, although there was no one around.

Philippa picked Kimberly up as she was having difficulty walking up the shingley beach, and said, 'It's worth a lot, but how we go about spending it is a different matter.'

I tugged Paul into following us. 'How do you mean – we're rich now…aren't we?'

'We have a gold coin, yes, but how will we pay for a night's accommodation with that? No tavern will be able to give us change.'

I had not thought of that. If we could not break it into smaller coins we might as well not have it.

'We'll need to sell it I suppose.' Philippa said.

'Who's going to be able to buy a gold coin? Besides, as soon as the locals find out we're walking around with something this valuable we won't last long before…'

'Yes, yes,' she said, 'I know all that, I'm not stupid. So we'll need to find someone wealthy.'

'I didn't say you were stupid.' I kicked a stone and walked off. We had not been back on English soil for five minutes and I was sulking.

We left the beach and followed a well-used path inland. It did not take long before we were passing local people who spoke our language. It was nice to be home and my mood brightened.

An elderly couple walked past and nodded a greeting to Philippa who was still dressed as a nun. She had managed to patch up the worst of the damage to the habit after the attack.

'Afternoon, Sister,' they said together.

She made the sign of the cross and said, 'Tell me my friends, what place is this?'

They stopped. 'Why, this is Pevensey, Sister.' The man pointed in the direction from which they had come. 'The castle is about half a mile that way – you can't miss it.'

She thanked them. 'And who is lord there these days?'

They looked surprised that we did not know.' It is owned by The Duke of Lancaster, John of Gaunt, Sister.'

She blessed them and we continued. Even I understood why she asked that question. The lord would be wealthy.

A few minutes later we arrived at the boundary of the castle. It was enormous, far bigger than the one in our hometown of

Tonebricge. It was encircled by a wide moat that was fed from the marshland which covered most of the surrounding area. I later discovered it was built on the site of an existing Roman fort, the Norman builders incorporated parts of it into their structure.

We crossed the narrow causeway up to the lowered drawbridge and were met by a bored-looking guard holding a gleaming halberd.

'State your business.'

'We have come to speak to The Duke of Lancaster,' I replied with as much confidence as I could muster.

This was funny. When he stopped laughing, he said, 'Queen Philippa is staying here at the moment while King Edward is travelling home from France, would you like to chat to her too?'

I went to say that I would, but Philippa intervened. 'Forgive our forthrightness my child, but we are not asking for an audience this minute.' She put on a false laugh. 'And that's a humorous jape about our beloved queen, if I may say so.'

The guard smiled at her flattery. 'I'm afraid it is out of the question to speak to Lord Gaunt, Sister, he never holds assembly with common serfs outside prearranged council meetings. Now, be on your way.'

But Sister Philippa was not to be deterred. 'If you might relay our request I think he will have a change of heart. It is to his advantage and if he finds you were the cause of this missed opportunity he will not take kindly to it.'

He stared hard at Philippa and me. Paul stood behind us mumbling in French to himself and watching birds fly in and out of the gate tower's arrow loopholes. A look of puzzlement crossed his face. 'Where do I know you from?' Paul looked back with a blank expression. 'I swear I know you from somewhere.'

Philippa pressed her point before the guard recognised Paul. 'We have a gold Ecu we would consider bartering with Lord Gaunt.' It was enough to force his attention onto her again. 'He is interested in gold, is he not?'

The guard stopped studying Paul and laughed. ‘Who isn’t! Let me see it.'

'I have it secured in a private and personal place, Sir, and I will only retrieve it in the company of Lord Gaunt.'

The guard laughed again and called over a young squire who was walking nearby. 'Get word to the Lord that there is a nun with gold shoved up her...' He saw the look on Sister Philippa's face. '...has gold upon her person and requests an audience.'

Philippa smiled.

The squire nodded and hurried off towards the inner keep.

'Go and wait outside until I get an answer,' he said and brushed us aside to speak to a man with a mangy horse pulling a cart of loaves.

We walked back over the causeway and waited.

Hours.

'You there, Golden Nun.'

We looked over. The guard had been replaced by a younger soldier who beckoned us over. We had been sitting on a grass verge watching people come and go as Kimberly got bored and demanded continual attention. There was only a certain number of games you could play with a toddler before the novelty wore off.

The squire was standing next to the guard. 'He will see you now. Follow this boy.'

The squire smiled and nodded. 'This way, Sister.'

He led us through the courtyard and into the main entrance of the keep. It was a blustery day in late September and the wind whistled through the structure. As he opened the doors to the passageway leading into the great hall, two armed guards greeted us.

'Leave them with us,' one said, and the squire bowed and left. He looked us up and down. 'Is he simple?' He nodded towards Paul who was looking towards the ground and counting from one to ten then starting over again.

'He's my brother, Sir, and I am his carer.' It was the first time I had faced up to the reality of my situation. 'He has been injured in battle serving his King.' I was not sure that was the right thing to say but I said it anyway. Philippa looked at me and frowned.

'Where?'

'We have returned from France, Sir. We fought at the battle of Sluys and at Arques.' I did not mention Tournai.

He stared at Paul. 'Who was his Lord?'

'Lord Hugh le Despenser, Sir.'

The guard relaxed. 'Sir Hugh is a fine Lord. I had the honour of serving him when we put down the Welsh uprisings a few years back.' He looked at Paul again. 'But I will ask this man to remain out here when you are given an audience with Lord Gaunt. He does not need reminding of the unpleasant consequences of war.'

I bet he did not.

I looked at Philippa. She nodded. 'Of course, Sir, I said and turned to Paul. 'Stay here with these nice men, Paul. We will not be long.'

He looked up and said something in French. The guard led him to a stool nearby and he sat and continued counting.

The second guard stepped forward and checked me for weapons, patting me down and lifting my tunic. When he was satisfied he said, 'Follow me.' He looked at Philippa. 'And you better not be wasting the Lord's time, Sister.'

She bowed her head. 'Lead on, my child.'

He led us down the passageway and into the Great Hall. It was not called the Great Hall for nothing. The walls were covered with tapestries and paintings and it had a roaring fireplace at the far end behind the raised dais, where sat Lord John of Gaunt, Duke of Lancaster. He was sitting in a high-backed nobleman's chair with two deerhounds sprawled in front of him, our entrance causing them to look up. A servant stood by his side, impassive.

We walked across the shining floor tiles, our footsteps echoing around the high roof and its latticework of carved wooden beams.

I had never seen such grandeur.

'Approach,' he commanded. We did as we were told and I knelt before him while Philippa remained standing. 'I am told you have gold you would like to exchange?'

He was a middle-aged man wearing casual clothing. I had expected robes and gowns. He was lounging back on his chair and eating a chicken leg. He stripped the last of the meat with his teeth and threw the bone to one of the dogs who caught it midair and ran across the floor being chased by the second. He laughed to himself.

Before I could answer his question, Philippa did. 'Yes, my lord, we have a gold Ecu coin from France.'

He leaned forward on his chair and looked interested. He glanced at Philippa. 'Is it true this gold is shoved up your…?' He stopped himself. '...is it on your person?'

Philippa gave a knowing smile. 'No, Sire, that was a little white lie. My companion here has it.'

He sat back and sighed. 'That's a relief.' He fiddled with one of the rings on his fingers. 'I have yet to see one of these coins – but I have heard good things about them.' His eyes darted between the two of us. 'You have my undivided attention.'

I took it from my pocket. 'Would you like to see it?' I asked.

That got the response it deserved. 'Well, if you want to sell it to me it might be a good idea.' He shook his head.

The servant walked forward and took it from me, passing it to Lord Gaunt. He studied it, nodding to himself. He turned his head and shouted, 'HENRY, COME AND GIVE ME YOUR OPINION.'

Seconds later a well-dressed young man entered the hall from a side door at one end of the dias. He wore a gold chain around his neck and an earring in each ear. Walking across the raised wooden platform he stood next to his Lordship. 'Sire?'

Lord Gaunt passed him the coin and he examined it, turning and rubbing it between his fingers.

'It is genuine, Sire, and a lovely piece. I have only seen two such coins before and this is superior to both.' He handed it back to the Lord.

'It would seem we can do business, Sister.'

I felt a little insulted at being overlooked but said nothing.

'How much are you willing to pay for it, Lord?'

He laughed. 'Let's come straight to the point shall we, Sister – I like that in a woman of God.' He glanced at Henry. 'Shall we say one hundred pennies? I think that is more than a fair price.'

I saw Philippa's posture drop. She let out a sigh, to which Lord Gaunt looked irritated.

'I think it is worth more than that, Sire, and I think you know it,' she said, letting her annoyance get the better of her.

'A haggling nun with no manners, what is this world coming to?'

The voice came from the door where Henry had entered. We looked. There stood a tall woman in a loose green gown, hands on hips. Her hair was coiled high and fixed with gold pins on top of her head.

Lord Gaunt and Henry knelt as she walked towards us. I did likewise.

'Will you not kneel to your queen, Sister?' she asked as she drew level with Lord Gaunt.

Philippa bowed her head. 'I am a servant to God, my Queen. He is whom I pledge my life to.'

She was playing a dangerous game and I fidgeted.

'That is your choice, Sister, and I respect it. You are a woman who knows her mind.'

I let out a gasp of relief.

'Rise, people. Pretend I am not here.' She moved in front of the fire and called one of the hounds to her side, stroking its head.

'As you wish, my Queen,' Lord Gaunt said. 'Where were we?'

'You had just offered her fifty pennies, Lord Gaunt.' The Queen was far from a silent observer.

Lord Gaunt glanced at Philippa. 'Ah yes, Sister, as our Queen has so graciously reminded me, fifty pennies was my offer.'

Philippa looked from the queen to Lord Gaunt to me. She had gambled and lost. She knew it.

I bore the insult for her. 'Your Highness and Lord Gaunt are too kind. We accept and are grateful for your indulgence.'

They both smiled.

'Henry, pay these good people and...guard,' he snapped his fingers and flicked his wrist, 'escort them from the castle if you would be so kind.'

The guard moved forward and led us out. Before we knew what was happening he had reunited us with a blissful Paul and ushered us out of the castle and into the surrounding town.

*

It was not until we booked into and entered our room at The Star Inn near the castle that Philippa cried. It was the first time I had seen her in tears. It hurt.

'Don't fret, darling.'

She laughed and cried together, snot spraying over the side of my face as I hugged her. She put on a weak impression of me. 'Don't fret, darling! You've never called me that before – you sound like a love-struck teenage girl.'

I looked towards the filthy ceiling. 'Gee, thanks.'

Kimberly was fast asleep in the corner of the room on a large sack filled with straw and I could hear Paul's snoring coming from the room next to us. Since his change in personality, he would spend hours sleeping when he had the chance. I think it was another symptom.

'Don't beat yourself up,' I said.

There was a short silence and then I laughed.

She blew her nose on my shoulder. 'What's there to laugh about?'

'If you'd have let me do the talking we'd have given them the Ecu *and* owed them money too!'

That broke her gloom. She hugged me.

'Both our children are asleep,' I said, stroking her bottom through her long habit.

She sniffed and took off her coif. It was the first time I had seen her head uncovered for days and watched as she stood back and ruffled her hair into life. Her demeanour changed.

'Take that off, Norman, and let me see how much you love your nun.'

She was back. I liked it when she was in charge. I stared at her eyes as they drilled into me. She crossed herself and planted her feet apart in a powerful stance. 'Your dirty nun is waiting. She needs adulation.'

I pulled my tunic over my head and threw it onto the bed, standing naked and rigid in front of her.

She looked down at me with wide eyes. 'You show great pleasure for your woman of God – now, kneel and praise me.'

She released herself from the black habit and stood naked. I stepped forward and she placed her hands on my head and eased me to the ground in front.

I dropped to my knees and worshipped her until she was screaming for God's forgiveness.

*

I will go no further as Brother Michael has disappeared with the parchment. I had to drink a mug of wine until he returned, flushed in the face. Yes, Brother, I have to tell them that part, and yes, you must write it – you know the rules.

*

However much noise Philippa and I made neither Paul nor Kimberly woke. We were thirsty and so went downstairs to the tavern to drink. Even though we had been sold short by the Lord and Queen Philippa, we still had coinage. Enough to pay for this night and many others so drank good ale from the black barrel.

'Ain't never seen you two round 'ere before.' The landlord had just thrown a drunken customer from the premises as his son watched returned men from the war in France drink and grope the local whores.

Philippa was in an afterglow following our passionate session. My tongue ached. I'll be honest with you – I was in the afterglow. She was no different from before, although she was not dressed as a nun now.

'No, sir, we are just passing through,' she said in answer to his question. It was obvious she did not want to speak.

He spoke anyway. 'There's a nun upstairs.'

We had checked into the tavern with the man's wife, although I doubt he would have recognised Philippa even if they had spoken earlier. She looked that different without the veil.

'Is there?' I asked. I was wondering how to shut him up.

He bent into me and beckoned me closer. He had a secret to tell, that was clear. 'Have you heard of Paul Christian?'

My blood went cold. 'No, Sir.'

He looked surprised. 'He was one of the leading figures in France. Said to have attacked Arques on his own.'

I sat back. 'Can't say I've heard of him.'

Philippa jumped in. 'What about him? Sounds like a hero to me.'

He sniffed and wiped away beer spillage from the rotting wooden bar we were leaning against.

'He was, only he and his brother murdered an archdeacon outside Tournai.' He shook his head as though he was there remembering the act. 'He's due to hang. I'm told he's here with a nun and another man. One of the guards from the castle was in here a while ago. He's gone to fetch help. This Paul fella is a bit of a savage by all accounts so they'll need all the men they can muster.' He winked. 'Keep it under your hat. I'd finish that and leave if I was you – it could get nasty.'

We pushed our drinks to one side and rose. I said, 'Thanks for the warning,' and tossed a penny onto the bar. 'Keep the change.'

He nodded thanks and scooped the coin into his pocket.

We dashed upstairs.

I noticed the door to Paul's room was open. 'Get Kimberly,' I said to Philippa but need not have bothered as she was already doing so.

I stepped into Paul's room. The landlord's son was standing over Paul. He had a short knife and was holding it to Paul's throat. Paul was sitting on the edge of his bed looking at the man.

'This is my capture, now fuck off. I'm not sharing the reward.'

I played dumb. 'I can help you if you like, I don't want any money.'

He looked at me with suspicion. 'Do you know who this is?'

'No, Sir. I was just passing the room. I want to help. Is he dangerous?'

He relaxed. 'Yeah, this is Paul Christian. He murdered a man of the cloth and I'm arresting him until the Lord gets here.' He stood back from Paul, safe in the knowledge there were two of us if he tried to escape.

I awaited the inevitable violence. It did not

come. Paul did not move.

'He's a pussycat,' the man said, nudging Paul and laughing. 'I thought he was supposed to be some sort of madman.'

Any second now, I thought.

He kicked Paul in the knee. Still nothing.

This is it.

He slapped Paul hard across the face.

Now?

He lowered his hand and went to pass me the knife. 'Wait here with him.' He withheld it for a second. 'This doesn't mean you helped capture him, you understand?' I nodded and he passed the dagger to me. 'I'll go and fetch Pa.'

I moved with speed. I bent down and cajoled Paul into standing. At least he still listened to me to a degree. There was nothing else other than his clothing in the room and I had undressed him before he got into bed. I needed to slip his tunic back on. I got him to raise his arms but as soon as I reached for the tunic he dropped them again.

It was too late.

'Here he is, Pa – he ain't dangerous.'

The son and the landlord stood behind me in the doorway.

'How do you know he ain't dangerous – you should have waited for the Lord,' the landlord said. He sounded nervous and confused. He looked at me holding the knife. 'Do you know who this man is?'

'No, Sir, I just happen to be passing. Whoever

Paul Christian is, I doubt this is him.'

The son looked at me and frowned. 'You don't know who Paul Christian is but think it's not him?' I saw recognition on his face. 'You're the one he's travelling with, aren't you?' He lunged for the knife.

I had no choice. I had hoped to avoid this next scene. If Paul was not capable of defending himself, I had to. I stood back and dodged his grasp as he fell onto Paul. The landlord moved forward to help his son. I thrust the blade into the son's armpit and punctured his lung as he tried to regain balance. He let out a loud cry of pain. At that moment, Philippa entered the room and stood horrified at the door. The landlord was torn between aiding his gasping son and fleeing. He settled for the latter. Pushing Philippa to one side, he dashed towards the stairs a little way down the hallway. If he managed to get down those he would raise help. We would all hang. I tried to run after him but Philippa was in my way and I slipped on the pooling blood on the slatted wooden floor.

I heard a child's scream and a thud. I regained my feet and hurried to the door with Philippa. The landlord was lying helpless in the corridor and Kimberly was crying next to him. He had been upended by her as he ran away. He looked dazed. As Philippa scooped Kimberly into her arms I grabbed the landlord's leg and dragged him back into the room. He did not struggle. I threw him next to his wheezing son and beat him unconscious with the stool lying on the floor nearby. He would have a headache if he ever woke.

I turned to Philippa and breathed hard. 'We must get out of here fast.' I stroked Kimberly's hair as she buried her head into her mother's chest. 'You saved our lives, young lady. I owe you a drink when you're old enough.' I moved over to Paul, stepping over the still body of the son, and continued dressing him. Philippa rushed back into our room and packed what little we had, and, after shutting Paul's door, the four of us rushed down the stairs and through the back entrance of the tavern. Once outside I found a scabby horse harnessed to a cart. It was the one I had seen entering the castle earlier. I had seen the owner in the tavern earlier, drunk. It would not take long for the landlord's wife to notice her husband and son were missing and Lord Guant was en route. We needed to get as far away as possible.

We stole off into the night as fast as a scabby harnessed horse can travel.

*

By the next morning, the horse was as good as dead and we were miles away. I unharnessed the poor beast and set it free in a nearby field. It would never recover from the stress we had driven it to that night so had no reason to keep it.

'What now?' Philippa asked before I had the

chance.

'They'll come looking for us,' I replied. I had tied one of Paul's hands to a long length of rope I found and led him like a mule. He had deteriorated that much. 'We must keep moving.'

Philippa stopped. 'Yes, but where? We can't continue like this.'

I tugged Paul to a halt. 'We need to get Paul somewhere he can be looked after.' I was tired of caring for him. It had got to the point where I did everything for him. Some things were revolting and I had come to the end of my tether. Just as Kimberly had grown out of one phase of her life Paul was entering it. I am not proud of my lack of compassion.

'That costs money, Al.' Philippa started walking again.

'We have money.' I pulled out what remained of the coins we had been given for the Ecu.

Philippa sighed. She was used to my lack of forethought but it still irked her. 'He needs long-term care. That will last a few months – if that.'

I thought hard but came up with nothing. Philippa did.

'Do you remember the monk from that abbey in Wales?' she said. 'The one we met when we were going to Cardiff – what was his name?'

I shrugged. 'I have no idea.'

I do not think that surprised her.

Then her face brightened. 'Oh, I remember now – his name was Brother Rhosier and he was from Tintern Abbey!'

Again, I shrugged. 'And?'

She had that look in her eyes she got when she had a good idea. It was something I never experienced. 'Don't you remember him telling us his abbey cared for people like Paul?'

'That does ring a bell,' I replied. And it did. 'I remembered him saying it was the only abbey he knew that gave long-term care.'

I felt hope. Then guilt. I was desperate to offload my own flesh and blood. Philippa saw it, and said, 'It's the only course of action we can take.' She looked at Paul. 'We've lost him, Al. He needs more than we can give now.'

She was right. He could not look after himself and I could not expect a young mother to dedicate her life to helping me nurse him – Kimberly deserved more. I feared I might lose her. There was only one course of action left open to us. We were going to Tintern Abbey in Wales.

CHAPTER 18

Nice of you to turn up, Brother Michael. By the look of your face, you lost the fight. You never learn, do you? You are confusing the ability to get into violent confrontations with the skills to win them. And what is that smell? Please do not tell me you have been cavorting with those ladies of the night again. Oh, and one more thing – when are you going to tell me your 'exciting news'? Later? So be it.

Now, pick up that quill and set these words to parchment if you would be so kind.

*

We reached Reigate Priory a week later. It was where Philippa had given birth when we first travelled to Tintern Abbey. We had taken a slow methodical journey until then, keeping off the main thoroughfares where possible, sleeping rough and out of sight. Life had turned full circle. It had been a couple of years since we had last stepped foot inside the priory and we were worried that no one would remember us. We need not have.

'LITTLE KIMBERLY, IS THAT YOU?' An excited Prioress came over as we entered the gates. We had been admitted by one of the novice monks whom we did not recognise and who did not recognise us. The Prioress would have run to us if decorum had permitted so, that much was obvious.

Philippa beamed. 'Kimberly darling, this is who you were named after.'

Kimberly buried herself into Philippa's legs and hid her face while the two embraced. I shook her hand before hugging her. I was not sure if that was permitted, but there you go – I am sure God will forgive my informality.

She took us on a tour of the priory, greeting those who remembered us. Many did. Kimberly lost her inhibitions after a short while and revelled in her favourite pastime – being the centre of attention.

Paul was taken away and cared for by some older nuns. We appreciated the break. I asked if there was any way he could remain with them long-term but was assured they did not have the facilities or know-how to deal with someone in his condition. It was worth a try. Prioress Kimberly confirmed that Tintern Abbey was indeed the place to take him. The monks were experienced and had a good record of curing problematic souls. 'God works harder healing the mind in Tintern,' she said, but I thought him beyond help. She gave us hope.

Then, as we sat with a group of nuns in the refectory, Prioress Kimberly told us something that surprised us.

'There will be a cost for leaving your brother with the monks at Tintern.' Philippa and I looked up in surprise. It had not occurred to us that there might be. 'If he is accepted, and that's a big if, he will be required to take the vows of a monk.'

'He has to become a monk?' I asked. It did not seem possible. 'You can't just monk someone up if they don't have the calling, surely?'

Philippa shook her head in despair. 'What I think he means is, you can't bypass the Postulancy and novitiate periods and get him to take his Monastic Vows just like that, can you?'

I nodded. 'Wasn't that what I said?'

Mother Kimberly frowned. 'In most cases of course not, but in the case of the insane the closer to God they are the more chance they have of being cured. He will be dressed and treated like any other of God's chosen people. He will lead a full and spiritual life until he meets his maker and is cleansed of any sin he may have acquired until now.'

All the nuns present said, 'Amen' to that, as did we.

I baulked at the word, insane, but had to face reality. 'Can I be honest with you, Mother Kimberly?' I asked.

'Of course, My Son, I would have it no other way – speak your mind.'

'He carries a great deal of sinful baggage. He has killed, he has robbed, he has...'

But she stopped me.

'That is between Paul and his God, My Child. Do not involve yourself in that intimate relationship.'

She made me feel good about my desire to leave Paul at Tintern. She made me feel good about myself. I loved her for it.

'Did you allude that they might not take Paul at all?' Philippa asked, picking up on something she had said in passing.

'Yes, as Tintern is such a specialised abbey people come from all over to seek help.' She sighed. 'It is a sad fact that insanity is the Devil's work and he uses it on a large scale. I have heard of people travelling from far-off lands, only to be turned away.'

Philippa looked concerned, mirroring my thoughts. 'Is there a way to guarantee access, Mother?'

She finished supper and pushed the bowl away, nodding to a nearby novice to clear our table. 'I'm afraid not, although a recommendation from a senior member of the church goes a long way.'

'Would you give such advocacy, Mother Kimberly?' I asked.

'I would, and will,' she replied, 'but if you can persuade Father John de Pyrie to...'

'Father John de Pyrie!' I cut in in dismay, 'he has such a bad reputation in that part of the world – he spent years putting down the Welsh uprisings. They'll not listen to him...'

'You did not allow me to finish, Ailred,' she said, raising her finger to silence my outburst. '...if you could persuade Father John de Pyrie to have the Archbishop of York, William de la Zouche do your bidding you will have far more sway.'

That took me aback somewhat. 'Who? And why him?'

'Because, young Ailred Norman, he is staying here at the priory this very day by invitation of our own Father John de Pyrie.' She looked at me and smiled. 'You made a fine impression on him when you stayed with us before. He liked you a great deal. If you rekindle that affection he may petition the Archbishop on your behalf.'

We thanked her and after attending prayers in the great church of the Blessed Virgin and the Holy Cross, we parted company for the night.

It seemed I had some grovelling to attend to the next day.

We spent that night in the same accommodation as our previous stay. And yes Brother Michael, we made love again but I will not share the details with you on this occasion. And no, Philippa did not have another baby.

That would come as a result, nine months later.

*

The following day after breakfast, Philippa, Kimberly and I again went to church, and we only attended with the monks this time.

Father John de Pyrie and the Archbishop of York, William de la Zouche were also present.

Philippa had schooled me as to what to say but I did not have to worry.

'Ailred and Philippa Norman, it is so wonderful to see you again.' Father John walked over and shook my hand. He looked at Philippa and Kimberly and smiled. 'And oh how she's grown.'

'Yes Father, little Kimberly's shot up too.'

He looked at me quizzingly before realising I was joking and chuckled. 'You always did make me laugh, Ailred.' He gestured to the tall powerful man of the cloth who was standing back, awaiting an introduction. 'May I introduce the Archbishop of York, Father Zouche?'

I bowed low, as did Philippa, while Kimberly playfully mimicked us. Father Zouche nodded recognition and smiled at Kimberly's antics.

'I am happy to make your acquaintance,' he said in a deep guttural tone.

Father John said, 'You must tell me what you and your good lady wife and this adorable child have been up to since we last had the pleasure of your company, Ailred.' He stared at me. 'Your face says you have been through a great deal of hardship.'

'I would be honoured to tell my story to you, your grace.' I expected him to dismiss us and continue his conversation with the Archbishop, but he continued. 'I have an hour or so to spare this afternoon if that is acceptable with you. It will be like old days – and I am sure Father Zouche will be interested.'

Father Zouche nodded.

'Then I will seek you out later, Fathers. I look forward to the opportunity.' They turned to leave and we bowed again.

He hesitated. 'Oh, and don't forget to bring wine, Ailred. We always had our deepest discourse over that.'

We parted.

When we were over an earshot away, Philippa said, 'I am jealous, Ailred.'

I laughed. 'Don't worry, wife, I will put a good word in for you now I mix with powerful men.'

She was silent for a moment, giving me time to glory in my newfound position of importance. It was not every day you were invited to drink wine with a Priorer and an Archbishop.

Only Philippa could dampen that.

'Why?' She asked.

'Why what?'

'Why is he asking you to attend a meeting with the Archbishop and himself?'

'Was he? I thought he wanted a chat and be updated on our…'

'Al, think about it. I'm sure an Archbishop has no interest in an archer returned from France. He has more important things to think about.'

I slumped. 'Couldn't you have let me enjoy the moment a little longer before throwing cold water on me?'

'Nope.'

*

I found them later that afternoon. Paul was still being cared for by the nuns and we had been to visit him. They had him in the infirmary. He had been asleep most of the time, only waking once and showing no recognition towards me. It was heartbreaking.

I carried a jug of wine and met them in the empty refectory. They were sitting at a round table with three empty cups. It was drizzling outside and I took my cape off as I joined them.

'Good to see you again, Ailred,' Father John said, tapping a bench opposite them.

I sat. The looks on their faces told me this was no informal catch-up.

'Wine, Fathers?'

They both nodded and thanked me.

'It has come to our attention…' Father Zouche started.

And there it was, Philippa was right. Again.

'...it has come to our attention that you are travelling with an insane man.'

I lost my enthusiasm for the wine. 'He is an ill man, Father, yes, but still a man.'

He fell silent and waited.

I waited.

He sipped his wine.

I sipped mine.

Archbishop Zouche spoke next. 'He is Paul

Christian, murderer of Archdeacon Rhys.' I stopped drinking my wine. 'Which makes you and Philippa accomplices to that vile crime.'

I looked at Father John who would not meet my eye. It was no use denying the truth. If they wanted us hung we would have been met by soldiers by now, not sitting here drinking wine. 'You are well informed, Father.' I sat back. 'Do you know why Paul did what he did, and what Father Rhys was doing to the local boys in France – because if you did you would...'

The Archbishop swigged deep and refilled his cup. 'We do. It is why, you are speaking to us now and not hanging from the local scaffolding.' He stared at me. He had a hard face, the face of someone comfortable with violence and who had seen plenty. It is funny how you can extract such information from the positioning of a man's eyes, nose and mouth. But it's invariably correct. It was in this case.

He continued to stare. 'Are you a good archer?' he asked as I was beginning to feel uncomfortable.

'I am.'

'Do you like the Scots?'

Now that was an unexpected question. 'I don't think I ever met one, Father, so do not know.'

Father John leaned forward. 'You've met plenty of Welsh from what I hear.' He poured himself and me more wine. 'Well, the Scots are worse, if that's possible.'

I could not see where this conversation was going and Father Zouche sensed that. I wished I had Philippa there – she would have understood long before.

He came to the point. 'Father John and I have been summoned to join the defence of the north from the Scots. They have mounted an invasion.' It was the first I had heard of it and questioned the information. 'It is solid. The French have asked for help to split King Edward's priorities and weaken his army. If they attack while he is down south threatening France the King is compromised.

It made sense. 'And where does my brother and I come into this?' I should have realised but did not.

'We need all the archers and men-at-arms we can muster,' Father John said.

So that was it. 'Paul is no use to you, Your Grace. He can barely stand.'

He shook his head. 'No, Ailred, it is you I am asking. If you agree to join us we will recommend Paul's inclusion into Tintern Abbey's programme and overlook any misdemeanours committed by your brother and yourself.' He looked behind me towards where he considered Philippa and Kimberly to be waiting out of sight. 'And your wife and child are also culpable in those crimes through association.'

*

'What choice did I have?'

Philippa sat in despair. 'All I want to do is find somewhere to settle down and raise Kimberly. Is that too much to ask?'

'This will be the final obstacle,' I assured her, although I spoke without conviction.

'Of course it is. You're going to fight the Scots now – what could go wrong?'

I knew that was a trick question so did not answer.

I filled Philippa in on the last part of my interrogation.

Archbishop Zouche had told me he was travelling north with his entourage, four in total, and had introduced me to them after the meeting. They were some of the toughest-looking warriors I had seen and were staying in the monks' dormitory. Despite appearances, they were a decent enough bunch. They were knights, men-at-arms, and had not travelled to France with King Edward. I recognised one from my days back in Tonebricge. He was Sir Louis de Cliffton and I had seen him and his wife with Lord Thomas de Clare on many occasions. The King had required them and many other seasoned knights to stay in England in case of any infraction by the Scots to the north. It had been expected. He was right to do so and understood that men of this calibre leading an army would instil confidence. As an archer, I understood the value of seeing men of extreme violence by your side when your back was against the wall. King Edward recognised that importance.

Sir Louis and another knight had wives with them. The plan was to travel to Barnard Castle which was far north, further than I had ever been, and join an army being assembled by Lord Ralph Neville to oppose the rampant Scots.

They were led by the charismatic King David the Second and had invaded in early October with a substantial army of twelve thousand men, plus a few French men-at-arms. Their army was financed in part by the French as it was to both nations' advantage to see King Edward stretched on two fronts.

Philippa was disappointed. 'When do we leave?'

'First thing tomorrow. A couple of the men-at-arms want us to meet them in the town later for a drink. They've heard stories about Paul's antics and want to know if they're true.' I looked away so she could not see my face as I said, 'Oh, and the wives want to meet you. There's a tavern called the White Lion and we'll get there...'

'Hold on, Al – the wives want to meet me? Am I some sort of exhibit now– a prize pig at a fair?'

I knew it was coming. 'The knights are good men, Philippa, especially Sir Louis. I spoke to his wife the other day and I think you'd like her.'

'How do you know I'd like her?' she snapped, scrunching her face. 'I might hate her.'

'Nice face,' I laughed. 'Is there anything you can't argue about?'

She stuck her tongue out and went to hit me. 'Yes, I'll meet my new best friend – if I have to.'

'That's the spirit. You can blame me if she's the bitch from hell!'

'Don't worry about that, Mr Norman – I will. 'I'll see if one of the nuns can look after Kimberly while we're gone.'

'There'll be no shortage of volunteers,' I guessed.

I was right, she had four to keep her occupied as we left the monastery and walked the short distance to the tavern.

The two knights were already there, sitting in one corner at a large table with their wives. We walked over and I introduced Philippa to the men and they in turn did likewise with their wives.

I was right – Philippa was nattering and exchanging gossip within minutes.

I noticed the landlord looked nervous and I did not blame him as we looked like a fearsome group. Two of the men had missing fingers and one had a deep scar running down his cheek. And that was only the wounds we could see.

Philippa did what Philippa did best, and that was talk. By the end of the night, she had won both wives over and was on first-name terms with the men. I did my best but could not match her wit and creative conversational skills.

I think the landlord was happy to see us leave

at the end of the night, although these wealthy men had spent a small fortune and neither Philippa nor I were allowed to contribute.

'You were right Al, they are a decent bunch, and I got on well with the women, especially Sir Louis's wife, Lady Maud.' Philippa said as we snuggled into the palliasse, as a worn-out Kimberly slept nearby. 'It will be nice to have company on the trip.'

I closed my eyes. 'It will be safer too. No one in their right mind will attack us with these men around.'

She cuddled up next to me, moulding herself into my back. 'Nope, something tells me those men are animals.' She thought for a second before adding, 'Decent animals.'

I am sure she said lots of other things but did not hear them as I was asleep.

*

Kimberly woke us at first light as she always did. Did that girl ever sleep on? We joined the Lauds prayer service, albeit towards the end. Coming out of the church, we met Father Zouche, Father John, the knights and the two wives. The knights looked blurry-eyed after our night out but were in good spirits. They were keen to get moving.

Father Zouche had dispensed with his formal monks' clothing, as had Father John, and they were all dressed in the Archbishop of York's livery.

Father Zouche was very much in charge on this

morning, his monk's servitude surrendered to his position of commander and soldier.

'Maud, take Philippa and the child and ready them for the journey if you please.' He nodded towards the older of the four knights and waved his hand in the direction of the monks' dormitory where they had been residing. 'And Sir Louis, find Ailred here suitable livery, will you? We don't want you hacking the poor boy to pieces because you confused him with an enemy now, do we?'

Sir Louis obeyed without question. 'Follow me, Ailred.'

Philippa and Kimberly were taken away and I was kitted out. I looked the part, even if I do say so myself. I was given a sword, light mail and a snug-fitting helmet. Philippa and I would have to walk the first part of the journey as there were only horses enough for the original retinue but Father Zouche promised to purchase more when we found a suitable sale. He said I would be provided with a war bow when we joined the army that was being assembled at Barnard Castle.

And then they fetched Paul. He had been dressed. One of the nuns led him by the hand into the early morning sunlight and Sir Louis sat him on his horse. It looked like he would be walking too.

So we waved goodbye to the nuns and monks of Reigate Priory and set off. The first stop –

Tintern Abbey.

CHAPTER 19

By the time we disembarked from the ferry at Beachley after crossing the River Severn we had enough horses to carry us all. Lord Zouche, as he preferred to be called now, had made good on his promise to buy more. It had taken us three days to travel the distance, stopping only to sleep at night. He drove us hard.

'It's good to be back,' Father John said, sniffing the air. 'I can smell the Welsh and their love for me already.' He laughed.

I noticed a few Welsh passengers on the crossing take sly looks at him but put that down to curiosity. He was as much at home on his horse with a sword strapped to his waist as he was back at the priory. He was fighting for God now, as he was keen to express at every opportunity. The Welsh and the Scots were heretical and required conversion to the true faith.

Once across the river, we turned east. Father Rhosier, the monk from Tintern Abbey, had given us directions the last time Philippa and I had crossed so we relayed these to Lord Zouche.

'I don't think it's far,' I concluded as we

meandered our way along a quiet path, Paul's horse being led by one of the younger knights at the rear.

As we approached a small town we were met by a group of men carrying weapons. The eldest-looking man amongst them stepped forward, held up his hand and said, 'Pwy ydych chi a beth ydych chi eisiau?'

'He wants to know who we are and what we want,' Father John said. 'I picked up enough of the language when I was here last time, taming these savages.' He laughed. 'If they knew who I was I doubt they'd be so accommodating.' He thought hard and then picked his words in reply. 'Rydym yn deithwyr syml sy'n pasio trwodd. Nid ydym yn golygu unrhyw niwed.'

I was impressed by his pronunciation. They seemed to understand him and stood aside to let us pass. 'What did you say, Father?' I asked.

Before he could answer, the Welshman replied in his stead. 'He claims you are simple travellers passing through and mean no harm.' He stared at Father John. 'Welcome back, John Y Diafol.'

Father John touched his sword's hilt and scoured back but the man and his companions lingered, their weapons remaining by their sides.

We tapped the flanks of our horses and trotted on through the village, watched by its inhabitants.

'Stay alert,' Lord Zouche hissed.

All eyes followed Father John de Pyrie. He was

far from forgotten.

We reached the far side of the village.

'I thought we were in trouble there,' I said to Philippa who was riding on a smaller pony next to me. She had been talking to Lady Maud and the other woman most of the journey but nerves silenced them.

'Don't speak too soon, Al, they know who Father John is – did you see the hatred in their faces? They won't accept that he's just walked through their village.'

'Move the women and Paul to the front right now,' Lord Zouche commanded without raising his voice. He sensed something was brewing and wanted to shield the vulnerable amongst us with his fighting men if attacked from the rear.

We did as we were instructed but nothing happened.

We left the village and continued. After a while, the path led into a forest, tall trees cutting out the sunlight.

'If they're going to attack, it will be here,' Lord Zouche said, looking around. 'They will have organised themselves now. Dismount.' We did as we were told. Philippa and the other women stopped their mounts too, but the Lord said, 'You continue with Paul. Wait for us on the far side of the forest – we will meet you there.'

I could see Philippa looked unsure but obeyed without speaking. The Lord spoke with confidence, reassuring us.

He split us into two groups, Lord Zouche, Father John and myself on one side of the path and the other four knights on the other. We tethered the horses in the undergrowth out of sight and waited. The Lord was gambling on the group following us and attacking us here, so he was going to strike first. He said it was gut instinct.

I thought he had misjudged the situation, but it did not take long before we heard footsteps and low voices.

As they drew level to where we were hiding I saw about ten of them, all armed and smeared with warpaint. Half had war bows. Even I could work out their intended tactic – cut us down with arrows and then slaughter the remainder when we were defenceless. It might have worked too if Lord Zouche had not been so perceptive.

'NOW,' he shouted and we sprung our trap from both sides. We attacked the men without bows first. Once we killed those with swords and maces the archers would be isolated. Killing at close quarters is best left to men-at-arms, and ours were ruthless.

I sliced my first opponent down the side of his head, cutting deep and taking much of his facial skin off as the blade struck his skull and slid down to his neck. My seax dagger finished the job by opening his belly and exposing his intestines. The speed we hit them with made the difference. I looked across and watched as our other men ripped into their warriors with such venom that a couple of the archers were running away before we could tackle them. As one man ran past me, panic etched into his young face, I managed to trip him and he fell. I was on him in seconds, my sword hacking and gouging deep into his flesh, ripping holes. He screamed in pain and terror but I continued until he stopped. He would have done the same to me – that is something you have to always remember if you are to live. Those last few who stood their ground showed bravery but received no mercy, the final man standing being the leader who had recognised John the Devil. He remained defiant to the end, spitting in Father John's face before having his skull stoved in from behind by Sir Louies's spiked mace.

Only one man had escaped and it was he who Lord Zouche focused on. 'Damn, that bastard coward for running away. I hate it when we don't complete a full set.'

We looked at one another and the carnage we had inflicted and laughed.

We picked through the dead men's possessions but found nothing of worth except I now had a choice of war bows. The archers had left bows of reasonable quality and I took the best I could find from the grasp of a mutilated body.

I was an archer again.

*

Father John did not enter Tintern Abbey. He waited outside alone.

Lord Zouche turned back into Archbishop William de La Zouche the second he stepped into the abbey and was greeted by Brother Rhosier with great reverence.

'And what do we owe this unexpected honour?' Brother Rhosier asked after we were made welcome and our horses stabled by the attending monks.

We were sitting outside the refectory drinking ale. It had been a thirst-provoking journey. The women were receiving constant attention from the monks as this was a male Benedictine abbey and females were a rare sight.

'I am here to ask a favour of you, Brother.'

Brother Rhosier looked at Paul who was sitting and being spoon-fed by a novice monk. 'I had an inkling you might. We are having difficulty caring for the poor devils we already board, Your Grace.'

Archbishop Zouche looked serious. 'I am afraid I need to be blunt with you, Brother Rhosier. We are required forthwith in Durham and cannot linger. The Scots are invading our northern counties and we must see them from our lands.'

'Our lands?' he replied. '*You* are in *our* lands.' He realised his belligerent tone and softened. 'I have heard of such incursions to the north. I also hear they are making good headway and have already sacked Liddell Peel and murdered all inside.'

The Archbishop looked shocked, as did we all. 'You are well informed, Brother. I had not heard of these shocking turn of events, which makes my swift onward journey more imperative.' He turned towards Paul. 'I beseech you to take him into your care. I will direct additional funds to this abbey when I have routed these Scots and sent them to their heathen gods.'

Brother Rhosier went to speak but knew he was beaten. The Norman rule was too powerful to oppose.

'In that case, I am sure we can find room for this lost soul. I am only a sub-Prior here but as Abbott Bryn is away on business I am empowered to enact such decisions.' He looked at Philippa and me. 'And I remember you two. I said there would always be a welcome here for you, and it still holds true.' He glanced at the archbishop. 'Can I assume you will stay the night? I see a few of you have slight injuries.'

Father Zouche looked skyward. 'We have a good couple of hours of daylight left and after your shocking news we must make haste, but thank you regardless.'

'As you wish, Archbishop. I will ask the kitchen to gather provisions together for you to take on your journey.' He looked at Philippa and me again. 'Maybe another time?' He looked towards the front entrance of the abbey. 'But maybe come without the Devil who stalks the grounds outside as we speak.' He sniffed the air. 'His brimstone surrounds this sanctuary.'

He was a sharp observer.

I said goodbye to Paul. He showed no recognition. I had lost him and felt guilty that I was happy to leave him behind. Our years of struggle were over. I consoled myself that he was still alive, although he was a shadow of his former self.

The provisions were loaded onto the refreshed horses. I took one final look at Paul. The ends of his mouth may have turned up into a smile. I am not sure. I like to think they did.

*

By the time we reached Richmond in North Yorkshire, there was little I did not know about our travelling companions. Philippa had become close to Lady Maud, Sir Louis's wife, to the point she had offered her employment when all this was over. We had no further hostilities after we left the wild valleys of Wales and were hearing disturbing news of the invaders from the north. I killed deer and rabbits with my bow as we travelled so we had eaten well, arriving in good health. My archery skills were still sharp.

There was no time for rest. Lord de la Zouche was in no mood to compromise. He had been charged by King Edward with the responsibility of seeing off the invaders and lost no time in setting about that task. He was an inspirational figure – any thoughts of defeat were soon banished. He would lead us to victory.

He journeyed to the surrounding counties, moving from town to town, speaking in churches, in marketplaces – anywhere people gathered. His message was clear and unwavering. Every able-bodied man of fighting age was required in the defence of this great land. The puppet heathens from Scotland were under the control of the French and were invading – killing your kinsfolk and raping your wives and daughters. There was only one way to stave off such atrocities and that was to kill and drive them back over the border – back to their hovels in the mud. It was a set speech that he used time and again, each sermon delivered with passion and histrionics and always resulting in wild applause and volunteers.

In a few short days, and with the call going out to the barons from the north of England, he had mustered about three thousand men, which included twelve hundred fellow archers. There was a promise of another three thousand men from South Yorkshire.

The crisis was moving at pace. The Scots avoided attacking Carlisle after the city paid a huge ransom but headed towards Durham, ransacking and murdering all that stood in their way. They destroyed the hallowed place of worship, Hexham Abbey. This was the final straw and the rallying call to any undecided men. They stopped short of Durham at Beaurepaire Priory and prepared to attack the wealthy city.

Lord Zouche could wait no more. He had word that Baron Ralph Neville and Lord Henry Percy were gathering their respective armies under one banner to the south of Durham, so we set off.

We were going to war.

*

We reached a town called Merrington and with great relief, Baron Ralph Neville was already there. He had a similar sized army to ours and it was agreed he, being the most experienced campaigner, should take overall command. I saw a moment of disappointment in the eyes of Lord Zouche, but he agreed and took a supporting role – the outcome far outweighing any sense of pride.

We were a short distance from Durham City and it was there that the two wives, Philippa, and Kimberly were to be taken.

'Take care,' Philippa said as we embraced and Kimberly stood back without her usual attempt to take the attention. It was as if she understood the importance of the moment. I hugged her.

This could be the last time I saw them and feared I would miss our future together but said nothing. 'Don't worry about me, neither of you.' I gestured towards our travelling companions as they said goodbye to their wives. 'I have these people to look after me. Besides, I'll be firing arrows a long way away from the Scots.'

She tried but failed to smile. 'I know, but please be careful. I know I don't always show it but I do love you.' She kissed me. 'Come back to us – I'll share my good news with you when you do.'

With that, she took Kimberly's hand and led her away.

'I love you too.'

She did not hear me.

*

Mid-October. It was a cold and foggy night which continued long into the morning, dampening everything and cutting our visibility to a few feet. Baron Neville had us up early. The Scots were camped a short distance away, only a waterlogged bog separating us, and as far as he was aware they had no idea we were here. King David was under the impression all the fighting men of England were down south either waiting to travel to France or already there. The Truce of Esplechin was redundant already. It was his perfect opportunity.

I was standing with Lord Zouche and the men-at-arms we had travelled with, eating breakfast. Baron Ralph Neville and a couple of his senior knights approached us.

'Greetings, Lord Zouche. I want you and a small group of your men to go tease the damned Scots out of their beds. My sources confirmed William Douglas is leading a division of about five hundred camped a few miles to the north. They've been raiding at will and are isolated from the main army. They think they're untouchable.' He smiled. 'Let's educate them, shall we?'

Our Lord agreed and together they set a plan

into action.

I was loaned out to the archers. They were from Lancashire and were desperate to see action. When they heard I had been at Sluys and in France they wanted to hear every detail. How many had I killed? Were the French as stupid as they had been led to believe? Had I met a man called Paul Christian? The questions were endless.

'You will have your own bloody stories to tell come the end of this day,' was my closing statement. This made them happy.

Under cover of the mist, Baron Neville split us archers into two groups, sending one set to the east of his chosen battlefield and the other, led by me, to the west. He planned to lure the over-confident Scots into the waterlogged area and hit them from both sides. Simple. There was no reason for them to have ventured far south from their camp where the bog was as all the towns and plunderable sites were to their north. They would be aware it was there but not its size and consistency. Lord Zouche had wagered on it.

It was twilight as we positioned ourselves onto the flanks. Durham City was awash with arrows, King Edward having flooded the city with them as insurance for just such an occasion, and the residents had supplied us with thousands. Lord Zouche's men-at-arms were charged with confronting the Scots and making a stand on the firm ground between their camp and the bog. Once the Scots were mobilised our men were to back off and retreat across the sapping waterlogged ground. It would take courage to allow themselves to be used as bait and require perfect timing. If they ran too soon the Scots might not give chase, and too late would allow the outnumbering foe to cut them down. At the south end of the bog where the ground raised and firmed, we had placed carts and barrels and anything we could find that could be used as a barricade. That was where our exhausted pursued men could take refuge if necessary. The plan was for no Scot to be standing by that time.

The men around me were nervous but excited as we lay flat, our arrows embedded in the ground around us for quick access and stored in quivers behind. All we could do was wait for the fog to lift enough and the men-at-arms in the centre to move forward and entice the hordes out.

Baron Neville had reserves on the flanks and at the southern end in anticipation of a Scottish retreat once they had realised their mistake.

A cry went up and we looked across the boggy ground in front of us. I knew there were hundreds of English archers on the opposite side to us but could not see them as the thinning mist prevented it. But I could see halfway across and guessed the other side could see similarly – between us we had the killing ground covered.

The cry was from our men-at-arms. They

had crossed the ground in silence and were in position. I could just about make out their battle standards. There were about two hundred, enough to put up a defence but not enough to discourage a full-scale assault.

The English rally cry went up. 'SAINT GEORGE...'

All hell broke loose. I heard the blare of Scottish pipes calling men to arms and as the mist cleared I could make out crazed Scots, many half-dressed, charging into the thin shield wall set up in defence by the English. Time and again individuals would attempt acts of bravery, each being bounced off the shield formation and hacked or pierced by English pikes. But it did not take long before they organised themselves. I could see one man at the front directing his men. William Douglas, I guessed. They were forming into battle units and amassing in huge numbers. They would charge into the shields and be pushed from behind, the men at the front trying to climb over or under, but always being stabbed or bludgeoned.

'Any second now – our boys can't hold them much more,' I hissed. 'Stay down. Stay hidden.'

The dam burst. They held beyond what I thought possible, their bloodlust and adrenaline causing them to fight on, but now was the time to retreat.

They dropped their shields and ran backwards into the mud. An almighty cheer went up from the Scots and I could hear cries of 'cowards' and laughter. Now was their turn to avenge the dozens of dead and wounded lying by the discarded weaponry.

Our men, without their heavy shields and wearing light armour, found the terrain slow but manageable. I could see them struggling but they had a good few yards advantage from the howling Scots who poured onto the ground and gave chase.

'Wait,' I called.

Our men churned the mud as they ran, leaving a trail of quagmire conditions in their wake as the Scots struggled to catch up. Some threw spears and a small number fired crossbows from the camp. I saw one of our men hit in the leg by a bolt and fall. He regained his feet and was helped by one of his comrades, but his wound slowed him too much. He and his companion were caught and hacked to pieces. There were hundreds of Scots now wading through the mud. The fastest of our men had reached the barricades and enough Scots were bogged down.

It was our turn to kill.

'LOOSE...'

We unleashed our barbed tips of death. Both flanks opened up, ripping into their floundering men. I could sense their realisation that they had been fooled into a trap. They could not move. Arrow after arrow thumped into their bodies. Some tried to retreat backwards and some tried to attack us on the flanks but whichever way they turned they met pain. My fingers bled with the number of flights that left my bow. I saw men trying to pull barbs embedded in flesh, only to tear great chunks with them. The fog was almost clear now and I could see the expressions on their faces. They went from frustration at not being able to fight hand-to-hand to the realisation that they had no protection from death. I saw men hold their hands in front of their faces in a vain attempt to protect their eyes.

'KILL THEM...' I screamed.

So we killed. The ground turned red. Some had managed to escape, William Douglas being one, but so many lay stuck with arrows in the mud as our men-at-arms took up the cause and finished the job. Each wounded man was dispatched without mercy and the remainder were routed and sent running to join their main army back at Beaurepaire Priory.

It was time to loot the bodies and celebrate. First blood to Baron Ralph Neville and the English.

CHAPTER 20

We rested. Killing men is stressful work. More so for the Scots.

As we searched through the pockets of the dead, Baron Neville and Lord Zouche wandered. They congratulated us on a job well done and we in turn praised their tactics.

'We are far from finished here boys but when Percy troubles himself to join us we will move to our chosen battleground.'

An hour later, Lord Henry Percy of Alnwick arrived with his men. He was furious to have missed our earlier sortie. Time waits for no man.

We now had three divisions. We were still outnumbered, but, although our leaders respected the Scots' headstrong approach, they were convinced it could be used to our advantage.

They also had us archers.

After a short council of war, we were hurried towards a site just outside Durham City where intelligence predicted the Scots would make battle. We strived to arrive first and choose our positioning. It was a short distance but, to Baron Neville's dismay, the Scots had beaten us there. I was standing close to Lord Zouche and heard his conversation with the Baron and Lord Percy.

‘I don’t know what King David is thinking fellows, but I won’t complain.’ The others acknowledged his words and agreed. ‘He could have claimed any defensive position he wanted – and chose that one!' He shrugged. 'So be it. Let us stake ours before he changes his mind. You know the plan, now stick to it and *do not* deviate.’

His words sent confidence through me. I was not privy to his thinking but with men of such experience leading we had every chance.

There was only one definite that day – there would be mass slaughter before either side’s battle standards prevailed.

In the hour before the battle we took the opportunity to eat, drink, and sharpen our blades. Again, local men and women arrived bearing thousands of good-quality arrows. We had thirty arrows or more for every Scot. The majority of my fellow archers were newly blooded men and the earlier engagement had given them the taste for more. They looked to me as a seasoned campaigner, which compared to them I was, and I felt a level of expectation on my shoulders.

I found myself within a circle of expectant faces. They needed a speech. I gave them one.

'Remember, do not take a backward step – and listen to the commanders. The Scots will come at us like wild animals but we are here to put them down.' I watched their eyes. They were listening. 'The advantage we have is our discipline. If we hold firm and together, we will flight these bastards.' There were nods of agreement. I laughed and held up my war bow. 'Oh, and we have thousands of these too!'

That drew the roar I was seeking and they reached for their weapons.

It was a speech I had heard many times when I was new to this game so cannot take credit for it, but it always holds true.

These men were fired up. I so wished Paul could be here to reap the rewards.

*

We were spread across our chosen position, each commander controlling his own battle. I remained with Lord Zouche's battalion. He positioned me and a couple of hundred fellow archers on his left flank, whilst a similar number protected his right. In the centre, he placed himself and his men-at-arms. No man outside his reserve remained on horseback. The initial stages of this confrontation were to be conducted in the mud.

Lord Percy and Baron Neville had similar setups. Baron Neville had placed us to the far left, with Lord Percy to the right and himself covering the centre.

The terrain favoured us. If the Scots were to assault they had to attack up a slope. The river Browney with its fast-flowing currents covered our left side, and a steep slope our right. He had us dig in, always stressing discipline and reminding us of how we had smashed William Douglas earlier. Morale was high.

I scanned the enemy as they moved into position. They were stretched across a vast area and I realised this would be a far more complex battle than anything I had encountered until now. There was a deep ravine in the centre of their situation, spitting their army, so they gathered on either side. There was a low tumbled-down wall stretching across parts of their land too, making movement restrictive.

As I concentrated on the deployment of their forces I noticed something moving in the ravine. My first suspicion was it was a small group of Scots attempting a surprise attack but a closer inspection revealed that whoever they were, they were not armed. They were wearing the brown capes of monks. They were chanting.

Earlier that morning, two monks from Durham Cathedral had visited King David at Beaurepaire and pleaded for peace. Some chance. In return, the King had ordered their beheading. He claimed they were spies. They had escaped unharmed due to some of the heathens having a conscience. I found that hard to believe but that was the story. As time went by, those chanting monks turned into singing monks, followed by praying monks, but whichever guise they took made no difference. King David was here to kill

Englishmen. His favourite pastime.

We waited.

They waited.

We listened to the psalms sung by monks in a ditch.

Hours passed. Families from Durham brought us more arrows. They also supplied us with baskets of fresh bread, dried fish and barrels of weak ale.

'Eat and drink, boys – we have all day.' I looked around and saw Lord Zouche wandering towards the back of our battle. He had left his position at the front to speak and bolster spirits. 'Remember men, we can wait here until the next coming of Christ if need be. These good folk from the town will keep us sustained until these heretics get bored or have the good grace to attack.' He laughed. 'No one will be supplying them with food and drink unless it is laced with poison.'

We joined his merriment.

There was a period of silence before Lord Zouche cleared his throat and started to sing. We looked at him in dumb amazement. He sang the first verse of Angelus ad Virginem in a strong and clear voice. 'SING MY BEAUTIES, SHOW THESE BASTARDS HOW ENGLISH SPIRITS SOAR.'

We sang.

It worked. They attacked.

*

We had kept up a steady barrage of arrows all morning in an attempt to antagonise them and lure them onto us. Even at this distance, I could tell they were itching to charge, only being held back by their command, Patrick de Dunbar, Earl of March. His division, the one opposing us, consisted of men-at-arms with a scattering of light horsemen and a few archers. When the tones from our hymn washed over them it was the final straw. Without Earl Patrick's permission, one of his commanders, John Graham, Earl of Menteith, rallied his own horsemen and men-at-arms and burst from the ranks. They charged us alone.

'Good for you,' I thought. 'You could be French with that lack of discipline.'

'This is it,' I heard Lord Zouche say as he hurried back into position at the front of his battle.

It was the moment we had been waiting for. We loosed. Thousands of English arrows were drawn back and sent skyward, the sound of a great flock of geese soaring as the goose-fletched shafts with points of death took the air. It was a mesmerising sight.

And then the arrows struck. And down they went, like hunks of meat on a butcher's slab. Horses whinnied and men screamed. We lost a small number of men as they returned fire, but not enough to stop us from edging forward, keen to meet them head-on.

'NO – NOT YET.' Shouted Lord Zouche, so we eased back.

Undaunted by their losses, the men from Scotland came. The horsemen, now followed by men-at-arms, struggled to bypass the low wall, their frustration at boiling point. Another volley struck, this time with more venom as they were at closer range. Few horses now stood, most thrashing and coughing blood as our arrows struck their necks, sinking into the soft carotid artery and pumping blood into the ground where they lay. It was grotesque and beautiful. By the time the remaining few men were within feet of us, Lord Zouche gave the order. With effortless efficiency, men linked shields into a wall and like a giant single organism moved forward. The Scots hacked with their axes and stabbed with their pikes but the wall rolled on. Any fallen man was devoured, sucked into the grinding cogs. Every fifth step they halted and cleansed the mechanism of human tissue.

Earl Patrick could watch no longer. His remaining disciplined men had already started moving so he led them forward. Good. Fresh meat. They too scrambled over walls and tripped over hedges and we brought them down. We littered the land before us with their writhing bodies. Seeing the shields' efficiency, they skirted towards the flanks but were met by our defiant hail of arrows, so they funnelled back into the killing zone.

By the time our men-at-arms had finished their shift only one Scotsman remained standing. That was Lord John Graham.

'DO NOT KILL THAT MAN,' shouted Lord Zouche.

A young man beside me in the euphoric phase of bloodlust snatched an arrow and nocked it. He aimed at Lord Graham. He wanted one more kill – a famous one. I stepped forward and grabbed the arrow before he had time to loose.

'No...'

He looked at me with wild eyes.

'That man's ransom is worth our wages for a year.' I waited until his face softened. 'You don't want to be the cause of us not being paid, do you?' I grinned. He nodded and lowered his bow.

John Graham was surrounded. He knew he was beaten but did not want to show fear or face humiliation. He held a defiant stance, swinging his blood-dripping sword at anyone who came close.

Lord Zouche broke the circle of men and stood before him.

'You have shown spirit, my Lord, but you are now my prisoner.' He sheathed his sword and held out his hand. 'Please pass me your weapon, Lord, your day is finished.'

Lord Graham was furious. In a near incomprehensible voice, he started screaming about how he was going to rape the daughters of every Englishman alive, starting with Lord Zouche's.

After he blew himself out, Lord Zouche said,

'Have you quite finished, Lord Graham?'

'Ya wee lassie will be suckin' me cock by nightfall, ya dirty English bastard, I'll make her...'

But he did not finish. Lord Zouche stepped forward and with incredible speed punched him with his gauntleted fist, breaking his teeth and twisting his nose across his face.

'Manners maketh the man...' he said.

The Scots in the other divisions were far from beaten. John Randolph, Earl of Moray, had watched in despair as Lord John Graham's day collapsed and decided to teach us the art of warfare. He brought his larger division forward and charged into the front of Baron Neville's battle. There were fewer obstacles in their path so even after being struck by the Baron’s supporting archers there were enough Scots left to cause serious damage. This was what Lord Randolph had been waiting for – the chance to go toe-to-toe with the hated English. He knew the ferocity his men would unleash. He counted on it. He was forever lambasting the English for their hesitancy in battle and always turning to their archers. 'Fuck those bastards' was his favourite term. He did not have a vast vocabulary. Now was his turn to show how to kill with honour. And so he did.

From where we stood we could not help. The ravine where the monks still remained and sang verse was between us and them so our support was impossible.

'YOU STAY PUT,' shouted Lord Zouche. He could understand our frustrations but was working to the battle plan.

But Baron Neville's men did not flinch. Whatever Lord Randolph threw at them they matched. I could see the four men we had travelled with, led by Sir Louis, their shields interlocked, their chain maces and morning stars whipping over the top or swiping below, hollowing skulls and splitting tendons. They held their ground. It was remarkable. The Scots' brutality was matched by the staunch discipline of the English defenders. I could see Lord Randolph to the fore, smashing through the unprotected, his double-handed broadsword cutting and bludgeoning with dual action. It remained a stalemate for some time. How those men continued with such stamina was astonishing.

Lord Henry Percy, never one to stand back and admire the view, moved forward under covering fire from his archers and engaged King David. It was time to turn the screw.

There were thousands of men hacking and killing each other across the landscape. We were just one small part.

Again we felt impotent as we were under orders to remain put.

Lord Zouche was now talking to his advisers. A shout went up and it was time to enact part two of the plan. He moved us onward. We had destroyed the division in front of us so he took us forward, killing the wounded enemy as we moved towards the long broken-down wall that had so hampered the Scots in their earlier assault. Now we could use it as a barricade. We were attempting to flank Lord Randolph's battle as they continued to strike into Baron Neville's forces. From the cover of the wall, we had a clear shot across the ravine and could strike the flanks of his men.

So we did. We had a free hand. Again, our archers tore into them. The men towards the back of Randolph's battle wheeled around and tried to cross the ravine to engage us. They were big bearded men, most carrying long pikes or heavy axes and they moved down the slope. At that point, the monks moved out. It was a wise decision. As these laden men entered the ravine we poured death into them. Their fury had got the better of their judgment and they were caught in the hollow. We did not need the cover of the wall anymore as what few archers the Scots had were deployed towards the front of Lord Randolph's battle.

Every man who attempted to cross that divide was killed. At first, they could not wait to run down the slope in their bid to clamber up and slaughter us, but, as each man was struck in the face, the abdomen, the neck, reality dawned. They were penned in. The bank towards us was too steep and the return slope was filled with crazed men charging down. So we killed them. It was like spearing fish in a barrel. My fingers bled as old soars reopened. I felt a tug on my tunic and looked down. A small boy was holding a bundle of fresh arrows and offering them to me. He looked over the lip and watched with fascination as men screamed and died. He smiled and ran off to get more. He would be an archer one day.

When there was no one left to kill, we took breath. The ravine was a mass of twitching bodies and our men slithered down and slit the throats of the wounded and looted the bodies. I did too.

With our help, Baron Neville drove deep into the dwindling ranks of Lord Randolph's battle. They withered. The hard men at the front, the men who held an army together, questioned themselves. They fought on but glanced backwards for the first time. They eyed routes of escape.

That was all it took. Baron Neville, sensing their hesitancy, called up his reserves. It was time to finish the job. He had a division of mounted cavalry and they smashed into the Scots from every direction, breaking what was left of their resolve.

We had finished robbing the dead and moved to flank the battle opposing Lord Percy – King David's. The jewel in the crown. When we arrived both sides had fought each other to a standstill.

It had been a long murderous day. This time we discarded our bows and drew our side arms. It was time to move in and kill at close range. When King David's men saw us attack their rear with our axes and maces their war cries turned to death rattles. We had out-maneuvered them. They could hardly stand, the mud and heavy weaponry sapping every ounce of strength. We crashed into them in a wedge formation, burying ourselves deep into the body of the living beast. I tore limbs from bodies and eyes from heads, no man given quarter. Some begged for life and others shit themselves in the throes of death as they were dismembered.

War is not glamorous. It is killing. And that day we butchered on a large scale.

*

By the end of that day, we had wiped out swathes of their army and captured or killed most of King David's Barons and his military leadership. The King included. He had run from the field of battle and hidden beneath a bridge that crossed the river Browney. John de Coupland, a squire from Northampton, found and captured him, although not before the King had knocked out two of his teeth despite having two arrow wounds to the head. Even tough bastards' luck runs out sometimes.

In comparison to the Scots, our casualties were low.

*

That night, Baron Ralph Neville dined out with his fellow commanders in Durham City where he was granted the freedom of the city. The next morning they attended service in Durham Cathedral where the Archbishop of York, Lord William de la Zouche himself, administered and read the sermon.

Thousands of local people waited outside the cathedral, eager to give thanks.

I was there with Philippa and Kimberly.

I had gone straight from the battlefield to search for them. They were not hard to find. They were waiting outside the main gates to the city and Philippa burst into tears when she saw me and ran into my arms. Kimberly burst into tears too, although that was a reaction to her mother's behaviour. As we kissed I cried. It was the first time I had ever cried out of love.

That night she told me her good news and I cried again. How many times can one man cry in a day? At least two.

'That's the last time we enter that Priory in Reigate,' she laughed after I drank my second tankard from the black barrel. 'I either go in pregnant and come out with a child or go in without and have one thrust into me.'

That night, after Kimberly went to sleep, Philippa showed me the pleasures to be had without a war bow in my hand.

It was good to be alive.

CHAPTER 21

We spent the week in Durham City. We were more than welcome. Then we were not. It never lasts long. Soon the locals were turning soldiers away from hostelries and asking the injured to move on when they embarrassed the patrons.

I was one of the luckier survivors. I had plundered a few coins from dead Scots and still had enough left from the sale of the Ecu gold to live comfortably. But it would not last long.

Philippa had spent the day of the battle with Lady Maud and shared her fears. Sir Louis had come away with honours as he had been with John de Coupland when King David had been captured. He had helped subdue him and hoped to share in the ransom. The four of us had bonded over that week and I realised why I had seen the couple in Tonebricge so often back in the day. Lady Maud was Lord Thomas de Clare's daughter. Small world.

'I can't do this anymore,' I said.

Philippa and I were sitting outside a small tavern in the backstreets of Durham. It was early afternoon and we had just finished eating. Sir Louis and Lady Maud were off buying new clothes and had taken Kimberly with them. They loved her. They were spending the ransom money they had yet to receive. I was not convinced they would see any of it but kept that to myself.

Philippa leaned back and basked in the weak October sun. 'You can't do what anymore?'

'Soldier. Kill men for money.'

She snorted. 'How much have you been paid for all that time on the battlefields in France and over here, Al?'

I thought hard. 'Nothing,' I replied. 'King Edward hasn't paid me a penny.'

She laughed. 'Then you're not killing men for money, are you! And you've only just realised?' She tapped me on the head. 'Hello, is anyone in there?'

I ignored her. 'If I carry on doing this I'm going to be killed. My luck can only hold out so long.'

'Good – that's the most intelligent thing I've heard you say in a long time.' She made a quizzical face. 'It might be the only intelligent thing you've ever said.'

I ignored her. 'But what else can I do? We need money. And now you've gone and got yourself pregnant again...!'

She chuckled, then thought for a few seconds. 'We can go back to the tavern in Tonebricge. We were good at that.'

'After what happened last time? Lord Thomas hates me, and Benedict and his huntsman tried to kill us.' I took a penny from my tunic pocket. 'Besides, we can't live on the wages your parents would pay – we have children to raise.' I put the coin on the table and waited for the serving girl to attend. 'Oh, and what about your brother, Richard? He's bound to be back home now we've gone. I can't live with that piece of shit – and you shouldn't even consider...'

'I know all that, but I've been thinking. I might have the solution.'

'I'm all ears.'

She looked at my ears and nodded. 'I hope the new kid doesn't inherit them.' She leaned forward. 'Look, Lady Maud is a friend now. She's even offered me employment.'

'You can't go back to being a servant for a Lady, even if she is...'

'Don't interrupt. She's Lord Thomas's daughter. He'll do anything for her, and he's a reasonable Lord.' I looked blankly at her. She shook her head. 'I'll ask her to persuade him to accept us back into Tonebricge. Maybe if we... and I mean, you...apologise, he'll allow us back without stringing us...and I mean, you...up.' I looked doubtful but she nodded her head. 'We can offer to pay him extra tax from the tavern.'

I laughed. 'Yeah right – your parents will agree to that! And besides, Richard will be there and you know what will happen...'

She sat back with a serious face. 'He won't be there.'

'You don't know that.'

'I do.'

'How?'

'Because I'm the reason he left. I told him if I ever saw him again I would cut his throat.' Her eyes bore into me. 'After what he'd done to me in the past and what he did to you, he knew I was serious.' She nodded to herself. 'I would have, too.' Her eyes cleared. 'So we can forget about that bastard.' She picked up the knife from the table. 'Although I hope he is there.'

'Remind me not to upset you. Why didn't you tell me?'

'I was hoping to never have to speak about him again. The memories still hurt.'

'If you didn't cut his throat I know I would have.'

She shrugged. 'You can have his balls.'

'It's a deal.' I nodded and smiled. 'You make it seem so simple. A throat cut here, a set of balls removed there – we still won't be earning enough, you can't deny that.'

'How long before my parents retire?' she said. She had an answer for everything. 'Without Richard, I'm the sole heir.' She tapped the table while she thought. 'Anyway, we could buy them out if need be.'

'Buy them out? I thought I was the dreamer here.' I handed the penny to the serving girl and took the change. 'But inheriting the tavern would give a good reason to go back I suppose.'

Her face lit up. 'You never know, we might find enough money. Shall I ask Lady Maud to get a message to Lord Thomas?'

'You're asking me? You seem to have this all worked out.'

She patted my head. 'One of us needs to use this thing up here. It might as well be me.'

She was annoying.

I stood and helped her to her feet. 'It looks like we're going home.'

*

Lady Maud and Sir Louis left a few days before us. They wanted to visit her father in Tonebricge, so said they would go ahead and pave the way for our return. Considering we were of a lower class it was astonishing they even spoke to us. Friendship forged in adversary is a powerful bond.

Sir William de la Zouche gave me his blessing to leave, spiritually and militarily. We had been through a great deal together, although he needed reminding of who I was. Maybe it was more on my part than his. John de Pyrie's goodbye was genuine. He said he would go back to the priory and resume his life as Father John. I would miss his devilish ways.

The journey south was unremarkable. It made a nice change. We had enough money to stay in half-decent accommodation, and I was able to hold court in many a tavern and recount stories of the battle at Durham. Even Philippa was impressed by my storytelling.

So when we entered Tonebricge it felt like a homecoming. Because it was. The first stop would be The Chequers Tavern and a visit to Philippa's parents. Sir Louis had loaned us a horse which Philippa and Kimberly shared, so we needed to feed and water that while we reintroduced ourselves to the town. We were not sure we would be welcome after being run out a couple of years earlier. Had it been that long? So much had happened in the interim.

We arrived about midday. Philippa was moaning about her arse being sore and I was moaning about Philippa's moaning about her arse. Kimberly was happy mind you.

Philippa was excited about seeing her mother and father again, but as soon as we set eyes on the tavern her enthusiasm died. It was boarded up. We stood outside and stared. It had not occurred to us they might not be there.

'What do you want?'

The voice was sharp and coming from the butchers next door. We turned and looked. It was Simon's mother. He had been murdered and I was prime suspect for her and her family.

'Good afternoon, Mrs Butcher, where are Tom and Emma?' I asked gesturing towards the tavern.

'Don't you Mrs Butcher me, you murdering piece of shit. They're gone. Sold the tavern to Lord de Clare and left.' She spat on the floor.

'They couldn't stand being associated with you and that filthy daughter who ran off with you.'

That hurt. Not the insults towards me, I was used to it, but towards Philippa. I went to defend her but did not get the chance.

'I'm sitting right here, Mrs Butcher. For your information, we had nothing to do with your son's death and you'll have to accept that as we have come home for good.' She passed Kimberly down to me and clambered from the horse. She walked over to her. She softened. 'As one mother to another, I swear to God we do not know who killed your son.' She held her hands.

Mrs Butcher stared at her with bitterness, then relented and burst into tears. 'I don't know what to think anymore,' she sobbed. 'It's been years and the pain never goes away. I just want to know the truth.'

Philippa comforted her. This return was never going to be easy.

I took the horse around the back of the tavern and forced the barn door open. It brought back memories, as it had been my home for so long. It seemed a lifetime ago.

I stalled the horse, collected some old food that was scattered about the floor, and watered the beast. It was not ideal but it was something. By the time I returned to Philippa, Mrs Butcher was smiling and playing with Kimberly. That child could melt the heart of the devil himself.

We discovered that Philippa's parents had left

town a few months back. As far as Mrs Butcher was aware no one knew where they had gone. Philippa was sad. She had hoped to introduce Kimberly to them. They would have loved her.

Mrs Butcher went back to her shop.

We sat together on the steps of the tavern. I was dejected. 'What are we going to do now? We were relying on your parents still being here.'

She threw a bundle of rags that were tightly wrapped into a ball that Mrs Butcher had given Kimberly to play with.

'If they sold the tavern to Lord Thomas for a fair price they should be wealthy,' she said, 'it might be worth searching for them.' Kimberly returned the ball and she threw it again.

I frowned. 'They could be anywhere. I don't reckon they'd stay round the Tonebricge area.'

Philippa went silent. Kimberly returned the ball but she did not throw it again. She looked as though her mind was miles away.

'Here, give me the ball, Kimberly – I think your mum's gone to sleep.' I reached over and took the ball from her hand and threw it. 'Fetch, doggie.' I laughed as Kimberly made a barking sound.

Philippa stood. 'I'll see if I can find anyone who knows where my parents are,' she said. 'Someone in the town must have an idea. They wouldn't just leave without telling anybody where they were going. I'll ask their friends.'

'It's worth a try. Let's go.'

She held up her hand. 'It's all right – I'll go. You

two stay here.' She nodded towards the stables. 'Someone needs to keep an eye on the horse. I won't be long.'

I agreed. My little doggie was having too much fun.

We had promised to return the horse to Sir Louis and Lady Maud as soon as we arrived and I did not want to insult them by being late, so hoped Philippa would not be long.

She was. Hours passed. I was beginning to worry that something might have happened to her when I heard a friendly voice. It was Sir Louis.

'There you are, Ailred. I'd heard you'd been seen skulking about town.' His tone changed. 'I thought you were supposed to come and see us at the castle? My father-in-law is expecting you.' He looked around. 'Where's the horse – you've not sold it, have you?' He was only half joking.

'No, nothing like that.' Kimberly ran over and held up her hands wanting to be picked up by him. He smiled and obliged, tossing her into the air. 'Philippa's off searching for her parents. They sold the tavern to Lord...'

'So I heard,' he cut in, 'Lord Thomas was telling us earlier. You do need to go see him now though, Ailred. We've done our part and I think he'll give you a pass and accept your apology. Maud has vouched for you – don't let her down.' He looked at me, waiting for me to move. 'Now, if you please, Ailred.'

'Can we wait a bit longer for Philippa, I doubt she'll be long?'

'You don't even know where she is, she could be hours. Come on, grab the horse and we'll go without her. It's you he wants to speak to.' He was growing impatient.

I had no choice. I went to fetch the horse and cleaned myself up in a water trough. I had made Lord Thomas wait, so the least I could do was look clean and respectable. Rejoining them again, I smoothed my hair down and together we walked towards the castle, Kimberly on Sir Louis's shoulders.

It was time to grovel. How was I going to do this alone? I realised at that moment how much I relied on Philippa.

As we approached the castle gates I heard a shout from behind. My heart leapt. Thank God.

'Wait for me you three.'

Kimberly looked down from up high and said, 'Mamma.'

I pulled her aside.

'Where have you been? We have to go see Lord Thomas right now.' I stood back and looked at her. 'At least I had the chance to wash up – you look filthy.'

She wiped her dirty hands on her tunic. 'Thanks,' she said. 'Let's hope we're not being judged on our appearances, shall we?'

I tried to help brush her down but she tutted and pushed me away. 'Did you find out where they were?' I asked.

'Where who were?'

'Your parents, who else?'

'Oh them, sorry, I was preoccupied. You've made me worry about my appearance now.' She finished combing her hair. 'Better?'

'You'll do – and what about your parents, did you find out where they are?'

'No, no one knows. Never mind, let's go see Lord Thomas.' And with that, she linked arms with Sir Louis and led on.

I shook my head and followed.

We were led into the grounds and towards the grand hall where Lord Thomas would receive us. Sir Louis handed us over to a couple of guards, one who checked me over for weapons while Philippa and Kimberly charmed the other.

We were led into the hall. It was similar to the hall where Lord John of Gaunt had relieved us of our gold Ecu coin. At least this would be less humiliating. We had nothing left to lose.

Lord Thomas was standing near the large fireplace with his daughter, Lady Maud. He turned as we approached and fixed his stare on me. I smiled. He did not.

'BENEDICT,' he shouted, 'I have some guests for you.'

My blood froze. The last time I had seen him he was hanging my friend, Bartholomew, and threatened to do the same to Philippa and me.

Philippa had the same thoughts and looked

at me, casting her gaze towards the doors suggesting we might run, but I shook my head. How far would we get?

‘Oh daddy, stop teasing them…’ Lady Maud slapped Lord Thomas on the arm.

He looked at my face and laughed. ‘It’s good to see you again, Ailred Norman.’ He looked towards Philippa and Kimberly. ‘And you, Mrs Norman and baby Norman. It seems we are in for another Norman invasion.’

I laughed. I could not help myself. ‘Thank you for seeing us, my Lord. It has been a long time, Sire.’

‘It has indeed. Last time I saw you you were vomiting on Lord Knole’s feet if I recall.’ He stroked his beard. ‘And you left me humiliated and in debt to him, too. You won’t know that part as you ran away and joined a division of Welsh archers to escape my wrath.’

'If I'm honest, Lord, It was Benedict we were escaping, not you. He turned into a monster. We have always respected your fairness.'

He looked serious for a second. 'Yes, I heard what he did to that boy and I punished him for it.'

I looked to the floor in embarrassment. ‘Your Lordship is well informed, if I may say so.'

‘There is little that goes on that I do not know, Mr Norman.’ He looked at his daughter. ‘You seemed to have neglected to tell my daughter here great swathes of your back story too.’

I looked at her and she looked back and

grimaced.

'I am here to apologise, my Lord.'

'Apologise away, my good fellow.'

I cleared my throat.

'You're not going to throw up on my feet now, are you? I know it's something you like to do.'

'Umm, no Sire.'

'Well, that's good of you, Ailred. I always said to my children when they were growing up 'Try not to vomit on people's feet when you meet them.' He looked at Lady Maud. 'Isn't that right Maud?'

She chuckled. 'Yes, Father, you were always telling us that.'

I gulped. This was not going well.

'Ahh, the old "swallow the vomit before speaking" technique. Great work, Ailred my boy.'

Philippa laughed out loud. Then Lady Maud.

'Quiet girls, Ailred here is making an apology. Don't distract him.'

That was my opening. 'I'm sorry, my Lord, from the bottom of my heart for all the foolish things I did.'

'There, that wasn't difficult was it? I accept your apology, Ailred.' He looked at his daughter who smiled and nodded. 'You can thank my daughter and Sir Louis for my change of heart.' He looked me in the eyes. 'But no one gets a second chance – do I make myself clear?'

I nodded. 'As clear as a...' I could not think of anything.

'A clear thing?' he prompted.

'Oh yes, one of those.'

I heard Philippa groan. Then she dug me out of my hole. 'We would like to speak to you about the Chequers Tavern, Lord.'

'I thought you might. You want to buy it back from me?' He laughed. 'Sorry, I'm joking. Do you want to work there when I open it? I think you would be good for...'

She stopped him, and added, 'No, Lord, we *do* want to buy it back.'

He looked a little taken aback.

I looked a little taken aback.

'I see. And you wish to pay me off by working there and deducting the...'

'No, Lord, a one-off payment.'

I looked at her and put my finger to my lips, trying to hush her. What was she doing?

'I see. And how would you intend to pay for this?'

She shuffled. 'We have money,' she said with confidence.

'I see. And would you by chance have any of this invisible money with you? Invisible money is my favourite type.'

His sarcasm was annoying but expected. It was my time to save Philippa. 'When she says we have money, what she means is...' I ran out of ideas.

'Will this do as a downpayment?'

We looked at Philippa. She was holding two

gold Doubloons. My jaw dropped. Lord Thomas showed no surprise.

'May I see them, young lady?' he asked, reaching out.

'Certainly, Sire.' She passed them over.

I was staring at her but she did not acknowledge my gaze.

'They seem a little dirty, but they're genuine. Can I assume the mud will be removed before any transaction?' He spat on one and shined it, holding it up to the light. He looked at me and said, 'I would ask you where you got them but something tells me you might not know, so I'll ask your good lady wife.' He looked at her and waited.

'He does know, my Lord.' But before I could say anything she continued. 'Ailred looted them from a French commander at the battle of Sluys.'

He looked at me, raised his eyebrows, and smiled. 'I see. Well done Ailred. Can I enquire as to which commander, or would I be better off asking Mrs Norman?'

I looked at Philippa. By this time I did not know what was going on, but Philippa seemed to have it under control.

'He never found out his name, Sire, as there were too many men trying to rob him after they discovered his lucky find. He ran away and hid the money until he could get it home safely. Isn't that so, Ailred darling?'

Lord Thomas laughed so hard that he had to sit

down. When he finished he said, 'So let's get this clear shall we?' He turned to Lady Maud and the two guards who were standing nearby. 'Would you mind leaving us for a while – we have a few things to discuss?' They left. He continued. 'This newfound wealth is rather fortunate, is it not?'

We both nodded and I went to speak but both Philippa and Lord Thomas waved a finger at me.

'Yes, Lord it is,' Philippa answered.

'I see. And it all came from a French commander of unknown identity, yes?'

'Yes, Lord, that sums it up,' she said.

'Which means it has nothing to do with, say, off the top of my head, for example, a robbery that took place a few years ago?'

There was silence.

I heard a noise in my head go "ping" and a light flashed in front of me. I jumped and pointed to Philippa. She glared back and stamped her foot. I lowered my arm. 'No, Lord, nothing whatsoever.' I scratched my head. 'What robbery?'

Philippa groaned.

He stroked his beard and stared at Philippa. 'If I sold you the tavern it would be quite a price, you understand? More than I paid your parents.'

She nodded. 'That would seem fitting.'

'And I would expect a larger tax offering at the end of each year.'

Again she agreed.

'Well then, under the circumstances I think we have a deal.' He stepped forward and shook her hand, then looked at me. 'Congratulations, Ailred. You'll be a wealthy man for the rest of your life if the sum you looted from the unknown French commander is worth what I think it is.'

I finally caught up. 'Yes, my Lord, we can all do very well out of this.'

'That we can, Ailred.' He called the others back in.

As we left, Lord Thomas said, 'Hold on to this little lady, Ailred Norman. Take her to Mary Magdalene's Priory and give thanks to God you found her. Maybe even marry her!' He laughed. 'Oh, and leave a decent contribution.'

CHAPTER 22

I looked at Paul. He wore the same brown cowl as every other monk at Tintern Abbey, his shaved hair and mannerisms identical. His inquisitive look was a far cry from the last time I had seen him. We sat on a low wall in the east wing of the cloister overlooking the central garden. A low mist dampened the air. 'Typical Welsh weather,' Father Rhosier had called it after he had welcomed us in. He was now Abbot Rhosier of Tintern Abbey and had aged since we last met. We all had. He had collected Paul from the church where he was attending None, one of the monks' daily services, and brought him to me, leaving us alone to speak.

Philippa, Kimberly and the twins, Timothy and Frederick, had given me space too. We had made the journey in a few days after receiving a message from Abbott Rhosier. He had confirmed that Paul was well enough to accept visitors. Of my many enquiries, this was the first correspondence he had replied to for years.

We stopped in at Reigate Priory to say hello but found many of our old friends had died or moved on. It was sad but inevitable.

'Hello, Paul, remember me?'

He studied my face. 'You look familiar, my child, what is your name?'

'I'm your brother, Ailred.' I smiled.

'Ah, Brother Ailred, I have not seen you around this abbey before. You are most welcome.'

I was unsure if he was joking, but his face confirmed my fears. 'No, sorry Paul, you misunderstand – I am your blood brother.' He looked sceptical. 'We have the same father and mother.'

He grinned. 'I know what a blood brother is, Ailred. I am only just learning to piece together my old life and connect it to my new.'

I felt foolish. 'I am sorry, I didn't mean to…'

He shook his head and touched my shoulder. 'I take no offence.' He continued to stare into my eyes, studying me. I felt self-conscious and looked away. 'Yes, I do recognise you,' he said, 'but I can't for the life of me picture a time and place.' He shook his head. 'It is so frustrating. God is testing my resolve, but it is difficult.' He looked at me again. 'I feel we had a strong bond before – am I right? The tenderness in your eyes gives you away, brother.'

I found it hard not to cry. 'We were brothers, Paul – close brothers. We kept each other alive. Without you, I would have died long ago.'

He lowered his eyes. 'I suspect I would not be here without you either, but I just do not recall. I *so* want to.'

There was a moment's silence. I broke it.

'Are you happy here?'

'It is all I know, Ailred. It is my home. All memories from before this abbey are a blur. I have been told nothing of my former life.' He looked sad. 'I feel a great void in my soul.'

'I think that is the purpose of my visit, Brother Paul.' It felt strange calling him that. 'Abbott Rhosier says he wants you to know who and what you were. It is the final part of your rehabilitation. I know your life – and he feels you need to come to terms with that.'

His eyes brightened. 'You can fill that void?' A tear ran down his cheek. I had never seen him emotional before. Even as a child.

This was going to be difficult.

*

I told him everything, much of it I have already told you. At first, I played down aspects but he insisted on the truth, however uncomfortable. So I told it. He sat listening without saying a word. The mist turned to rain and the day turned to night, and still we sat. Abbott Rhosier would come out to check Paul was feeling all right on occasion and Philippa would do likewise to me, but we did not move.

And then I reached the end. Now.

'And you kept the money?'

I looked at the floor. 'Yes, I am not proud, but it has transformed our lives. We own businesses in Tonebricge now and our children are set for life.'

I held his hands. 'And we work hand in hand with the priory, doing charitable work, so they benefit too.' I realised that sounded like a hollow excuse. 'But, yes, it is ill-gained wealth.'

'Gained through my barbarism. And you say I confessed this to your wife?'

'Yes, although you thought she was a nun at the time.'

He looked at me. 'I should report this.'

I knew this moment would come. 'That is a decision only you can make.' I nearly pointed out the ramifications of such an action but decided against it. Our fate was in his hands.

He thought long and hard. 'It was a long time ago and would serve only to destroy your lives and my own.' He stood. 'Come brother, introduce me to your family. I want them to meet their Uncle Paul.'

I stood and he faced me.

'Thank you,' he said and then embraced me. 'I will keep this secret until I meet my God and he can judge me then. I am happy now – the weight is lifted and I am complete. I love you, Ailred.'

*

You do not have to keep writing everything I say now, Brother Michael. I have finished. Yes, I know you are not a monk anymore but I have spent so long in your company that calling you Brother comes naturally. I feel a sense of guilt that my confessions have had the opposite effect on you. Those accounts of death and battle have turned you into the soldier you have become. Not to mention your womanising. I hope you will accept this money. You have earned it. A bribe? You may call it that – but I call it an appreciation of your continued silence.

I will miss you too.

Are you still writing? Please stop – we are at the end.

Thank you.

Printed in Great Britain
by Amazon